THE ZAFFRE BOOK OF OCCULT FICTION

EDITED BY

BRENDAN CONNELL

THE ZAFFRE BOOK
OF OCCULT FICTION

Brendan Connell was born in Santa Fe, New Mexico, in 1970. His works of fiction include *The Architect* (PS Publishing, 2012), *Lives of Notorious Cooks* (Chômu Press, 2012), *Miss Homicide Plays the Flute* (Eibonvale Press, 2013), *Cannibals of West Papua* (Zagava, 2015), and *Against the Grain Again: The Further Adventures of Des Esseintes* (Tartarus Press, 2021). As editor he has worked on various projects, including *The World in Violet: An Anthology of English Decadent Poetry* (Snuggly Boos, 2022), and *The Neo-Decadent Cookbook* (Eibonvale Press, 2020), which was co-edited by Justin Isis. As translator his efforts include *Alcina and Other Stories* (Snuggly Books, 2019), by Guido Gozzano, which was co-translated by his wife Anna.

CONTENTS

EDITORIAL NOTE

THE current volume, to a large degree, takes off where *The Zinzolin Book of Occult Fiction* left off, though with some overlap in years. That volume concerned itself primarily with the occult revival of the British Isles, as it manifested itself in fiction produced under that impulse from 1888-1911. This selection contains occult fiction published or created from 1908-1937, either in the British Isles or by those believed to be native to them.

The contents of this book are arranged chronologically. I have presented the various pieces, as much as possible, in a format that aligns with their original publication, though an infrequent correction has been made where an obvious error was present, and seldomly an adjustment to a spelling or bit of punctuation has been made for the regularity of the volume.

I have, furthermore, as in *The Zinzolin Book of Occult Fiction*, taken a somewhat broad view of the word "fiction," as, in my view, is necessary in a project such as the present one. The reader will find a number of peculiar inclusions, but I felt it was important to include strains which tend to be left out of similar productions, so that the current series can encompass a broad spectrum of styles and be truly representative of what the occult fiction of the period actually was, having in it items by those who were the deepest practitioners.

I would like to conclude by thanking Daniel Corrick for supplying the text for "The Ghost Friend."—B.C.

THE ZAFFRE BOOK
OF OCCULT FICTION

ROSA ALCHEMICA

by W. B. Yeats

O blessed and happy he, who knowing the mysteries of the gods, sanctifies his life, and purifies his soul, celebrating orgies in the mountains with holy purifications.

—Euripides.

I

IT is now more than ten years since I met, for the last time, Michael Robartes, and for the first time and the last time his friends and fellow students; and witnessed his and their tragic end, and endured those strange experiences, which have changed me so that my writings have grown less popular and less intelligible, and driven me almost to the verge of taking the habit of St. Dominic. I had just published *Rosa Alchemica*, a little work on the Alchemists, somewhat in the manner of Sir Thomas Browne, and had received many letters from believers in the arcane sciences, upbraiding what they called my timidity, for they could not believe so evident sympathy but the sympathy of the artist, which is half pity, for everything which has moved men's hearts in any age. I had discovered, early in my researches, that their doctrine was no merely chemical phantasy, but a philosophy they applied to the world, to the elements and to man himself; and that they sought to fashion gold out of common metals merely as part of an universal transmutation of all things into some divine and imperishable substance; and this enabled me to make my little book a fanciful reverie over the transmutation of life into art, and a cry of measureless desire for a world made wholly of essences.

I was sitting dreaming of what I had written, in my house in one of the old parts of Dublin; a house my ancestors had made almost famous through their part in the politics of the city and their friendships with the famous men of their generations; and was feeling an unwonted happiness at having at last accomplished a long-cherished design, and made my rooms an expression of this favourite doctrine. The portraits, of more historical than artistic interest, had gone; and tapestry, full of the blue and bronze of peacocks, fell over the doors, and shut out all history and activity untouched with beauty and peace; and now when I looked at my Crevelli and pondered on the rose in the hand of the Virgin, wherein the form was so delicate and precise that it seemed more like a thought than a flower, or at the grey dawn and rapturous faces of my Francesca, I knew all a Christian's ecstasy without his slavery to rule and custom; when I pondered over the antique bronze gods and goddesses, which I had mortgaged my house to buy, I had all a pagan's delight in various beauty and without his terror at sleepless destiny and his labour with many sacrifices; and I had only to go to my bookshelf, where every book was bound in leather, stamped with intricate ornament, and of a carefully chosen colour: Shakespeare in the orange of the glory of the world, Dante in the dull red of his anger, Milton in the blue grey of his formal calm; and I could experience what I would of human passions without their bitterness and without satiety. I had gathered about me all gods because I believed in none, and experienced every pleasure because I gave myself to none, but held myself apart, individual, indissoluble, a mirror of polished steel: I looked in the triumph of this imagination at the birds of Hera, glowing in the firelight as though they were wrought of jewels; and to my mind, for which symbolism was a necessity, they seemed the doorkeepers of my world, shutting out all that was not of as affluent a beauty as their own; and for a moment I thought as I had thought in so many other moments, that it was possible to rob life of every bitterness except the bitterness of death; and then a thought which had followed this thought, time after time, filled me with a passionate sorrow. All those forms: that Madonna with her brooding purity, those rapturous faces singing in the morning light, those bronze divinities with their passionless dignity, those wild shapes rushing from despair to despair, belonged to a divine world wherein I had no part; and every experience, however profound, every perception, however exquisite, would bring me the bitter dream of a limitless energy I could never know, and even in my most perfect moment I would be two selves, the one watching with heavy eyes the other's moment of content. I had heaped about me the gold born in the crucibles of others; but the supreme dream of the alchemist, the transmutation of the weary heart into a weariless spirit, was as far from me as, I doubted not, it had been from him also. I turned to my last purchase, a set of alchemical apparatus which, the dealer in the Rue le Peletier had assured me, once belonged to Raymond Lully, and as I joined the *alembic* to the *athanor* and laid the *lavacrum maris* at their side, I understood the alchemical doctrine, that all beings, divided from the great deep where spirits wander, one and yet a multitude, are weary; and sympathized, in the pride of my connoisseurship, with the consuming thirst for destruction which made the alchemist veil under his symbols of lions and dragons, of eagles and ravens, of dew and of nitre, a search for an essence which would dissolve all mortal things. I repeated to myself the ninth key of Basilius Valentinus, in which he compares the fire of the last day to the fire of the alchemist, and the world to the alchemist's furnace, and would have us know that all must be dissolved before the divine substance, material gold or immaterial ecstasy, awake. I had dissolved indeed the mortal world and lived amid immortal essences, but had obtained no miraculous ecstasy. As I thought of these things, I drew aside the curtains and looked out into the darkness, and it seemed to my troubled fancy that all those little points of light filling the sky were the furnaces of innumerable divine alchemists, who labour continually, turning lead into gold, weariness into ecstasy, bodies into souls, the darkness into God; and at their perfect labour my mortality grew heavy, and I cried out, as so many dreamers and men of letters in our age have cried, for the birth of that elaborate spiritual beauty which could alone uplift souls weighted with so many dreams.

II

My reverie was broken by a loud knocking at the door, and I wondered the more at this because I had no visitors, and had bid my servants do all things silently, lest they broke the dream of my inner life. Feeling a little curious, I resolved to go to the door myself, and, taking one of the silver candlesticks from the mantlepiece, began to descend the stairs. The servants appeared to be out, for though the sound poured through every corner and crevice of the house there was no stir in the lower rooms. I remembered that because my needs were so few, my part in life so little, they had begun to come and go as they would, often leaving me alone for hours. The emptiness and silence of a world from which I had driven everything but dreams suddenly overwhelmed me, and I shuddered as I drew the bolt. I found before me Michael Robartes, whom I had not seen for years, and whose wild red hair, fierce eyes, sensitive, tremulous lips and rough clothes, made him look now, just as they used to do fifteen years before, something between a debauchee, a saint, and a peasant. He had recently come to Ireland, he said, and wished to see me on a matter of importance: indeed, the only matter of importance for him and for me. His voice brought up before me our student years in Paris, and remembering the magnetic power he had once possessed over me, a little fear mingled with much annoyance at this irrelevant intrusion, as I led the way up the wide staircase, where Swift had passed joking and railing, and Curran telling stories and quoting Greek, in simpler days, before men's minds, subtilized and complicated by the romantic movement in art and literature, began to tremble on the verge of some unimagined revelation. I felt that my hand shook, and saw that the light of the candle wavered and quivered more than it need have upon the Maenads on the old French panels, making them look like the first beings slowly shaping in the formless and void darkness. When the door had closed, and the peacock curtain, glimmering like many-coloured flame, fell between us and the world, I felt, in a way I could not understand, that some singular and unexpected thing was about to happen. I went over to the mantlepiece, and finding that a little chainless bronze censer, set, upon the outside, with pieces of painted china by Orazio Fontana, which I had filled with antique amulets, had fallen upon its side and poured out its contents, I began to gather the amulets into the bowl, partly to collect my thoughts and partly with that habitual reverence which seemed to me the due of things so long connected with secret hopes and fears. "I see," said Michael Robartes, "that you are still fond of incense, and I can show you an incense more precious than any you have ever seen," and as he spoke he took the censer out of my hand and put the amulets in a little heap between the *athanor* and the *alembic*. I sat down, and he sat down at the side of the fire, and sat there for awhile looking into the fire, and holding the censer in his hand. "I have come to ask you something," he said, "and the incense will fill the room, and our thoughts, with its sweet odour while we are talking. I got it from an old man in Syria, who said it was made from flowers, of one kind with the flowers that laid their heavy purple petals upon the hands and upon the hair and upon the feet of Christ in the Garden of Gethsemane, and folded Him in their heavy breath, until He cried against the cross and his destiny." He shook some dust into the censer out of a small silk bag, and set the censer upon the floor and lit the dust which sent up a blue stream of smoke, that spread out over the ceiling, and flowed downwards again until it was like Milton's banyan tree. It filled me, as incense often does, with a faint sleepiness, so that I started when he said, "I have come to ask you that question which I asked you in Paris, and which you left Paris rather than answer."

He had turned his eyes towards me, and I saw them glitter in the firelight, and through the incense, as I replied: "You mean, will I become an initiate of your Order of the Alchemical Rose? I would not consent in Paris, when I was full of unsatisfied desire, and now that I have at last fashioned my life according to my desire, am I likely to consent?"

"You have changed greatly since then," he answered. "I have read your books, and now I see you among all these images, and I understand you better than you do yourself, for I have been with many and many dreamers at the same cross-ways. You have shut away the world and gathered the gods about you, and if you do not throw yourself at their feet, you will be always full of lassitude, and of wavering purpose, for a man must forget he is miserable in the bustle and noise of the multitude in this world and in time; or seek a mystical union with the multitude who govern this world and time." And then he murmured something I could not hear, and as though to someone I could not see.

For a moment the room appeared to darken, as it used to do when he was about to perform some singular experiment, and in the darkness the peacocks upon the doors seemed to glow with a more intense colour. I cast off the illusion, which was, I believe, merely caused by memory, and by the twilight of incense, for I would not acknowledge that he could overcome my now mature intellect; and I said: "Even if I grant that I need a spiritual belief and some form of worship, why should I go to Eleusis and not to Calvary?" He leaned forward and began speaking with a slightly rhythmical intonation, and as he spoke I had to struggle again with the shadow, as of some older night than the night of the sun, which began to dim the light of the candles and to blot out the little gleams upon the corner of picture-frames and on the bronze divinities, and to turn the blue of the incense to a heavy purple; while it left the peacocks to glimmer and glow as though each separate colour were a living spirit. I had fallen into a profound dream-like reverie in which I heard him speaking as at a distance. "And yet there is no one who communes with only one god," he was saying, "and the more a man lives in imagination and in a refined understanding, the more gods does he meet with and talk with, and the more does he come under the power of Roland, who sounded in the Valley of Roncesvalles the last trumpet of the body's will and pleasure; and of Hamlet, who saw them perishing away, and sighed; and of Faust, who looked for them up and down the world and could not find them; and under the power of all those countless divinities who have taken upon themselves spiritual bodies in the minds of the modern poets and romance writers, and under the power of the old divinities, who since the Renaissance have won everything of their ancient worship except the sacrifice of birds and fishes, the fragrance of garlands and the smoke of incense. The many think humanity made these divinities, and that it can unmake them again; but we who have seen them pass in rattling harness, and in soft robes, and heard them speak with articulate voices while we lay in deathlike trance, know that they are always making and unmaking humanity, which is indeed but the trembling of their lips."

He had stood up and begun to walk to and fro, and had become in my waking dream a shuttle weaving an immense purple web whose folds had begun to fill the room. The room seemed to have become inexplicably silent, as though all but the web and the weaving were at an end in the world. "They have come to us; they have come to us," the voice began again; "all that have ever been in your reverie, all that you have met with in books. There is Lear, his head still wet with the thunder-storm, and he laughs because you thought yourself an existence who are but a shadow, and him a shadow who is an eternal god; and there is Beatrice, with her lips half parted in a smile, as though all the stars were about to pass away in a sigh of love; and there is the mother of the God of humility who cast so great a spell over men that they have tried to unpeople their hearts that he might reign alone, but she holds in her hand the rose whose every petal is a god; and there, O swiftly she comes! is Aphrodite under a twilight falling from the wings of numberless sparrows, and about her feet are the grey and white doves." In the midst of my dream I saw him hold out his left arm and pass his right hand over it as though he stroked the wings of doves. I made a violent effort which seemed almost to tear me in two, and said with forced de-termination: "You would sweep me away into an indefinite world which fills me with terror; and yet a man is a great man just in so far as he can make his mind reflect everything with indifferent precision like a mirror." I seemed to be perfectly master of myself, and went on, but more rapidly: "I command you to leave me at once, for your ideas and phantasies are but the illusions that creep like maggots into civilizations when they begin to decline, and into minds when they begin to decay." I had grown suddenly angry, and seizing the *alembic* from the table, was about to rise and strike him with it, when the peacocks on the door behind him appeared to grow immense; and then the *alembic* fell from my fingers and I was drowned in a tide of green and blue and bronze feathers, and as I struggled hopelessly I heard a distant voice saying: "Our master Avicenna has written that all life proceeds out of corruption." The glittering feathers had now covered me completely, and I knew that I had struggled for hundreds of years, and was conquered at last. I was sinking into the depth when the green and blue and bronze that seemed to fill the world became a sea of flame and swept me away, and as I was swirled along I heard a voice over my head cry, "The mirror is broken in two pieces," and another voice answer, "The mirror is broken in four pieces," and a more distant voice cry with an exultant cry, "The mirror is broken into numberless pieces"; and then a multitude of pale hands were reaching towards me, and strange gentle faces bending above me, and half wailing and half caressing voices uttering words that were forgotten the moment they were spoken. I was being lifted out of the tide of flame, and felt my memories, my hopes, my thoughts, my will, everything I held to be myself, melting away; then I seemed to rise through numberless companies of beings who were, I understood, in some way more certain than thought, each wrapped in his eternal moment, in the perfect lifting of an arm, in a little circlet of rhythmical words, in dreaming with dim eyes and half-closed eyelids. And then I passed beyond these forms, which were so beautiful they had almost ceased to be, and, having endured strange moods, melancholy, as it seemed, with the weight of many worlds, I passed into that Death which is Beauty herself, and into that Loneliness which all the multitudes desire without ceasing. All things that had ever lived seemed to come and dwell in my heart, and I in theirs; and I had never again known mortality or tears, had I not suddenly fallen from the certainty of vision into the uncertainty of dream, and become a drop of molten gold falling with immense rapidity, through a night elaborate with stars, and all about me a melancholy exultant wailing. I fell and fell and fell, and then the wailing was but the wailing of the wind in the chimney, and I awoke to find myself leaning upon the table and supporting my head with my hands. I saw the *alembic* swaying from side to side in the distant corner it had rolled to, and Michael Robartes watching me and waiting. "I will go wherever you will," I said, "and do whatever you bid me, for I have been with eternal things." "I knew," he replied, "you must need answer as you have answered, when I heard the storm begin. You must come to a great distance, for we were commanded to build our temple between the pure multitude by the waves and the impure multitude of men."

III

I did not speak as we drove through the deserted streets, for my mind was curiously empty of familiar thoughts and experiences; it seemed to have been plucked out of the definite world and cast naked upon a shoreless sea. There were moments when the vision appeared on the point of returning, and I would half-remember, with an ecstasy of joy or sorrow, crimes and heroisms, fortunes and misfortunes; or begin to contemplate, with a sudden leaping of the heart, hopes and terrors, desires and ambitions, alien to my orderly and careful life; and then I would awake shuddering at the thought that some great imponderable being had swept through my mind.

It was indeed days before this feeling passed perfectly away, and even now, when I have sought refuge in the only definite faith, I feel a great tolerance for those people with incoherent personalities, who gather in the chapels and meeting-places of certain obscure sects, because I also have felt fixed habits and principles dissolving before a power, which was *hysterica passio* or sheer madness, if you will, but was so powerful in its melancholy exultation that I tremble lest it wake again and drive me from my new-found peace.

When we came in the grey light to the great half-empty terminus, it seemed to me I was so changed that I was no more, as man is, a moment shuddering at eternity, but eternity weeping and laughing over a moment; and when we had started and Michael Robartes had fallen asleep, as he soon did, his sleeping face, in which there was no sign of all that had so shaken me and that now kept me wakeful, was to my excited mind more like a mask than a face. The fancy possessed me that the man behind it had dissolved away like salt in water, and that it laughed and sighed, appealed and denounced at the bidding of beings greater or less than man. "This is not Michael Robartes at all: Michael Robartes is dead; dead for ten, for twenty years perhaps," I kept repeating to myself. I fell at last into a feverish sleep, waking up from time to time when we rushed past some little town, its slated roofs shining with wet, or still lake gleaming in the cold morning light. I had been too pre-occupied to ask where we were going, or to notice what tickets Michael Robartes had taken, but I knew now from the direction of the sun that we were going westward; and presently I knew also, by the way in which the trees had grown into the semblance of tattered beggars flying with bent heads towards the east, that we were approaching the western coast. Then immediately I saw the sea between the low hills upon the left, its dull grey broken into white patches and lines.

When we left the train we had still, I found, some way to go, and set out, buttoning our coats about us, for the wind was bitter and violent. Michael Robartes was silent, seeming anxious to leave me to my thoughts; and as we walked between the sea and the rocky side of a great promontory, I realized with a new perfection what a shock had been given to all my habits of thought and of feelings, if indeed some mysterious change had not taken place in the substance of my mind, for the grey waves, plumed with scudding foam, had grown part of a teeming, fantastic inner life; and when Michael Robartes pointed to a square ancient-looking house, with a much smaller and newer building under its lee, set out on the very end of a dilapidated and almost deserted pier, and said it was the Temple of the Alchemical Rose, I was possessed with the phantasy that the sea, which kept covering it with showers of white foam, was claiming it as part of some indefinite and passionate life, which had begun to war upon our orderly and careful days, and was about to plunge the world into a night as obscure as that which followed the downfall of the classical world. One part of my mind mocked this phantastic terror, but the other, the part that still lay half plunged in vision, listened to the clash of unknown armies, and shuddered at un-imaginable fanaticisms, that hung in those grey leaping waves.

We had gone but a few paces along the pier when we came upon an old man, who was evidently a watchman, for he sat in an overset barrel, close to a place where masons had been lately working upon a break in the pier, and had in front of him a fire such as one sees slung under tinkers' carts. I saw that he was also a voteen, as the peasants say, for there was a rosary hanging from a nail on the rim of the barrel, and I saw I shuddered, and I did not know why I shuddered. We had passed him a few yards when I heard him cry in Gaelic, "Idolaters, idolaters, go down to Hell with your witches and your devils; go down to Hell that the herrings may come again into the bay"; and for some moments I could hear him half screaming and half muttering behind us. "Are you not afraid," I said, "that these wild fishing people may do some desperate thing against you?"

"I and mine," he answered, "are long past human hurt or help, being incorporate with immortal spirits, and when we die it shall be the consummation of the supreme work. A time will come for these people also, and they will sacrifice a mullet to Artemis, or some other fish to some new divinity, unless indeed their own divinities, the Dagda, with his overflowing cauldron, Lug, with his spear dipped in poppy-juice lest it rush forth hot for battle. Aengus, with the three birds on his shoulder, Bodb and his red swineherd, and all the heroic children of Dana, set up once more their temples of grey stone. Their reign has never ceased, but only waned in power a little, for the Sidhe still pass in every wind, and dance and play at hurley, and fight their sudden battles in every hollow and on every hill; but they cannot build their temples again till there have been martyrdoms and victories, and perhaps even that long-foretold battle in the Valley of the Black Pig."

Keeping close to the wall that went about the pier on the seaward side, to escape the driving foam and the wind, which threatened every moment to lift us off our feet, we made our way in silence to the door of the square building. Michael Robartes opened it with a key, on which I saw the rust of many salt winds, and led me along a bare passage and up an uncarpeted stair to a little room surrounded with bookshelves. A meal would be brought, but only of fruit, for I must submit to a tempered fast before the ceremony, he explained, and with it a book on the doctrine and method of the Order, over which I was to spend what remained of the winter daylight. He then left me, promising to return an hour before the ceremony. I began searching among the bookshelves, and found one of the most exhaustive alchemical libraries I have ever seen. There were the works of Morienus, who hid his immortal body under a shirt of hair-cloth; of Avicenna, who was a drunkard and yet controlled numberless legions of spirits; of Alfarabi, who put so many spirits into his lute that he could make men laugh, or weep, or fall in deadly trance as he would; of Lully, who transformed himself into the likeness of a red cock; of Flamel, who with his wife Parnella achieved the elixir many hundreds of years ago, and is fabled to live still in Arabia among the Dervishes; and of many of less fame. There were very few mystics but alchemical mystics, and because, I had little doubt, of the devotion to one god of the greater number and of the limited sense of beauty, which Robartes would hold an inevitable consequence; but I did notice a complete set of facsimiles of the prophetical writings of William Blake, and probably because of the multitudes that thronged his illumination and were "like the gay fishes on the wave when the moon sucks up the dew." I noted also many poets and prose writers of every age, but only those who were a little weary of life, as indeed the greatest have been everywhere, and who cast their imagination to us, as a something they needed no longer now that they were going up in their fiery chariots.

Presently I heard a tap at the door, and a woman came in and laid a little fruit upon the table. I judged that she had once been handsome, but her cheeks were hollowed by what I would have held, had I seen her anywhere else, an excitement of the flesh and a thirst for pleasure, instead of which it doubtless was an excitement of the imagination and a thirst for beauty. I asked her some question concerning the ceremony, but getting no answer except a shake of the head, saw that I must await initiation in silence. When I had eaten, she came again, and having laid a curiously wrought bronze box on the table, lighted the candles, and took away the plates and the remnants. So soon as I was alone, I turned to the box, and found that the peacocks of Hera spread out their tails over the sides and lid, against a background, on which were wrought great stars, as though to affirm that the heavens were a part of their glory. In the box was a book bound in vellum, and having upon the vellum and in very delicate colours, and in gold, the alchemical rose with many spears thrusting against it, but in vain, as was shown by the shattered points of those nearest to the petals. The book was written upon vellum, and in beautiful clear letters, interspersed with symbolical pictures and illuminations, after the manner of the *Splendor Solis*.

The first chapter described how six students, of Celtic descent, gave themselves separately to the study of alchemy, and solved, one the mystery of the Pelican, another the mystery of the green Dragon, another the mystery of the Eagle, another that of Salt and Mercury. What seemed a succession of accidents, but was, the book declared, the contrivance of preternatural powers, brought them together in the garden of an inn in the South of France, and while they talked together the thought came to them that alchemy was the gradual distillation of the contents of the soul, until they were ready to put off the mortal and put on the immortal. An owl passed, rustling among the vine-leaves overhead, and then an old woman came, leaning upon a stick, and, sitting close to them, took up the thought where they had dropped it. Having expounded the whole principle of spiritual alchemy, and bid them found the Order of the Alchemical Rose, she passed from among them, and when they would have followed she was nowhere to be seen. They formed themselves into an Order, holding their goods and making their researches in common, and, as they became perfect in the alchemical doctrine, apparitions came and went among them, and taught them more and more marvellous mysteries. The book then went on to expound so much of these as the neophyte was permitted to know, dealing at the outset and at considerable length with the independent reality of our thoughts, which was, it declared, the doctrine from which all true doctrines rose. If you imagine, it said, the semblance of a living being, it is at once possessed by a wandering soul, and goes hither and thither working good or evil, until the moment of its death has come; and gave many examples, received, it said, from many gods. Eros had taught them how to fashion forms in which a divine soul could dwell, and whisper what they would into sleeping minds; and Ate, forms from which demonic beings could pour madness, or unquiet dreams, into sleeping blood; and Hermes, that if you powerfully imagined a hound at your bedside it would keep watch there until you woke, and drive away all but the mightiest demons, but that if your imagination was weakly, the hound would be weakly also, and the demons prevail, and the hound soon die; and Aphrodite, that if you made, by a strong imagining, a dove crowned with silver and had it flutter over your head, its soft cooing would make sweet dreams of immortal love gather and brood over mortal sleep; and all divinities alike had revealed with many warnings and lamentations that all minds are continually giving birth to such beings, and sending them forth to work health or disease, joy or madness. If you would give forms to the evil powers, it went on, you were to make them ugly, thrusting out a lip, with the thirsts of life, or breaking the proportions of a body with the burdens of life; but the divine powers would only appear in beautiful shapes, which are but, as it were, shapes trembling out of existence, folding up into a timeless ecstasy, drifting with half-shut eyes, into a sleepy stillness. The bodiless souls who descended into these forms were what men called the moods; and worked all great changes in the world; for just as the magician or the artist could call them when he would, so they could call out of the mind of the magician or the artist, or if they were demons, out of the mind of the mad or the ignoble, what shape they would, and through its voice and its gestures pour themselves out upon the world. In this way all great events were accomplished; a mood, a divinity, or a demon, first descending like a faint sigh into men's minds and then changing their thoughts and their actions until hair that was yellow had grown black, or hair that was black had grown yellow, and empires moved their border, as though they were but drifts of leaves. The rest of the book contained symbols of form, and sound, and colour, and their attribution to divinities and demons, so that the initiate might fashion a shape for any divinity or any demon, and be as powerful as Avicenna among those who live under the roots of tears and of laughter.

IV

A couple of hours after Sunset Michael Robartes returned and told me that I would have to learn the steps of an exceedingly antique dance, because before my initiation could be perfected I had to join three times in a magical dance, for rhythm was the wheel of Eternity, on which alone the transient and accidental could be broken, and the spirit set free. I found that the steps, which were simple enough, resembled certain antique Greek dances, and having been a good dancer in my youth and the master of many curious Gaelic steps, I soon had them in my memory. He then robed me and himself in a costume which suggested by its shape both Greece and Egypt, but by its crimson colour a more passionate life than theirs; and having put into my hands a little chainless censer of bronze, wrought into the likeness of a rose, by some modern craftsman, he told me to open a small door opposite to the door by which I had entered. I put my hand to the handle, but the moment I did so the fumes of the incense, helped perhaps by his mysterious glamour, made me fall again into a dream, in which I seemed to be a mask, lying on the counter of a little Eastern shop. Many persons, with eyes so bright and still that I knew them for more than human, came in and tried me on their faces, but at last flung me into a corner with a little laughter; but all this passed in a moment, for when I awoke my hand was still upon the handle. I opened the door, and found myself in a marvellous passage, along whose sides were many divinities wrought in a mosaic, not less beautiful than the mosaic in the Baptistery at Ravenna, but of a less severe beauty; the predominant colour of each divinity, which was surely a symbolic colour, being repeated in the lamps that hung from the ceiling, a curiously-scented lamp before every divinity. I passed on, marvelling exceedingly how these enthusiasts could have created all this beauty in so remote a place, and half persuaded to believe in a material alchemy, by the sight of so much hidden wealth; the censer filling the air, as I passed, with smoke of ever-changing colour.

I stopped before a door, on whose bronze panels were wrought great waves in whose shadow were faint suggestions of terrible faces. Those beyond it seemed to have heard our steps, for a voice cried: "Is the work of the Incorruptible Fire at an end?" and immediately Michael Robartes answered: "The perfect gold has come from the athanor." The door swung open, and we were in a great circular room, and among men and women who were dancing slowly in crimson robes. Upon the ceiling was an immense rose wrought in mosaic; and about the walls, also in mosaic, was a battle of gods and angels, the gods glimmering like rubies and sapphires, and the angels of the one greyness, because, as Michael Robartes whispered, they had renounced their divinity, and turned from the unfolding of their separate hearts, out of love for a God of humility and sorrow. Pillars supported the roof and made a kind of circular cloister, each pillar being a column of confused shapes, divinities, it seemed, of the wind, who rose as in a whirling dance of more than human vehemence, and playing upon pipes and cymbals; and from among these shapes were thrust out hands, and in these hands were censers. I was bid place my censer also in a hand and take my place and dance, and as I turned from the pillars towards the dancers, I saw that the floor was of a green stone, and that a pale Christ on a pale cross was wrought in the midst. I asked Robartes the meaning of this, and was told that they desired "To trouble His unity with their multitudinous feet." The dance wound in and out, tracing upon the floor the shapes of petals that copied the petals in the rose overhead, and to the sound of hidden instruments which were perhaps of an antique pattern, for I have never heard the like; and every moment the dance was more passionate, until all the winds of the world seemed to have awakened under our feet. After a little I had grown weary, and stood under a pillar watching the coming and going of those flame-like figures; until gradually I sank into a half-dream, from which I was awakened by seeing the petals of the great rose, which had no longer the look of mosaic, falling slowly through the incense-heavy air, and, as they fell, shaping into the likeness of living beings of an extraordinary beauty. Still faint and cloud-like, they began to dance, and as they danced took a more and more definite shape, so that I was able to distinguish beautiful Grecian faces and august Egyptian faces, and now and again to name a divinity by the staff in his hand or by a bird fluttering over his head; and soon every mortal foot danced by the white foot of an immortal; and in the troubled eyes that looked into untroubled shadowy eyes, I saw the brightness of uttermost desire as though they had found at length, after unreckonable wandering, the lost love of their youth. Sometimes, but only for a moment, I saw a faint solitary figure with a Rosa veiled face, and carrying a faint torch, flit among the dancers, but like a dream within a dream, like a shadow of a shadow, and I knew by an understanding born from a deeper fountain than thought, that it was Eros himself, and that his face was veiled because no man or woman from the beginning of the world has ever known what love is, or looked into his eyes, for Eros alone of divinities is altogether a spirit, and hides in passions not of his essence if he would commune with a mortal heart. So that if a man love nobly he knows love through infinite pity, unspeakable trust, unending sympathy; and if ignobly through vehement jealousy, sudden hatred, and unappeasable desire; but unveiled love he never knows. While I thought these things, a voice cried to me from the crimson figures: "Into the dance! there is none that can be spared out of the dance; into the dance! into the dance! that the gods may make them bodies out of the substance of our hearts'; and before I could answer, a mysterious wave of passion, that seemed like the soul of the dance moving within our souls, Alchemica took hold of me, and I was swept, neither consenting nor refusing, into the midst. I was dancing with an immortal august woman, who had black lilies in her hair, and her dreamy gesture seemed laden with a wisdom more profound than the darkness that is between star and star, and with a love like the love that breathed upon the waters; and as we danced on and on, the incense drifted over us and round us, covering us away as in the heart of the world, and ages seemed to pass, and tempests to awake and perish in the folds of our robes and in her heavy hair.

Suddenly I remembered that her eyelids had never quivered, and that her lilies had not dropped a black petal, or shaken from their places, and understood with a great horror that I danced with one who was more or less than human, and who was drinking up my soul as an ox drinks up a wayside pool; and I fell, and darkness passed over me.

V

I awoke suddenly as though something had awakened me, and saw that I was lying on a roughly painted floor, and that on the ceiling, which was at no great distance, was a roughly painted rose, and about me on the walls half-finished paintings. The pillars and the censers had gone; and near me a score of sleepers lay wrapped in disordered robes, their upturned faces looking to my imagination like hollow masks; and a chill dawn was shining down upon them from a long window I had not noticed before; and outside the sea roared. I saw Michael Robartes lying at a little distance and beside him an overset bowl of wrought bronze which looked as though it had once held incense. As I sat thus, I heard a sudden tumult of angry men and women's voices mix with the roaring of the sea; and leaping to my feet, I went quickly to Michael Robartes, and tried to shake him out of his sleep. I then seized him by the shoulder and tried to lift him, but he fell backwards, and sighed faintly; and the voices became louder and angrier; and there was a sound of heavy blows upon the door, which opened on to the pier. Suddenly I heard a sound of rending wood, and I knew it had begun to give, and I ran to the door of the room. I pushed it open and came out upon a passage whose bare boards clattered under my feet, and found in the passage another door which led into an empty kitchen; and as I passed through the door I heard two crashes in quick succession, and knew by the sudden noise of feet and the shouts that the door which opened on to the pier had fallen inwards. I ran from the kitchen and out into a small yard, and from this down some steps which descended the seaward and sloping side of the pier, and from the steps clambered along the water's edge, with the angry voices ringing in my ears. This part of the pier had been but lately refaced with blocks of granite, so that it was almost clear of seaweed; but when I came to the old part, I found it so slippery with green weed that I had to climb up on to the roadway. I looked towards the Temple of the Alchemical Rose, where the fishermen and the women were still shouting, but somewhat more faintly, and saw that there was no one about the door or upon the pier; but as I looked, a little crowd hurried out of the door and began gathering large stones from where they were heaped up in readiness for the next time a storm shattered the pier, when they would be laid under blocks of granite. While I stood watching the crowd, an old man, who was, I think, the voteen, pointed to me, and screamed out something, and the crowd whitened, for all the faces had turned towards me. I ran, and it was well for me that pullers of the oar are poorer men with their feet than with their arms and their bodies; and yet while I ran I scarcely heard the following feet or the angry voices, for many voices of exultation and lamentation, which were forgotten as a dream is forgotten the moment they were heard, seemed to be ringing in the air over my head.

There are moments even now when I seem to hear those voices of exultation and lamentation, and when the indefinite world, which has but half lost its mastery over my heart and my intellect, seems about to claim a perfect mastery; but I carry the rosary about my neck, and when I hear, or seem to hear them, I press it to my heart and say: "He whose name is Legion is at our doors deceiving our intellects with subtlety and flattering our hearts with beauty, and we have no trust but in Thee"; and then the war that rages within me at other times is still, and I am at peace.

THE PERFUME OF EGYPT

by C. W. Leadbeater

IT is a curious life, that of a man in chambers, though very pleasant in many ways. Its great charm is its absolute liberty—the entire freedom to go out and come in, or *not* to go out and come in, exactly as one pleases. But it is terribly lonely. Probably most people remember Dickens's ghastly tale (founded, I believe, on fact) of a man who was struck by apoplexy when on the point of opening his door, and lay propped up against it for a whole year, until at the expiration of that time it was broken open, and his skeleton fell into the arms of the locksmith. I do not think I am a nervous man, but I confess that during my residence in chambers that story haunted me at times; and indeed, quite apart from such unusual horrors, there is a wide field of uncomfortable possibility in being left so entirely to oneself.

All the most unpleasant things that happen to people, both in fiction and real life, seem to occur when they are alone; and though no doubt the talented American author is right when he "thanks a merciful heaven that the unendurable extreme of agony happens always to man the unit, and never to man the mass," one feels that it is probably easier to re-echo his sentiment heartily when one is not the unit in question.

On the other hand, when a man in chambers locks his door on a winter night and settles down cosily by the fire for an evening's reading, he has a sense of seclusion and immunity from interruption only to be equalled by that of a man who has sported his oak in a top set in college.

Just so had I[1] settled down—not to reading, however, but to writing—on the evening on which occurred the first of the chain of events that I am about to relate. In fact, I was writing a book—my first book—*On the Present State of the Law on Conveyancing*. I had published several essays on various aspects of the subject, and these had been so well received by high legal authorities, that I was emboldened to present my views in a more ambitious form. It was to this work, then, that I was applying myself with all a young author's zeal on the evening in question; and my reason for mentioning this fact is to show the subject on which my thoughts were fixed with a special intentness—one far enough, surely, from suggesting anything like romantic or unusual adventure.

I had just paused, I remember, to consider the exact wording of a peculiarly knotty sentence, when suddenly there came over me that feeling which I suppose all of us have experienced at one time or another—the feeling that I was not alone—that there was some one else in the room. I knew that my door was locked, and that the idea was therefore absurd; yet the impression was so strong that I instinctively half-rose from my chair and glanced hurriedly round. There was nothing visible, however, and with a half-laugh at my foolishness I was turning to my sentence again, when I became conscious of a faint but very peculiar odour in the room. It seemed familiar to me, yet for some few moments I was unable to identify it;

---

1 The narrator of this remarkable series of incidents (whom I have called Mr. Thomas Keston) is—or rather was—a barrister of considerable repute in London. I have thought it best to leave him to tell his own story in his own words, reserving comments until the end.—C. W. L.

then it flashed across my mind where I had met with it before, and my surprise was profound, as will be readily understood when I explain.

I had spent the long vacation of the preceding year in wandering about Egypt, peering into odd nooks and corners, and trying to make myself acquainted with the true life of the country—keeping as far as possible out of the beaten track and away from bands of tourists. While in Cairo I had the good fortune to make the acquaintance of a certain Sheikh (so he was called, though I am unable to say whether he had any right to the title) who proved to be a perfect mine of information as to ancient manners and customs, and the antiquities of the place generally—as regards relics of the glory of the mediaeval Caliphs, I mean, not the *real* antiquities of the old Egyptian dynasties. My servant warned me to beware of this man, and said he had the reputation of being a magician and dealing extensively with the evil one; however, I always found him very friendly and obliging, and he certainly pointed out to me many objects of interest that I should inevitably have missed but for him.

One day, going to call on him at an unusual hour, I was struck on entering his room by a most peculiar odour. It was altogether unlike anything I had ever smelt before—indescribably rich and sweet—almost oppressively so—and yet its effects seemed stimulating and exhilarating. I was so much pleased with it that I pressed the Sheikh strongly either to give me a little of it or tell me where I could obtain it; but to my surprise he refused courteously but firmly to do either. All he would say was that it was a sacred perfume, used only in certain incantations; that its manufacture was a secret handed down from the remotest ages and known only to a chosen few; and that not all the gold in the world would ever buy a single grain of it.

Naturally this excited my curiosity immensely, but he would give me no further information either as to the scent itself or the purpose for which he had been using it. Sitting talking with him for an hour or so, my garments became permeated with its alluring fragrance, and when I returned to my hotel my servant, in brushing my coat, perceived it and started back with horror. Startled out of his usual impassivity and imperturbable courtesy, he asked hurriedly:

"Effendi, where have you been? How comes this devil-scent upon your clothes?"

"What do you mean?" said I. "What is the smell that excites you so strangely?"

"O sir, be careful!" replied my man, almost weeping. "You do not know, you do not believe; you English do not understand the awful power of the old magic of Egypt. I do not know where you have been, but O sir! never go there again, for you have been in terrible danger. Only magicians use this scent, and no magician can make it for himself; it is prepared by devils, and for every phial there must be a human sacrifice, so we call it virgin's blood."

"Nonsense, Mustapha," I said; "you cannot expect me to believe such a tale as that. Cannot you get me some of this mysterious substance?"

"Not for the world," answered Mustapha, with every appearance of mortal dread upon his countenance. "No one can get it—no one, I assure you! and I dare not touch it for my life, even if they could. Effendi, keep away from these things, for your soul's sake."

I laughed at his fear for me, but there could be no doubt that he was in deadly earnest; and it is certainly true that I could find no perfume in the least like that which I remembered so well, though I tried every scent-merchant in Cairo.

When I say that it was this mysterious aroma—faint, but quite unmistakable—that greeted my nostrils in my own chambers in London on that memorable night, it will be seen that I had good reason to be surprised. What could it mean? Was it anyhow possible that the smell could have lingered in some article of clothing? Obviously not, for had it done so I must certainly have discovered the fact in much less time than the fourteen or fifteen months that had elapsed. Then whence could it come? For I was well convinced that nothing in the least like it could be obtained in England. The problem appeared so difficult that when I could no longer perceive the odour I was half inclined to doubt whether after all it might not have been a hallucination; and I turned to my work again, resolved to throw it entirely off my mind.

I worked out the knotty sentence to my satisfaction, and had written perhaps a page more, when quite suddenly and without warning I felt again, more strongly than ever, that unpleasant consciousness of some other presence in the room; but this time, before I could turn to look, I felt—distinctly felt—a soft breath or puff of wind on the back of my neck, and heard a faint sigh. I sprang from my chair with an inarticulate cry, and looked wildly round the room, but there was nothing unusual to be seen—no trace remained of my mysterious visitant. No trace, did I say? Even in the moment that passed while I was regaining my self-possession there stole again upon my astonished sense that strange subtle perfume of ancient eastern magic!

It would be folly to deny that I was seriously startled. I rushed to the door and tried it—shook it vigorously; but it was locked, exactly as I had left it. I turned to the bedroom; there was no one there. I then searched both the rooms thoroughly looking under bed, sofas, and tables, and opening every cupboard or box large enough to hold even a cat; still there was nothing. I was completely puzzled. I sat down and tried to think the matter out, but the more I thought the less could I see my way to any rational solution of these occurrences.

At length I decided to shake off their influence for the time, and postpone all consideration of them until the morning. I tried to resume my work, but I was out of tune for writing—my mind had been too much disturbed. The haunting consciousness of another presence would not leave me; that soft sad sigh seemed yet sounding in my ears, and its unutterable sorrow provoked a feeling of sympathetic depression. After a few unavailing efforts I gave up the attempt to write, threw myself into an arm-chair by the fire, and began to read instead.

Though simple enough, I believe, in most of my habits, I am rather a Sybarite about my reading; for that purpose I always use the most comfortable arm-chair that money can procure, with that most blessed of inventions, the "Literary Machine," to hold my book at exactly the right angle, shade the light from my face and concentrate it on the page, and give me a desk always ready to my hand if I wish to make notes.

In this luxurious manner, then, I settled myself down on this occasion, choosing as my book Montaigne's *Essays*, in the hope that their cleverness and marvellous flexibility of style might supply just the mental tonic that I felt I needed. Ignore them as I might, however, I had still as I read two under-currents of consciousness—one of that ever-haunting presence, and the other of occasional faint waftings of the perfume of Egypt.

I suppose I had been reading for about half an hour when a stronger whiff than ever greeted my nostrils, and at the same time a slight rustle caused me to raise my eyes from my book. Judge of my astonishment when I saw, not five yards from me, seated at the table from which I had so lately risen, and apparently engaged in writing, the figure of a man! Even as I looked at him the pen fell from his hand, he rose from the chair, threw upon me a glance which seemed to express bitter disappointment and heart-rending appeal, and—vanished!

Too much stupefied even to rise, I sat staring at the spot where he had stood, and rubbed my eyes mechanically, as though to clear away the last relics of some horrible dream. Great as the shock had been, I was surprised to find, as soon as I was able to analyse my sensations, that they were distinctly those of relief; and it was some minutes before I could comprehend this. At last it flashed across me that the haunting sense of an unseen presence was gone, and then for the first time I realised how terrible its oppression had been. Even that strange magical odour was rapidly fading away, and in spite of the startling sight I had just seen, I had a sense of freedom such as a man feels when he steps out of some dark dungeon into the full bright sunlight.

Perhaps it was this feeling more than anything else that served to convince me that what I had seen was no delusion—that there had really been a presence in the room all the time which had at last succeeded in manifesting itself, and now was gone. I forced myself to sit still and recall carefully all that I had seen—even to note it down on the paper which lay before me on the desk of my literary machine.

First, as to the personal appearance of my ghostly visitor, if such he were. His figure was tall and commanding, his face expressing great power and determination, but showing also traces of a reckless passion and possible latent brutality that certainly gave on the whole the impression of a man rather to be feared and avoided than loved. I noticed more particularly the firm setting of his lips, because running down from under one there was a curious white scar, which this action caused to stand out conspicuously; and then I recollected how this expression had broken and changed to one in which anger, despair, and appeal for help were strangely mingled with a certain dark pride that seemed to say:

"I have done all I could; I have played my last card and it has failed; I have never stooped to ask help from mortal man before, but I ask it from you now."

A good deal, you will say, to make out of a single glance; but still that was exactly what it seemed to me to express; and, sinister though his appearance was, I mentally resolved that his appeal should not have been made in vain, if I could in any way discover who he was or what he wanted. I had never believed in ghosts before; I was not even quite sure that I did now; but clearly a fellow-creature in suffering was a brother to be helped, whether in the body or out of the body. With such thoughts as these all trace of fear vanished, and I honestly believe that if the spirit had reappeared I should have asked him to sit down and state his case as coolly as I should have met any other client.

I carefully noted down all the events of the evening, appended the hour and date, and affixed my signature; and then, happening to look up, my eye was caught by two or three papers lying on the floor. I had seen the wide sleeve of the long dark gown that the spectre wore sweep them down as he rose, and this for the first time reminded me that he had appeared to be writing at the table, and consequently might possibly have left there some clue to the mystery. At once I went and examined it; but everything was as I had left it, except that my pen lay where I had seen it fall from his hand. I picked up the papers from the floor, and then—my heart gave a great bound, for I saw among them a curious torn fragment which had certainly not been on my table before.

The eagerness with which I seized upon it may be imagined. It was a little oblong slip about five inches by three, apparently part either of a longer slip or a small book, for its edge at one end was extremely jagged, suggesting that considerable force had been required to tear it off; and indeed the paper was so thick and parchment-like that I could not wonder at it. The curious thing was that while the paper was much discoloured—water-stained and yellow with age—the jagged edge was white and fresh, looking as though it had been but just torn off. One side of the paper was entirely blank—or at least, if there ever had been any writing upon it, it had disappeared through the influence of time and damp; on the other were some blurred and indistinct characters, so faded as to be scarcely distinguishable, and, in a bold hand-writing in fresh black ink the two letters "Ra".

Since the ink with which these letters were written corresponded exactly with that which I was in the habit of using, I could hardly doubt that they had been written at my table, and were the commencement of some explanation that the spectre had wished, but for some reason found himself unable, to make. Why he should have taken the trouble to bring his own paper with him I could not understand, but I inferred that probably some mystery was hidden beneath those undecipherable yellow marks, so I turned all my attention to them. After patient and long-continued effort, however, I was unable to make anything like sense out of them, and resolved to wait for daylight.

Contrary to my expectations, I did not *dream* of my ghostly visitor that night, though I lay awake for some time thinking of him. In the morning I borrowed a magnifying glass from a friend, and resumed my examination. I found that there were two lines of writing, apparently in some foreign language, and then a curious mark, not unlike a monogram of some kind, standing as if in the place of a signature. But with all my efforts I could neither distinguish the letters of the monogram nor discover the language of the two lines of writing. As far as I could make it out it read thus:

Qomm uia daousa sita eo uia uiese quoam.

Some of these words had rather a Latin look; and I reflected that if the memorandum were as old as it appeared to be, Latin was a very likely language for it; but then I could make out nothing like a coherent sentence, so I was as far off from a solution as ever. I hardly knew what steps to take next. I shrank so much from speaking of the events of that evening that I could not bring myself to show the slip to any one else, lest it should lead to enquiries as to how it came into my possession; so I put it away carefully in my pocket-book, and for the time being my investigations seemed at a standstill.

I had not gained any fresh light on the subject, nor come to any definite conclusion about it, by the time the second incident of my story occurred, about a fortnight later. Again I was sitting at my writing-table early in the evening—engaged this time not upon my book but in the less congenial pursuit of answering letters. I dislike letter-writing, and am always apt to let my correspondence accumulate until the arrears assume formidable proportions, and insist on attention; and then I devote a day or two of purgatory to it, and clear them up. This was one of these occasions, further accentuated by the fact that I had to decide which of three Christmas invitations I would accept. It had been my custom for years always to spend Christmas when in England with my brother and his family, but this year his wife's health compelled them to winter abroad. I am conservative—absurdly so, I fear—about small things like this, and I felt that I should not really enjoy my Christmas at any house but his, so I cared little to choose in the matter. Here, however, were the three invitations; it was already the fourteenth of December, and I had not yet made up my mind. I was still debating the subject when I was disturbed by a loud knock at my door. On opening it I was confronted by a handsome sunburnt young fellow, whom at first I could not recognise; but when he called out in cheery tones:

"Why, Keston, old fellow, I believe you've forgotten me!"

I knew him at once as my old school-fellow Jack Fernleigh. He had been my fag at Eton, and I had found him such a jolly, good-hearted little fellow that our "official" relation had glid-ed into a firm friendship—a very rare occurrence; and though he was so far junior to me at Oxford that we were together there only a few months, still our acquaintance was kept up, and I had corresponded with him in a desultory sort of way ever since. I knew, consequently, that some years ago he had had some difference with his uncle (his only living relation) and had gone off to the West Indies to seek his fortune; and though our letters had been few and far between, I knew in a general way that he was doing very well there, so it was with no small surprise that I saw him standing at the door of my chambers in London.

I gave him a hearty welcome, set him down by the fire, and then asked him to explain his presence in England. He told me that his uncle had died suddenly, leaving no will, and that the lawyers had telegraphed the news to him. He had at once thrown up his position and started for England by the next steamer. Arriving in London too late to see his lawyers that day, and having after his long absence no other friends there, he had come, as he expressed it, to see whether I had forgotten my old fag.

"And right glad I am that you did, my boy," said I; "where is your luggage? We must send to the hotel for it, for I shall make you up a bed here for tonight."

He made a feeble protest, which I at once overruled; a messenger was found and despatched to the hotel, and we settled down for a talk about old times which lasted far into the night. The next morning he went betimes to call upon his lawyers, and in the afternoon started for Fernleigh Hall (now his property), but not before we had decided that I should run down and spend Christmas there with him instead of accepting any of my three previous invitations.

"I expect to find everything in a terrible state," he said; "but in a week's time I shall be able to get things a little to rights, and if you will turn up on the twenty-third I will promise you at least a bed to sleep in, and you will be doing a most charitable action in preventing my first Christmas in England for many a year from being a lonely one."

So we settled it, and consequently at four o'clock on the afternoon of the twenty-third I was shaking hands again with Jack on the platform of the little country station a few miles from Fernleigh. The short day had already drawn to a close by the time we reached the house, so I could get only a general idea of its outside appearance. It was a large Elizabethan mansion, but evidently not in very good repair; however, the rooms into which we were ushered were bright and cheerful enough. We had a snug little dinner, and after it Jack proposed to show me over the house. Accordingly, preceded by a solemn old butler with a lamp, we wandered through interminable mazes of rambling passages, across great desolated halls, and in and out of dozens of tapestried and panelled bedrooms—some of them with walls of enormous thickness, suggestive of all sorts of trap-doors and secret outlets—till my brain became absolutely confused, and I felt as though, if my companions had abandoned me, I might have spent days in trying to find my way out of the labyrinth.

"You could accommodate an army here, Jack!" said I.

"Yes," he replied, "and in the good old days Fernleigh was known all over the county for its open hospitality; but now, as you see, the rooms are bare and almost unfurnished."

"You'll soon change all that when you bring home a nice little wife," I said; "the place only wants a lady to take care of it."

"No hope of it, my dear fellow, I'm sorry to say," replied Jack; "there is not enough money for that."

I knew how in our school-days he had worshipped with all a boy's devotion lovely Lilian Featherstone, the daughter of the rector of the parish, and I had heard from him at college that on his part at least their childish intimacy had ripened into something deeper; so I asked after her now, and soon discovered that his sojourn in the tropics had worked no change in his feelings in this respect, that he had already contrived to meet her and her father out riding since his return, and that be had good reason to hope from her blush of pleasure on seeing him that he had not been forgotten in his absence. But alas! her father had only his living to depend on, and Jack's uncle (a selfish profligate) had not only let everything go to ruin, but had also so encumbered the estate that, by the time all was paid off and it was entirely free, there was but little money left—barely sufficient to support Jack himself, and certainly not enough to marry upon.

"So there is no hope of Lilian yet, you see," he concluded; "but I am young and strong; I can work, and I think she will wait for me. You shall see her on Thursday, for I have promised that we will dine with them then; they would have insisted on having me on Christmas day, but that I told them I had an old school-fellow coming down."

Just then we reached the door of the picture-gallery, and the old butler, having thrown it open, was proceeding to usher us in, but I said:

"No, Jack, let us leave this until tomorrow; we cannot see pictures well by this light. Let us go back to the fire, and you shall tell me that old legend of your family that was so much talked about at college; I never heard more than the merest fragments of it."

"There is nothing worth calling a legend," said Jack, as we settled down in the cosy little room he called his study; "nor is it very old, for it refers only to the latter part of the eighteenth century. The interest of the story, such as it is, centres round Sir Ralph Fernleigh, the last baronet, who seems by all accounts to have been a somewhat questionable character. He is said to have been a strange, reserved man—a man of strong passions, iron will, and indomitable pride; he spent much of his time abroad, and was reported to have acquired enormous wealth by means that would not bear too close examination. He was commonly known as "wicked Sir Ralph," and the more superstitious of his neighbours firmly believed that he had studied the black art during his long absences in the East. Others hinted that he was owner of a privateer, and that in those troubled times it was easy for a reckless man to commit acts of piracy with impunity.

"He was credited with a great knowledge of jewels, and was reported to possess one of the most splendid private collections of them in the world; but as none were found by his successor, I conclude that unless they were stolen the story was a myth, like that which represented him as having bars of gold and silver stacked up in his cellars. It seems certain that he was really tolerably rich, and that during his later years, which he spent here, he lived a remarkably retired life. He discharged all servants but a confidential man of his own, an Italian who had accompanied him in his wanderings; and these two lived a sort of hermit-life here all by themselves, holding no intercourse with the outer world. The universal report was that, though he had stored up great hoards of ill-gotten wealth, Sir Ralph lived like a miser. The few people who had seen him whispered darkly of a haunted look always to be seen on his proud face, and talked beneath their breath of some terrible secret crime; but I do not know that anything was ever really proved against him.

"One morning, however, he mysteriously disappeared; at least such was the story of the Italian servant, who came one day to the village asking in a frightened way in his broken English whether any one had seen his master. He said that, two days before, Sir Ralph had in the evening ordered his horse to be saddled early on the following morning, as he was going on a short journey alone; but when the morning came, though the horse was ready, *he* was not. He did not answer to his servant's calls, and though the latter searched through every room in the great old house, not a trace of his master could he find. His bed, he said, had not been slept in that night, and the only theory he could offer was that he had been carried away by the demons he used to raise. The villagers suspected foul play, and there was a talk of arresting the servant—which, coming to the latter's ears, seems to have alarmed him so much (in his ignorance of the customs of the country) that *he* also mysteriously disappeared that night, and was never seen again.

"Two days afterwards an exploring party was formed by the more adventurous of the villagers. They went all over the house and grounds, examined every nook and corner, and shouted themselves hoarse; 'but there was no voice, neither any that answered,' and from that day to this no sign either of master or man has ever revisited the light of the sun. Since the explorers could find none of the rumoured hoards of money either, it was an accepted article of faith among them that 'that there furriner' had murdered his master, hidden his body, and carried off the treasure, and of course a story presently arose that Sir Ralph's ghost had been seen about the place.

"They whispered that his room might be known from all the rest in this dark old house by a peculiar atmosphere of its own, caused by the constant haunting of the unquiet spirit of the owner; but this soon became a mere tradition, and now no one knows even in what part of the house his room was, nor have I ever heard of the ghost's appearance in my uncle's time, though I know he half-believed in it and never liked to speak of it. After Sir Ralph's disappearance the place was unoccupied and neglected for some years, till at last a distant cousin put in a claim to it, got it allowed by the lawyers, and took possession. He found, it is said, but a small balance after all to Sir Ralph's credit at his bankers'; but he had money of his own, apparently, for he proceeded to refit and rearrange the old place, and soon had it in respectable order. From him it descended to my uncle, who has let every thing run to seed again, as you see."

"That is a very interesting family legend after all, Jack," said I, "though perhaps rather lacking in romantic completeness. But have you no relics of this mysterious Sir Ralph?"

"There is his portrait in the picture-gallery along with the rest; there are some queer old books of his in the library, and one or two articles of furniture that are reported to have been his; but there is nothing to add to the romance of the story, I am afraid."

Little he thought, as he uttered those words just as we were separating for the night, what the real romance of that story was, or how soon we were to discover it!

My bedroom was a huge panelled chamber with walls of prodigious thickness, and with some very beautiful old carving about it. A border of roses and lilies that ran round the panels especially attracted my attention as one of the finest examples of that style of work that I had ever seen. There is always, I think, something uncanny about great Elizabethan bedrooms and huge four-post bedsteads, and I suppose my late ghostly experience had rendered me specially alive to such influences; so, though the roaring fire which Jack's hospitable care had provided for me threw a cheery light into every corner, I found myself thinking as I lay down in bed:

"What if this should turn out to be Sir Ralph's forgotten chamber, and he should come and disturb my rest, as that other visitor came to me in town!"

This idea returned to me again and again, until I really began to fancy that I could distinguish the peculiar atmosphere of which Jack had spoken—a sort of subtle influence that was gradually taking possession of me. This I felt would never do, if I was to have a comfortable night, so I roused myself from this unhealthy train of thought and resolutely put it away from me; but do what I would, I could not entirely shake off ghostly associations, for (recalled I suppose by my surroundings) every detail of the strange occurrence at my chambers passed before my mind over and over again with startling distinctness and fidelity.

Eventually I fell into a troubled sleep, in which my late mysterious visitor and the idea I had formed of Sir Ralph Fernleigh seemed to chase each other through my brain, till at last all these confused visions culminated in one peculiarly vivid dream. I seemed to myself to be lying in bed (just as I really was), with the fire burnt down to a deep red glow, when suddenly there appeared before me the same figure that I had seen in my chambers, habited in the same loose black robe; but now it held in its left hand a small book—evidently that to which the slip in my possession had belonged, for I could see the very place from which the missing leaf had been torn—and with the forefinger of the right hand the spectre was pointing to the last page of the book, while it looked eagerly in my face. I sprang up and approached the figure; it retreated before me until it reached one of the panelled walls, through which it seemed to vanish, still pointing to the page of its book, and with that imploring gaze still on its face. I woke with a start, and found myself standing close to the wall at the spot where the figure had seemed to disappear, with the dull red glow of the fire reflected from the carving, just as I had seen it in my dream, and my nostrils filled once more with that strange sweet Oriental perfume! Then in a moment a revelation dawned upon my mind. There *was* a peculiarity in the atmosphere of the room—I had been quite right in fancying so; and that peculiarity, which I could not recognise before, consisted in the faintest possible permanent suggestion of that magical odour so faint that I had not been able to identify it until this stronger rush of the scent made it clear.

Was it a dream, I asked myself; or had I really seen my mysterious visitor once more? I could not tell, but at any rate the smell in the room was an undoubted fact. I went and tried the door, but, as I expected, found it as I left it fast locked. I stirred up my fire into a bright blaze, threw fresh coals on it, and went to bed again—this time to sleep soundly and refreshingly till I was awakened in the morning by the servant bringing hot water.

Reviewing my last night's adventure in the sober light of day, I was disposed to think that something of it at least might be due to overheated imagination, though I still fancied I could detect that faint peculiarity of atmosphere. I decided to say nothing to Fernleigh, since to speak of it would involve describing the apparition in my chambers, which I shrank from discussing with any one; so when Jack asked me how I had slept, I replied:

"Very well indeed towards morning, though a little restless in the earlier part of the night."

After breakfast we walked about the park, which was very extensive, and studied the stately old house from different points of view. I was much struck with the great beauty of its situation and surroundings; and, though there were sad traces of neglect everywhere, I saw that the expenditure of what was comparatively but a small amount of money for so large a place would make it fully worthy to rank with any mansion and estate of its size in the kingdom. I enthusiastically pointed out the various possibilities to Jack, but he, poor fellow, sorrowfully remarked that the sum required to make the improvements, though no doubt comparatively small, was absolutely pretty large, and far beyond his present means.

After some hour's ramble we returned to the house, and Jack proposed that we should look over the picture-gallery and some other rooms that we had not seen on the previous night. We took the gallery first, and Jack told me that it had once contained many almost priceless gems of the old Flemish and Italian masters; but his dissolute uncle had sold most of them, often at merely nominal prices, to raise money for his riotous life in town, so that what were left were, generally speaking, comparatively valueless. There was the usual collection of ancestral portraits—some life-like and carefully executed, others mere daubs; and we were passing them over with scant interest, when my eye was caught by one which instantly riveted my attention and sent a cold thrill down my spine, bright midday though it was; for there, out of the canvas, looked the very face I had seen so vividly in my dream last night—the face of the mysterious visitant at my chambers in London!

The commanding look of iron will and dauntless courage was there, and the same indefinable air of latent passion and cruelty; there too, though tenderly treated by the artist and made less prominent than it was in reality, was the curious white scar running down from the lower lip. Except that he was here dressed in rich court costume instead of the plain black robe, nothing but the pleading look of appeal was wanting to make the resemblance exact. I suppose something of the emotion I felt showed itself in my face, for Jack seized me by the arm, crying:

"Bless me, Tom, what is the matter? Are you ill? Why are you glaring at the portrait of Sir Ralph in that awful manner?"

"Sir Ralph? Yes, the wicked Sir Ralph. I know him. He came into my room last night. I've seen him twice."

Muttering these disjointed sentences, I staggered to an ottoman and tried to collect my scattered senses. For the whole truth had flashed upon me, and it was almost too much for me. Of course it has occurred to the intelligent reader long ago, but until this moment absolutely no suspicion had ever crossed my mind that Sir Ralph and my spectral visitor in London were identical; now I saw it all. The word commencing with "Ra" that he had tried so hard to write was his own name; he had somehow (heaven alone knows how) foreseen that I should visit Fernleigh, and so had tried to make an impression on my mind—introduce himself to me, as it were—beforehand. I was now obliged to tell Jack the whole story, and was relieved to find that instead of laughing at me, as I more than half expected, he was deeply interested.

"I never believed in a ghost before," he said, "but here there seems no room for doubt. A perfect stranger shows himself to you in London, you recognise his portrait at once on sight down here at Fernleigh, and he turns out to be the very man whom tradition points out as haunting this place! The chain of evidence is perfect."

"But why should he have come to *me*?" I said. "I know nothing about ghosts and their ways; I am not even what these spiritualists call mediumistic. Would it not have been much more straightforward to appeal to you direct? Why should *I* be singled out for such a visitation?"

"Impossible to say," replied Jack; "I suppose he liked your looks; but what could he have wanted? We are no nearer discovering that than we were before. Where is that scrap of paper? For it strikes me that the solution of its mystery will yield the answer to our riddle."

I pulled out my pocket-book and handed the slip to Jack.

"Ha!" he exclaimed, the moment he glanced at it, "this is certainly Sir Ralph's monogram; I know it well, for I have seen it in several of the books in the library."

We at once adjourned to the library and compared the writing in some of Sir Ralph's books with that on the slip; the resemblance was perfect, though the writing on the slip seemed more carefully done, as though with a special effort to make every letter legible: while in the monogram (a very complicated one) every line and stroke were exactly similar. With Jack's guidance I was able to make out of it the initials

"R.F.," but I should certainly never have discovered them without assistance. We now concentrated our attention on the two lines of writing.

Jack took a powerful glass from a drawer and scrutinized them long and carefully.

"Your reading of the letters seems quite correct," he said at length; "but what language can this possibly be? It is not Spanish, Portuguese, nor Italian, I know; and you, who are acquainted with several Oriental dialects, do not recognise it either. I don't believe it is a language at all, Tom; it looks much more like a cryptograph."

"Scarcely, I think," I remarked; "you know, in a cryptograph one always gets utterly impossible combinations of consonants which betray its nature at once."

"Not invariably," replied Jack; "that depends upon the system on which it is constructed. I happen, though only by way of pastime, to have made this subject a rather special study, and I do not think there are many cryptographs which I could not, with sufficient time and patience, manage to make out."

"Then, Jack, if you think this may be one, by all means proceed to exercise your talents upon it at once."

Jack set to work, and I must say I was really amazed at the ingenuity he displayed, and the facility with which he seized upon and followed up the most seemingly insignificant clues. I need give no particulars of his processes; thanks to Edgar Allen Poe, everybody in these days knows how a cryptograph is solved. Suffice it to say that this, though really extremely simple, gave a good deal of trouble and led us off on a false scent, in consequence of the fact that a double system is employed in its construction. The rule is to substitute for every consonant the letter succeeding it in the alphabet, but for every vowel—not the letter, but—the *vowel* next *preceding* it in the alphabet. By a reversal of this process the reader will easily discover that its signification is as follows:

Our excitement may be imagined when this was deciphered. I knew at once to what it referred, for I remembered the carved border of roses and lilies round the panels in my bedroom of last night. The butler came in to announce luncheon, but we cared little for that; we rushed upstairs like a couple of school-boys and dashed into the panelled room.

"The third panel from which end?" asked Jack.

But I had not the slightest doubt; I remembered that the spectre had vanished through the wall on the left of the fireplace, so I walked up to that spot without hesitation, put my hand on the third panel from the corner, and said:

"This is it."

So large was the panel, however, that the centre rose was above our reach, and it was necessary to drag a table underneath it to stand upon. Jack sprang upon it and gave an energetic pull at the centre rose, but no result followed.

"Get down again," I said; "let us try the other side of the panel."

We moved the table, and Jack tried again, and this time with success. A small piece of the border had been cut out and hinged at the top, and the pull upon the rose lifted this and disclosed a cavity about six inches each way, in which was a large knob—evidently a handle. For some time this resisted our efforts, the machinery attached being probably rusty; but eventually we succeeded in turning it, and the whole huge panel swung into the room like a door, showing behind it a dark arched recess with steps leading downward, up which came, stronger than ever, that strange sweet smell of the perfume of Egypt which had haunted my thoughts so long. Jack was springing in, but I held him back.

"Stay, my dear fellow," I said; "curb your impatience. That place probably has not been opened for a very long time, and you must first let the fresh air penetrate it; you don't know what noxious gases may have accumulated down in that dreadful hole. Besides, we must first lock the door of the bed-room, that we may not be interrupted in our investigation."

Finally I persuaded him to wait five minutes, though in our excited condition it was a hard thing to do. Meantime we could not but admire the enormous strength of the walls, and the care that had been taken to make the moving panel safe by a massive backing of oak that prevented it from giving anything like a hollow sound if accidentally struck, and indeed made it as capable of resisting any conceivable blow as any other por-tion of the wall. When we noticed, too, the immense size and strength of the lock it had to move, we no longer wondered at the trouble it had cost us to turn the handle.

When the five minutes had expired we lighted a couple of candles that stood on the mantel-piece, and with mingled feelings of awe and pleasure entered the secret passage. The stairs turned abruptly to the left, and descended in the thick-ness of the wall. My fears as to want of ventilation seemed groundless, for there was quite a strong draught, proving that there must be an opening of some kind in the passage.

At the bottom of the steps we found ourselves in a long narrow vault or chamber, scarcely six feet in width, but perhaps thirty in length, and certainly fourteen or fifteen in height. Floor and walls were alike stone, and at the extreme end near the roof, quite out of reach, was a small slit such as those made of old for the convenience of archers, through which came a certain amount of light, and the current of air that we had noticed. On the floor at the further end were two large chests—the only furniture of this dungeon—and on one of them lay a black heap that by the flickering light of our candles looked horribly like a shrouded corpse.

"What can that be?" said I, shrinking back instinctively; but Jack pushed on to the end of the vault, and then dropped his candle with a smothered cry and came back towards me with a very white face.

"It is a dead body," he said in a horror-stricken whisper; "it must be Sir Ralph."

"Then," said I in the same tone, "he must have been shut in here somehow and starved to death."

"Good heavens!" cried Jack; and he rushed past me and up the stairs at full speed. At first I thought he had lost his nerve and deserted me, but in a few moments he was back again, though still pale with emotion.

"Just think, Tom," he said; "suppose a gust of wind had shut that door, the very same thing might have happened to us! No one knows of the existence of this place, so they would never think of looking here for us; and with such a massive door as that, it would be hopeless to dream of forcing our way out or making ourselves heard. Now I have fixed it open, and we are safe."

"Horrible as it is, I suppose we must examine this thing," I said.

We approached it, Jack picking up and relighting his candle. The sight that met our eyes was truly an awful one, for there, stretched on the top of one of the chests, and wrapped in a loose black robe with wide sleeves, lay a skeleton, with its grinning face turned upwards and its arm thrown carelessly over the side as if in ghastly imitation of sleep. Beside it on the floor lay a curiously shaped wide-mouthed bottle, and on the other chest—and I shuddered afresh as I recognised it—the very memorandum-book that the spectre had carried in my dream! I took it up, and we at once proceeded to examine it. It opened at the place where a leaf had been newly torn out, but I turned hastily to those last pages at which the figure had pointed so earnestly, and there read the following words:

I, Ralph Fernleigh, Bart., do here indite these my last dying words. By the judgment of God or by some foul treachery I am fast shut up in this mine own secret place, from which is no escape. Here I have lain three days and three nights, and forasmuch as I see naught before me but to die by hunger I am now resolved to put an end to this my so miserable existence by eating of those poisonous gums, whereof I have happily some store. But first will I confess the deadly sin that lieth upon my soul, and will lay solemn charge upon him who shall here find my body and shall read this my writing.[1]

. . . .

And if he who reads these my words shall fail to make such restitution as I have charged upon him, or shall reveal ever to mortal man this my deadly sin that I have here confessed, then shall my solemn curse rest upon him for ever, and my spirit shall dog him even to his grave. But if he shall do faithfully this my behest, then do I hereby freely give and bequeath to him such wealth as he will here find, hoping that he may use it to better purpose than I have done. And so may God have mercy on my soul.

RALPH FERNLEIGH.

How deeply we were affected by thus, in the very presence of his mortal remains, reading this strange message from the

---

1 The document itself explains why my friend was compelled to omit some part of it.—C. W. L.

dead, may easily be imagined. Jack had picked up the wide-mouthed bottle, at the bottom of which still remained some dark-coloured resinous matter—evidently the "poisonous gums" of the writing; but on hearing of its terrible association he dashed it on the floor in horror, and it was broken into a thousand pieces. Nor could I censure him for the act, though I knew that it contained the perfume of Egypt that I had so long desired. (I may here mention that I afterwards recovered a few grains and subjected it to analysis; it proved to be the 7 Persian *lôbhán*, but mixed with belladonna, Indian hemp, and some other vegetable ingredients whose exact nature I was unable to determine.)

Our next duty was the examination of the chests; but to perform this it was necessary first to remove the skeleton, and that we shrank from touching or even looking at. Still it had to be done, so we fetched a sheet from the bedroom, laid the ghastly relic reverently upon that, and so lifted it from the bed where it had lain so long. Then, not without a feeling of excitement, we opened the chests—a work of no difficulty, for the key that was in the lock of one fitted that of the other as well. The first was closely packed with bags and smaller boxes, the former of which, to our astonishment, we found to contain chiefly gold and silver coin of various countries; while the latter proved the truth of at least one of the popular rumours about Sir Ralph, for arranged carefully in them was a collection of gems, cut and uncut, some of which even our inexperienced eyes could tell to be almost priceless.

"Jack, my boy," said I grasping his hand (for not even the presence of the skeleton could altogether restrain my joy), "you shall soon wed your Lilian now! Even after carrying out Sir Ralph's wishes you will still be a rich man."

"Yes, Tom," answered he; "but remember, half of this is yours; without you I should never have known of its existence."

"No, no," replied I; "not a penny will I touch; I have enough and to spare, and besides it is all yours by right, for you are Sir Ralph's heir."

But he insisted, and at last to pacify him I had to consent to accept one or two of the larger jewels as mementos. The other chest contained a great quantity of family plate, some of it very rich and massive, and half a dozen small bars of gold, probably the basis of the wild myth that I mentioned before.

By the time our investigations were finished evening had come on; and, as may be supposed, we sat down to dinner with an appetite, and after it was over sat talking and planning far into the night. Very happily, though very quietly, we spent our Christmas day, and on the Thursday we dined at the rectory as arranged. Certainly Jack had not exaggerated the charms of his fair Lilian, and when in the course of the evening I saw them come out of the conservatory together, both looking greatly discomposed but deliciously happy, I knew that I might safely offer the dear fellow my congratulations.

I have little more to tell. The dying charge of Sir Ralph was scrupulously obeyed. Jack and I paid a visit to a somewhat out-of-the-way part of the Continent, and spent some time in searching through old records and unravelling forgotten genealogies; but after much toil we met with gratifying success, and at long last atonement was made—so far as in such cases atonement ever can be made—for the sin of the previous century, and the traditional hatred which certain families bore to the memory of a magic-working English lord was changed into a vivid and surprised gratitude. All was done that could be done; indeed, Jack was most lavishly generous, and we have every reason to hope that Sir Ralph was satisfied. At any rate, he has never since shown himself, either to praise or to blame us; so we trust that his long-tormented soul is at peace.

Three months later, in the sweet early spring-time, I went down to Fernleigh again to act as "best man" at a wedding, and as we passed down the churchyard the happy bridegroom silently pointed out to me a white marble cross bearing simply the words:

SIR RALPH FERNLEIGH, BART.
1795.

✳

Though not myself an eye-witness of the events of this story, I received them on unimpeachable testimony; in fact I may say that I had evidence for them such as would have satisfied any ordinary jury. With the narrator I had the pleasure of an intimate acquaintance of some years' duration. His friend Mr. Fernleigh I have seen only once, when he was in town for a few days; but on that occasion he fully and circumstantially corroborated Mr. Keston's account of these strange events, and gave me a warm and hearty invitation to come down and spend a fortnight at the Hall, so as to examine the theatre of their occurrence at my leisure; and further, as my engagements compelled me regretfully to forego the pleasure of this interesting visit, he was good enough to take the trouble to send up to Mr. Keston (for my inspection) the curious old memorandum-book and the torn leaf containing the cryptograph which occupies so prominent a place in the narrative.

Whether or not my friend is right in describing himself as not mediumistic in the ordinary sense of the word is uncertain. There are certain peculiarities in his character which may help to explain what seems to have puzzled him so much—the reason why Sir Ralph should have selected *him* to receive his communication. He is preeminently a man of deep feeling, of intense and ready sympathy, as indeed may be seen from the narrative; a man who reminds one of those lines of Beranger:

Probably this capability of sympathy attracted Sir Ralph as a channel through which his purpose could be carried out.

The story seems to me to differ from other accounts of the visitations of "earthbound souls" only (1) in the appearance of the wraith in the first place at a distance from the scene of death and to a person in no way specially connected with it, and (2) in the foreknowledge which the dead man seems to have possessed of that person's visit to his former home—not only before the invitation was given, but even before the *idea* of the invitation (which, as far as we can see, was quite accidental) could possibly have existed in the mind of either host or guest. This latter is the point which seems to me most difficult to explain, since such foreknowledge would appear to indicate a power of prevision much more considerable than that with which men in such a condition can usually be credited. It is probable that Sir Ralph's attention was attracted to Mr. Keston in consequence of the bond of friendship existing between him and Mr. John Fernleigh, and that, finding him to be sufficiently impressionable to receive his communication, he endeavoured to deliver his message to him in his chambers; but, failing in that attempt, he influenced Mr. Fernleigh (as he might easily do) to invite him into his own peculiar domain, where his power was naturally greater. The fact that the strange rare and magical perfume of Egypt was known to both men must be regarded simply as a coincidence, though a dramatic one.

THE CONFESSION OF CHARLES LINKWORTH

by E. F. Benson

R. TEESDALE had occasion to attend the condemned man once or twice during the week before his execution, and found him, as is often the case, when his last hope of life has vanished, quiet and perfectly resigned to his fate, and not seeming to look forward with any dread to the morning that each hour that passed brought nearer and nearer. The bitterness of death appeared to be over for him: it was done with when he was told that his appeal was refused. But for those days while hope was not yet quite abandoned, the wretched man had drunk of death daily. In all his experience the doctor had never seen a man so wildly and passionately tenacious of life, nor one so strongly knit to this material world by the sheer animal lust of living. Then the news that hope could no longer be entertained was told him, and his spirit passed out of the grip of that agony of torture and suspense, and accepted the inevitable with indifference. Yet the change was so extraordinary that it seemed to the doctor rather that the news had completely stunned his powers of feeling, and he was below the numbed surface, still knit into material things as strongly as ever. He had fainted when the result was told him, and Dr. Teesdale had been called in to attend him. But

the fit was but transient, and he came out of it into full consciousness of what had happened.

The murder had been a deed of peculiar horror, and there
was nothing of sympathy in the mind of the public towards
the perpetrator. Charles Linkworth, who now lay under
capital sentence, was the keeper of a small stationery store in
Sheffield, and there lived with him his wife and mother. The
latter was the victim of his atrocious crime; the motive of it
being to get possession of the sum of five hundred pounds,
which was this woman's property. Linkworth, as came out at
the trial, was in debt to the extent of a hundred pounds at the
time, and during his wife's absence from home on a visit to re-
lations, he strangled his mother, and during the night buried
the body in the small back-garden of his house. On his wife's
return, he had a sufficiently plausible tale to account for the
elder Mrs. Linkworth's disappearance, for there had been constant jarrings and bickerings between him and his mother for
the last year or two, and she had more than once threatened
to withdraw herself and the eight shillings a week which she
contributed to household expenses, and purchase an annuity
with her money. It was true, also, that during the younger
Mrs. Linkworth's absence from home, mother and son had
had a violent quarrel arising originally from some trivial point
in household management, and that in consequence of this,
she had actually drawn her money out of the bank, intending
to leave Sheffield next day and settle in London, where she
had friends. That evening she told him this, and during the
night he killed her.

His next step, before his wife's return, was logical and
sound. He packed up all his mother's possessions and took
them to the station, from which he saw them despatched to
town by passenger train, and in the evening he asked several
friends in to supper, and told them of his mother's departure.
He did not (logically also, and in accordance with what they

probably already knew) feign regret, but said that he and she had never got on well together, and that the cause of peace and quietness was furthered by her going. He told the same story to his wife on her return, identical in every detail, adding, however, that the quarrel had been a violent one, and that his mother had not even left him her address. This again was wisely thought of: it would prevent his wife from writing to her. She appeared to accept his story completely: indeed there was nothing strange or suspicious about it.

For a while he behaved with the composure and astuteness which most criminals possess up to a certain point, the lack of which, after that, is generally the cause of their detection. He did not, for instance, immediately pay off his debts, but took into his house a young man as lodger, who occupied his mother's room, and he dismissed the assistant in his shop, and did the entire serving himself. This gave the impression of economy, and at the same time he openly spoke of the great improvement in his trade, and not till a month had passed did he cash any of the bank-notes which he had found in a locked drawer in his mother's room. Then he changed two notes of fifty pounds and paid off his creditors.

At that point his astuteness and composure failed him. He opened a deposit account at a local bank with four more fifty-pound notes, instead of being patient, and increasing his balance at the savings bank pound by pound, and he got uneasy about that which he had buried deep enough for security in the back-garden. Thinking to render himself safer in this regard, he ordered a cartload of slag and stone fragments, and with the help of his lodger employed the summer evenings when work was over in building a sort of rockery over the spot. Then came the chance circumstance which really set match to this dangerous train. There was a fire in the lost luggage office at King's Cross Station (from which he ought to have claimed his mother's property) and one of the two boxes was partially burned. The company was liable for compensation, and his mother's name on her linen, and a letter with the Sheffield address on it, led to the arrival of a purely official and formal notice, stating that the company were prepared to consider claims. It was directed to Mrs. Linkworth's and Charles Linkworth's wife received and read it.

It seemed a sufficiently harmless document, but it was endorsed with his death-warrant. For he could give no explanation at all of the fact of the boxes still lying at King's Cross Station, beyond suggesting that some accident had happened to his mother. Clearly he had to put the matter in the hands of the police, with a view to tracing her movements, and if it proved that she was dead, claiming her property, which she had already drawn out of the bank. Such at least was the course urged on him by his wife and lodger, in whose presence the communication from the railway officials was read out, and it was impossible to refuse to take it. Then the silent, uncreaking machinery of justice, characteristic of England, began to move forward. Quiet men lounged about Smith Street, visited banks, observed the supposed increase in trade, and from a house near by looked into the garden where ferns were already flourishing on the rockery. Then came the arrest and the trial, which did not last very long, and on a certain Saturday night the verdict. Smart women in large hats had made the court bright with colour, and in all the crowd there was not one who felt any sympathy with the young athletic-looking man who was condemned. Many of the audience were elderly and respectable mothers, and the crime had been an outrage on motherhood, and they listened to the unfolding of the flawless evidence with strong approval. They thrilled a little when the judge put on the awful and ludicrous little black cap, and spoke the sentence appointed by God.

Linkworth went to pay the penalty for the atrocious deed, which no one who had heard the evidence could possibly doubt that he had done with the same indifference as had marked his entire demeanour since he knew his appeal had failed. The prison chaplain who had attended him had done his utmost to get him to confess, but his efforts had been quite ineffectual, and to the last he asserted, though without protestation, his innocence. On a bright September morning, when the sun shone warm on the terrible little procession that crossed the prison yard to the shed where was erected the apparatus of death, justice was done, and Dr. Teesdale was satisfied that life was immediately extinct. He had been present on the scaffold, had watched the bolt drawn, and the hooded and pinioned figure drop into the pit. He had heard the chunk and creak of the rope as the sudden weight came on to it, and looking down he had seen the queer twitchings of the hanged body. They had lasted but a second for the execution had been perfectly satisfactory.

An hour later he made the post-mortem examination and found that his view had been correct: the vertebrae of the spine had been broken at the neck, and death must have been absolutely instantaneous. It was hardly necessary even to make that little piece of dissection that proved this, but for the sake of form he did so. And at that moment he had a very curious and vivid mental impression that the spirit of the dead man was close beside him, as if it still dwelt in the broken habitation of its body. But there was no question at all that the body was dead: it had been dead an hour. Then followed another little circumstance that at the first seemed insignificant though curious also. One of the warders entered, and asked if the rope which had been used an hour ago, and was the hangman's perquisite, had by mistake been brought into the mortuary with the body. But there was no trace of it, and it seemed to have vanished altogether, though it a singular thing to be lost: it was not here; it was not on the scaffold. And though the disappearance was of no particular moment it was quite inexplicable.

Dr. Teesdale was a bachelor and a man of independent means, and lived in a tall-windowed and commodious house in Bedford Square, where a plain cook of surpassing excellence looked after his food, and her husband his person. There was no need for him to practise a profession at all, and he performed his work at the prison for the sake of the study of the minds of criminals. Most crime—the transgression, that is, of the rule of conduct which the human race has framed for the sake of its own preservation—he held to be either the result of some abnormality of the brain, or of starvation. Crimes of theft, for instance, he would by no means refer to one head; often it is true they were the result of actual want, but more often dictated by some obscure disease of the brain. In marked cases it was labelled as kleptomania, but he was convinced there were many others which did not fall directly under the dictation of physical need. More especially was this the case where the crime in question involved also some deed of violence, and he mentally placed underneath this heading, as he went home that evening, the criminal at whose last moments he had been present that morning. The crime had been abominable, the need of money not so very pressing, and the very abomination and unnaturalness of the murder inclined him to consider the murderer as lunatic rather than criminal. He had been, as far as was known, a man of quiet and kindly disposition, a good husband, a sociable neighbour. And then he had committed a crime, just one, which put him outside all pales. So monstrous a deed, whether perpetrated by a sane man or a mad one, was intolerable; there was no use for the doer of it on this planet at all. But somehow the doctor felt that he would have been more at one with the execution of justice, if the dead man had confessed. It was morally certain that he was guilty, but he wished that when there was no longer any hope for him he had endorsed the verdict himself.

He dined alone that evening, and after dinner sat in his study which adjoined the dining-room, and feeling disinclined to read, sat in his great red chair opposite the fireplace, and let his mind graze where it would. At once almost, it went back to the curious sensation he had experienced that morning, of feeling that the spirit of Linkworth was present in the mortuary, though life had been extinct for an hour. It was not the first time, especially in cases of sudden death, that he had felt a similar conviction, though perhaps it had never been quite so unmistakable as it had been today. Yet the feeling, to his mind, was quite probably formed on a natural and psychical truth. The spirit—it may be remarked that he was a believer in the doctrine of future life, and the non-extinction of the soul with the death of the body—was very likely unable or unwilling to quit at once and altogether the earthly habitation, very likely it lingered there, earth-bound, for a while. In his leisure hours Dr. Teesdale was a considerable student of the occult, for like most advanced and proficient physicians, he clearly recognised how narrow was the boundary of separation between soul and body, how tremendous the influence of the intangible was over material things, and it presented no difficulty to his mind that a disembodied spirit should be able to communicate directly with those who still were bounded by the finite and material.

His meditations, which were beginning to group themselves into definite sequence, were interrupted at this moment. On his desk near at hand stood his telephone, and the bell rang, not with its usual metallic insistence, but very faintly, as if the current was weak, or the mechanism impaired. However, it certainly was ringing, and he got up and took the combined ear and mouth-piece off its hook.

"Yes, yes," he said, "who is it?"

There was a whisper in reply almost inaudible, and quite unintelligible.

"I can't hear you," he said.

Again the whisper sounded, but with no greater distinctness. Then it ceased altogether.

He stood there, for some half minute or so, waiting for it to be renewed, but beyond the usual chuckling and croaking, which showed, however, that he was in communication with some other instrument, there was silence. Then he replaced the receiver, rang up the Exchange, and gave his number.

"Can you tell me what number rang me up just now?" he asked.

There was a short pause, then it was given him. It was the number of the prison, where he was doctor.

"Put me on to it, please," he said.

This was done.

"You rang me up just now," he said down the tube. "Yes; I am Doctor Teesdale. What is it? I could not hear what you said."

The voice came back quite clear and intelligible.

"Some mistake, sir," it said. "We haven't rang you up."

"But the Exchange tells me you did, three minutes ago."

"Mistake at the Exchange, sir," said the voice.

"Very odd. Well, good-night. Warder Draycott, isn't it?"

"Yes, sir; good-night, sir."

Dr. Teesdale went back to his big arm-chair, still less inclined to read. He let his thoughts wander on for a while, without giving them definite direction, but ever and again his mind kept coming back to that strange little incident of the telephone. Often and often he had been rung up by some mistake, often and often he had been put on to the wrong number by the exchange, but there was something in this very subdued ringing of the telephone bell, and the unintelligible whisperings at the other end that suggested a very curious train of reflection to his mind, and soon he found himself pacing up and down his room, with his thoughts eagerly feeding on a most unusual pasture.

"But it's impossible," he said, aloud.

He went down as usual to the prison next morning, and once again he was strangely beset with the feeling that there was some unseen presence there. He had before now had some odd psychical experiences, and knew that he was a "sensitive"—one, that is, who is capable, under certain circumstances, of receiving supernormal impressions, and of having glimpses of the unseen world that lies about us. And this morning the presence of which he was conscious was that of the man who had been executed yesterday morning. It was local, and he felt it most strongly in the little prison yard, and as he passed the door of the condemned cell. So strong was it there that he would not have been surprised if the figure of the man had been visible to him, and as he passed through the door at the end of the passage, he turned round, actually expecting to see it. All the time, too, he was aware of a profound horror at his heart; this unseen presence strangely disturbed him. And the poor soul, he felt, wanted something done for it. Not for a moment did he doubt that this impression of his was objective, it was no imaginative phantom of his own invention that made itself so real. The spirit of Linkworth was there.

He passed into the infirmary, and for a couple of hours busied himself with his work. But all the time he was aware that the same invisible presence was near him, though its force was manifestly less here than in those places which had been more intimately associated with the man. Finally, before he left, in order to test his theory he looked into the execution shed. But next moment with a face suddenly stricken pale, he came out again, closing the door hastily. At the top of the steps stood a figure hooded and pinioned, but hazy of outline and only faintly visible. But it was visible, there was no mistake about it.

Dr. Teesdale was a man of good nerve, and he recovered himself almost immediately, ashamed of his temporary panic.

The terror that had blanched his face was chiefly the effect of startled nerves, not of terrified heart, and yet deeply interested as he was in psychical phenomena, he could not command himself sufficiently to go back there. Or rather he commanded himself, but his muscles refused to act on the message. If this poor earth-bound spirit had any communication to make to him, he certainly much preferred that it should be made at a distance. As far as he could understand, its range was circumscribed. It haunted the prison yard, the condemned cell, the execution shed, it was more faintly felt in the infirmary. Then a further point suggested itself to his mind, and he went back to his room and sent for Warder Draycott, who had answered him on the telephone last night.

"You are quite sure," he asked, "that nobody rang me up last night, just before I rang you up?"

There was a certain hesitation in the man's manner which the doctor noticed.

"I don't see how it could be possible, sir," he said. "I had been sitting close by the telephone for half an hour before, and again before that. I must have seen him, if anyone had been to the instrument."

"And you *saw* no one?" said the doctor with a slight emphasis.

The man became more markedly ill at ease.

"No, sir, I *saw* no one," he said, with the same emphasis.

Dr. Teesdale looked away from him.

"But you had perhaps the impression that there was some one there?" he asked, carelessly, as if it was a point of no interest.

Clearly Warder Draycott had something on his mind, which he found it hard to speak of.

"Well, sir, if you put it like that," he began. "But you would tell me I was half asleep, or had eaten something that disagreed with me at my supper."

The doctor dropped his careless manner.

"I should do nothing of the kind," he said, "any more than you would tell me that I had dropped asleep last night, when I heard my telephone bell ring. Mind you, Draycott, it did not ring as usual, I could only just hear it ringing, though it was close to me. And I could only hear a whisper when I put my ear to it. But when you spoke I heard you quite distinctly. Now I believe there was something—somebody—at this end of the telephone. You were here, and though you saw no one, you, too, felt there was someone there."

The man nodded.

"I'm not a nervous man, sir," he said, "and I don't deal in fancies. But there was something there. It was hovering about the instrument, and it wasn't the wind, because there wasn't a breath of wind stirring, and the night was warm. And I shut the window to make certain. But it went about the room, sir, for an hour or more. It rustled the leaves of the telephone book, and it ruffled my hair when it came close to me. And it was bitter cold, sir."

The doctor looked him straight in the face.

"Did it remind you of what had been done yesterday morning?" he asked suddenly.

Again the man hesitated.

"Yes, sir," he said at length. "Convict Charles Linkworth."

Dr. Teesdale nodded reassuringly.

"That's it," he said. "Now, are you on duty tonight?"

"Yes, sir, I wish I wasn't."

"I know how you feel, I have felt exactly the same myself. Now whatever this is, it seems to want to communicate with me. By the way, did you have any disturbance in the prison last night?"

"Yes, sir, there was half a dozen men who had the nightmare. Yelling and screaming they were, and quiet men too, usually. It happens sometimes the night after an execution.

I've known it before, though nothing like what it was last night."

"I see. Now, if this—this thing you can't see wants to get at the telephone again tonight, give it every chance. It will probably come about the same time. I can't tell you why, but that usually happens. So unless you must, don't be in this room where the telephone is, just for an hour to give it plenty of time between half-past nine and half-past ten. I will be ready for it at the other end. Supposing I am rung up, I will, when it has finished, ring you up to make sure that I was not being called in—in the usual way."

"And there is nothing to be afraid of, sir?" asked the man.

Dr. Teesdale remembered his own moment of terror this morning, but he spoke quite sincerely.

"I am sure there is nothing to be afraid of," he said, reassuringly.

Dr. Teesdale had a dinner engagement that night, which he broke, and was sitting alone in his study by half past nine. In the present state of human ignorance as to the law which governs the movements of spirits severed from the body, he could not tell the warder why it was that their visits are so often periodic, timed to punctuality according to our scheme of hours, but in scenes of tabulated instances of the appearance of *revenants*, especially if the soul was in sore need of help, as might be the case here, he found that they came at the same hour of day or night. As a rule, too, their power of making themselves seen or heard or felt grew greater for some little while after death, subsequently growing weaker as they became less earth-bound, or often after that ceasing altogether, and he was prepared tonight for a less indistinct impression. The spirit apparently for the early hours of its disembodiment is weak, like a moth newly broken out from its chrysalis—and then suddenly the telephone bell rang, not so faintly as the night before, but still not with its ordinary imperative tone.

Dr. Teesdale instantly got up, put the receiver to his ear. And what he heard was heart-broken sobbing, strong spasms that seemed to tear the weeper.

He waited for a little before speaking, himself cold with some nameless fear, and yet profoundly moved to help, if he was able.

"Yes, yes," he said at length, hearing his own voice tremble. "I am Dr. Teesdale. What can I do for you? And who are you?" he added, though he felt that it was a needless question.

Slowly the sobbing died down, the whispers took its place, still broken by crying.

"I want to tell, sir—I want to tell—I must tell."

"Yes, tell me, what is it?" said the doctor.

"No, not you—another gentleman, who used to come to see me. Will you speak to him what I say to you?—I can't make him hear me or see me."

"Who are you?" asked Dr. Teesdale suddenly.

"Charles Linkworth. I thought you knew. I am very miserable. I can't leave the prison—and it is cold. Will you send for the other gentleman?"

"Do you mean the chaplain?" asked Dr. Teesdale.

"Yes, the chaplain. He read the service when I went across the yard yesterday. I shan't be so miserable when I have told."

The doctor hesitated a moment. This was a strange story that he would have to tell Mr. Dawkins, the prison chaplain, that at the other end of the telephone was the spirit of the man executed yesterday. And yet he soberly believed that it was so, that this unhappy spirit was in misery and wanted to "tell." There was no need to ask what he wanted to tell.

"Yes, I will ask him to come here," he said at length.

"Thank you, sir, a thousand times. You will make him come, won't you?"

The voice was growing fainter.

"It must be tomorrow night," it said. "I can't speak longer now. I have to go to see—oh, my God, my God."

The sobs broke out afresh, sounding fainter and fainter. But it was in a frenzy of terrified interest that Dr. Teesdale spoke.

"To see what?" he cried. "Tell me what you are doing, what is happening to you?"

"I can't tell you; I mayn't tell you," said the voice very faint. "That is part——" and it died away altogether.

Dr. Teesdale waited a little, but there was no further sound of any kind, except the chuckling and croaking of the instrument. He put the receiver on to its hook again, and then became aware for the first time that his forehead was streaming with some cold dew of horror. His ears sang; his heart beat very quick and faint, and he sat down to recover himself. Once or twice he asked himself if it was possible that some terrible joke was being played on him, but he knew that could not be so; he felt perfectly sure that he had been speaking with a soul in torment of contrition for the terrible and irremediable act it had committed. It was no delusion of his senses, either; here in this comfortable room of his in Bedford Square, with London cheerfully roaring round him, he had spoken with the spirit of Charles Linkworth.

But he had no time (nor indeed inclination, for somehow his soul sat shuddering within him) to indulge in meditation. First of all he rang up the prison.

"Warder Draycott?" he asked.

There was a perceptible tremor in the man's voice as he answered.

"Yes, sir. Is it Dr. Teesdale?"

"Yes. Has anything happened here with you?"

Twice it seemed that the man tried to speak and could not. At the third attempt the words came "Yes, sir. He has been here. I saw him go into the room where the telephone is."

"Ah! Did you speak to him?"

"No, sir: I sweated and prayed. And there's half a dozen men as have been screaming in their sleep tonight. But it's quiet again now. I think he has gone into the execution shed."

"Yes. Well, I think there will be no more disturbance now. By the way, please give me Mr. Dawkins's home address."

This was given him, and Dr. Teesdale proceeded to write to the chaplain, asking him to dine with him on the following night. But suddenly he found that he could not write at his accustomed desk, with the telephone standing close to him, and he went upstairs to the drawing-room which he seldom used, except when he entertained his friends. There he recaptured the serenity of his nerves, and could control his hand. The note simply asked Mr. Dawkins to dine with him next night, when he wished to tell him a very strange history and ask his help. "Even if you have any other engagement," he concluded, "I seriously request you to give it up. Tonight, I did the same. I should bitterly have regretted it if I had not."

Next night accordingly, the two sat at their dinner in the doctor's dining-room, and when they were left to their cigarettes and coffee the doctor spoke.

"You must not think me mad, my dear Dawkins," he said, "when you hear what I have got to tell you."

Mr. Dawkins laughed.

"I will certainly promise not to do that," he said.

"Good. Last night and the night before, a little later in the evening than this, I spoke through the telephone with the spirit of the man we saw executed two days ago. Charles Linkworth."

The chaplain did not laugh. He pushed back his chair, looking annoyed.

"Teesdale," he said, "is it to tell me this—I don't want to be rude—but this bogey-tale that you have brought me here this evening?"

"Yes. You have not heard half of it. He asked me last night to get hold of you. He wants to tell you something. We can guess, I think, what it is."

Dawkins got up.

"Please let me hear no more of it," he said. "The dead do not return. In what state or under what condition they exist has not been revealed to us. But they have done with all material things."

"But I must tell you more," said the doctor. "Two nights ago I was rung up, but very faintly, and could only hear whispers. I instantly inquired where the call came from and was told it came from the prison. I rang up the prison, and Warder Draycott told me that nobody had rung me up. He, too, was conscious of a presence."

"I think that man drinks," said Dawkins, sharply.

The doctor paused a moment.

"My dear fellow, you should not say that sort of thing," he said. "He is one of the steadiest men we have got. And if he drinks, why not I also?"

The chaplain sat down again.

"You must forgive me," he said, "but I can't go into this. These are dangerous matters to meddle with. Besides, how do you know it is not a hoax?"

"Played by whom?" asked the doctor. "Hark!"

The telephone bell suddenly rang. It was clearly audible to the doctor.

"Don't you hear it?" he said.

"Hear what?"

"The telephone bell ringing."

"I hear no bell," said the chaplain, rather angrily. "There is no bell ringing."

The doctor did not answer, but went through into his study, and turned on the lights. Then he took the receiver and mouthpiece off its hook.

"Yes?" he said, in a voice that trembled. "Who is it? Yes: Mr. Dawkins is here. I will try and get him to speak to you." He went back into the other room.

"Dawkins," he said, "there is a soul in agony. I pray you to listen. For God's sake come and listen."

The chaplain hesitated a moment.

"As you will," he said.

He took up the receiver and put it to his ear.

"I am Mr. Dawkins," he said.

He waited.

"I can hear nothing whatever," he said at length. "Ah, there was something there. The faintest whisper."

"Ah, try to hear, try to hear!" said the doctor.

Again the chaplain listened. Suddenly he laid the instrument down, frowning.

"Something—somebody said, 'I killed her, I confess it. I want to be forgiven.' It's a hoax, my dear Teesdale. Somebody knowing your spiritualistic leanings is playing a very grim joke on you. I *can't* believe it."

Dr. Teesdale took up the receiver.

"I am Dr. Teesdale," he said. "Can you give Mr. Dawkins some sign that it is you?"

Then he laid it down again.

"He says he thinks he can," he said. "We must wait."

The evening was again very warm, and the window into the paved yard at the back of the house was open. For five minutes or so the two men stood in silence, waiting, and nothing happened. Then the chaplain spoke.

"I think that is sufficiently conclusive," he said.

Even as he spoke a very cold draught of air suddenly blew into the room, making the papers on the desk rustle. Dr. Teesdale went to the window and closed it.

"Did you feel that?" he asked.

"Yes, a breath of air. Chilly."

Once again in the closed room it stirred again.

"And did you feel that?" asked the doctor.

The chaplain nodded. He felt his heart hammering in his throat suddenly.

"Defend us from all peril and danger of this coming night," he exclaimed.

"Something is coming!" said the doctor.

As he spoke it came. In the centre of the room not three yards away from them stood the figure of a man with his head bent over on to his shoulder, so that the face was not visible. Then he took his head in both his hands and raised it like a weight, and looked them in the face. The eyes and tongue protruded, a livid mark was round the neck. Then there came a sharp rattle on the boards of the floor, and the figure was no longer there. But on the floor there lay a new rope.

For a long while neither spoke. The sweat poured off the doctor's face, and the chaplain's white lips whispered prayers. Then by a huge effort the doctor pulled himself together. He pointed at the rope.

"It has been missing since the execution," he said.

Then again the telephone bell rang. This time the chaplain needed no prompting. He went to it at once and the ringing ceased. For a while he listened in silence.

"Charles Linkworth," he said at length, "in the sight of God, in whose presence you stand, are you truly sorry for your sin?"

Some answer inaudible to the doctor came, and the chaplain closed his eyes. And Dr. Teesdale knelt as he heard the words of the Absolution.

At the close there was silence again.

"I can hear nothing more," said the chaplain, replacing the receiver.

Presently the doctor's man-servant came in with the tray of spirits and syphon. Dr. Teesdale pointed without looking to where the apparition had been.

"Take the rope that is there and burn it, Parker," he said.

There was a moment's silence.

"There is no rope, sir," said Parker.

A LEGEND OF LIFE

by William T. Horton

PROLOGUE

THE Spirit of Man wandering in barren places finds no rest. Blindly he seeks hither and thither but cannot find happiness and truth, for his eyes are closed except to the things of this life, and the shackles binding him to the ground, shackles that he must wear for a season.

One day as he wanders a ray of light shows him the Kingdoms that he may win, visioned before him. Like a traveller whose eyes have seen the land to which he is bound, but who sees also the high mountains he must pass over and the far distance he must travel, he loses heart and is well-nigh despairing even to the point of death.

He is awakened by a Voice speaking within himself, yet arising from without, of one who in vision, the ideal of his dreams, now stands radiant by his side and breathes into him new hopes, showing how near is the Kingdom, and how the shackles are not lasting, and how by faith and patience he shall come to the City on which his hopes are set.

His thirsting soul is satisfied, but the fight is in nowise finished. Many times his heart shall fail and his foot stumble, but, having seen the Vision, he cannot forget or fail.

THERE WAS A TRAVELLER

There was a Traveller who set out with staff and wallet to search for a maiden who should bring him all joy and happiness.

As he travelled he met many whom he loved, but of whom, after a little while, he grew weary. So he ever passed on.

One day, as he prayed in anguish of loneliness, he looked upward towards a high mountain, round the foot of which he would pass, and saw the sky of clouds breaking, and in the break he saw a face looking down upon him, calm and quiet, radiant and wonderful, and he cried out in joy, "I will come unto thee," and began to ascend the mountain.

Faint and exhausted he fell and was lying dead, but the Father of Life carried him in His arms to the precincts of a new life and breathed into his nostrils, and he lived again.

Then the Father left him, and there came to him the beautiful woman whose face he had seen in the break of the clouds, and she bade him arise.

Throwing her arms around him she carried him away to a plain whence he could behold the Cities of the Sun. And she told him he must come to them journeying alone before they might meet again.

Thereupon she left him, and on the breast of a storm-cloud he was borne to Earth.

Often he would wander under the stars, and in the moonlight, crying to his Beloved for help.

"Surely my Beloved I have conquered Fear, even strangling him as he grappled with me down in the Valley of the Shadow of Death. I am ready to come to thee. Thou prayest for me. Let my prayer mingle with thine, and let me enter the Heavenly City where thou dwellest."

Then he looked for a glimpse of the City where she dwelt,

but he was bound to Earth in the prison-house of his own body and by the cruelties of circumstance.

In anguish he prayed for deliverance, and after many days the Sunlight of Life came upon him through the working of his Beloved and the shackles of Earth fell from him, and he was free.

Free, he flung himself into the Sea of Hope which stretched before him and opened to him the way to his Beloved. Sorely was he tossed upon the waves, but reaching the shore he was received and tended by her.

Into the gates of the Palace of Time they entered, for the Mother of Souls had prevailed by Her prayers that they should come again to Earth together and knowing one another. And She took them into Her arms and blessed them, before their journey, as they waited in the Palace.

And the Mother of Souls stood as guardian, with a flaming sword and shield held over the two who were about to be born again to Earth, and cast round them a sanctifying halo which many men and women should feel but not see consciously.

Then the Father of Life took them into His hand and placed them on an Earth-bound storm-cloud.

But the storm-cloud broke, separating them one from the other. The man was tossed into a low-lying plain where the marsh-land surrounded him and the mountains lowered beyond and round, and he tried to walk but his feet ever slipped, and often he nearly fell and sank, and he desired wings so that he might fly to the heights. Then wings were given him, but they were too heavy for him so that he could neither fly nor walk.

He cried out in agony and a vision was vouchsafed him of his Beloved whom he had lost, and he heard her voice saying, "Behold I am with thee even though I wander lonely looking for thee even as thou dost for me."

Then he saw her sitting on the high cliff whither she had been cast by the bursting storm-cloud, and he was comforted and determined to make his way to her.

Slowly and painfully he arose, but now he could move more easily for his heavy wings were gone, only the invisible ones of his Spirit remained. So he renewed his journey, helped and inspired by the vision.

Black shapes flew round and about him, but he was swifter than they, and was confident in his own strength, now he knew and had seen the wings that bore him forward, and no longer cried out for earthly wings which only weighed him downwards.

Soon he came and reached the summit where he had seen his Beloved waiting for him, and the sun shone behind her and through her so that she appeared to him to be radiant with light.

And she took his hand and showed him the City, where they should dwell, into which she had not yet entered, since she had waited for him.

Entering in they partook of perfect happiness and wandered unhurt by any of the forces of evil, knowing that the Angel of Perfect Purity walked with them.

After a while a craving came upon both of them for the glory of the Cities of Heaven, whence the Father of Life had sent them forth, and they wandered to the edge of the world to entreat the Guardian Angel of Life to let them pass and swim the dark river between the Earth and the Heavens.

But the Angel answered "Not yet, my children, there is work yet for you to do according to your own wisdom. See here for your comfort." And they were shown how even as on Earth so were their Spirits in Heaven.

Then they turned once more to life and, setting their feet firmly, they made their way joyfully up the steep paths, knowing that they were linked in wondrous fashion to their Spirit forms in Heaven.

THE GHOST-FRIEND

by Jack Edwards

JIM SHANNON, when he first came to the up-river station, looked about him with much of the same interest
that any of the beasts captured in the adjacent forests might
have exhibited on being transferred to a new cage after a year's
captivity in a zoo.

He felt he had gone out of one part of a prison into another and worse one. All tropical Africa was a prison to him,
with the trading stations on the river for cells and the farthest
station the worst cell of all.

It was up here in the clutch of the great forests that Mayhew
had died, Cleaver had gone mad, and Lind had disappeared.

Doubtless, too, there were other tragedies that he had
heard nothing about.

Not that he had heard much of these. He had picked up
a thing or two from the talk of the other prisoners of circumstance, who, like himself, sweated under a tropical sky
for an emolument which was larger than salaries in a more
genial climate in proportion as the risk to life was greater. But
few of them were loquacious on the subject of the up-river
tragedies, and the history of that far post whither Shannon,
in due course, was sent, was one implied rather than indicated
whenever, in desultory conversations, reference was made to
the station of the Upper Ahili.

A man might be drafted there from a lower depot any day, and it would hardly be "the game" to make him sick with his destination before he got there. Such, roughly, was the vague feeling in the back of the public mind causing this irritating reticence with regard to the Upper Ahili.

Shannon, a "call-a-spade" type of man was inclined to fulminate against this well-meant conspiracy of omission when once he had reached the "U.A."—the initials of the post were generally used instead of the full name—and he searched his memory for such scraps of information as he had gleaned in the past eighteen months.

Mayhew had died of fever; that he knew. Fever is a wide term, and in the tropics is a polite euphemism for many forms of demise, from alcoholism to carelessness in handling a revolver. Shannon was curious as to Mayhew's end. It might have been quite conventional. It was whispered that he had blown his brains out, but Shannon had not been able to verify that statement. Anyway, it didn't trouble him over much.

So Cleaver had gone "dotty." In the loneliness and isolation of the upper reaches of West African rivers that has been heard of before; trade has its heroes as well as war.

It was the mystery of Lind's fate that appealed to his imagination. No one seemed to know what had become of Lind. He had gone up to the U.A. He had never come back. Other men followed him, and they had returned, fever-shaken and a little more grim, a little more silent than they had gone there; but Lind had never come back. It was surmised that he was dead. He might have gone out into the bush and died there, or been killed by natives. He might have fallen into the river on one of the black, starless nights. He, like Cleaver, might have passed the borderland of sanity and have gone—goodness knows where! It was a matter in which one's fancy had a wide field; anyway; Lind's end was a mystery.

But on the upper reaches of the river trade had to be looked after, and therefore other white men passed on to the undesirable post, and finally Shannon, in his turn, was drafted for the U.A.

When he left England Shannon would have felt the word "imaginative," as applied to himself would have conveyed a subtle form of insult. He had been fined at Bow Street as the result of a Boat-Race night "rag"; he had enjoyed a small reputation as an athlete; his size had incommoded fellow-passengers in tubes and 'buses; his literary horizon had been bounded by sporting papers and the light fiction that is barred by the libraries; it was left to the Upper Ahili to prove to him that he had an imagination. Up there in the shadow of great trees, in the embrace of malaria-haunted glades, in the silence of tropical forests, men had died or gone mad of heart-break and loneliness.

Shannon was lonely too. He knew what it was to watch the progress of dreadful days from fierce dawn to fiercer sunset, like a universe afire, with nothing to do but to wait for that trickle of trade for which the post had been established. He knew what it was to watch the remote and hostile stars wheel through the blackness of the African night, and realise, in watching them, that he was utterly alone—lost, on the edge of the world.

He knew that it was this isolation that had broken men like Mayhew and Cleaver—and Lind.

They, aided by fate, had found a way out, and Lind's way was a secret one. The other two had gone by way of doors that were known, but Lind had flown his prison by an unknown portal.

In the stillness that came at the end of the burning day Shannon would dwell on the stealthy exit of his predecessor and check himself in the midst of speculation. He acquired the habit of talking out loud to himself in the silence of the wide-verandahed bungalow that was in reality little more than a hut.

"Oh, rot, rot!" he might have been heard to exclaim, and speech would degenerate into a whistle as he resolutely sought to change the channel of his thoughts. Words would come back after an interval.

"Wonder what they are doing now down at the Bend? Wonder if Simpson's got that roulette-wheel he was sending home for? Wonder if——"

He did not yearn for the society of any of his former associates. He had no friendships. In an ordinary way one man was as good as another as far as companionship went. He missed not any particular individual or group of individuals, but the atmosphere of a community. People were to him somewhat like furniture in a room—to be used for different purposes. It was the social room himself he sighed for. For the social room had comfortable limitations; walls that bounded vision, a roof that excluded the sky. There were things to hinder the flow of thought, to prevent a chap going too far into regions not profitable for exploration. Up at the U.A. he had no such protective influences. He felt himself mentally wall-less, roofless.

There were no other minds to tether his own to the comfortable common places of human intercourse. His mind flowed out to a dark horizon: The dark horizon sent in a constant flow of influences upon him that detached him from every-day events. His spirit was like a toy balloon on the string of his common sense; inflated with the hot air of imagination, it tugged at its string and sought to fly free. The wind fluttered it, played with it, lured it. The night wanted to take it to itself.

Shannon had a banjo upon which he had learnt to strum. In the earlier days of his exile he had often fingered it of evenings, playing such simple tunes as appealed to his not very cultivated taste. Now he never touched it. Somehow he felt forbidden, by whom or what he could not have said.

A watcher, however fearless, in a haunted house might have felt a similar feeling—a sense that such frivolous sounds would be an impertinence to be justly resented by whatever mysterious influence inhabited the place.

Shannon's mental state was not unlike that of a child punished often, and always unjustly, and who is at length wholly possessed by an unconscious, but ever present fear of asserting itself in any way lest it call attention to itself. Such a child might at length come dimly to realise that not its actions but its existence was at fault, and would insensibly shrink from being observed, and learn to move with stealth and become furtive, secret, and subtle.

Shannon became a changed man. His talkative overflow, copious in exclamation and expletive, during the day, dried up at night like a stream absorbed in arid soil. The creaking of his cane-chair was a noise to be avoided; it seemed to him that it attracted the attention of invisible and inimical forces that surrounded the lonely dwelling and slowly, as night drew on, invaded it, penetrating farther and farther into its recesses as though searching, groping, feeling for him.

"I'm a kid—a bally kid!" he told himself, with deep contempt. "Frightened of the dark——"

He had an immense scorn of himself, a contempt that refused to allow him to find comfort in anything that had formerly palliated his exile—the banjo, the few books, the diary that he laboriously kept, making entries of the trifles that, in the place of more stirring events, marked the currentless flow of his days.

He was in a bad case now; angry and impatient with himself by day for the fears that possessed him at night, and fever-shaken always.

A Presence that he dreaded was always close to him, and he felt a shuddering in the air, as though something invisible and immense was shaking great wings. Sometimes it passed him by, and he felt the air trail in its wake, sucked after it in its progress as it went looking for him. The idea was strong in his mind that the hostile influences were blind to him; could not see him, having no eyes; could not feel him, having no members with which to feel; could not hear him, having no aural sense. He felt that they only come in contact with him by vibrations; that when he plucked the banjo strings and his spirit yielded to the appeal in the cadences he evoked from the instrument, the change in his psychic atmosphere was a change of which the invisible influences were aware. When fear overmastered, and his muscles were flabby with terror, and his brain swam with a sickening realisation of his helplessness, he felt that the Things came perceptibly nearer. He came at length to the idea that his safety depended upon his mental and psychical attitude, that his spiritual expansion, either in the sadness produced by music or in the purely phys-ical terror that overmastered him at moments, he was setting up vibrations by which the haunting Influences could detect his presence; that he was creating a road in the air by means of which "They" could approach.

His safety, he felt sure, could only be preserved by closing his mind and his senses at one and the same time to any in-dication, fancied or otherwise, of the activity of the invisible forces he dreaded. By this means alone could he hold them at bay.

But how to compass the neutrality of mind, the negation of feeling, that he felt alone could safeguard him, was more than he could discover. He was asking himself to achieve the impossible; to be dispassionately calm when he was passion-ately engaged in a struggle to preserve himself from powers that he felt were bent upon his destruction.

In the torrid hours of the day he told himself that these fears were the signs of incipient mania; that fever, an intense love of life, and a wild passion for self-preservation, were the factors that were combining with solitude and a new-born and hither-to unsuspected gift of self-analysis to destroy him; that the very excess of his craving to survive was the begetter of chimeras that had no existence save in his over-anxious brain.

"That is the way that poor devil, Cleaver, may have begun," he told himself. "He fancied things; soon he saw them; his brain transformed his fears into actualities. He ended being a gibbering idiot."

He increased his daily dose of quinine.

Sunset found him with a thudding heart, telling himself to be brave.

"Now then, buck up," he would address himself, smiling foolishly and endeavouring to force himself to a stoical calm. "Nothing has happened to you yet. Each night's bally funk is so much wasted energy. You know, you silly fool, that intangible things, if they exist, cannot produce tangible effects. It's all moonshine!"

But all his endeavours melted away when the black night, like a swarthy tide, swept over the land and he sat in his bungalow fearing to enter the next room and go to bed, and equally afraid to sit still and stem the current of antagonistic and occult influences that pressed-upon him.

One night his terror took a fresh form.

He heard a sound he could not explain.

It was quite near him. It was the sound of something shaking. He listened and only silence beat upon his ears in waves through which the thudding of his heart, the racing pulses, as his blood swept through his veins, made themselves heard. When that other sound came again, fainter—in a far corner of the room. He waited in a death-like stillness. It sounded nearer. It was not unlike the whirring of a fly-wheel, he fancied. A moment later, and he found a better description. It was more like the trembling of wings, or quills shaken by a great bird in anger. The quivering, shaking sound made by the feathers of a peacock when the bird, with spread tail, dances in rage and agitates his plumage, was somewhat akin to it. It was harsher than the humming of a top, not so sustained and even there was a sibilation in it, almost a hissing. Although distinct, it was not loud; it seemed to be muted, as though veils of atmosphere lay between it and his ear.

At the first moment of hearing he did not at once connect it with the boding terror that surrounded him. He looked about to find some physical explanation, he half expected to see something fluttering in an unexpected current of air.

But there was no wind to cause such a sound, nor indeed, anything in the gaunt room to be shaken by a draught had any arisen. No bird had found entry to disturb him by any flutter or beating of its wings. He recognised immediately that it was too steady, too definitely centred to be caused by a bird or a bat seeking egress from a room into which it had strayed. At the same time, it was, in spite of its distinctness, not absolutely at hand. It seemed to be at the far end of the avenue of air that transmitted the sound to his ear, without affording his other senses any clue to its origin. In a moment he had grasped its significance. It was a spirit sound, and it was the first direct revelation to the physical senses of the brooding, hostile forces that encompassed him, and which he felt were engaged in a stealthy hunt for him.

It was his conviction that they had come a step nearer. They had almost located him. In this sound lay evidence that they had passed one of the barriers dividing the material and the spiritual; they had established a point of contact with one sense; soon he might expect them to become visible, tangible——

"Good God!" he muttered, the anguish of his soul finding piteous expression in speech, "I'm doomed——doomed!"

Immediately the ghastly, whirring, fluttering, shaking sound sprang into existence so near him that his muttering died away in horror and he shrank back, putting out his hands before him as though to ward off the attack of some material assailant.

He did not spring from his chair. He felt that to do so would draw his invisible enemy in pursuit down the shuddering trail of his terrified flight. Instead, he crept from his chair stealthily and withdrew to the farther side of the room.

Upright near the opposite wall he listened, and, with anguish of soul, heard the ghostly pursuit hum in his wake. It came nearer, and broke into a hideous, purring sound almost at his shoulder.

He was off again instantly, still stealthily, moving as unobtrusively possible, utterly obsessed with fear, yet realising that to break into panic-stricken flight would invite the final disaster—would give him over to his ghostly antagonists, and reveal him plainly to them beyond the hope of ever again finding concealment and shelter.

Orestes, on hearing the breathing of the Furies in the temple at the moment when he had thought he had escaped them and found sanctuary, could not have been more despairing and hopelessly forsaken than Shannon when, in the next pause, he found himself tracked by his invisible enemies and the hateful sound broke out, not on one side of him as before, but all around him.

It was in a vortex of sound, not loud, but horribly distinct, and with a new quality added to the sibilant whirring; a deeper humming note, that gave him a conviction that his enemies were concentrating upon him, and that the moment of horror would progress to some revelation of them in form and a demonstration of their malignant power.

Almost with the reflection there came to him the discovery that the room appeared filmy and indistinct, as though he were looking at it through tinted glasses. The darkness was not due to the fading of the lamp, nor was it caused by a mist coming in at the open door. The space near the door was comparatively clear; it was near him that the diminution of light was caused by, as it were, a thickening of the air or by the spinning of an intangible web.

And suddenly he saw that while the air became every second more misty, the mist was vibrated as though thin veils of gauze were being agitated around him, and on the filmy background darker spots appeared, like eyes that were concentrating a dark gaze upon him. The air was full of these eyes radiating from him as the eyes in a peacock's tail radiate from the bird's body.

He was the centre of a filmy fan through which he distinctly saw details of the room, and which contained thousands of watching eyes.

He covered his face with his hands, and before his eyes were hidden saw simultaneously with the upward movement of his arms the net of shadows shudder nearer, as though his actions drew the encompassing veil closer.

The mist deepened round him, and the edges of everything seen through the veil became wavy and blurred.

And the vibrating, humming rose grew to a shrill din.

Waiting, with his eyes hidden, for he knew not what, Shannon felt the spirit siege ebb and faint suddenly at the moment when he had waited for touch to add its eclipsing horror to the evidence of eye and ear.

Raising his head, he saw a man standing just within the door.

He recognised two things at once. One was that the evil and menacing influences had melted away, and were gone; and the other, that the man at whom he was staring was no man, but an apparition.

It was smiling, it was kindly, it was reassuring.

Almost as soon as he realised its presence it was gone, and Shannon found himself alone in the room with the evil influences that had haunted and pursued him suddenly neutralised and an atmosphere of calm and peace pervading the apartment.

He was safe, and he knew, without any discussion of the matter in his mind, that a spirit intervention had saved him, and that to the apparition he owed his rescue.

Shannon's diary at this point gives the plainest possible testimony to his feelings:

Dec. 15th. Saw the ghost once more last night. "They" were after me again. The noise is at first very faint, and often breaks out in a different part of the room, as if they were having a kids' game with me—blind-man's-buff or something. I notice that the sound grows loud at once when I concentrate on it. But for the life of me I cannot help it! I must listen! I know my fear makes it easy for them to find me, but it is impossible for me to keep my mind off them when they are hunting for me. And then I begin to see those eyes. They are a darkish blue. I can see through them. They are rather like specks that float before one's vision when one is bilious, only of course much larger. Round every eye there is a ring of light. These are like the eyes of a peacock's tail, only dull in colour, and hazy. They swim round me. Last night they were closer than before. I bolted into my bedroom, and they were after me. I saw them all round me—close. And the noise was a deep, steady hum. And then "He" came. I saw him through the door of in room. "He" stood in the lamplight. One hand was up, and he faced me. The infernal racket died at once and the eyes faded. I stayed in my room looking out at him, and "He" stared in at me. It seemed a long time. And then "He" faded. But the noise did not return. "They" cannot stay when "He" comes.

Dec. 16th. I wonder who "He" is. Is he Mayhew's ghost or Lind's? Of course, I don't know if Lind is dead. No one knows. I was told that Mayhew shot himself. Put the muzzle of his revolver in his mouth and fired. This isn't the spirit of a suicide. One would expect Mayhew's ghost to have a dreadful face—blood-stained. "He" is very calm—not at all dreadful. When "He" came last night I was glad. "He" was early, and I knew "They" couldn't come then. "They" didn't. Why has "He" appeared? Has "He" come to save me?

Dec. 20th. "He" has come each night. When sunset comes I almost pray for him, but each night "He" has come, and then I have been safe. I think he must be Lind's ghost. Lind must be dead. Perhaps he died of fright, or "They" killed him, and he has come back to save me from them. I see him now more plainly than first. "He" stays longer, too. Last night I had been sitting waiting, wondering if "He" would come, or if that awful whirring noise would come instead. I looked round, and there "He" was close beside me. I don't know how long "He" had been there. Must have been some time, for I did not feel "Them" in the room at all. I am not afraid of "Him."

Dec. 22nd. "They" caught me on the edge of the forest today. I had gone out with my gun. Right ahead of me was a peacock in a sunlit glade, spreading his tail and courting a pea-hen a little way off from him in the shade. The eyes on his tail made me think of those eyes that circle round me at night. I had no sooner thought that than I heard the sound "They" make. My mind had drawn them by its fear. Never had I heard the noise so loud, and never before had they been after me in the day-time. I turned and ran. The noise was all around me, and, like veils of gauze falling in a stage scene, darkness began to obscure the sunlight, For the first time I felt "Them"—actually felt the touch of "Them." The world seemed airless; I couldn't breathe. I stumbled and picked myself up several times. God knows where I dropped the gun! Every time I felt the noise subsided, as though "They" were a flight of birds that had settled on me; every time I picked myself up and ran on again the noise began once more, like the whirring and beating of wings. And all the time I was choking, stifling, strangling.

I had fallen for the tenth time, I should think, and the world had gone almost quite dark, when "He" came. I could just make out glints of light on trees and bushes in the same way one can see through a thin bandage over one's eyes in places where the fabric is worn. But "They" were round me, sucking my life, drawing my breath. "They" had me. Then "He" came.

"I have never seen him in the day-light till today. I couldn't see him so plainly as I can by night, but I knew it was "He" from the way they dispersed, and I was able to breathe again. "He" was gone again in a moment.

Last night "He" came again. "He" was very distinct. Every time "He" comes "He" is plainer to be seen, more substantial, more life-like, Last night I was able to see into his eyes. They are like no eyes I have ever seen. When "He" went "He" beckoned me to follow to the door. But I dared not go. In the open "They" might get me.

Dec. 23rd. Each night now "He" comes and beckons. Whereas when first I saw him "He" was shadowy, a figure I could look right through, now "He" is substantial. "He" is materialising. "He" has colouring even. Fair hair, grey eyes. I can even see the shape of his finger-nails—they are what people call "filbert shape." "He" is peaceful—splendid. "He" calms the air. "He" is like a star shining on a dark pool. But now "He" beckons me to follow, and I daren't obey. I want to go with him, but I daren't.

Dec. 24th. I hate to deny him. I feel that it hurts him. "He" saves me from "Them," and yet I won't trust him and go where. "He" wants me to go. His eyes are not reproachful, but they are sad. It makes me feel that I am betraying a friend.

I know who "He" is. I cannot say how I know. Knowledge comes to me from him without speech. What "He" wants me to know I know. "He" is Lind—Lind, who died horribly somewhere near at hand. "He" has come back to save me from "Them" because in life "He" fought "Them" too.

He wants me to follow him, and to perform some office I cannot understand. Either "He" cannot tell me, or does not want to. All I know is that "He" entreats me to follow.

Tomorrow is Christmas Day—perhaps the last I shall ever see!

Dec, 25th. Christmas morning. Everybody all the world over wishing each other "A Merry Christmas." People at home being jolly. Holly, mistletoe, cards, church in the morning, "Hark the herald angels," and all that; greetings, handshakings, good wishes; dinner, turkey, pudding with brandy blazing. All the usual sort of thing, and not one soul in all the world to know that a poor, spook-haunted devil on the edge of an African forest is nearly dead with fever and loneliness and fear. Will "He" come tonight! I pray that "He" may.

Later. I am sitting alone. I have seen him. "He" is near me. If I look round "He" will go. "He" always goes soon after I look at him. And as "He" goes "He" beckons me to follow. If I don't look round 'He' stays till I do, waiting for me.

"I will not look round. I will go on writing, and pretend "He" isn't there. Then, perhaps, I can keep him all evening. It is a funny Christmas. Here am I, thousands of miles from anywhere, on the devil haunted Ahili River, keeping Christmas with a ghost.

If "He" beckons me tonight I will follow.

✳

It happened that there was a missionary station on a confluent of the Ahili, and one of the missionaries, Anderson by name, animated with the spirit of the season, called together three natives, who were good oarsmen, and swept down the tributary and into the main stream, intent on paying a call upon the white man, whoever he might be, at that time in charge of the U.A. post.

Anderson was delayed on his journey by an accident to the canoe in rounding a bend of the river. A snag under water ripped a hole in the bottom of the boat. In consequence of the delay in executing the repairs, which took the better part of a day, the missionary arrived, not upon Christmas Day, as he intended, but upon the day after.

Shannon was not to be found. Anderson, who understood the lingo of the tribe, heard enough to make him go alone, and unattended, into the bush in search of the missing man. He went alone for the reason that he could not prevail on any of the natives to accompany him.

There was the track of a man, a white man, who wore boots—so the natives said—in the bush leading to the Grove of Great Devils.

The white man must have gone there alone and at night.

None had seen him go. He had been seen the day before, but not that day. And there was the track showing whither he had gone.

Anderson did not wait for further parley. He followed the trail. Several times he lost it, but at length, deep in the heart of the forest, he found a clear space. In the thick grass he found the bones of a man—a white man, from the shape of the skull and the gold-filling of some of the teeth—and by the skeleton lay Shannon!

He was not dead, but at first Anderson thought he was.

He was mosquito-bitten, insect-stung and unsightly, but he breathed. Anderson had to leave him beside the grass-cradled skeleton and to return to the station for help.

Bribery and threats induced the boatmen to return with him bearing a hammock slung on poles and thus Shannon came to the scene of his haunting. But not for long.

There was a deeper medicine-chest and better facilities for nursing a sick man at the mission. Anderson risked the river journey for his patient, and transferred him thither, although he confidently expected Shannon to die on the way. Feeling sure he would die anyway, he thought he might as well accept the risk.

But Shannon did not die. His splendid physique and tough constitution pulled him through.

But he never returned to the U.A.

Years later he narrated the whole affair to a man who had some reputation as a specialist in occult matters.

To him Shannon described the end of his Christmas Day on the Ahili.

"When 'He' came," said Shannon, "I sat for a long time without looking at him. 'He' was my friend; I felt it, and somehow I knew 'He' meant me to feel it. 'He' had come to me on a special mission to save me from dangers that had menaced him living. But in saving me 'He' asked for a return. There was something I could do for him, and I dreaded to do it. For two reasons I dreaded it. I was afraid that 'They' would get hold of me out there in the open, and I was afraid, too, that if I did him the service, whatever it was, that 'He' wanted of me, I should lose him. 'He' might never come again, and I should be left defenceless. And apart from that—it sounds silly to say it—but I had a passion of gratitude to him; to lose him would have been like losing a friend one loved. Sounds silly to talk like this about an apparition, doesn't it?"

The scientist made no answer at first.

"Tell me what you did," he said quietly, after a pause.

"I waited without turning my head," said Shannon, "and all the time I could see him with the tail of my eye. It was like sitting with a living man. It was more than that, for I cannot imagine any living being radiating such calm—such——" He paused, seeking for words.

"'He' was god-like," he went on presently; "'He' stilled me to utter peace. And after a bit I knew that, great as my terror was, my feeling for him was stronger than my fear. I looked full at him at last, and I shall never forget the look I got in return. It went into me. It went into my very soul, and I rose with my hands out. As I touched him my eyes seemed to be opened, and I saw things I never dreamed a man could see. I saw us ringed about with all the horrors that had oppressed me. I cannot describe them. They are indescribable. They were all around us and they came near because of him. But they were avid and hungry and loathsomely evil. But they were afraid because of the shining of him.

"We went through them, and they broke and fled as a pack of hyenas might fly before a brandished torch, and we went out of the room and across the verandah and down the steps.

"I was not afraid now. I had to go where 'He' wanted me to go, and to do something 'He' wanted me to do, and I knew 'He' would keep me safe.

"We went on and on. I don't remember walking. I seemed to float through air. With every moment I felt lighter and happier. I was going on towards something happy. I did not know what.

"At last we came to a point where 'He' floated from me. I know no more. Everything is blank after that, except that in his going from me I realised that something still lay ahead of me. The thing I was to do. The service I had to render. I knew that our association was not ended but that 'He' would come again and my duty would be made plain."

"Is that all?" asked the scientist.

"That is all," answered Shannon. "I was found in the forest beside a heap of bones. They were Lind's bones. Lind, you know, was the man who was lost. The mission people who rescued me sent a party to bury the skeleton decently. Now, what I want to ask you is this: how was it that Lind's ghost saved me, and what were those awful things he saved me from?"

The scientist threw out his hands in a gesture that seemed to pass on the query.

"Who can say for certain?" he returned. "You tell me a man died or shot himself there; another man went mad; this man Lind also died, no one knows how. How many other men may not have died there? There may have been terrible deeds done on the river by the natives before ever white man came. There may have been torturing, murders, and massacres. It is only too probable. All these terrible things carry with them certain spiritual consequences. Men who die in agony leave thought forms behind them in the place where they have died. Men who commit crimes leave thought forms in the scenes of those crimes. These thought forms haunt those who come after. You were unconsciously throwing yourself open to these influences. Every day you gave them the power to haunt you. Without knowing it you made yourself a medium——"

Shannon broke: "Yes, that would account for the dark fine influences, but what about my ghost-friend?"

"He was the spirit of the man who had died in the forest," answered the scientist slowly, "and who desired that you should give his bones burial."

"But," affirmed Shannon warmly, "that wasn't what he came for. He came for more than that. He came to save me."

"Lind," returned the scientist gravely, "when alive was without doubt a great and good man. And the spirit of a good man is stronger than many evil spirits. Just as living he would have helped you, so in spirit he was ready to come to your aid. For the spirits of the good, did we but realise it, are ever mindful of us."

And to this Shannon made no reply, having none that he cared to make.

THE WINGS OF HORUS

by Algernon Blackwood

BINOVITCH had the bird in him somewhere: in his features, certainly, with his piercing eye and hawk-like nose; in his movements, with his quick way of flitting, hopping, darting; in the way he perched on the edge of a chair; in the manner he pecked at his food; in his twittering, high-pitched voice as well; and, above all, in his mind. He skimmed all subjects and picked their heart out neatly, as a bird skims lawn or air to snatch its prey. He had the bird's-eye view of everything. He loved birds and understood them instinctively; could imitate their whistling notes with astonishing accuracy. Their one quality he had not was poise and balance. He was a nervous little man; he was neurasthenic. And he was in Egypt by doctor's orders.

Such imaginative, unnecessary ideas he had! Such uncommon beliefs!

"The old Egyptians," he said laughingly, yet with a touch of solemn conviction in his manner, "were a great people. Their consciousness was different from ours. The bird idea, for instance, conveyed a sense of deity to them—of bird deity, that is: they had sacred birds—hawks, ibis, and so forth—and worshipped them." And he put his tongue out as though to say with challenge, "Ha, ha!"

"They also worshipped cats and crocodiles and cows," grinned Palazov. Binovitch seemed to dart across the table at his adversary. His eyes flashed; his nose pecked the air. Almost one could imagine the beating of his angry wings.

"Because everything alive," he half screamed, "was a symbol of some spiritual power to them. Your mind is as literal as a dictionary and as incoherent. Pages of ink without connected meaning! Verb always in the infinitive! If you were an old Egyptian, you—you"—he flashed and spluttered, his tongue shot out again, his keen eyes blazed—"you might take all those words and spin them into a great interpretation of life, a cosmic romance, as they did. Instead, you get the bitter, dead taste of ink in your mouth, and spit it over us like that"—he made a quick movement of his whole body as a bird that shakes itself—"in empty phrases."

Khilkoff ordered another bottle of champagne, while Vera, his sister, said half nervously, "Let's go for a drive; it's moonlight." There was enthusiasm at once. Another of the party called the head waiter and told him to pack food and drink in baskets. It was only eleven o'clock. They would drive out into the desert, have a meal at two in the morning, tell stories, sing, and see the dawn.

It was in one of those cosmopolitan hotels in Egypt which attract the ordinary tourists as well as those who are doing a "cure," and all these Russians were ill with one thing or another. All were ordered out for their health, and all were the despair of their doctors. They were as unmanageable as a bazaar and as incoherent. Excess and bed were their routine. They lived, but none of them got better. Equally, none of them got angry. They talked in this strange personal way without a shred of malice or offence. The English, French, and Germans in the hotel watched them with remote amazement, referring to them as "that Russian lot." Their energy was elemental. They never stopped. They merely disappeared when the pace became too fast, then reappeared again after a day or two, and resumed their "living" as before. Binovitch, despite his neurasthenia, was the life of the party. He was also a special patient of Dr. Plitzinger, the famous psychiatrist, who took a peculiar interest in his case. It was not surprising. Binovitch was a man of unusual ability and of genuine, deep culture. But there was something more about him that stimulated curiosity. There was this striking originality. He said and did surprising things.

"I could fly if I wanted to," he said once when the airmen came to astonish the natives with their biplanes over the desert, "but without all that machinery and noise. It's only a question of believing and understanding——"

"Show us!" they cried. "Let's see you fly!"

"He's got it! He's off again! One of his impossible moments."

These occasions when Binovitch let himself go always proved wildly entertaining. He said monstrously incredible things as though he really did believe them. They loved his madness, for it gave them new sensations.

"It's only levitation, after all, this flying," he exclaimed, shooting out his tongue between the words, as his habit was when excited; "and what is levitation but a power of the air? None of you can hang an orange in space for a second, with all your scientific knowledge; but the moon is always levitated perfectly. And the stars. D'you think they swing on wires? What raised the enormous stones of ancient Egypt? D'you really believe it was heaped-up sand and ropes and clumsy leverage and all our weary and laborious mechanical contrivances? Bah! It was levitation. It was the powers of the air. Believe in those powers, and gravity becomes a mere nursery trick—true where it is, but true nowhere else. To know the fourth dimension is to step out of a locked room and appear instantly on the roof or in another country altogether. To know the powers of the air, similarly, is to annihilate what you call weight—and fly."

"Show us, show us!" they cried, roaring with delighted laughter.

"It's a question of belief," he repeated, his tongue appearing and disappearing like a pointed shadow. "It's in the heart; the power of the air gets into your whole being. Why should I show you? Why should I ask my deity to persuade your scoffing little minds by any miracle? For it is deity, I tell you, and nothing else. I know it. Follow one idea like that, as I follow my bird idea—follow it with the impetus and undeviating concentration of a projectile—and you arrive at power. You know deity—the bird idea of deity, that is. They knew that. The old Egyptians knew it."

"Oh, show us, show us!" they shouted impatiently, wearied of his nonsense-talk. "Get up and fly! Levitate yourself, as they did! Become a star!"

Binovitch turned suddenly very pale, and an odd light shone in his keen brown eyes. He rose slowly from the edge of the chair where he was perched. Something about him changed. There was silence instantly.

"I *will* show you," he said calmly, to their intense amazement; "not to convince your disbelief, but to prove it to myself. For the powers of the air are with me here. I believe. And Horus, great falcon-headed symbol, is my patron god."

The suppressed energy in his voice and manner was indescribable. There was a sense of lifting, upheaving power about him. He raised his arms; his face turned upward; he inflated his lungs with a deep, long breath, and his voice broke into a kind of singing cry, half prayer, half chant:

"O Horus,
Bright-eyed deity of wind,
Feather my soul[1]
Though earth's thick air,
To know thy awful swiftness——"

---

1 The Russian is untranslatable. The phrase means, "Give my life wings."

He broke off suddenly. He climbed lightly and swiftly upon the nearest table—it was in a deserted card-room, after a game in which he had lost more pounds than there are days in the year—and leaped into the air. He hovered a second, spread his arms and legs in space, appeared to float a moment, then buckled, rushed down and forward, and dropped in a heap upon the floor, while every one roared with laughter.

But the laughter died out quickly, for there was something in his wild performance that was peculiar and unusual. It was uncanny, not quite natural. His body had seemed, as with Mordkin and Nijinski, literally to hang upon the air a moment. For a second he gave the distressing impression of overcoming gravity. There was a touch in it of that faint horror which appals by its very vagueness. He picked himself up unhurt, and his face was as grave as a portrait in the academy, but with a new expression in it that everybody noticed with this strange, half-shocked amazement. And it was this expression that extinguished the claps of laughter as wind that takes away the sound of bells. Like many ugly men, he was an inimitable actor, and his facial repertory was endless and incredible. But this was neither acting nor clever manipulation of expressive features. There was something in his curious Russian physiognomy that made the heart beat slower. And that was why the laughter died away so suddenly.

"You ought to have flown farther," cried some one. It expressed what all had felt.

"Icarus didn't drink champagne," another replied, with a laugh; but nobody laughed with him.

"You went too near to Vera," said Palazov, "and passion melted the wax." But his face twitched oddly as he said it. There was something he did not understand, and so heartily disliked.

The strange expression on the features deepened. It was arresting in a disagreeable, almost in a horrible, way. The talk stopped dead; all stared; there was a feeling of dismay in everybody's heart, yet unexplained. Some lowered their eyes, or else looked stupidly elsewhere; but the women of the party felt a kind of fascination. Vera, in particular, could not move her sight away. The joking reference to his passionate admiration for her passed unnoticed. There was a general and individual sense of shock. And a chorus of whispers rose instantly:

"Look at Binovitch! What's happened to his face?"

"He's changed—he's changing!"

"God! Why he looks like a—bird!"

But no one laughed. Instead, they chose the names of birds—hawk, eagle, even owl. The figure of a man leaning against the edge of the door, watching them closely, they did not notice. He had been passing down the corridor, had looked in unobserved, and then had paused. He had seen the whole performance. He watched Binovitch narrowly, now with calm, discerning eyes. It was Dr Plitzinger, the great psychiatrist.

For Binovitch had picked himself up from the floor in a way that was oddly self-possessed, and precluded the least possibility of the ludicrous. He looked neither foolish nor abashed. He looked surprised, but also he looked half angry and half frightened. As some one had said, he "ought to have flown farther." That was the incredible impression his acrobatics had produced—incredible, yet somehow actual. This uncanny idea prevailed, as at a séance where nothing genuine is expected to happen, and something genuine, after all, does happen. There was no pretence in this: Binovitch had flown.

And now he stood there, white in the face—with terror and with anger white. He looked extraordinary, this little, neurasthenic Russian, but he looked at the same time half terrific. Another thing, not commonly experienced by men, was in him, breaking out of him, affecting *directly* the minds of his companions. His mouth opened; blood and fury shone in his blazing eyes; his tongue shot out like an ant-eater's, though even in that the comic had no place. His arms were spread like flapping wings, and his voice rose dreadfully:

"He failed me, he failed me!" he tried to bellow. "Horus, my falcon-headed deity, my power of the air, deserted me! Hell take him! Hell burn his wings and blast his piercing sight! Hell scorch him into dust for his false prophecies! I curse him—I curse Horus!"

The voice that should have roared across the silent room emitted, instead, this high-pitched, bird-like scream. The added touch of sound, the reality it lent, was ghastly. Yet it was marvellously done and acted. The entire thing was a bit of instantaneous inspiration—his voice, his words, his gestures, his whole wild appearance. Only—here was the reality that caused the sense of shock—the expression on his altered features was genuine. *That* was not assumed. There was something new and alien in him, something cold and difficult to human life, something alert and swift and cruel, of another element than earth. A strange, rapacious grandeur had leaped upon the struggling features. The face looked hawk-like.

And he came forward suddenly and sharply toward Vera, whose fixed, staring eyes had never once ceased watching him with a kind of anxious and devouring pain in them. She was both drawn and beaten back. Binovitch advanced on tiptoe. No doubt he still was acting, still pretending this mad nonsense that he worshipped Horus, the falcon-headed deity of forgotten days, and that Horus had failed him in his hour of need; but somehow there was just a hint of too much reality in the way he moved and looked. The girl, a little creature, with fluffy golden hair, opened her lips; her cigarette fell to the floor; she shrank back; she looked for a moment like some smaller, coloured bird trying to escape from a great pursuing hawk; she screamed. Binovitch, his arms wide, his bird-like face thrust forward, had swooped upon her. He leaped. Almost he caught her.

No one could say exactly what happened. Play, become suddenly and unexpectedly too real, confuses the emotions. The change of key was swift. From fun to terror is a dislocating jolt upon the mind. Some one—it was Khilkoff, the brother—upset a chair; everybody spoke at once; everybody stood up. An unaccountable feeling of disaster was in the air, as with those drinkers' quarrels that blaze out from nothing, and end in a pistol-shot and death, no one able to explain clearly how it came about. It was the silent, watching figure in the doorway who saved the situation. Before any one had noticed his approach, there he was among the group, laughing, talking, applauding—between Binovitch and Vera. He was vigorously patting his patient on the back, and his voice rose easily above the general clamour. He was a strong, quiet personality; even in his laughter there was authority. And his laughter now was the only sound in the room, as though by his mere presence peace and harmony were restored. Confidence came with him. The noise subsided; Vera was in her chair again. Khilkoff poured out a glass of wine for the great man.

"The Czar!" said Plitzinger, sipping his champagne, while all stood up, delighted with his compliment and tact. "And to your opening night with the Russian ballet," he added quickly a second toast, "or to your first performance at the Moscow Théâtre des Arts!" Smiling significantly, he glanced at Binovitch; he clinked glasses with him. Their arms were already linked, but it was Palazov who noticed that the doctor's fingers seemed rather tight upon the creased black coat. All drank, looking with laughter, yet with a touch of respect, toward Binovitch, who stood there dwarfed beside the stalwart Austrian, and suddenly as meek and subdued as any mole. Apparently the abrupt change of key had taken his mind successfully off something else.

"Of course—'The Fire-Bird,'" exclaimed the little man, mentioning the famous Russian ballet. "The very thing!" he exclaimed. "For *us*," he added, looking with devouring eyes at Vera. He was greatly pleased. He began talking vociferously about dancing and the rationale of dancing. They told him he was an undiscovered master. He was delighted. He winked at Vera and touched her glass again with his. "We'll make our début together," he cried. "We'll begin at Covent Garden, in London. I'll design the dresses and the posters 'The Hawk and the Dove!' *Magnifique!* I in dark grey, and you in blue and gold! Ah, dancing, you know, is sacred. The little self is lost, absorbed. It is ecstasy, it is divine. And dancing in air—the passion of the birds and stars—ah! they are the movements of the gods. You know deity that way—by living it."

He went on and on. His entire being had shifted with a leap upon this new subject. The idea of realising divinity by dancing it absorbed him. The party discussed it with him as though nothing else existed in the world, all sitting now and talking eagerly together. Vera took the cigarette he offered her, lighting it from his own; their fingers touched; he was as harmless and normal as a retired diplomat in a drawing-room. But it was Plitzinger whose subtle manœuvring had accomplished the change so cleverly, and it was Plitzinger who presently suggested a game of billiards, and led him off, full now of a fresh enthusiasm for cannons, balls, and pockets, into another room. They departed arm in arm, laughing and talking together.

Their departure, it seemed, made no great difference at first. Vera's eyes watched him out of sight, then turned to listen to Baron Minski, who was describing with gusto how he caught wolves alive for coursing purposes. The speed and power of the wolf, he said, was impossible to realise; the force of their awful leap, the strength of their teeth, which could bite through metal stirrup-fastenings. He showed a scar on his arm and another on his lip. He was telling truth, and every-body listened with deep interest. The narrative lasted perhaps ten minutes or more, when Minski abruptly stopped. He had come to an end; he looked about him; he saw his glass, and emptied it. There was a general pause. Another subject did not at once present itself. Sighs were heard; several fidgeted; fresh cigarettes were lighted. But there was no sign of boredom, for where one or two Russians are gathered together there is always life. They produce gaiety and enthusiasm as wind pro-duces waves. Like great children, they plunge whole-heartedly into whatever interest presents itself at the moment. There is a kind of uncouth gambolling in their way of taking life. It seems as if they are always fighting that deep, underlying, national sadness which creeps into their very blood.

"Midnight!" then exclaimed Palazov, abruptly, looking at his watch; and the others fell instantly to talking about that watch, admiring it and asking questions. For the moment that very ordinary timepiece became the centre of observa-tion. Palazov mentioned the price. "It never stops," he said proudly, "not even under water." He looked up at everybody, challenging admiration. And he told how, at a country house, he made a bet that he would swim to a certain island in the lake, and won the bet. He and a girl were the winners, but as it was a horse they had bet, he got nothing out of it for him-self, giving the horse to her. It was a genuine grievance in him. One felt he could have cried as he spoke of it. "But the watch went all the time," he said delightedly, holding the gun-metal object in his hand to show, "and I was twelve minutes in the water with my clothes on."

Yet this fragmentary talk was nothing but pretence. The sound of clicking billiard-balls was audible from the room at the end of the corridor. There was another pause. The pause, however, was intentional. It was not vacuity of mind or absence of ideas that caused it. There was another subject, an unfinished subject that each member of the group was still considering. Only no one cared to begin about it till at last, unable to resist the strain any longer, Palazov turned to Khilkoff, who was saying he would take a "whisky-soda," as the champagne was too sweet, and whispered something beneath his breath; whereupon Khilkoff, forgetting his drink, glanced at his sister, shrugged his shoulders, and made a curious grimace. "He's all right now"—his reply was just audible—"he's with Plitzinger." He cocked his head sidewise to indicate that the clicking of the billiard-balls still was going on.

The subject was out: all turned their heads; voices hummed and buzzed; questions were asked and answered or half answered; eyebrows were raised, shoulders shrugged, hands spread out expressively. There came into the atmosphere a feeling of presentiment, of mystery, of things half understood; primitive, buried instinct stirred a little, the kind of racial dread of vague emotions that might gain the upper hand if encouraged. They shrank from looking something in the face, while yet this unwelcome influence drew closer round them all. They discussed Binovitch and his astonishing performance. Pretty little Vera listened with large and troubled eyes, though saying nothing. The Arab waiter had put out the lights in the corridor, and only a solitary cluster burned now above their heads, leaving their faces in shadow. In the distance the clicking of the billiard-balls still continued.

"It was not play; it was real," exclaimed Minski vehemently. "I can catch wolves," he blurted; "but birds—ugh!—and human birds!" He was half inarticulate. He had witnessed something he could not understand, and it had touched instinctive terror in him. "It was the way he leaped that put the wolf first into my mind, only it was not a wolf at all." The others agreed and disagreed. "It was play at first, but it was reality at the end," another whispered; "and it was no animal he mimicked, but a bird, and a bird of prey at that!"

Vera thrilled. In the Russian woman hides that touch of savagery which loves to be caught, mastered, swept helplessly away, captured utterly and deliciously by the one strong enough to do it thoroughly. She left her chair and sat down beside an older woman in the party, who took her arm quietly at once. Her little face wore a perplexed expression, mournful, yet somehow wild. It was clear that Binovitch was not indifferent to her.

"It's become an *idée fixe* with him," this older woman said. "The bird idea lives in his mind. He lives it in his imagination. Ever since that time at Edfu, when he pretended to worship the great stone falcons outside the temple—the Horus figures—he's been full of it." She stopped. The way Binovitch had behaved at Edfu was better left unmentioned at the moment, perhaps. A slight shiver ran round the listening group, each one waiting for some one else to focus their emotion, and so explain it by saying the convincing thing. Only no one ventured. Then Vera abruptly gave a little jump.

"Hark!" she exclaimed, in a staccato whisper, speaking for the first time. She sat bolt upright. She was listening. "Hark!" she repeated. "There it is again, but nearer than before. It's coming closer. I hear it." She trembled. Her voice, her manner, above all her great staring eyes, startled everybody. No one spoke for several seconds; all listened. The clicking of the billiard-balls had ceased. The halls and corridors lay in darkness, and gloom was over the big hotel. Everybody was in bed.

"Hear what?" asked the older woman soothingly, yet with a perceptible quaver in her voice, too. She was aware that the girl's arm shook upon her own.

"Do you not hear it, too?" the girl whispered.

All listened without speaking. All watched her paling face. Something wonderful, yet half terrible, seemed in the air about them. There was a dull murmur, audible, faint, remote, its direction hard to tell. It had come suddenly from nowhere. They shivered. That strange racial thrill again passed into the group, unwelcome, unexplained. It was aboriginal; it belonged to the unconscious primitive mind, half childish, half terrifying.

"What do you hear?" her brother asked angrily—the irritable anger of nervous fear.

"When he came at me," she answered very low, "I heard it first. I hear it now again. Listen! He's coming."

And at that minute, out of the dark mouth of the corridor, emerged two human figures, Plitzinger and Binovitch. Their game was over: they were going up to bed. They passed the open door of the card-room. But Binovitch was being half dragged, half restrained, for he was apparently attempting to run down the passage with flying, dancing leaps. He bounded. It was like a huge bird trying to rise for flight, while his companion kept him down by force upon the earth. As they entered the strip of light, Plitzinger changed his own position, placing himself swiftly between his companion and the group in the dark corner of the room. He hurried Binovitch along as though he sheltered him from view. They passed into the shadows down the passage. They disappeared. And every one looked significantly, questioningly, at his neighbour, though at first saying no word. It seemed that a curious disturbance of the air had followed them audibly.

Vera was the first to open her lips. "You heard it *then*," she said breathlessly, her face whiter than the ceiling.

"Damn!" exclaimed her brother furiously. "It was wind against the outside walls—wind in the desert. The sand is driving."

Vera looked at him. She shrank closer against the side of the older woman, whose arm was tight about her.

"It was *not* wind," she whispered simply. She paused. All waited uneasily for the completion of her sentence. They stared into her face like peasants who expected a miracle.

"Wings," she whispered. "It was the sound of enormous wings."

And at four o'clock in the morning, when they all returned exhausted from their excursion into the desert, little Binovitch was sleeping soundly and peacefully in his bed. They passed his door on tiptoe. But he did not hear them. He was dreaming. His spirit was at Edfu, experiencing with that ancient deity who was master of all flying life those strange enjoyments upon which his own troubled human heart was passionately set. Safe with that mighty falcon whose powers his lips had scorned a few hours before, his soul, released in vivid dream, went sweetly flying. It was amazing, it was gorgeous. He skimmed the Nile at lightning speed. Dashing down headlong from the height of the great Pyramid, he chased with faultless accuracy a little dove that sought vainly to hide from his terrific pursuit beneath the palm trees. For what he loved must worship where he worshipped, and the majesty of those tremendous effigies had fired his imagination to the creative point where expression was imperative.

Then suddenly, at the very moment of delicious capture, the dream turned horrible, becoming awful with the nightmare touch. The sky lost all its blue and sunshine. Far, far below him the little dove enticed him into nameless depths, so that he flew faster and faster, yet never fast enough to overtake it. Behind him came a great thing down the air, black, hovering, with gigantic wings outstretched. It had terrific eyes, and the beating of its feathers stole his wind away. It followed him, crowding space. He was aware of a colossal beak, curved like a scimitar and pointed wickedly like a tooth of iron. He dropped. He faltered. He tried to scream.

Through empty space he fell, caught by the neck. The huge spectral falcon was upon him. The talons were in his heart. And in sleep he remembered then that he had cursed.

He recalled his reckless language. The curse of the ignorant is meaningless; that of the worshipper is real. This attack was on his soul. He had invoked it. He realised next, with a touch of ghastly horror, that the dove he chased was, after all, the bait that had lured him purposely to destruction, and awoke with a suffocating terror upon him, and his entire body bathed in icy perspiration. Outside the open window he heard a sound of wings retreating with powerful strokes into the surrounding darkness of the sky.

The nightmare made its impression upon Binovitch's impressionable and dramatic temperament. It aggravated his tendencies. He related it next day to Mme. de Drühn, the friend of Vera, telling it with that somewhat boisterous laughter some minds use to disguise less kind emotions. But he received no encouragement. The mood of the previous night was not recoverable; it was already ancient history. Russians never make the banal mistake of repeating a sensation till it is exhausted; they hurry on to novelties. Life flashes and rushes with them, never standing still for exposure before the cameras of their minds. Mme. de Drühn, however, took the trouble to mention the matter to Plitzinger, for Plitzinger, like Freud of Vienna, held that dreams revealed subconscious tendencies which sooner or later must betray themselves in action.

"Thank you for telling me," he smiled politely, "but I have already heard it from him." He watched her eyes for a moment, really examining her soul. "Binovitch, you see," he continued, apparently satisfied with what he saw, "I regard as that rare phenomenon—a genius without an outlet. His spirit, intensely creative, finds no adequate expression. His power of production is enormous and prolific; yet he accomplishes nothing." He paused an instant. "Binovitch, therefore, is in danger of poisoning—himself." He looked steadily into her face, as a man who weighs how much he may confide. "Now," he continued, "if we can find an outlet for him, a field wherein his bursting imaginative genius can produce results—above all, visible results"—he shrugged his shoulders—"the man is saved. Otherwise"—he looked extraordinarily impressive—"there is bound to be sooner or later——"

"Madness?" she asked very quietly.

"An explosion, let us say," he replied gravely. "For instance, take this Horus obsession of his, quite wrong archæologically though it is. *Au fond* it is megalomania of a most unusual kind. His passionate interest, his love, his worship of birds, wholesome enough in itself, finds no satisfying outlet. A man who *really* loves birds neither keeps them in cages nor shoots them nor stuffs them. What, then, can he do? The commonplace bird-lover observes them through glasses, studies their habits, then writes a book about them. But a man like Binovitch, overflowing with this intense creative power of mind and imagination, is not content with that. He wants to know them from within. He wants to feel what they feel, to live their life. He wants to become them. You follow me? Not quite. Well, he seeks to be identified with the object of his sacred, passionate adoration. All genius seeks to know the thing itself from its own point of view. It desires union. That tendency, unrecognised by himself, perhaps, and therefore subconscious, hides in his very soul." He paused a moment. "And the sudden sight of those majestic figures at Edfu—that crystallisation of his *idée fixe* in granite—took hold of this excess in him, so to speak—and is now focusing it toward some definite act. Binovitch sometimes—feels himself a bird! You noticed what occurred last night?"

She nodded; a slight shiver passed over her.

"A most curious performance," she murmured; "an exhibition I never want to see again."

"The most curious part," replied the doctor coolly, "was its truth."

"Its truth!" she exclaimed beneath her breath. She was frightened by something in his voice and by the uncommon gravity in his eyes. It seemed to arrest her intelligence. She felt upon the edge of things beyond her. "You mean that Binovitch did for a moment—hang—in the air?" The other verb, the right one, she could not bring herself to use.

The great man's face was enigmatical. He talked to her sympathy, perhaps, rather than to her mind.

"Real genius," he said smilingly, "is as rare as talent, even great talent, is common. It means that the personality, if only for one second, becomes everything; becomes the universe; becomes the soul of the world. It gets the flash. It is identified with the universal life. Being everything and everywhere, all is possible to it—in that second of vivid realisation. It can brood with the crystal, grow with the plant, leap with the animal, fly with the bird: genius unifies all three. That is the meaning of 'creative.' It is faith. Knowing it, you can pass through fire and not be burned, walk on water and not sink, move a mountain, fly. Because you are fire, water, earth, air. Genius, you see, is madness in the magnificent sense of being superhuman. Binovitch has it."

He broke off abruptly, seeing he was not understood. Some great enthusiasm in him he deliberately suppressed.

"The point is," he resumed, speaking more carefully, "that we must try to lead this passionate constructive genius of the man into some human channel that will absorb it, and therefore render it harmless."

"He loves Vera," the woman said, bewildered, yet seizing this point correctly.

"But would he marry her?" asked Plitzinger at once.

"He is already married."

The doctor looked steadily at her a moment, hesitating whether he should utter all his thought.

"In that case," he said slowly after a pause, "it is better he or she should leave."

His tone and manner were exceedingly impressive.

"You mean there's danger?" she asked.

"I mean, rather," he replied earnestly, "that this great creative flood in him, so curiously focused now upon his Horus-falcon-bird idea, may result in some act of violence——"

"Which would be madness," she said, looking hard at him.

"Which would be disastrous," he corrected her. And then he added slowly: "Because in the mental moment of immense creation he might overlook material laws."

✳

The costume ball two nights later was a great success. Palazov was a Bedouin, and Khilkoff an Apache; Mme. de Drühn wore a national head-dress; Minski looked almost natural as Don Quixote; and the entire Russian "set" was cleverly, if somewhat extravagantly, dressed. But Binovitch and Vera were the most successful of all the two hundred dancers who took part. Another figure, a big man dressed as a Pierrot, also claimed exceptional attention, for though the costume was commonplace enough, there was something of dignity in his appearance that drew the eyes of all upon him. But he wore a mask, and his identity was not discoverable.

It was Binovitch and Vera, however, who must have won the prize, if prize there had been, for they not only looked their parts, but acted them as well. The former in his dark grey feather tunic, and his falcon mask, complete even to the brown hooked beak and tufted talons, looked fierce and splendid. The disguise was so admirable, yet so entirely natural, that it was uncommonly seductive. Vera, in blue and gold, a charming head-dress of a dove upon her loosened hair, and a pair of little dove-pale wings fluttering from her shoulders, her tiny twinkling feet and slender ankles well visible, too, was equally successful and admired. Her large and timid eyes, her flitting movements, her light and dainty way of dancing—all added touches that made the picture perfect.

How Binovitch contrived his dress remained a mystery, for the layers of wings upon his back were real; the large black kites that haunt the Nile, soaring in their hundreds over Cairo and the bleak Mokattam Hills, had furnished them. He had procured them none knew how. They measured four feet across from tip to tip; they swished and rustled as he swept along; they were true falcons' wings. He danced with Nautch-girls and Egyptian princesses and Rumanian Gipsies; he danced well, with beauty, grace, and lightness. But with Vera he did not dance at all; with her he simply flew. A kind of passionate abandon was in him as he skimmed the floor with her in a way that made everybody turn to watch them. They seemed to leave the ground together. It was delightful, an amazing sight; but it was peculiar. The strangeness of it was on many lips. Somehow its queer extravagance communicated itself to the entire ball-room. They became the centre of observation. There were whispers.

"There's that extraordinary bird-man! Look! He goes by like a hawk. And he's always after that dove-girl. How marvellously he does it! It's rather awful. Who is he? I don't envy *her*."

People stood aside when he rushed past. They got out of his way. He seemed forever pursuing Vera, even when dancing with another partner. Word passed from mouth to mouth. A kind of telepathic interest was established everywhere. It was a shade too real sometimes, something unduly earnest in the chasing wildness, something unpleasant. There was even alarm.

"It's rowdy; I'd rather not see it; it's quite disgraceful," was heard. "I think it's horrible; you can see she's terrified."

And once there was a little scene, trivial enough, yet betraying this reality that many noticed and disliked. Binovitch came up to claim a dance, programme clutched in his great tufted claws, and at the same moment the big Pierrot appeared abruptly round the corner with a similar claim. Those who saw it assert he had been waiting, and came on purpose, and that there was something protective and authoritative in his bearing. The misunderstanding was ordinary enough—both men had written her name against the dance—but "No. 13, Tango" also included the supper interval, and neither Hawk nor Pierrot would give way. They were very obstinate. Both men wanted her. It was awkward.

"The Dove shall decide between us," smiled the Hawk politely, yet his taloned fingers working nervously. Pierrot, however, more experienced in the ways of dealing with women, or more bold, said suavely:

"I am ready to abide by her decision"—his voice poorly cloaked this aggravating authority, as though he had the right to her—"only I engaged this dance before his Majesty Horus appeared upon the scene at all, and therefore it is clear that Pierrot has the right of way."

At once, with a masterful air, he took her off. There was no withstanding him. He meant to have her and he got her. She yielded meekly. They vanished among the maze of coloured dancers, leaving the Hawk, disconsolate and vanquished, amid the titters of the onlookers. His swiftness, as against this steady power, was of no avail.

It was then that the singular phenomenon was witnessed first. Those who saw it affirm that he changed absolutely into the part he played. It was dreadful; it was wicked. A frightened whisper ran about the rooms and corridors:

"An extraordinary thing is in the air!"

Some shrank away, while others flocked to see. There were those who swore that a curious, rushing sound was audible, the atmosphere visibly disturbed and shaken; that a shadow fell upon the spot the couple had vacated; that a cry was heard, a high, wild, searching cry: "Horus! bright deity of wind," it began, then died away. One man was positive that the windows had been opened and that something had flown in. It was the obvious explanation. The thing spread horribly. As in a fire-panic, there was consternation and excitement. Confusion caught the feet of all the dancers. The music fumbled and lost time. The leading pair of tango dancers halted and looked round. It seemed that everybody pressed back, hiding, shuffling, eager to see, yet more eager not to be seen, as though something dangerous, hostile, terrible, had broken loose. In rows against the wall they stood. For a great space had made itself in the middle of the ball-room, and into this empty space appeared suddenly the Pierrot and the Dove.

It was like a challenge. A sound of applause, half voices, half clapping of gloved hands, was heard. The couple danced exquisitely into the arena. All stared. There was an impression that a set piece had been prepared, and that this was its beginning. The music again took heart. Pierrot was strong and dignified, no whit nonplussed by this abrupt publicity. The Dove, though faltering, was deliciously obedient. They danced together like a single outline. She was captured utterly. And to the man who needed her the sight was naturally agonizing—the protective way the Pierrot held her, the right and strength of it, the mastery, the complete possession.

"He's got her!" some one breathed too loud, uttering the thought of all. "Good thing it's not the Hawk!"

And, to the absolute amazement of the throng, this sight was then apparent. A figure dropped through space. That high, shrill cry again was heard:

"Feather my soul . . . to know thy awful swiftness!"

Its singing loveliness touched the heart, its appealing, passionate sweetness was marvellous, as from the gallery this figure of a man, dressed as a strong, dark bird, shot down with splendid grace and ease. The feathers swept; the wings spread out as sails that take the wind. Like a hawk that darts with unerring power and aim upon its prey, this thing of mighty wings rushed down into the empty space where the two danced. Observed by all, he entered, swooping beautifully, stretching his wings like any eagle. He dropped. He fixed his point of landing with consummate skill close beside the astonished dancers. He landed.

It happened with such swiftness it brought the dazzle and blindness as when lightning strikes. People in different parts of the room saw different details; a few saw nothing at all after the first startling shock, closing their eyes, or holding their arms before their faces as in self-protection. The touch of panic fear caught the entire room. The nameless thing that all the evening had been vaguely felt was come. It had suddenly materialised.

For this incredible thing occurred in the full blaze of light upon the open floor. Binovitch, grown in some sense formidable, opened his dark, big wings about the girl. The long grey feathers moved, causing powerful draughts of wind that made a rushing sound. An aspect of the terrible was about him, like an emanation. The great beaked head was poised to strike, the tufted claws were raised like fingers that shut and opened, and the whole presentment of his amazing figure focused in an attitude of attack that was magnificent and terrible. No one who saw it doubted. Yet there were those who swore that it was not Binovitch at all, but that another outline, monstrous and shadowy, towered above him, draping his lesser proportions with two colossal wings of darkness. That some touch of strange divinity lay in it may be claimed, however confused the wild descriptions afterward. For many lowered their heads and bowed their shoulders. There was terror. There was also awe. The onlookers swayed as though some power passed over them through the air.

A sound of wings was certainly in the room.

Then some one screamed; a shriek broke high and clear; and emotion, ordinary human emotion, unaccustomed to terrific things, swept loose. The Hawk and Vera flew. Beaten back against the wall as by a stroke of whirlwind, the Pierrot staggered. He watched them go. Out of the lighted room they flew, out of the crowded human atmosphere, out of the heat and artificial light, the walled-in, airless halls that were a cage. All this they left behind. They seemed things of wind and air, made free happily of another element. Earth held them not. Toward the open night they raced with this extraordinary lightness as of birds, down the long corridor and on to the southern terrace, where great coloured curtains were hung suspended from the columns. A moment they were visible. Then the fringe of one huge curtain, lifted by the wind, showed their dark outline for a second against the starry sky. There was a cry, a leap. The curtain flapped again and closed. They vanished. And into the ball-room swept the cold draught of night air from the desert.

But three figures instantly were close upon their heels. The throng of half-dazed, half-stupefied onlookers, it seemed, projected them as though by some explosive force. The general mass held back, but, like projectiles, these three flung themselves after the fugitives down the corridor at high speed—the Apache, Don Quixote, and, last of them, the Pierrot. For Khilkoff, the brother, and Baron Minski, the man who caught wolves alive, had been for some time keenly on the watch, while Dr. Plitzinger, reading the symptoms clearly, never far away, had been faithfully observant of every movement. His mask tossed aside, the great psychiatrist was now recognised by all. They reached the parapet just as the curtain flapped back heavily into place; the next second all three were out of sight behind it. Khilkoff was first, however, urged forward at frantic speed by the warning words the doctor had whispered as they ran. Some thirty yards beyond the terrace was the brink of the crumbling cliff on which the great hotel was built, and there was a drop of sixty feet to the desert floor below. Only a low stone wall marked the edge.

Accounts varied. Khilkoff, it seems, arrived in time—in the nick of time—to seize his sister, virtually hovering on the brink. He heard the loose stones strike the sand below. There was no struggle, though it appears she did not thank him for his interference at first. In a sense she was beside—outside—herself. And he did a characteristic thing: he not only brought her back into the ball-room, but he *danced* her back. It was admirable. Nothing could have calmed the general excitement better. The pair of them danced in together as though nothing was amiss. Accustomed to the strenuous practice of his Cossack regiment, this young cavalry officer's muscles were equal to the semi-dead weight in his arms. At most the onlookers thought her tired, perhaps. Confidence was restored—such is the psychology of a crowd—and in the middle of a thrilling Viennese waltz he easily smuggled her out of the room, administered brandy, and got her up to bed. The absence of the Hawk, meanwhile, was hardly noticed; comments were made and then forgotten; it was Vera in whom the strange, anxious sympathy had centred. And, with her obvious safety, the moment of primitive, childish panic passed away. Don Quixote, too, was presently seen dancing gaily as though nothing untoward had happened; supper intervened; the incident was over; it had melted into the general wildness of the evening's irresponsibility. The fact that Pierrot did not appear again was noticed by no single person.

But Dr. Plitzinger was otherwise engaged, his heart and mind and soul all deeply exercised. A death-certificate is not always made out quite so simply as the public thinks. That Binovitch had died of suffocation in his swift descent through merely sixty feet of air was not conceivable; yet that his body lay so neatly placed upon the desert after such a fall was stranger still. It was not crumpled, it was not torn; no single bone was broken, no muscle wrenched; there was no bruise. There was no indenture in the sand. The figure lay sidewise as though in sleep, no sign of violence visible anywhere, the dark wings folded as a great bird folds them when it creeps away to die in loneliness. Beneath the Horus mask the face was smiling. It seemed he had floated into death upon the element he loved. And only Vera had seen the enormous wings that, hovering invitingly above the dark abyss, bore him so softly into another world. Plitzinger, that is, saw them, too, but he said firmly that they belonged to the big black falcons that haunt the Mokattam Hills and roost upon these ridges, close beside the hotel, at night. Both he and Vera, however, agreed on one thing: the high, sharp cry in the air above them, wild and plaintive, was certainly the black kite's cry—the note of the falcon that passionately seeks its mate. It was the pause of a second, when she stood to listen, that made her rescue possible. A moment later and she, too, would have flown to death with Binovitch.

THE SWAYING VISION

by Jessie Douglas Kerruish

CHADWICK bought the desirable semi-detached residences, Nos. 75 and 77, Herald Crescent, Willingborough, to fulfil the ideal of middle-class retirement; a house to live in and another to pay rates and taxes and the coal bill. He was not a man to buy a pig in a poke, or a house in a strange town in a hurry; he held strict inquest on the birth and death rates of the locality, and on the drains of his prospective purchase, its damp courses, and the character of the immediate neighbourhood. He welcomed a two days' downpour that triumphantly vindicated the watertightness of the buildings, and he found that the pair were the only ones to let in the Crescent.

What else, within the limits of the normal Three Dimensions, could a man have done further?

On March 25 he, with his family consisting of Mrs. Chadwick and their two daughters, moved into No. 75. On the 26th he consorted with his next-door neighbour and learnt the worst.

"It was really nobody's affair," the next-door neighbour protested. "How could anybody warn you? Of course you might," he added, as the aggrieved Chadwick breathed threats relating to the ex-landlord of his new demesne and the house agent. "Still, I must remind you it's a penal of-fence to kill people, even if they have landed you with one of the most notorious haunted houses in England."

It was bad enough, the worst. No. 77—under an alias for the law of libel's sake—had figured five times in the pages of a certain psychic review, and times innumerable in magazines of a sensational tendency. It had been let twelve times in eight years; no tenant stayed out his term. The first one paid up to avoid trouble, and reimbursed himself by spreading information concerning his experiences. He stayed a month. The second, at the end of a week, wanted to horsewhip the landlord for letting in his wife for nervous breakdown. So the tale went on, the last occupants had left at the half-quarter before Chadwick acquired the treasure; they had refused to pay for the remainder of the year they had agreed on, and had dared the landlord to sue them and embellish the reputation the place already owned. So there had been nothing left for the landlord to do but to sell to some stranger while he removed to a far city.

Local house-agents, consulted, confirmed the tale. They said they would try to get a tenant, but mentioned, pessimistically, that No. 79 was let at thirty per cent below the regular rent in the road because only the detaching tradesmen's entrances divided from No. 77. Yes, the Psychic Society had investigated, they had even taken up the flooring in the noted front room. And they had found no explanation.

Chadwick was no coward; he spent that evening in the front room of No. 77. At 3 a.m. he stumbled into his own parlour in the throes of panic. Next day he repaired to London to seek aid from Lester Stukeley.

Stukeley and Chadwick were old schoolfellows. Chadwick at fifty was a   retired merchant, with gardening for his hobby; Stukeley, at near the same age, still adorned the Civil Service, and had taken to psychic investigation.

"It was utterly beastly, Stukeley," said Chadwick, mopping his ample bald brow at the recollection.

"We will go into it systematically," said his friend. "To begin, the house is of modern construction!'

"Built twenty years ago."

"Of new materials, if you know?"

"I know. Yes. Why, Stukeley?"

"Because I've known things happen in modern houses built out of the debris of old ones. You say twelve tenants have lived there in eight years, that leaves twelve since the building of the place to be accounted for."

"It was in the hands of two tenants; neither complained of any disturbance; the first stayed his full term of five years, the second, by renewals, stayed for seven in all."

"So it was after the departure of this second tenant that the trouble began? That looks suspicious."

"I know his address. He is an old Frenchman, and by the house-agents' accounts most harmless and above-board. He declared, when questioned, that he never noticed anything wrong, nor did his family."

"There's always the possibility that they were merely of a solid and unsusceptible nature. Still, I'll remember this Frenchman. It is somewhat unusual to encounter occult manifestations in a house of such recent construction with no sinister tale attached to it. Has anyone died in it?"

"It happens no death has so far taken place in it."

"This increases the mystery. Now, if you know, Chadwick, what was the site like before the building took place?"

"My communicative neighbour remembers it; it was a meadow."

"Were there any knolls that had to be levelled for the building—if you know?"

"My informant describes it as perfectly flat."

"I must congratulate you, Chadwick, on your foresight in procuring such exhaustive information. I confess I thought a burial barrow might have been disturbed for the builders' benefit. You watched last night?"

Chadwick got scarlet, then blurted out, "I watched for a while. Then—then I bolted. It was just what all the other people described—the unutterably abominable smell—faugh!—and I knew I'd be compelled to turn out the light in a minute—I just hurled myself through the doorway."

"To turn out the light?" repeated Stukeley inquiringly.

"Yes," Chadwick answered explosively. "Everybody agreed about that. It can't be seen in the dark distinctly, and it can't be seen at all in full light, a faint light is what suits it. You feel it's there, and you smell it—heavens, that's the horrible part of it! Not strong, you'll understand, but beastly—viscid—and—and—a sort of pale yellow-green, sticky stench."

"I understand. A strongly developed colour sense is useful in description. And what is seen?"

"I didn't see. I knew it would give me the horrors. But the people who saw it because they hadn't gumption to run away all agreed. 'Pon my word, Stukeley, it sounds absurd, but I thought the description of the first feeling absurd, too, before I'd experienced it, and now I've experienced that, and know how utterly loathsome it is, I can believe the rest is as bad."

"One moment," said Stukeley, with the air of one struck by a sudden thought. "Do not tell me what is said about the ocular manifestation. Let me try with an open mind, and see if what I see agrees with the other accounts. Will you watch with me?"

"Will you draw the protective thing, the what d'ye call it?" Chadwick hesitated.

"The pentacle? Most certainly I will erect it. With no reason for occult manifestations to be found there is always room for hoaxing, but it is well to take precautions."

"I'll watch then—inside the pentacle. I don't believe it is hoaxing, Stukeley, but as nobody has received bodily harm, beyond shock, so far, I feared you would not trouble with the pentacle."

"I know, Chadwick, that one can never tell when occult manifestations may become dangerous to life. Tomorrow night, then, I hope it will prove a hoax."

"Tomorrow night," Chadwick repeated. "We'll have the house to ourselves. Mary and the girls got hold of the tale soon enough. The servants we brought left this morning, they'd heard it, too, and we are staying at the nearest hotel while I decide what is to be done. They all drew the line at even being next door to the thing."

When Stukeley unloaded his bag from the cab next evening and took a look up and down Herald Crescent, nothing could have presented a more reassuring appearance. The place shouted of respectability, leisure, and fish-and-soup-course-dinners. The kind of place where occult manifestations were the very last things that might be expected to happen. Two rows of three-storey, semi-detached residences sloped before his gaze to a quiet twilight sky, every house a replica of its fellows, white-curtained, brass-plated, trim and commonplace.

No. 77 was only singled out from its neighbours because it was the only one to let, and was plus a brace of notice boards and minus plate and curtains.

In the dining-room of No. 75 the table awaited the dinner for two which a near-by restaurant was to furnish in an hour, the brave charwoman who had agreed to stop till sunset and return at sunrise to see to the wants of the two men was in attendance, and Chadwick was ready for a preliminary daylight inspection of the scene of forthcoming vigil.

Under Chadwick's key the front door of No. 77 swung open with a reassuring squeak.

Stukeley and his aide went through to the back and inspected the garden.

Then they locked and sealed the back door, and set out on an exhaustive tour of the house, leaving the front room to the last, and making a species of drive down to it from the garret.

As each room was overhauled the door was shut, locked, and sealed behind them until of all the apartments in the house only the front one was open. The windows even were closed and sealed, and narrow strips of paper sealed in a network across the register of every chimney.

Chadwick stood nervously by the open door as Stukeley went round the front room.

The occultist raised the blinds, flooding the place with harsh reflected sunset light from the windows opposite.

The apartment was the largest in the house, measuring some twenty feet by thirty, the ceiling was high, the walls painted dull olive-green, the floor oak-stained and polished. Stukeley went round several times, tapping walls and floor questingly, peered up the chimney, then nodded gravely.

"Once we have locked ourselves in this bare room, nothing outside of the Fourth Dimension could get us without our knowledge," he commented.

"Lock ourselves in?" Chadwick repeated, without relish.

"Within the pentacle, old chap. Now what is the spot at which the manifestations begin?"

"Between the chimney and the west wall," Chadwick answered.

The room was bounded at one side by the entry-lobby, the wall opposite was conterminous with the passage of the tradesmen's entrance outside, the east wall contained the large bay window, the west one separated it from the next room.

Stukeley stamped and tapped the flooring at the indicated spot, but elicited no more signs of hollowness than the ventilation space beneath would justify. They then returned to No. 75, locking the front door of No. 77 carefully behind them.

Dinner put more heart into Chadwick. At eleven, the charwoman having long departed, they locked No. 75 up and adjourned to No. 77 again.

Gas was laid on. Stukeley went all over again, ascertaining that the seals were unbroken before opening each door. Satisfying himself that nobody had been in, he lit the gas all over the place, and repeated the drive of the earlier hour, leaving the light on full cock in each room and the doors open, and seeing that the chimneys and windows were well sealed.

With the blaze of light Chadwick's courage was augmented. The front room was furnished with an incandescent burner in a hanging chandelier set in the centre of the ceiling. When it was lit the whole apartment was plain and bare to the view. Chadwick shuddered a little as the door was closed. Stukeley laid his bag in the middle of the floor together with a pair of camp stools.

"Now, we will stay here while I make my arrangements," he said, and Chadwick felt emboldened as he watched the said arrangements.

Producing a little bundle of twigs from the bag, the occultist swept the floor in a circle, extending nearly to the walls, keeping himself within the limit of it. Then, in the same way he drew a pentacle with charcoal within the bounds of the swept space.

"It's charred rowan wood," he explained over his shoulder, as he traced with a continuous line the five-pointed figure. "Now just remember, Chadwick, that if either of us should step outside the line, or even touch it sufficiently to break the continuity of it, the pentacle will lose its protective power. Should danger threaten safety lies within this line. But if even a match should fall across it linking the space within to the space without, the virtue of the pentacle is gone."

In the five points of the star he placed five crusts, each wrapped in a slip of linen, and between, in the five angles, five pinches of white powder.

"Bread and salt, with charcoal, are great protective influences," he said, standing up. "I'll guarantee that within this we will be safe from all molestation."

They established themselves on the camp stools, full in the light of the gas, and waited. Chadwick's courage oozed. Herald Crescent is a quiet thoroughfare, and before midnight traffic in it practically ceased.

Silence settled down; with it Chadwick knew that darkness—wholesome, respectable darkness—also came to the other houses, with drawn blinds and extinguished lights. Now and then a chance cab rattled past, clattering eerily over the wood-paving between the hushes that followed and preceded its progress.

A couple of strayed revellers fared homewards, none too steadily, their footsteps ringing irregularly; the policeman, who had been apprised of the reason for the lights in No. 77, passed by with a slow tramp of ample boots.

An hour passed. Stukeley sat quiet. Chadwick copied him outwardly, and inwardly quaked. His imagination shudderingly played with the fancy that they were sitting in an island of light in the dark street; it felt as though everybody else in the world were dead; there was no help to be had if help were needed.

A rogue horror, a muddle-headed sense of the bounds of matter, began to grip him. He tried to reassure himself by thoughts of the nearness of his kind. It was a failure.

Looking before him at the brightly illuminated wall, he told himself that beyond the wall was a narrow passage, an open passage full of the blessed free air of heaven, then another wall, and beyond that the merry family of children who, with a jolly father and cheery mother, lived in No. 79. The thought was of no use, the family would not be in the room beyond the dividing passage now, but upstairs, ever so many walls away, and that boundary passage full of open air—it was a terrible place, with no bound between it and the stars, and the void beyond the stars. It was a continuation of space, it was an immeasurable sundering gap between himself in the haunted room and his kind, as represented by the jolly family in the next house.

Chadwick shuddered and tried another tack. His back was to the door, but if he slewed round there would be nothing but the room wall, the width of the passage, and another wall to divide him from the refuge of No. 75.

Nothing but two walls and the passage—a thousand miles would be no more barrier—he could not leap through solid walls if the need for refuge came when the lights had to be lowered. He must open the door of the room, traverse the passage, open the front door—heavens! It was a tremendous way to go if need pressed and something was after him.

New Zealand came into his mind. It seemed within nearer reach, for all the hours of train journeying and half a world of sea between, than his own home next door, with but the six-foot width of passage and two walls between.

He came to himself with a little cry and sat bristling. By his side Stukeley turned with a little cool nod.

"Do you feel it?" Chadwick gasped.

Stukeley nodded again, holding up a hand for silence. Chadwick braced himself and steadied his quivering under-jaw.

"My God, don't you taste it?" he cried suddenly.

Stukeley made no answer. A faint, thin viscid flavour in the air was but too perceptible to him. He sat with his eyes turned to the front of him. Chadwick followed his gaze to the floor, and sat tense with expectation. The burner high above and somewhat behind the men cast the shadows before them. The shadows were clear-cut, reflected light from the walls lit them to a dark transparency. In them the lines where the floor-boards met were defined blackly. Stukeley's extended the farthest, nearly to the wall by the fireplace, it went over that side of the pentacle, a sharp cut patch of clear dark.

Within the span of this cast shadow one of the angles and half a point of the pentacle were included, the intersecting charcoal lines clear black, the little heap of salt in the angle dusky grey, half the wrapped crust in the point in shadow, a dirty, white little mass, the other half dazzling white against the lit boards beyond the shadow edge.

Chadwick looked at these details until his gaze swam, then his senses woke and his scalp drew together, chilled and twitching. He had become aware of another bit of darkness on the floor, a flood of black that was creeping steadily forward towards them across Stukeley's shadow.

It began, clear cut, as the edge of the shadow, and was spreading in a little stream, about a hand-breadth in width, progressing with the lazy, rolling deliberation of spilt ink. For several moments the men sat immovable. Stukeley speculated, clear-brained, as to its origin. Where could it come from, starting, as it apparently did, at the edge of his shadow?

As they watched it languidly split into two irregular branches and so continued on its way.

"It will touch our feet!" Chadwick screamed, springing up and retreating a pace.

Stukeley got up more quietly to join him. The move brought them immediately beneath the gas, and their shadows were concentrated under their feet. The floor around was all in light, no sign of the creeping shadow stream was visible.

Chadwick trembled violently.

"Do you hear it?" he quavered.

Stukeley's eyes searched the floor. "A little hissing and bubbling near the fireplace," he said gravely.

"And the—the stench?" gulped his companion. "Blood—and—corruption——"

"No, new blood," said Stukeley. "It is like the scent of the drain pit in a Dakhma I examined near Bombay."

"A Dakhma?"

"Tower of Silence. A Parsee, corpse-exposing building."

The occultist stepped forward; his shadow ran over the floor to its old place.

The creeping stain appeared as before, further advanced to them. "It is only visible in the dark," he commented.

"Come before it touches us," Chadwick mouthed.

"Stay in the pentacle," Stukeley commanded sternly. "It is our safety—see!"

Chadwick, half-frantic with horror, glanced along his indicating finger. The stream touched the point of the pentacle, turned as though it had encountered a wall, and ran along outside against the charcoal mark. In its flow it met the pile of salt and laved it without penetrating the absorbent stuff. It continued to spread itself along against the charcoal line. Chadwick understood, and felt less dread: it could not penetrate the pentacle.

Stukeley stepped forward, keeping his shadow crosswise over the mystic one, and advancing parallel to it. As he advanced the edge of his shadow still remained the edge of the other. At last the shadow of his head was low on the wall by the fireplace and that of his shoulders on the floor beneath.

And right in the middle of the shadowed left shoulder was the beginning of the dark stream—a rectangular spot that hissed softly and gave forth bubbles of shadow which rose from it and broke sibilantly.

He moved his shadow away, and the bubbling stream was gone; he moved the shadow back and it reappeared. Behind him Chadwick suddenly cried out in a shrill tone, "Stukeley, there's something over the stream! It will be on us! I can't stand it—invisible! I must see it!'

He snatched upwards and turned the gas low. From both men came a gasp.

Over the bubbling stream, now clearly defined in the gloom, lay a figure.

It was stretched apparently on the floor, some ten feet from them; they saw it clearly; it was solid to view, yet they could not exactly define details. To each it appeared as though he was wearing spectacles unsuited to his eyes. The figure, naked and flaccid, was half-corpse, half-skeleton. In parts the bones protruded, but the head was untouched; a handsome young head, a face young behind its ashiness, hollow-cheeked and unshaven. As they looked it slowly rose in the air almost as high as the ceiling, then swept down again to the floor.

Again it rose, canted at a different angle, and descended at another tilt, so that for several seconds it seemed to stand upright before them, the jaw dropping with a jerk. Then it went up and turned so that it appeared to stand head down with its back to them.

A dozen times these gyrations were repeated, and at each repetition the form was displayed at a slightly varying angle; the movements were accomplished with a horrible lazy deliberation, then with a jar the figure stopped in mid-air, level with their eyes, and was jerked double, so that it appeared to be sitting up bent forward from the hips, the head almost butting on its knees.

"It will fall on us!' screamed Chadwick. He turned for the door, but Stukeley caught him.

"Stay in the pentacle!' he shouted. Chadwick looked over his shoulder. The figure had risen and was almost over them and almost flat against the ceiling, face up. He gave a little whimpering cry, and fainted.

Chadwick issued from his swoon all sore and cramped.

He was lying full-length within the limits of the pentacle; Stukeley's folded coat was under his head, and his friend was sitting on a stool beside him, chin on palm and eyes full of thought. Daylight was striking in through the chinks of the blinds; the room was bare and empty of anything outside the five-pointed star.

He sat up and stared, terrified, towards the fireplace. Walls, floor, and ceiling were plain and prosaic. Meeting his eyes, Stukeley stepped out of the pentacle and stamped questingly on the very boards whence the horror had issued.

"I'd advise you to have this up, Chadwick," he advised.

His masterful tone was a tonic. Chadwick scrambled up, shuddering. "Let's get out of this," he shivered.

As he opened the front door Stukeley pointed to the unbroken seals. The rose and amber sunrise was billowing over the houses opposite; Chadwick stood by the gate basking in the clean morning air while Stukeley went over the house, putting out the lights.

"No seal disturbed," reported the occultist.

"I can't stand four walls at present," Chadwick groaned.

They passed into the back garden of 75 and paced up and down between the laurels.

"That's just what all the tenants said," Chadwick burst out suddenly. "A decayed corpse that sprang up and down, and threatened to topple over on you—ugh!'

"It was not decayed, and it did not spring up and down," Stukeley corrected.

"Eh?"

"I watched it until at the first streak of daylight the bubbling ceased and it vanished. It was not decayed at all."

"Eh? The scent——'

"Scent of death, but of new death."

"The bones——'

"The flesh had been purposely removed."

"Mangled by beasts or birds?"

"No. Cut off neatly. Partly dissected, in a word."

"What do you make of it, then?"

"I'm nonplussed."

"Well, it jumped up and down," Chadwick said ruminatively.

"No. It swayed and dipped with the exact motion a ship in a heaving sea would display."

"By George——"

"It was just as though the thing was lying on the deck of a vessel, invisible to us, that swayed and jerked it about."

"But, Stukeley, what connection could that house have with a ship?"

"I don't know. What I say is—have the floor up."

✳

They had the workmen in that very morning, but with no more result than the Psychic Society had achieved before them. At two or three places by the walls, including the spot where the bubbling rose, the planking had been repaired; mouse-holes beneath explained that, however. Below was the innocuous ventilation space, and below they found virgin earth that revealed nothing though they dug it up for some depth.

"Chadwick, one thing struck me," said Stukeley, as they sat at lunch. "Did you notice any connection between the bubbling and the figure?"

"No. Truth is I was too frightened to notice much."

"You are not used to these investigations, as I am," the occultist replied charitably. "Wherever the figure moved a band of something like vapour rose, fanlike, from the bubbling, and always touched it. There should have been something under the floor." He seemed quite annoyed at the lack. "I wonder where the second tenant, the Frenchman, lives?"

"My neighbour, who knew him well, might know."

The neighbour, questioned, had lost touch with Monsieur Duhamel, but knew that he was an occasional contributor to *The One Weekly*.

That same afternoon saw Stukeley, fresh from a brief interview with the editor of *The One Weekly*, en route for Balham and the modest abode of M. Auguste Duhamel.

M. Duhamel was reassuring; a fat, genial old gentleman, prosy and cheery.

"Indeed, I regret the distress of the good M. Chadwick," he asseverated. "Ourselves, we never used the front room, so saw nothing."

"If I am not trenching on the impertinent, M. Duhamel, it seems strange that you did not use the large front room."

"I will explain. My late respected father was a collector of curiosities, and all of them he left to me. They were of value, but ugly; African witch-masks, mummy cases—*le bon Dieu* alone knows what! There was no inducement to live with them; the front room was the only one large enough to hold all, therefore we put them there. You understand, *monsieur*? We put them there in order that our friends might come to see them sometimes, but—*tiens!*—they are ugly, ugly as *le diable*—our friends preferred to glance at them by day, and our servant washed and dusted them by day likewise."

"Curios?" And Stukeley pricked up his ears.

"*Oui, monsieur*. Curiosities. My father loved them. I do not. This year I have sold all to a museum. I was nursing them for years while prices went up. That was all the good of them in my eyes." M. Duhamel made a gesture of large scorn.

"However, I kept the room in good repair, the landlord repaired the outside, the tenant the inside; that is the rule. When the mice ate holes in the flooring I mended it; I myself mended it. I am a great amateur carpenter."

"You mended the place by the fire? And you found nothing when you worked?" asked Stukeley eagerly.

M. Duhamel shook his head decisively, and Stukeley added, "It was from there the apparition rose."

"*En passant*, M. Stukeley, I have heard much about this apparition, but never have I had a good description of it. May I ask?"

Stukeley gave a sketch of his experience of the previous night. He came out of absorption in his own recital to find the Frenchman gaping with dawning enlightenment in his eyes.

"*Monsieur*," said Duhamel, "I myself am a man of rational cast of mind, but you who believe in the spirit world, you hold that the blood is the very vehicle of life and the soul, is it not? And that with blood many marvellous feats can be performed? I have read even that from the emanations of fresh blood spirit forms can be conjured."

"Some belief of the kind is current with certain people. And what, *monsieur*——"

"Mr. Stukeley, is it possible that old blood may have strange properties? Power, for instance, to show to living eyes what it once was?"

Stukeley answered affirmatively. The Frenchman slapped his thigh.

"Then, *m'sieur*, I will tell you. In my father's collection were many things whose bone fides it would be difficult to prove. Pieces of wood or stone from famous or infamous erections, for instance. As I care nothing for curios, and knew that it would be impossible to sell things of this species, I did not scruple to make practical use of them. It is said, *monsieur*, that in the famed Chicago pork-canning factories nothing of the pig is wasted but the squeak. I am more economical than that; I would make use of the squeak by calling in all the neighbours' little ones to enjoy the sound——"

He paused to laugh. Stukeley quivered, all impatience.

"Ah, M. Stukeley, the stone that forms so good a foundation for the little rockery in the back garden of our friend No. 77 is from the old Bastille. But who could have proved it? Who would have bought? The same with pieces of wood. When the mice ate holes in the floor I mended it,

and I said to myself, 'I will make that certain piece of wood
in the cabinet of use.' That piece cut down to a suitable size
to fit the place by the fire, the chips from it went into our
stove that same day. Now in the piece of wood a stain was
deeply sunk, and my father held that it was blood——"

"Where from? What from?" demanded the Englishman,
as the narrator paused.

"In a moment, *monsieur*. I mended it well. I am a good
amateur carpenter. Undoubtedly it is the piece from whence
your mysterious bubbling came."

"Where was that piece of wood from?" demanded
Stukeley hoarsely.

"From the raft of the *Medusa*, monsieur."

That evening, directly he had returned from the metropolis
to Willingborough, Stukeley took Chadwick into the dis-
membered room and hunted amidst the scattered planks.
It was easy to identify the piece that had mended the part
by the fireplace; it was small, thick, and was of a different
colour to the larger planks.

From the oak stain on top through half its thickness was
a deeper tint than that of the lower half.

"It's my opinion that the thing remained quiescent
until it was insulted by being put to a practical use," said
Stukeley. "When I've destroyed it—reverently—Chadwick,
I've every hope your house will become marketable property again."

In the back garden he kindled a fire, feeding it to a good
heat with shavings, and planted the piece of wood on it.
He further scratched a pentacle round the blaze. The wood
burnt slowly; Chadwick thought he detected a curious
acrid odour in the smoke from it.

" '*Requiescat in pace*'," muttered Stukeley. "So a collector of ghastly relics is to be blamed for it all! By Jove, one certainly never knows what the final reflex of one's actions may be!"

Chadwick looked puzzled.

"But Stukeley, I do not understand. What was the *Medusa*? And the raft? I seem to recollect the name vaguely, but nothing about it."

"You might recollect it through Géricault's famous picture of it—a monument of ill-taste. The *Medusa*, Chadwick, was a French vessel, and she happened to be wrecked, decades and decades ago. The survivors made a raft, and on it knocked about the open sea until—it's a horrible tale, Chadwick, need I tell it all? Can't you piece it together? They were starving—think of the wood with the indelible stain on it—and the man with a lot of flesh hacked off him—that's what a relic of the *Medusa*'s raft meant!'

THE PAPER MAN
(A DREAM)

by Neville Meakin

BELOW the great city lay like a map, its lights glimmering faintly, the river a silver thread winding out of gloom into gloom. At first nothing was clearly seen, the parks were but spaces of blackness, the loftiest buildings only hillocks in the plain of roofs, the widest of London's thoroughfares as furrows in a field. But gradually spires, columns, and towers shot up, the streets broadened, even men became visible as ants running to and fro, each full of unknown conflicting purpose. The river appeared, vanished and reappeared, now calm and desolate, gliding between quiet banks, now full of shipping, lined with crowded docks. I had passed over it from north to south; again I was crossing, south to north, nearer and nearer at each passing.

The whirlpool of London had caught me in its swirl and was drawing me deeper and deeper into its vortex.

But whence had I come and what was I? A floating wreath of grey mist, nothing more, a being without body, filmy, formless, more impalpable than air, yet something, some one, for I thought. From some other world I had descended, some world of which I remembered nothing, not even the manner of my descent; I knew only that I had come to behold and to learn, and I surrendered myself to the eddy without fear.

Faster and faster the soundless whirlpool rushed, smaller and smaller the circles, louder and louder the noise of the streets contended with the gusty night winds that tossed the smoke hither and thither, but the eddy that swept me on knew nothing of London's mirth nor the bubbling of her tortured air. I too, being of the swirl, heard the tumult of the place of men without heeding it, saw without noting, for on a sudden a loneliness smote me, and I sought for a being like myself, who might read me the riddle of the world in which I was and the world that was below.

It seemed that other wisps of mist floated round me, differing from the eddy as white of egg formed in water differs from the water. Their shape, too, was after the fashion of an egg, but they swept by careless of my presence. I could not greet them, perchance there was not language in their place, or perchance I had not the key. For it came to me that they were souls of men and women, dead and doomed to haunt the vortex of the whirl, while I was but a living soul brought within by chance or fate for a little space only and for an unknown end. Between them and me was a gulf fixed.

Down drew the vortex of the whirl, a blank and then stillness. I seemed to have passed the great eddy of void, though I was not of it, for still I remained bodyless, floating without motion above the pavement of a street, Piccadilly.

It was night, but yet early, neither the most crowded now nor yet the emptiest. Dowdy women of the pavement passed and repassed, men went in and out of cafés and clubs. Sometimes I thought that dark shapes of dead souls flitted below me, clinging round the women, striving to enmesh the men. I watched without attraction, without repulsion, for amid all these living souls and their attendant spirits accursed, I found no one who seemed to me akin.

Then suddenly a strange pair attracted me. One was an artist. He carried a portfolio under his arm and walked rapidly, threading his way through the crowd homewards. He was rather over the average height, young and strong with blue eyes and a fair Vandyke beard. He wore a black velvet jacket, a soft felt hat, and a loud flaring tie, yet despite his energy and look of intellect, there was a pucker of care between his brows; he was no stranger to trouble, hopeful though his step was now.

But his companion even more than himself arrested me. Beside him walked, or rather glided, a man, or the semblance of a man. This being, if being it was, seemed the very copy of the artist, but was a shape without substance, as though fashioned of the frailest tissue paper, and within but empty air. The face was the face of the artist, but all changed. Feature and feature was the same, yet the look of power, the strength of mind, was gone. The eyes were abstracted as in contemplated adoration; the lips parted a little, as though dwelling on the memory of a kiss. A pinkish glow seemed to suffuse from within suggesting a Japanese lantern faintly illuminated by a red lamp. Perhaps the heart of this being, if heart it had, glowed with undying fire.

For a little I floated over them, watching both, the artist and the Paper Man. The artist seemed unconscious of his strange comrade, and the Paper Man of him, yet never did they separate. Wherever the artist went, the Paper Man slid on beside him, without ever turning his head, following without effort of will, wrapped forever in his very dream. I noticed, too, that no one seemed to perceive the Paper Man.

Who, what was the Paper Man? Was he a phantom that I alone could behold, and why did he cling thus to the artist, a shadow yet not a shadow. I was consumed by the passion to know; but how?

The thought came to me that I myself was even less material than the Paper Man, that I could pass whither I would, through even the midst of men. I hovered over the artist, from him, through him, still baffled in my attempt to find the mystery.

Then shaking myself, as it were, into a cloud of unseen vapour I descended upon the artist, enveloping him. But he felt nothing. I willed to enter within him, and, gathering together, I absorbed myself within his body; but still he knew nothing, felt nothing. As a sponge holds water he held me all ignorantly. What his ears heard, his eyes saw, his mind thought, planned and willed, all was clear to me as the page of a printed book; I could read his inmost soul.

But over his doings I had no control, and my own senses remained my own thoughts, my own will. The sponge and the water are in one place, but not one. The first thing that I learned was that the artist did not perceive the Paper Man; that I saw, and watched he taught the artist nothing. He carried me and my question unheeding. He held in himself the answer, that I understood; and I vowed to remain till I found the truth.

I abandoned watching the streets and even the Paper Man, and watched instead the thoughts within my careless heart. I read that he was poor, that the struggle was hard, but that tonight a dealer had given him hope. He was to sell a few pictures, to get a commission for others. He saw bright prospects, built castles in Spain, and was bringing his dreams to his wife.

He walked on, and I watched all his thoughts. Once he stopped at a flower-girl's appeal. She offered him a dark rose for his sweetheart. The Paper Man stood by dimly illuminated, gazing ever at that vision wonderful. The artist bought the rose.

Quick was his mind, full of many fancies lightly started, but all moved inwards to one centre, the thought of the woman whom he loved. Long or short, straight or crooked the course, she was the bourne.

He lodged in a mean street, at the very top of the house. The staircase was dingy, unlit; but it was the stair of paradise to him. He ran up lightly, and by his side slid ever the Paper Man.

The attic formed his studio, I perceived, and also the chief living-room. The door was in the narrow side; in the opposite angle a small fireplace with a hob, to the right of which was an old armchair. A wooden stool, bearing a Utter of chalks and rags, stood in the corner where the roof sloped down. Overhead were glass windows, none in the walls. His easel and a stock of paints were behind the armchair; a few Turkish rugs relieved the bare boards; a helmet and shield glittered over the mantel-shelf, on which stood a meerschaum and a tin of Latakia.

In the midst of the room was a deal table with two places laid. Some sausages were frying over the tiny fire. Evidently with bread and cheese they were the entire meal. But the woman who was cooking it was the object of his thoughts, and at that I did not wonder. Her dress might be cheap, ill-fitting, even slatternly, that could only make her beauty seem out of its true sphere, but have no power to dim it. She stood up facing him as he came to kiss her. But to me it seemed that her lips were cold, the wealth of her red-brown hair that glowed in the firelight held no warmth for him.

He gave her the rose with a lover's speech and gesture. She accepted it indifferently with some muttered word about waste. Then they sat down to their supper, and he told her of his hopes.

Meanwhile the Paper Man had entered with us, and was near. He had not changed, only he seemed to look ever towards the woman, as did the artist himself. She did not see him, that I understood. Only once he altered, yet it might have been but a fancy. For when she received her husband's gift so hardly, I knew that there was a chill in the artist's heart, and I looked at the Paper Man. I thought that the glow within him seemed to flicker for an instant, and again I wondered what he was, what was the hidden meaning that with all my power I could not read aright.

The artist had gained a little money, a very little, for some of his sketches, and he built for her his castles in Spain. They were not new to me, I but dwelt in his body and watched the woman. She listened, saying little. She needed few words, for her beauty spoke for her.

But I noticed certain things. He talked of the days when fame should come and wealth, when she would not need to toil, hurting her hands and making her fingers rough that should wear other jewels than the plain gold ring. At this her eyes, dark dreamy eyes, kindled a little, and she smiled sleepily.

What the artist did not see, I saw. It was not only work that made her fingers rough, the one blemish on her loveliness. Fair was her face, shapely her form, but the soul within had shown one trace of its true self without.

Afterwards he went over to the fire, sat in the armchair, filled the meerschaum with his tobacco and smoked. Beside him, in the corner on the wooden stool that was covered with the fitter of the craft, sat the Paper Man, pinkly luminous, staring at his rosy dream, smiling his never-changing, childlike smile. They were happy, that strange pair, man and shadow, man and wraith; but wraith of what? They were happy, that was all I knew; and the artist's busy brains were bright pictures while the Paper Man dreamt of him.

Within the artist's body I turned to look behind him, towards the table where the woman was clearing the supper. I saw her counting over the few coins he had gained and given her. She pocketed them with a shrug, ungracefully. Then she looked at his unconscious back. Her face grew hard, stony with contempt; she despised him.

But he did not know, and still the Paper Man smiled like a child that nestles against his mother's bosom.

So in that attic studio we dwelt together—he, she, and I, and that other, the Paper Man. I knew too well their hearts, and only one thing was hid from me. She knew too, but nothing of my presence nor of the other's, and he nought at all. And the Paper Man existed unchanging, following his lord. Knowledge could never be his, that I understood, though not yet understanding why.

I stayed to learn. Their history was simple: a young artist, a beautiful model; a man with ideas, a woman with ambitions; he wedding for love below his class, she marrying that some day she might be raised above hers; poverty and struggle following. It was a common tale, yet a romance to him that might have been a poem for both, but she had no liking to make it so. From her nought fair could be born, by her dwelt nothing, not even so fragile a being as the Paper Man. Was she the cause, I wondered, that he was so frail, in all his mimicry to substance so nigh to nought. Could I have feared or sorrowed I had trembled for his life, if life he had, when I saw the hardness of her face. But without human body as I was, a sojourner in another's form, I had but the passion, the desire, to know.

Time passed. How long I do not know, for having no needs of the flesh, the change of day and night, the round of little earthly needs, had no claim upon me, and there was no call for me to count the passing hours. The Paper Man, too, ate not, nor slept, remaining ever the same, lost in beatitude. Yet sometimes I thought that he grew frailer, and that the glow within him sometimes failed. But it was only for an instant, when such things chanced as the giving of the rose.

Time passed, but brought no fortune to the artist. Sometimes he painted furiously, his brain creating noble things, which he dared not attempt, for he needed money,

154

and must work to sell. He wrought in black and white and sought vainly to find a buyer; he tried to teach his craft, but he was married and could get no post. Still he had one hope, in the dealer who had spoken him fair before I became his unknown guest. Of his failure he told her nothing; but she knew. And ever accompanied him the Paper Man. Surely, though his face never changed, surely he grew more frail.

One by one the Turkish rugs disappeared. He suffered, but she took the money, and while he smoked over the fire, would eye him with ever deepening contempt. I saw, but he never saw, and on the stool in the corner smiled happily the Paper Man.

The helmet and shield went too. They were relics of his race, his forefathers had carried them in battle, and it wrung his heart to bid them go. He smoked slowly and sadly that night, but it was for her sake. All his sorrows were for her, and she took the money, saying only that he had been cheated, they were worth more. I knew too well he had been cheated, robbed, in all ways, of his due. But the Paper Man, happy in having no power to know, sat ever in his corner glimmering roseate, frailer but smiling still.

She despised him more and more, and I watched her while he stared into the fire. I knew all his thoughts now, the centre ever the same, like the Paper Man, the ceaseless planning for money, that she might not starve, one unvarying endless round. He dared not create; it wasted time. Once art had reigned, taking him into a higher world of his own making. From that world now he shut himself out to scheme for her. He felt helpless, and he too despised himself, doubting himself. In the one test comprehended by the world, the test of making money, he was tried and found wanting, and he knew it. Yet he had still his love and trust, still his one gleam of life, still beside him the Paper Man. So he tortured himself vainly, like a beetle twirling on his pin, so ran the artist's mind. But knowing it all I watched her. A new look was in those sleepy eyes when his back was turned. She would play with her wedding ring, slipping it up and down. Hardness and scorn were in her glance, and something else, cunning.

He was starved, worn and thin, but she showed no sign of pinch or want. I turned to the Paper Man. So unsubstantial was he now that he was but the shadow of himself, the shadow of a shadow. Could nothing make him real, I wondered? Yet he smiled as of old. What was the secret of his being? Could she have made him real? I should know the answer soon.

The meerschaum had disappeared, in its place was a brier. There was no more Latakia in the jar on the mantelpiece, only shag, and she complained that it made her cough. The jar vanished too, and he ceased to smoke. On her lips, in her eyes, was that cunning craft, while the pucker of care deepened on his brow. There was no change in the face of the Paper Man.

At last came a night of rain and storm. With it came a letter from the dealer. He took it up trembling. She watched him oddly, while he tore it open, looking inside for what was not there. The note was polite, its words encouraging, but the pictures had not sold, the commission was not to be obtained. What use was it to him to be told that his work was full of promise? That was for years to come, not for now.

Then he told her, while at his side stood the Paper Man. Was I mistaken, or was there a change in that unchanging film of a face, a look in those abstracted eyes, as of one pleading for reality, for life, to be made true and no more a shadow.

The artist was speaking, slowly, brokenly, then with a rush of words the cry of a man broken on the wheel of fate, mourning not for himself, but for her whom he had brought to share his starvation and his ruin. Yet even in this depth one word, one caress from her could have lightened half his burden, healed the dumb prayer in the face of the Paper Man, that, fatuous as once it had seemed, was now tragic beyond telling.

But she only listened, mute, casting down her false eyes. Even I, remote from all human feeling, a mind dispassionate and detached, had almost thought she would respond. And she only listened, doing nothing, cruel in her immobility, harder than the nether millstone in her calm acceptance, without pity and without reproach.

She put out a little bread, some water, and a few parings of cheese for supper, that was all. He stopped at last, and gave her one look, all his heart in it. She turned away, with a slight shrug of her beautiful shoulders. He flung himself in his chair, before the expiring fire.

Without, the rising wind wailed like a sick child, and the rain splashed on the rattling skylights. Only a stump of a candle lit the attic, barely penetrating into the comer where lay heaped his unsold canvasses, and the nook where was wont to sit the Paper Man.

I glanced round to him. This once he had not followed the artist, but stood by the table. I beheld the woman slip off her ring. She put it on an unused plate, the artist's, and went from the room without a backward look. After her slid the Paper Man.

The fire died down, the candle burned lower, the storm raged. Water began to drip through the skylights, making little pools on the bare floor, spoiling the canvasses, beating at the litter of chalks upon the wooden stool. Want and gloom rained inside, wind and rain, and black night without, but darkest of all was the artist's soul.

He sat huddled, beyond power of thought, in numb agony. I had known that this must come to him, but the abyss was deeper than I could fathom. He knew not my presence, he had never known, and I had no comfort to offer him in this extremity of suffering. Yet I lingered, for I had yet something to learn, and here.

Gradually I began to diffuse from his body, as the water might evaporate on vapour from the sponge. I heard faint sounds, imperceptible to him; the woman moaned in their garret bedroom. After a time she descended the stairs, very quietly. The street door shut, then soon after the door of the attic studio opened, and there slid in the Paper Man. But he was changed, horribly changed. He was wet from the storm, the fight had died within him; he was pallid as the phantom of a corpse, his eyes white, staring and dead. Yet still he resembled the artist, more than ever maybe, for he was ghastly as the desolation in the artist's heart.

WHEN I WAS DEAD

by Prince Immanuel of Jerusalem

THEMIS, the goddess of justice, is depicted with a handkerchief over her eyes, so that the image of blindness may persuade those against the decrees of courts have been promulgated, that justice is impartial. The perennial miscarriage of justice has, however, long since convinced man that our goddess is Hybris in disguise. Justice is indeed blind, not blind to prejudice, but prestricted to right.

It is time that this deceptive bandage be torn away, and the dispensers of justice be given a sight of the litigants who appear before them. The perjury that has so long been permitted to influence the ears of the judges, might then be encountered by a view of the distorted beings that utter it.

But how vain this aspiration! There are none so blind as those who refuse to see! We all know that Hybris holds the scales.

"O dark, dark, dark, amid the blaze of noon."

✳

Yet I would lay my case before the bar of humanity, not that I expect justice, or am concerned about the verdict, but one day all human beings will be dead, and then able and anxious to judge equitably. My cause, as that of others, will then come back to them with all the force that it has accumulated through its comdemnation by mortals, and the dead will interact with the living on some other globe to vindicate truth and justice.

It is to you, living dead, that I turn my appeal primarily. Many of the noble souls among you told me of this day. And I should be betraying my trust, be unworthy of the death that elevated me to your sphere, if I did not reproduce your utterances recorded on my soul.

Of mortals I ask only that they lend me their ears, vouchsafe me the opportunity to add my experience to that of a man who enjoys universal respect. Even *blind* justice does not always refuse to listen to corroborative evidence. Let your justice then at last not bar me publicly though it diseredit my testimony. The curiosity that has commanded a perusal of *Raymond* proves that the subject is absorbing to you.

If my story be condemned, it at least has the sanction of the paramount religious, and it is well to remember that great men have not a monopoly on the truth.

Autobiographies have been written by mortals, autonecrologies never. I propose then to write an auto-obituary, and that this is not impossible, I refer to at least seven personages mentioned in Scripture:

The son of the woman of Zarephath raised by Elijah,
The Shunamite's son raised by Elisha,
The man who revived when he touched the bones of Elisha,
The son of the widow of Nain raised by Christ,
Lazarus raised by Christ,
Tabitha raised by Peter,
Christ.

I do not wish, however, to add weight to my recital by quoting Scripture. The races that attach so little importance to the teachings they profess that they have plunged the Old World into a holocaust of rapine and carnage, are not influenced by Scripture, though perchance to the bereft my words may bring the blessing of consolation. A *miracle* today to those who do read the Scriptures is blasphemy, yet mayhap those who do not read them may be led to consider the Bible miracles worthy of consideration when they hear that modern science is investigating and reproducing similar miracles. Those who believe nothing unless they see it with their own eyes, who deny the psychic differences between men, though they admit the physical and mental, will explain everything to their own satisfaction with the words: trance, coma, lethargy—words as inexplicable to the greatest scientist as life itself is.

Yet why should one man not be able to see or hear what others are deaf and blind to? Genius has been defined as the highest conceivable form of original ability, something altogether extraordinary and beyond even supreme educational prowess. Mozart was a composer when he was four years old. Will the most obdurate sceptic deny that he heard music to which others were totally deaf?

Similarly authors and painters see visions before they put them on paper or canvas. These sounds and sights do not reach the brain through the senses.

It may be answered that they are created in the brain. It is doubtful whether with a child as young as Mozart, the brain has the power of creation such as is engendered by education. We have the authority of geniuses themselves for the assertion that they really see and hear with their brains by some medium unknown to man.

If it be argued with Carlyle that genius is "transcendent capacity of taking trouble, first of all," the case for the difference between the psychic powers of men is not weakened but strengthened. It is demonstrable that the brain by education can be modified to excel other brains as the muscles are trained in the athlete, the ears in the musician. Why should not the eye be capable of increasing its perspicacity, why should not the brain be subject to development so as to be able to perceive the universe without the aid of organs of sense?

We have not reached the limits of the senses even, and if it only the fool who dare declare that nothing exists that is not perceptible to the senses. It has been proved scientifically that there are sounds which the human ear cannot hear even with any appliance that man has yet invented. The telescope and microscope have enlarged the range of vision, the microphone has quickened the tympanate, but the sounds above and below a certain number of vibrations are inaudible to the human ears.

It was my desire to develop these latent psychic powers that led to the extraordinary experience I am about to relate. I had argued with the sceptic that sensations which affect only specially endowed beings are irrational. I demanded the demonstration of the senses, and evidence that would be palpable to every rational mind. I was advised that every human being possesses in a greater or less degree the psychic power of communicating with the dead, and that if I would only exercise patience and diligence in my development, my efforts would be rewarded. To my own knowledge I possessed none of the qualities of the medium, and in my determination to keep a safe distance between me and the borders of hypnotism or insanity, I refused the advice of a special diet, though I was compelled to admit that if food affected the stamina of the athlete in training, it was reasonable to suppose it would influence the psychic.

✻

Some five years ago I was admitted to the séances of a few Greek friends in the Holy Land. We met in various places, some rendered immortal by the associations recorded in the Bible. At these reunions, one or other of our circle usually fell under the spell of some spirit who then dictated to us through the medium exhortations or information in an answer to our enquiries. Our secretary took these down and we were able to publish a few volumes of spiritual literature.

> Descend, and touch, and enter; hear
> > The wish too strong for words to name;
> > That in this blindness of the frame
> My Ghost may feel that thine is near.

> So word by word, and line on line,
> > The dead man touched me from the past,
> > And all at once it seemed at last
> The living soul was flashed on mine.
>
> —Tennyson

When conditions were favourable, the spirits would converse with us direct through the trumpet, or materialize for our delectation.

Usually the spirit of Saint Gregorias presided at our séances, and other spirits were brought to us by him when he deemed it wise and possible.

To all this I was merely a critical spectator trying to convince myself that all the phenomena I witnessed were subjective, auto-suggestion; or when I admitted an objective cause, I invented ingenious theories of vibrations to satisfy my reason.

The theory of light waves had taught me that the light of stars extinct millions of years ago was now illuminating the earth. Similarly, photographs of everything in existence were travelling through space eternally, and as the light of the extinct star vibrated on the retina of our eye, so the travelling photo of objects annihilated in past ages was reproduced on our brain like the film on the curtain. If the lantern is focused onto space, no picture will be seen though it is being transmitted, as an intervening screen will prove. Thus it requires a properly attuned organ, the brain, to intercept and reproduce the wave photos of departed beings.

The theory of sound waves had proved to me that sound is travelling indefinitely and might be reproduced by a suitable sounding-board, as a disc declaims the dead and would convince a savage that he was listening to a human being.

The theory of conservation of energy had demonstrated to me that every movement, every thought, every feeling produces vibrations on the surrounding media, and moves everlastingly as light and sound, and could effect suitable organs, as wireless waves may be regulated to vibrate one receiver and not another.

With the mental reservation of such theories, I agreed with my friends:

"Inspiration is as eternal as the stars. God is everywhere from sand to stars, to the suns that dot the immensities; and angels would speak as readily to God's living Americans as to His ancient Hebrews if the proper conditions were given them. Open the doors of your souls, O mortals, and invite the good angels in; invite your loved ones, propelling higher spheres, to come with their olive-leaf message of love and truth and wisdom. The universe is not dead. Every atom is afire with life. The universe is one. Conscious spirit is infinite, and if, as science teaches, every undulating wave in its rhythmic motion impinges upon every other wave in the vast, all-embracing sea of universal life, who can set limits to the bounds of thought, or will, or spirit influence, either within or without the mortal body? Believed or not, this peerless universe is one grand whispering gallery, and we are surrounded, as the apostle taught, by a great 'cloud of witnesses'—numberless multitudes—who delight under proper conditions to converse with earth's foot-weary travellers, by impression, inspiration, premonition, and vision. Precious fact, proving the perpetuity of intelligence, of love, and of law, beyond death's portal."

One of our séances was held at Mar Saha, about three hours' journey from the Holy City. This monastery, standing in the midst of grand and wild scenery, utterly barren and desolate, is a lofty structure, built in terraces in a kind of amphitheatre on the side of a mountain. Whether viewed from without or within, it is one of the most weird places in the world.

We arrived here one evening after sunset, while the full moon was casting long shadows across the valleys. The effect of this extraordinary mass of buildings is at all times exceedingly strange and wild, but on a moonlight night it is one of the most wonderful sights in the world. After allowing this marvellous scene to sink into our souls, we knocked at a small portal, and placed our letter of introduction, obtained from the superior of the Greek monastery at Jerusalem, in a basket which was lowered to us for purpose. Following a careful inspection and enquiries as to whether any ladies accompanied us, for ladies are never permitted under any circumstances to enter this monastery, we were allowed to pass. This was a special favour, as the doors are barred after dark, and most of the monks asleep at 6 p.m.

On entering the gate, there was a steep descent by stairs to a second gate, and another to a third. We then found ourselves in one of the strangest places that human ingenuity has ever contrived for a dwelling place.

It is a series of precipices with walls of natural rock and artificial battlements. You look down at buildings, and court-yards, and labyrinths of passages, and up at curious holes in the walls, with ledges in front, where are the cells and dwelling-places of monks.

The place is full of mystery. You see men walking upon these ledges of rock, and turning into these holes in the walls; and you look upon a little garden hanging in the air, as it seems, with a solitary palm-tree looking down in the chasm, in which are more buildings, and chapels, and cupolas. None but the initiated could ever find his way through these myste-rious labyrinths, and once within these strong walls, a stranger could never find his way out.

While we partook of the refreshments which were placed hospitably at our disposal, the superior gave us some informa-tion concerning the monastery:

"The founder of this remarkable monastery was one Sabas, who was born in Cappadocia, A.D. 437. He was famous for his sanctity, for his learning, and for his power of working miracles. The devout gathered round him in great numbers, and at last the Patriarch of Jerusalem made him abbot of all those who were named after him, Sabaites.

"He established the 'Great Laura;' and later the 'New Laura,' under St. Basil's Rule. In the Lauras the young monks lived a cenobitical life, but the elders, a semi-eremitical one, each in his own hut within the precincts of the Laura, attend-ing only the solemn church services.

"Many fierce struggles have been witnessed here. Its wealth being considered enormous, it was a tempting place to the Persian hordes, who plundered it in 614; and in the succeed-ing centuries, it was attacked for the same purpose. It was plundered as late as 1835, but in 1840 was made additionally safe and well protected by the Russians."

Our vegetarian repast over, the superior showed us our couches, and retired to his own bed. This was Monday night, one of the three on which the monks of Mar Saba are not permitted to eat any kind of animal food, such as eggs, milk, or cheese. At no time do they touch meat, and many of them live on bread and water. No wonder that the Greek hospital at Jerusalem is constantly receiving some of these fanatics for treatment, and that recalcitrant monks are sent to this spot for penance!

We were somewhat fatigued after our long ride on asses and as we made it a rule never to sit unless we felt perfectly reposed, we also lay down to sleep.

At one a.m. we were awakened by the nakus, or long plate, which is used by Eastern sects instead of a bell. We rose immediately and repaired to the church of the convent where we found already assembled the seventy odd monks who dwell here. Prayers lasted for five or six hours, after which we went to the refectory and shared in the frugal breakfast, bread and coffee.

The monks then withdrew to their quarters, not over-clean and very plain, at the back of the church, where they occupied themselves in the manufacture of souvenirs for travellers, often interrupting their labours to count a thousand beads and repeat a thousand prayers on their knees and beat their breasts with all the violence of their excitable temperaments.

We seized the opportunity to stroll about viewing the marvels of this abode of bigotry. From the turrets we looked down into the awful ravine of the Kidron and the maze of valleys that surrounded us, and watched some of the monks feed the beautiful black birds with yellow wings peculiar to the desert of Judah and the Jordan valley, and known as Tristam's grackles.

Next we went to the cave of St. Sabas, where the saint first took up his abode when the place was more desolate than it is now. A legend recounts that the place at that time was inhabited by a lion, and that the saint and the lion lived together for a while, but the latter not having those gifts and graces which would make him a suitable companion for long, the saint bade him leave, and he left accordingly.

Then in turn we visited the tomb of St. Sabas; the chapel of St. Nicolas, a grotto or cave, where, behind a screen, may be seen several hundreds of skulls of monks who were slaughtered by the Persians: the tomb of John of Damascus, the author of the well known English hymn, *The Day of Resurrection*. Stephen, who wrote the hymn, *Art thou weary, art though languid*, and Andrew, later on Archbishop of Crete, who composed the hymn, *Christian, dost thou see them, on the holy ground*, both spent part of their lives as monks in this monastery.

Towards noon we went across to the tower which St. Saba's mother occupied, and where the late queen of Austria halted when the monks refused her admission. It was very hot and sultry, and some of the hills were seemingly separated from their bases by the strata of which condenses in such weather.

We sat discussing our plans, when simultaneously we perceived a patriarchal figure suspended in the sky and apparently gazing at us benignly. My friends prostrated themselves in adoration, while I examined the apparition critically. It had nothing to distinguish it from the venerable Arabs we often noticed on our journeys, except in that it was inverted. I was going to draw this fact to the attention of my companions, when one of them was seized by some spirit influence and began to exhort us vicariously to forsake the desires of this world and devote ourselves to a life of poverty and piety. While he was speaking, the vision was gradually being dispelled and at last I interrupted my friend with an exclamation of regret:

"It's gone!"

My words seemed to break the spirit spell, and the admonition ceased.

"It must have been one of the saints," said one, reverently.

"The mirage of an ordinary Arab," I replied.

The others looked at me angrily.

"Perhaps Paul had a similar vision?" I continued half to myself.

"Blasphemy!" said another of my friends. "If you suggested such a thought in the presence of one of the monks they would stone you. Why do you say it was a mirage?"

"Because it was up-side-down, and dressed as a modern sheikh."

"I didn't notice it was up-side-down."

"That's because you did not take the trouble to look. If it had been the *Brockengespenst* with its chromatic halo, you would no doubt have sworn it was one of the apostles.

"This is not the first mirage I have seen. There you have something like it before your very eyes. Those hills seem to be suspended in the air, but you know they are not. It is an optical illusion due to variations in the refractive index of the atmosphere. I once saw the mirage of a lake in Turkestan, at another time I witnessed an oasis in the sky not far from the Pyramids. In the Polar regions, ships and icebergs are often seen as if inverted and suspended in the clouds. The Fata Morgana frequently seen in the Straits of Messina, and 'looming' as witnessed in mists and fogs, are other variations of this phenomenon."

"Perhaps," said my friends unconvinced. "You are always trying to argue us out of our faith. But remember what St. Gregorias said—Your proof will be more convincing than any we have hitherto been accorded."

"I am waiting patiently," I replied earnestly, then after a pause I continued: "I do not think you are justified in accusing me of trying to weaken your convictions. You know I am the most tolerant man in the world and think every one is welcome to his own creed. I am more anxious than any of you to know that we live after death. You have never heard me deny the possibility. But trance and inspirational speaking, psychometry and clairvoyance, clairaudience, healing—or writing mediumship, planchette and Ouija boards, even trumpet speaking and materializations, may have other forces besides departed souls as their causes.

"Often when I sit down to reflect or write, I close my eyes and see people and hear them as plainly as in my dreams, in fact, I am dreaming, though I am awake. I put these waking dreams on to paper. Years after, I pick up a volume that I remember to have read in my boyhood. The very words that I heard in my waking dreams stand before me. I recognize a person in the streets who appeared to me in my waking dreams; I tax my memory and am not sure that I did not see the same face many years before among the millions that have impressed themselves unconsciously upon my subliminal self. I examine what I have written and find it patchy, plagiaristic, often a literal repetition, page for page, of what I had read twenty years before.

"Socrates, through the doctrine of reminiscence, teaches that all knowledge is latent in the mind from birth and through kindred (or association of) ideas much may be recovered, if only a beginning is made.

"If it is not my memory that is bringing back these sights and sounds, there may be some force in nature able to affect several persons similarly and simultaneously. We are all parts of nature. We say 'ideas are in the air.' The great thought atmosphere, the plane of universal ideas, is open to those who are attuned to its vibrations. At the time Professor Bell was perfecting his telephone, at least three other inventors were developing the same thing. In wireless telegraphy, Marconi had three rivals, and who built the first liquid-air apparatus is at present in dispute.

"Of course you argue that they have tapped the thought-tides from the unseen and have been inspired by the combined influences of the thinkers of a certain grade or sphere. But Socrates has observed that rhapsodists and even poets have no definite knowledge of the things which they so powerfully represent. He brings the rhapsode so to admit this, and to conclude that he is the inspired medium of magnetic influence. The Muse is the chief magnet, and the poet is the first of a series of magnetic rings. Then follow the rhapsode and actor, who are rings of inferior power, and the last ring is the hearer or spectator.

"But why should ideas not be as contagious as gaping, or why should not the forces of nature, which you say are soulless, though I am not so sure of that, be creators of ideas? Socrates' magnetic influence is probably only what we should call a force of nature. To my mind these forces have always surpassed man in their productions. I am now taking your viewpoint that man is not a force of nature. My own opinion, as you know, is that life is merely a manifestation of nature.

"Crystalization, the frost on a window pane, clouds, flowers, a landscape, the planetary system, show more ideas and more beauty than all the inventors and artists of the earth have ever been able to produce.

"Spinoza says: 'I confess I cannot understand how spirits express God more than the other creatures, for I know that between the finite and the infinite there is no proportion, and that the distinction between God and the most excellent of created things differs not a whit from the distinction between Him and the lowest and meanest of them.'"

"There you are again with your pantheism," interrupted my friend. "Spinoza taught that God is the underlying spirit in everything. There is no room for eternal, personal spirits in Pantheism."

"All the spirits that have communicated with us," I retorted, "have not been able to tell us what happens on the highest planes. The human spirit may ultimately be absorbed into the Spirit of God, for all we know.

"Spinoza says again: 'If the infinite be the real, and the finite, so far as it is distinguished therefrom, the unreal, then the supposed substantiality or individuality of finite beings is an illusion. As we think ourselves free because we are conscious of our actions but not of their causes, so we think that we have an individual existence only because the infinite intelligence is not wholly but partially realized in us.'

"If all spirits were not of the same substance, I do not understand how they could communicate with one another. I believe it says somewhere in Genesis that God made man in His own image. To me this means that man contains part of the divine substance, and I therefore think that Pantheism instead of being opposed to, is really a strong argument in favour of Spiritualism.

"But let us return to the monastery and arrange with the superior for our séance tonight. We do not want any of those fanatical monks to interrupt us, or all of us may be stoned for witchcraft, not only myself for blasphemy, as you suggested. We must have a room that we can lock, where no monk can spy on us through a window or listen to us through a keyhole. I think it is a good suggestion that the superior be invited to the séance. If our spirit friends should create a disturbance, he will be able to anticipate any trouble with the monks by instructing them in advance that our chamber is not to be approached."

As no one objected to this arrangement, we walked leisurely back to the monastery and laid our plan before the superior. He showed himself to be much interested and readily agreed to be one of the séance. In reply to our enquiry as to what could be done to keep our meeting secret, he quieted our anxiety with the information that no one would be able to approach within hearing distance or our chamber. In a building constructed as Mar Saba is, and occupied by men with habits and discipline of the monks, it was a comparatively easy matter to find a cell where we could be as inaccessible as in a desert.

That night after the superior had assured us that all the brethren were asleep, we repaired to our cell adjoining the sepulchre where the monks are buried shrouded in their robes. Although a corpse had been laid on the slabs a few weeks before, we were not able to detect any unpleasant smell, when the superior admitted us for a few brief moments before the séance. This peculiarity of the sepulchre is considered one of the miracles of Mar Saba. The other is the belief that women who eat of the dates which grow on the solitary palm-tree already referred to will be cured of barrenness.

The room was not more than twelve feet square, there were no windows, but in the ceiling were placed the little discs of glass used in Oriental bath rooms. We took our seats in a circle on the seven stools we had brought with us, placed the trumpet in our midst, and asked the superior to offer a prayer. All our séances were begun in a similar manner.

After the prayer, we sat quietly waiting for some spirit to announce himself. Suddenly one of our number fell forward, and his hand began to move spasmodically as if wishing to write. In a few moments he raised his head and spoke calmly, but his hand continued to tremble.

"I am here."

"Who is here?" I inquired.

"St. Gregorias."

"Give me the oath."

There was a long pause and I repeated the command. Instead of giving the oath by which we had been taught all spirits should be tested, a terrible curse was hurled at me. I sprang to my feet and shouted at the medium:

"Get out, Satan! Your curses on your own head!"

The medium began to moan incoherently, and his whole body shook with violence. Then he uttered a cry, and some unseen hand seized the candle, and hurled it against the wall.

We were thrown into utter darkness, and the superior broke into prayer again, begging us in fear to let him out, as he was sure we had invoked some evil spirit.

One of my friends lit the candle again, and we tried to re-assure the priest with the information that such interruptions were not unusual. But he was deathly pale, and was held in our midst more by his fear of departing alone than by our words.

Our secretary now took a Bible from his pocket, and read several chapters, until we noticed again that the medium was falling under spirit influence.

I repeated the question I had asked previously, and the spirit took the required oath:

"I avow the incarnation of Christ."

"Then give me the sign."

"What sign?"

My suspicions were immediately aroused. Impersonating spirits trouble every séance, and we had been warned to put them to the severest test.

"If you can't give me the sign, depart!"

"I will not depart, I wish to speak, I have a right to speak!"

"Depart!"

After much persuading, the spirit left the medium, and finally a spirit took possession of him who gave the oath, and made the sign of the cross with a pencil that was put into the medium's hand. Although he had refused to give his name when he first spoke, he now replied when the question was put again.

"I am the Angel of Death."

Such an answer would only have amused us if had been given before the out and sign, but now the others no less than myself felt a thrill of fear pass through our bodies.

At last I found sufficient temerity to enquire:

"Why have you come to us?"

"Memento mori!"

Filled with that indefinable certainty that our curiosity would be satisfied without prompting, none of us dared enquire further. We sat motionless and silent, sentient of the presence of some other being.

Suddenly there was a small flash in our midst, and the trumpet was raised above our heads; then some shapeless form gradually materialized, and a voice came through the trumpet:

"Memento mori!"

Now, what appeared to be a human hand pointed in my direction, and I felt my hands and feet grow suddenly cold. I tried to rise to my feet, but all my members had become numb. I wished to call to my friends to seize me and hold me tight, but my tongue cleaved to the roof of my mouth.

"Momento mori!" again came through the trumpet, and I saw the materialization approach me with outstretched arms as if to envelop me. I felt the chill creeping along my arms and legs, and wished to shout defiantly:

"A free man thinks of nothing less than death, his wisdom is a meditation not of death but of life."

But I could not shake the incubus that had seized hold of all my muscles. My brain, however, seemed to be more alert than usual. I knew I was dying and tried to give myself courage.

"To fear death is to assume pretended knowledge," said Socrates. I was ignorant of the future, so why should I be afraid to die?

My friends and the objects in the room were now fading from my vision, I seemed to be falling through space at limitless speed, and thought I would wake up dead.

Stars were now sweeping past me; I looked down, expecting to be dashed to pieces against something, but nothing intercepted my descent. I looked up and around, the sky was as clear as crystal, translucent day seemed to pervade space, and my vision penetrated endless vistas of constellations.

My friends and the room in which we had sat had disappeared. I looked down again, and found myself lying on the grass amid brilliant flowers at the side of a rippling brook. The transition from motion to rest, from terrestrial environment to my present surroundings had taken place by some process that had escaped my perception.

My fear was dissipated and replaced by a peaceful calm, but I felt myself alone, and longed for some sound to break the silence, some living being to intrude on my solitude.

I felt the desire to rise to my feet, and found myself standing. I wished to feel the water of the brook, and my hand was kissed by the ripples. Every wish, every desire was instantaneously fulfilled, without the consciousness of effort, and I recalled the impatience I had felt in life at every obstacle that had intercepted my movements. On the pavements, every pedestrian who had blocked my rapid stride had been inwardly wished elsewhere, I had chafed at every means that had delayed an end, every hindrance that had stood between me and an object.

I now examined my body in the hope of discovering the secret of this metamorphosis, but it appeared to have undergone no change, except in that I could not feel the beat of my pulse or temple, and when I pinched myself my fingers and thumb came together without causing me any pain.

I was hungry and thirsty, and bent down to drink of the brook. The water tasted cool to me, and when I had satisfied my thirst, my hunger was also appeased.

Still I felt lonely, and wished for some human being to appear that I might ask a thousand questions. How was it that all my other desires were realized at their inception, while this one remained impossible of fulfillment? No doubt it was my ignorance, and Spinoza's words came to my mind:

"The range of possibility narrows as knowledge widens, until to perfect knowledge possibility is lost in necessity."

I would go in search of some being that could set my curiosity at rest, and banish my lonesomeness.

No sooner had this decision taken possession of me than I saw the brook disappear behind me. Beautiful landscapes flew by as they do when you are seated in an express train. I had no doubt that I was moving rapidly and that the scenes I saw were stationary, but I was too enthralled with the beauty of everything to try and discover whether I was moving or not. Awake in my life and dreams, the wonders of nature had always filled my soul with a foretaste of heaven, and I did not wish to lessen the effect now by analysis.

I did not remember noticing the first human soul, and when I saw many of them, it did not seem as if I had longed for their company, or had ever lacked their society. The hills and valleys, the peaks and precipices, the lakes and rivers, banked and bordered with moss and flowers and trees, were no longer moving past me, but I was walking among them, in search of some one.

I was climbing a mountain, hoping to be rewarded, when I reached the summit, by that exhilaration of vision which are the experience of climbers only. Suddenly I found myself looking down over hundreds, or was it thousands of miles hills and plains, with streams meandering away into obscurity!

I sat down to better enjoy this, and then noticed that I was on the edge of a transparent lake, and that a girl was seated close to me and looking into the depths of the water. She had long black hair which the breeze tossed playfully over the pebbles, her eyes were wonderfully large and also black, her lips ruby and full, contrasting artistically with the pure whiteness of her skin. I thought I had never seen such a beautiful woman, and although I was prompted to approach and speak to her, yet I was afraid, lest my boldness should prove unwelcome.

Whilst I stood aloof filled with doubt, she looked up abruptly, and seeing me gazing at her in wonder, the colour rushed to her brows and almost equalled the carmen of her lips.

I was moved as if about to withdraw and relieve her of the confusion I had caused her, when I noticed a sudden look of anxiety come into her eyes, her lips parted disclosing the pearly evenness of her teeth, but she checked in modesty whatever she had desired to say.

Encouraged by her demeanor, I came towards her. As I drew nearer, her eyelids drooped, and when I stood in front of her, her face was turned almost away from me in embarrassment.

"Forgive me if I speak to you," I said in English as reassuringly as I could, "but I think I am dead and want to ask some one about it. If you do not wish to answer me, tell me to go, and I shall leave you at once, and seek elsewhere, but please do not dismiss me without a word of advice.

"It seems to me that I have been wandering all my life, looking for someone like you to talk to me. The blank that has always filled my soul seems now effaced when I look at you. I longed for something undefined and now I long no more."

As I spoke, she turned timidly towards me, her eyelids slowly rising, until her dreamy orbs looked full and wonderingly into mine. When she spoke, her voice seemed strangely familiar, it thrilled me and sounded to my ears more harmonious than any music I had ever heard.

"While I was on earth I felt as you. I longed for something as you did, but never found it. Then I died, and it seems that

I have been wandering about in this world for aeons waiting for you to come, and praying that God might give me what I was deprived of when I was alive. On earth the want of love robbed me of all pleasure, here I waited in patience, for I know you would come.

"All the souls have told me that you and I will become one spirit and then as one we shall rise to a higher plane. When you find your compliment on earth, a third spirit is created. In heaven love does not create spirits but unites two so that they become one."

"I do not understand you," I said meekly.

"Sit down next to me," she invited ingenuously, "and let me try and explain."

I seated myself before her, so that I could look into her eyes and feel the power which they already exercised over me.

"We are composed of body, soul and spirit," she continued gravely. "Two bodies cannot unite, except metaphorically, though the spirits within them try to become one when they love each other. The soul is the house of the spirt in this world, and souls can unite. We are two souls, and we shall become one spirit, and leave our souls here, as you left your body on earth. You could not come here with your body, so we cannot go further with our souls."

"Are we going to love our identity?" I enquired almost fearfully.

"I have told you," she said quietly, placing her hand on mine, "that spirits who have a community of ideas are glad to lose their personality in each other, and that the highest spirts even lose themselves in God. But this will not be a mystery to you, if you have ever loved any one."

I caught the hand which she had laid on mine and held it to my lips. No feeling I had ever experienced on earth could express the bliss that the touch of her hand imparted to me. I wished to seize her in my arms, and press her to me, but some chivalrous respect for her modesty held me back, and I said:

"When you love some one, you are willing to die for her, I know. Self-sacrifice is the essence of love. With a woman I love in my embrace, I see only her, my own body disappears from my sight; her thoughts, her wishes are my thoughts and wishes; her pain is mine; her happiness is mine. I live only for her, and lose consciousness willingly of myself."

An angelic smile of happiness spread over her face.

"You see, you are perfectly willing to lose your identity."

"But only for the woman I love."

"Is not that very love the thing you most desire? What you have lacked most on earth you will obtain here. All our deficiencies are made good here."

I thought she was talking now to prevent the confession of love that was ready to burst from my lips. Her eyes fell again before my ardent looks. Yet she had admitted that she loved me, and I was compelled to hold my desire in leash before the spirit of dalliance that inspired her.

"Those who have lacked love, find it here, for love is no sin. The pitiless learn misericorde here; the miser generosity; pain is turned into pleasure; regret to content; dejection to cheerfulness; lamentation to rejoicing; fear to hope; coward-ice to courage; enmity to friendship; ingratitude to gratitude; revenge to forgiveness; impenitence to penitence; impurity to purity; even ugliness to beauty, for the blind see, the deaf hear, the cripples walk, amputated and paralyzed members are renewed. Vice is turned into virtue, guilt to innocence."

"Is there no punishment here?" I asked.

"Punishment?" she repeated. "Do you ask that question seriously, you who are so wise? I thought the earth had out-grown Hell and Priestcraft. You are turning your prisons into reformatories. When the criminal is reformed, do you send him to the gallows, or do you forgive him? If the earth can give the murderer a new lease of life, why cannot heaven, especially, when all the motives for sin are removed?"

"But if men were not afraid of punishment after death, they would commit many more crimes," I urged.

"Neither men, nor women," she added coyly, "are afraid of the punishment you mention. They do not believe in Hell. They are deterred by fear of earthly punishment or ostracism, by education, a thousand reasons. You don't expect us to treat criminals worse than you do. If you refuse to burn them alive, we are not going to pile them into cauldrons of fiery brimstone. That's what your priests ought to do, if they had the courage of their convictions. But I am sure the inquisitors took Hell with them when the earth purged itself of them."

"But do all these changes take place immediately?"

"No, of course not. We have teachers for the ignorant, doctors for the sick, guides for the erring, lovers for the forlorn."

She was looking again into my eyes as she said these last words. I caught her other hand in mine and, leaning forward, exclaimed impetuously: "I am no longer forlorn, since I have found you. Tell me your name that I may address you by it and tell you all I must."

"My name is Tilly," she replied softly, as if imparting a secret and fearing its consequence.

I started, then looked close into her face, and like an illuminating flash I recognized her.

"Tilly, my wife, Tilly!"

"Yes, Immanuel, my husband, I am your wife, Tilly."

"But you have changed, you have become more beautiful than any earthly woman . . ."

"And you have changed," she interrupted, "you have become more handsome than any earthly man. Look at yourself in the lake," and she turned my head towards the watery mirror.

I looked down and stared in wonder. I had indeed changed, and could barely recognize myself. I was again as I had been in my youth. The blemish a fall with my horse had caused was gone, and my nose was as regular as when my mother had playfully pressed her finger on it. I smiled and noticed that the teeth I had lost in the same accident had been replaced, and they were as white and as perfect as they had been in my twentieth year. I rubbed the hair of my right eyebrow which hid a scar I had received in a boyish quarrel—the scar had disappeared. My eyes laughed and sparkled, my skin glowed, as they did when I climbed the mountains in South Africa. Then I noticed my wife's hand caressing my hair, which again fell in long curls below my shoulders as it had done till my sixteenth year, and I turned and taking her in my arms cried excitedly:

"What has made us change?"

"Love," she whispered in my ear. "Our love has made us desire beauty, as it makes earthly beings long for it. Puberty makes girls beautiful, as it does animals and birds and flowers. When you courted me, did you not try to look your best?" she enquired slyly. "When a woman expects her lover, does she not use every artifice of dress, powder, paint and perfume to enthrall the man she loves? It is natural that love should crave for beauty. We asked for it unconsciously, and we received it."

"But why did you just say that you lacked love on earth?"

"You said the same," she retorted.

"But I loved you."

"And did I not love you?"

"It is true, you did love me, but I was too foolish to appreciate it, and that is why you thought I did not love you. But you know now that I loved you, and will forgive me."

I pressed her to me, and closing my eyes in happiness kissed her on those lips which even on earth had transported me with their form and ardour.

I thought I was dying again, but instead of falling, I seemed to be soaring upwards; instead of fear, I was now filled with courage. The union of two spirits was being made intelligible to me by a celestial impulse to cease to exist except in perfect absorption with the being I loved.

Then I heard my wife's voice coming to me softly as if from a distance.

"Why do you close your eyes? You used to do it on earth, and it makes me believe that you are picturing other loves with your wonderful imagination."

I opened my eyes to reassure her.

"No, I see nothing at all; I close them because I am happy. I was so happy that I thought we were going as a united spirit to that higher plane of which you told me."

"I also thought so, but you know I always wanted you to look at me when you hold me in your arms."

"I will not close them again," I replied. "But do you really believe we were undergoing another change?"

"It seemed so."

I was silent for some time, until my wife asked:

"I can see in your eyes that you are thinking; what is it?"

"I made a promise on earth, and I have just recalled it."

"What was it?" she asked quickly.

"I promised that my soul would return to my friends when they called me, and would give them further evidence of life after death. They seem to be drawing me towards them now, for I feel an uncontrollable urge to fly to them and tell them what has happened to me."

The same look of anxiety that I had noticed before spread over my wife's face, and she said almost inaudibly:

"Immanuel, my love, my life, you are going back to the earth, and I must stay here and wait till you come again."

She laid her head on my breast and looking up continued:

"Promise me also something, and I shall wait in patience."

"You need not require a promise, tell me what I must do, and it shall be done."

"Call my soul to you on earth. I could not come before, because I did not know whether you still wanted me, but now

I know. Our love has lasted beyond death. You are mine, and I am yours for ever. Immanuel, I love you." And she pressed me frantically to her heaving bosom.

I thought again that we were mounting to some higher sphere, when suddenly a voice behind me caused me to turn my head. A tall being robed in white stood before me and pointing its finger at me repeated the words of the Angel of Death:

"Memento mori!"

I tried to turn away and take a last look at my wife, but the eyes of the angel transfixed me and I could not move. Again the chill of death benumbed my members, a mist that blotted out the celestial panorama rose before my eyes. I began to fall and fall, and the terror of destruction took possession of me again.

Then I heard voices, someone praying in Greek, and the mist before my eyes began to evaporate. Like a moving picture that is being enlarged by a lens on a screen, I gradually recognized the cell at Mars Saba. My body lay on the flag stones, and my friends knelt and prayed. While they prayed for the repose of soul, the superior walked round them swinging his censer and filling the room with incense. At last they uttered their final amen.

"There is no more hope," said one. "He is dead. It is now four days since his soul departed, and the body is beginning to putrefy. We may as well bury him."

"It is punishment for his scepticism," said another sadly. "He would never accept the doctrines of our holy church, and he treated our spirit saints as if they were ordinary human beings worthy or unworthy of his attention as his earthly judgement deemed fit. Perhaps he is now suffering for this. Yet he was a loyal friend, honest, truthful, generous, brave, an ear and hand for every creed and its followers. May his soul rest in peace."

"Come then!"

Their words and actions interested me so much that I was

loath to intervene, though I felt the power within me to arrest them.

They scattered deodorizing spices over my body, lifted it on to a sheet, and bore it into the sepulchre, while I walked behind them apparently invisible and unperceived.

Then I heard the first knell of the passing bell, and wished to fly in search of the sexton and wrest the rope from his hand, but I heard the dirge of the approaching monks, and waited. They walked slowly and solemnly in double file, preceded by the cantors and incense bearers, and formed in a semicircle around the door of the sepulchre. My friends gathered around me within the tomb, forming another semicircle, and thus unwittingly they created such as the ancient Christians constituted when miracles were performed in their midst. I immediately felt the contact, and was only prevented from clasping my body by the superior who swung his censer across my mortal remains and seemed to interpose some obstacle between me and my purpose.

While he recited the service for the dead, I glanced hurriedly around, searching for some means to incite the superior away from my body. At the back of the sepulchre lay a heap of bones and skeletons, men who had died here or had had their corpses brought hither to repose near the tomb of St. Saba, and partake of the miracle that dissipated the effluvium of the dead. Near one lay the corpses of three monks with their robes stitched around them.

Suddenly the priest passed and stepped back to cover the mourners with incense. This was my opportunity. Bending down I seized my corpse in my arms and raised it to its feet. My soul seemed to sink into my body, or my body into my soul, I know not which, but we were no longer distinct.

I stretched out my hands to my friends, who stared aghast and I heard them exclaim:

"A resurrection! A resurrection!"

A third miracle had been added to the rubric of Mar Saba.

THE MAN WHO KILLED GOD

by Ralph Shirley

I WAS called in to see him on his deathbed. He was dying inch by inch, but though his mind was evidently deranged, I could find, no trace of an organic complaint. and was at a loss to account for the fact that the vital forces were slowly but surely ebbing away. Poor fellow, his delusion was that he was damned, and, finding himself on a high mountain amid all the glories of a gorgeous sunset, in his hallucination he took it to be the throne of God himself. This is the story that he gave me. I repeat it as near as I can, word for word, without comment or explanation.

"I knew," he said, "that I was damned. I had committed the unpardonable sin: the sin against the Holy Ghost. How I came to do it I cannot recall. It was done on the spur of the moment, in a fit of recklessness, alike without evil intent and without any understanding of the terrible crime that I was committing. I did not in truth realize what I was doing till the thing was accomplished, when it suddenly burst upon me that in sheer thoughtlessness I had damned myself to all eternity. In a flash I saw that I was condemned to everlasting torment, without hope of escape. Without hope of escape! That was the terrible conviction that burnt into my inmost soul. I raged helplessly at the sense of my own impotence. I raged

186

for how long I know not. It might have been days or weeks or months. To .me it seemed an eternity. I cursed the Deity who could punish one moment's lapse after a comparatively blameless life by a sentence which must endure through all the ages. I repeated to myself over and over again the terrible words: 'Without hope of escape I ' Was there, then, indeed no loophole by which I might avoid this terrible punishment? No possibility of forgiveness either in this world or the next? I kept on putting the question to myself again and again when suddenly a line flashed upon me, a line familiar to me in my earlier youth. though whence it came, I could not for the moment recall. nor could I gauge for some time what bearing it could have on my present awful predicament.

"The words seemed to be spoken to me by some voice from without; though whether this were so or whether it was merely my own memory or imagination that had conjured them up, I could not say. 'Had I,' said the voice, 'but served my God as I have served my king!' And then it stopped. 'Had I but served my God as I have served my king!' What could this mean? The words echoed and echoed through my brain like some refrain that had a meaning in relation to my present condition. that offered some clue or solution to the terrible problem with which I was confronted. As I kept repeating them, though the thought was present that they pointed out to me some mysterious way of escape, the words themselves conveyed no meaning to my brain. Whence did they come, and who had uttered them? For some time I could find no answer. Then suddenly some thing seemed to whisper to me the name 'Cromwell.'

"'Cromwell?' I said to myself. 'Cromwell? Cromwell?' What had Cromwell to do with these words? 'Had I but served my God as I have served my king!' How, then, did Cromwell serve his king? A sudden light dawned upon me. Why, he beheaded him! It was true beyond a doubt. And he regretted on his deathbed—what? What? That he had not served his God as he had served his king I For he too was damned like me beyond hope of reprieve.

"For him, indeed, it might be too late. He was on his bed of death. The opportunity had slipped past him. But I? how did it stand with me? Might I not succeed where Cromwell failed? What else was the meaning of these mysterious words that forced themselves unsought upon me? Who was this God, this 'fiend with names divine,' that was condemning me to an eternity of torment for so trifling an offence? Might not I get even with my Creator and my torturer? Must I like Cromwell be haunted by bitter regrets when it was too late to act? Nay! Rather let me strike while there was yet time— now!—now!—now! My father's dagger hung on the wall of a neighbouring room. I would fetch it and go in search of my enemy, the enemy of the whole human race, and bring these dreadful tortures to an end What did I stand to lose? Nothing! Nothing! The sentence had gone forth. I was damned to all eternity. I might do what I would. Worse could not befall me. I looked in the inner room where my father's dagger hung. I lifted it down and drew it from its sheath. It was still bright and keen. I would, I said to myself, go forth to the uttermost parts of the earth and track down my enemy, wherever he might be. Thus armed, I left the house on my sacrilegious quest. Sacrilegious did I call it? But why? Might not the victim measure his strength against the tyrant? Might not man, condemned to eternal flames. confront the God who had sentenced him, in his own defence? If there was justice in the universe, that justice was on my side, and not on that of an outraged Deity.

"I travelled on my quest in strange climes, and among races of mankind whose language and customs, were unknown to me; with one aim in· view. And still I travelled on, seeking my enemy and vengeance, the vengeance which was to be my salvation. Men deemed me mad, but few laid hands upon me. Once I was arrested and cast in prison on the charge of having been found in the possession of arms, and with no visible means of subsistence. I escaped from gaol and resumed my quest. If there was a hue and cry after me, I knew it not. I had left my gaolers far behind me before my escape was bruited abroad At length I came to a dark forest and beyond this was a high mountain which I climbed and climbed until I seemed well nigh to have attained the summit. I had eaten and drunk nothing for days, and in sheer exhaustion sank beside a stone near the mountain top. I seemed to lose consciousness; but whether I were awake or dreaming I did not know. I suddenly realized, as I looked up with a start, that I had attained the object of my quest. Right before me, bathed in the dazzling glow of the colours of the setting sun, stood the throne of God himself, as it seemed to my imagination, part and parcel of the sunset sky, illumined in all the glory of the sunset, in lurid red and gold and sapphire and topaz light. And on the throne was my arch-enemy, smiling serenely at the audacity of mortal man, who should venture to measure swords with his Creator!

"'Who are you?' he seemed to demand, ' that you should dare to question the divine fiat? 'Who are you that you should rebel against the doom appointed from all eternity for the sinner against God's law? 'Who are you that you should question when the word of Omnipotence has gone forth?'

"'I question," I replied, emboldened by my desperation, 'by the right of that divine reason which has been implanted in my brain, by the right of that eternal justice on the strength of which you can alone lay claim to the throne of the universe. By what other right, if not by justice and reason, do you sit, enthroned above a myriad worlds? I claim my right to be beard through my inheritance of the divine sonship, through my inheritance of those qualities of justice and reason which are the pillars on which the whole universe has been built. In repudiating these by your arbitrary fiat, you have forfeited the throne of Heaven. In the name of that justice and reason which you have forsworn, I call upon you to abdicate the throne of a universe whose pillars you have shattered and destroyed. Your hour has struck, in token whereof I now smite you with my father's dagger and doom you to eternal death.'

"Suiting the action to the word, I leaped up, and beheld the gigantic form of my arch enemy, his face now pale, whether with rage or terror I knew not, and smote him to the heart as he strove to rise from his throne of sapphire and trample under foot yet one more blaspheming mortal, in addition to the many millions who had already paid the debt of destiny.

"'The crushed worm turns at last,' I thought, 'and the tyrant falls,' as I watched my enemy in one last agony of despair fall prone on the mountain side. I stepped forward meaning to bestride my vanquished foe, but as I stood there upon the mountain steep I looked around and found myself alone. Throne and Deity had alike vanished. The sun had set deep down in the valley beneath, and the shadows of night were gathering fast around the mountain side. A damp chill crept over me. What had I done, in awe I asked myself, in slaying my Creator? in slaying the source from which all the worlds and all the universes drew their life? What could remain, now God was dead? Must not life itself perish at its source? Must not ' the great globe itself dissolve and like an insubstantial pageant fading, leave not a rack behind?' 'The heart of the universe is dead!' I exclaimed. Life, from this moment, must ebb out, and can never more be replenished. With life must· disappear, too, all that we deem the material world and foolishly imagine so solid, but which could have no existence apart from the life at the heart of all things. I have dared the deed for which the ages have been waiting, and which it was my destiny to fulfil. 'The inbreathing of Brahma' has begun. I must hasten home while yet I have a home to hasten to, and announce the end of all things. Ah! when they see that end approaching, how many will kneel down and pray! Fools! Fools! to pray to the God whom I have slain!"

At this point my patient sank back exhausted upon his bed. Then for a brief moment he looked up into my face, a gleam of maniacal joy in his eyes. "My friend," he said, "we are all equal today. There is true democracy at last. Doctor and patient, king and beggarman, all are equal at length. There is one horoscope for all-the horoscope of doom and eternal nothingness. There will be no news in the papers to-morrow, though the greatest event in history will have taken place, for there will be none to print the papers, and none to read them. The millionaires may save themselves the trouble of making their wills. There will be none richer tomorrow than the workhouse inmates.

"Doctor," he cried, as he gripped my hand in a last con-vulsive spasm. "there is only one patient left for you to treat today. If you can cure him you can cure all-God! God I God! whom I have slain. A pill for an earthquake a little oxygen for the Deity, and all may yet be well." He ended with a wild maniacal laugh, sank back once more upon his pillow, and all was over.

Poor fellow! the world has not yet come to an end, only one more prophet whose prophecy has miscarried has passed to his long home-one more champion of the divinity of rea-son has met his end among his fellow lunatics.

THE MOON-GAZER

by D.N.J.

MR. JONATHAN BUNCE was a Fellow of one of the more distinguished colleges of Cambridge. The precise period of his brief tenure of a Fellowship is immaterial to my tale, and for reasons which must be obvious in the reading of it I shall not further particularise his college than by christening it All Hallows. If any of my readers should be inquisitive, I briefly recommend them to apply their knowledge of the peculiarities of the various college courts of Cambridge to the passing details of the truthful chronicle that follows, and thence to draw their own conclusions. If they carry their curiosity further, and ask for the textual authorities for my tale, I will be even franker. They are two, and two only. The first is a manuscript diary, which Mr. Bunce was keeping at the time of his sudden death; it has, I am told, been published in parts by the Mathematical Society (1879), and the original manuscript is still in the possession of Mr. Bunce's great-nephew, a well-known and popular ecclesiastical dignitary in the county of Shropshire. The other is a volume, easily accessible to all members of the University, in the Library (enquire in Room Theta).

First, for the diary. Mr. Bunce lived in Cambridge at a time when the main duty of a college don was to amble up and down the Backs on a safe nag in pursuit of an appetite for the evening's port-wine. But it is clear from his diary that Mr. Bunce was youthful and enthusiastic and took a serious view of his studies. As his name would imply, these studies were devoted to the purest of pure mathematics, and from long-winded and profound entries in the diary, I gather that he was engaged upon a *magnum opus* at the time of his death, a mighty work upon astronomy and geometry which was to shake the stars in their complacent courses and to leave the moon dumfounded. I am not an expert in things mathematical, but I am given to understand that more than one of Bunce's assertions or conclusions or discoveries (I know not the right term) has been developed and amplified by a distinguished living mathematician of this University.

To the lay-mind, however, this diary, with its abstruse mathematical disquisitions, has very little interest. It is not until the last month of his life that poor Mr. Bunce seems to become a human being. Then, at last, he begins to complain of solitude, and to blame himself for having lost touch with his fellow-men in the first ardours of mathematical discovery. Perhaps, he was disillusioned; perhaps, he had over-worked. The entry "Bad dreams" comes over and over again. At first he does not describe his dreams, but one morning he writes, "all night long I kept seeing that wicked old fellow, Gerschovius, in my sleep; he kept prowling up and down the cloisters, hitting at the flags with his stick and a huge black dog came prowling behind him." Another time, he writes, "I really must fight these dreams. I dreamed last night a tall brown man, like an Egyptian Pharaoh, was standing by my bed, naked except for a loin cloth, with a white hood, like the pictures of Egyptians in books, on his head. He put his hand on my brow, and somehow I felt I must rise and go into my living-room and put out the candle which I was sure I had left alight. The worst of it was that when I woke up, I still felt I must go and see if the candle were really alight, which, of course, it wasn't, when I got to my living-room." A week or so after this, Bunce seems to have become seriously alarmed about the state of his health. "I found myself doing it *again*," he notes: "climbing into the New Court from my window, and shouting those hideous words from under the picture of Gerschovius in the cloisters. I can't keep them out of my mind, waking or sleeping". The very last entry of all, made on the evening of his death, runs as follows:

"I know I *must* do it; I can't hold out another night. I *know* he lives in that tree, and if I can climb it and find him when he calls, well, something for good or evil must happen."

So much for the diary for the moment. The book is a far more interesting compilation than the diary, and in its own way, every whit as learned. In fact, I cordially recommend it to all students of Old Teutonic mythology and medieval interpretations of some of the better known legends of classical antiquity. Bunce notes its title, *De Signis Mysticis*, in his diary, and so I had little difficulty in running it to earth. On the title page the scope of the work is conveyed with greater fullness: *De Conjuratione Daemonum, mortuûm aut eternûm, per Signa quattuor Mystica.* It is the work of one Doctor Jacobus Gerschovius, of the University of Wittenberg, and is divided up into four books, the *Liber de Signo Salamandrae,* the *Liber de Signo Undinae,* the *Liber de Signo Sylphae,* and the *Liber de Signo Incubi aut Coboldi.* The whole volume is dedicated in flowery and atrocious Latin to "*Amlodio, Danorum Principi ac praeclarissimo studenti Wittenbergiensi.*" The printer is a certain Johannes Fustus, likewise of the University of Wittenberg, and the date of publication is 1571.

At first sight, this book looks no more than a dull treatise in Latin upon the elements of Euclid. It is profusely garnished with circles and semi-circles, arcs, crescents, ellipses, rhomboids, oddly lettered triangles and strange pentagrams. But a more careful inspection produces a very different impression on the mind of the reader. To begin with, it has some most striking illustrations. Facing the title-page is a portrait of the learned Dr. Gerschovius himself, a fat puffy old gentleman with a bushy white beard and dull, sleepy eyes, not, you would say, a very remarkable personage. But if you turn to the other illustrations scattered up and down the book, you will certainly change your mind. In every one of them the portly figure of Dr. Gerschovius reappears, and they seem to picture some very strange incidents in his earthly career. In one we see him sitting peacefully at his studies, like St. Jerome in his cell, around him stuffed monkeys and dead lizards. Through a crack in the shuttered window, a thin shaft of moonlight falls on his bald pate, as though a cold, watchful eye from without were staring in upon him. In another picture, Dr. Gerschovius is on a midnight ramble through a desolate valley, following a clumsy black poodle up the mountain-side. In a third, he is apparently in a ruined crypt. Before him, standing shadowless within the limits of a circle chalked upon the ground, is a nun, pale, with parted lips and eyes in a trance. In yet another, he is in an orchard under a vacuous full-moon: in the centre of the picture is a tall tree, and against its trunk leans a rickety ladder. A first glance does not reveal the inevitable Dr. Gerschovius, but soon we descry him among the leaves in the tree, climbing, and stretching out his hand to touch—what is it? Just above his head, a dark naked leg hangs down as though someone were sitting astride a bough, and stretching down through the leaves towards the toiling Doctor is a long, thin hand.

But, in some ways (perhaps because of the reference to it in Bunce's diary) the most remarkable picture is one that stands half-way through the book. Dr. Gerschovius' travels seem to have brought him to Venice; he is wandering up and down the colonnade of some palace; an unseen moon floods the court with light, and as he paces under the arches we see that Dr. Gerschovius is beating upon the flags at his feet with a stout oaken cudgel, and strangely sinister he looks as he does it. Under this wood-cut come the mystic words:

Sator a repo tenet opera rotas.
Veni, veni, precor, Tophet-Amenhotas.

The contents of this volume are as fascinating as its wood-cuts. There is, it is true, a vast deal of incomprehensible jargon about the conjunction of the macrocosmus with the micro-cosmus, the marriage of the Red Lion and the Lily, and the birth of the Young Queen, which to me remains but jargon. But beyond this medieval mummery, Dr. Gerschovius shows himself a man deeply-read in the legendary lore of many climes and many ages, from the humble German *Hausmärchen* to the great fables of Greece and Rome. Some of the tales he tells are new to me, and for all he has an interpretation of his own, highly original and curious. At the risk of boring the reader I will briefly outline two of his tales, partly because they are typical, but more because, I think, they have some bearing on the life and death of Mr. Bunce.

In the *Book of the Undine* comes a chapter headed "*De Narcisso et Echone Nymphâ.*" This is the Gerschovian variant of the old tale of the beautiful youth, Narcissus. The nymph Echo, pining away for unrequited love of him, ere she dies, calls upon the Great Pan ("*vel Mephistophilis*", adds the Doctor) to avenge her upon Narcissus. The Great Pan hears her cry and promises her that, after death, she shall lure her heedless lover to his doom. In the meantime, Narcissus is away hunting the Calydonian Boar with his friend, the Duke Meleager. He out-strips all his companions in the ardour of the chase, and from sunrise to sundown, and after, he follows hard upon the tracks of the Boar, faintly seen galloping a-head of him. Then, suddenly, in a wild and desolate valley, skirted on one side by a dark forest, the Boar disappears from view and Narcissus finds himself alone, gaping up at the full-moon in an empty sky. And as he stands gaping, a violent and uncontrollable longing overcomes him, to shout and howl and bay the moon like one of his own dogs, and accordingly he shouts his own name to the moon, "*Narcisse! Narcisse!*" for several minutes on end. At last the fit dies away and he stops shouting as suddenly as he had begun, but far away, in the depths of the wood, he hears the voice of the dead Echo, crying imploringly, "*Narcisse! Narcisse!*" His one thought, now, was to escape from the "moon-struck shouting dingle" ("*ex valiolio lunatico ululanti*"), and so he dashed into the wood in search of the unseen Echo, crying out alternately "*Narcisse! Narcisse!*" and "*Echo! ai, Echo!*" as he went. The distant voice took up his cry, and lured him deeper and deeper into the wood, until at last he found himself by a lonely pool under high over-arching trees. Wearied out with his long night-wandering he flung himself down beside the pool and stooped to drink from its waters. As he did so, he heard the reeds whisper mockingly "*Narcisse! Narcisse!*" and reflected in the pool he saw, not his own image, but the image of a dark, brown face with a goat's beard and sprouting horns upon its forehead, and two lean, skinny arms rose, Excalibur-like, from the mere and drew him down beneath its surface. And so, like Hylas, Narcissus perished in a wood-land lake; but, says Dr. Gerschovius, it was not the nymph Echo that drew him down, and he adds some wise and profound remarks upon the folly of dallying with an echo when the moon is at its full. It may not be your own voice which replies to you.

The other tale follows almost immediately after. The chapter is headed "*De Fabricio filioque suo Vati.*" A hasty reader would English this as "Of the Smith and his son, the Poet (or the Seer)", but a closer study of the stories that Dr.

Gerschovius has to tell us, proves that we have to deal with far more interesting personages than the village blacksmith and a precocious sonneteering son. It is, apparently, the Doctor's contention that the Great Pan takes many forms in many countries according to the name and spell whereby he is conjured up: "*in Aegypto dicunt Amenhotaden, sed in Germaniâ nostrâ Fabricium (vel teutonice Junker Volant), aut per nomen filii sui, Vatem (vel teutonice Vata) eum vocant.*" Now, Squire Volant is none other than Weyland the Smith, familiar to all readers of Kenilworth and Icelandic Saga, and Vata is his son, Wade, the theme, we know, of many songs in olden days, and, in particular, of a song chanted by a fair Trojan dame in the gardens of Criseyde. Dr. Gerschovius has collected together many tales of the doings of this strange pair, but one, the last, I must transcribe at length:

"In the village of Berchtes," writes Dr. Gerschovius, "there lived a cow-herd whose duty it was to tend his master's herds all through the summer in a large field high above the village on the side of the mountain. Now one summer this cow-herd noticed that at the time of the full moon, every morning there came down from the mountain, twelve large oxen of more than usual size and beauty, which grazed the whole day long with his master's herds. In the evening it was his wont to stand upon a rock above the field and with loud and long shouts to call the cattle into the pound by his hut, but at this particular season, he noted that every time he ceased from shouting, a voice repeated his cry in the self-same tones from the mountain above him, whereat the twelve fair oxen would leave the other herd and climb up the mountain-side out of his view. For some time the cow-herd thought little of this matter but one day he was taken with a desire to steal these oxen for his master. He therefore drove them into the pound before the setting of the sun and tethered them down so that they could not stir. He then stood upon the rock and called in the other cattle as before. When he had done crying, he heard the other voice shouting from the mountain, whereat the twelve oxen bellowed aloud, as in distress, and sought to break their bonds, but could not. The cow-herd in derision cried up the hill to the other in his own tongue '*Stulte, stultissime pastor!*' but was much surprised to hear his own voice reply with great volume and in wrath: '*Stultissime pastor!*' That night he was unable to sleep in his hut for fear that the other cow-herd should descend and rob his master's herd. He therefore arose and went and sat on the side of the valley over against the cattle-pound, and as he sat there he was aware of a form of more than human stature advancing on him, as in wrath, down the opposite side of the valley. But when he looked in that direction he saw nothing but the bare rocks and the short trees. Nevertheless, while he looked he was aware that the twelve oxen in the pound were lowing with pleasure, and at the sound of their lowing the other cattle who had been sleeping, awoke with a loud scream of terror and rushed madly from the pound in two separate flocks to opposite ends of the valley, as though one of the old gods had passed through their midst. The cow-herd was so frightened that he turned tail and ran down the pass to the village of Berchtes. Nor were his master's herds ever seen again, though men say that they may yet be heard, lowing in the mountains above the field, where they are tended by the wicked demon, Wade."

How, you may ask, did this strange volume find its way into Mr. Bunce's hands? The diary explains that. He had gone to the University Library in quest of Ramsden's *Tractate on Rhomboids*, and had found to his disgust that the volume was out. In the faint hope that it might have slipped to the back of the bookcase, he had thrust his hand through the gap in the row of books and had pulled forth the work of Dr. Gerschovius, very dusty and rather mouldy. On opening its pages, like myself, he had been fascinated by its wood-cuts and had taken it home to his rooms to study more at leisure.

Mr. Bunce's rooms were on the south side of the cloister court of his college, overlooking, as he tells us, the New
Court, in the centre of which grew one solitary tree. Often, of
a night, between two bouts of brain-work, Mr. Bunce would
stand at his window, gazing meditatively at this tree. Or he
would pace the cloisters for an odd half-hour, deep in some
mathematical calculation. Now the cloisters of All Hallows'
College have one very remarkable peculiarity. As you walk
down the north side, you are aware of the deep dull echo
of your foot-steps following you behind, growing ever louder
as you draw nearer to the western end of the vault. College
porters still point out to cynical Yankees one particular flag-
stone in which all the echo seems concentrated to its loudest
volume. If you strike upon it with your stick, or stand upon it
and shout, the sound will be taken up with startling clearness
at the far end of the cloister.

Well, late one night, Mr. Bunce was pacing up and down
the north-side of this cloister, lost in thought and wholly deaf
to the echo of his own foot-steps. The moon was at its zenith,
and he stopped a moment to gaze at it abstractedly. As he did
so, a vague memory of Dr. Gerschovius in the picture, striking at the floor with his stick, floated across his mind. He was
standing on the fateful, mysterious flag-stone, and without
knowing why, he muttered to himself the curious formula in
the book:

> *Sator a repo tenet opera rotas.*
> *Veni, veni, precor, Tophet Amenhotas.*

and stamped thrice.

Scarcely had he done so, when he stood transfixed with
terror. The echo gave back not the sound of his own foot
stamping, but of naked feet running swiftly and pattering on
the stones of the cloister-walk, until it seemed they came to

rest just behind him. He veered round with a start and saw nothing but the empty moonlit cloister.

For a minute or two, Mr. Bunce stood blinking uneasily. Was he dreaming or awake? He looked up again at the placid moon, and, why he knew not, he felt that he was enmeshed in some horrible dream-world. If only he could shout and wake himself from his nightmare! Three times his voice refused to pass through his parched throat, and then, suddenly, he found himself howling and bellowing his own name to the moon, "Bunce! Bunce! Bunce!" like a frightened dog. The echo took up his cry and seemed to roll it back upon him in sardonic mockery from the shadowy walls of the cloister, and still he could not wake himself. At length he stopped, half in shame, and listened to the echo slowly dying away. Fainter and fainter it grew, and then, to his straining ear, there came a thin, clear cry down the cloister, "*Venio, domine, venio!*"

Mr. Bunce owns that he fled, like the foolish cow-herd, and did not recover his peace of mind, until he was seated in the comfortable lamp-light of his college rooms, with his papers on the table in front of him.

He would have liked to have forgotten his mad behaviour in the cloisters, but an unkind fate was against him. All the next day he felt vaguely aware of some unseen presence in the room, which seemed to mock and sneer at his abstruse astronomical calculations, and in the evening this feeling became insupportable. He rose from his table angrily and went to the large black-board that stood by his window, and, in a half-hearted way, began chalking some old proposition from Euclid upon it. His mind was still running on Dr. Gerschovius and his book, so that he scarcely noticed what his hand was drawing on the board. Tonight he could not banish from his thoughts the picture of the pale-faced nun standing in the ruined crypt. On the page facing that picture was the diagram of a circle with a large pentagram in its midst. Underneath this diagram was a short admonition in Latin, to the effect that the necromancer must be careful not to break his circle, else, in the words of Dr. Gerschovius, "the spook will escape into the common air, and there will be a fine scrimmage." From this picture with its diagram, Bunce's mind ran on to his sudden terror in the cloister the night before, and ere he could stop to think, he found himself again muttering, "*Veni, veni, precor, Tophet Amenhotas.*"

The moment the words were past his lips, he woke from his reverie with a start, and gazed upon the black-board. All unconsciously he had been tracing the circle and the pentagram of the pale-faced nun. With an angry oath for his foolish obsession he picked up the duster to rub it out. He made one clean sweep, and broke the chalk line of the circle's circumference. Even as he did so, the glass of his lamp broke with a startling crack and the room was plunged into darkness. Somehow, his foot seemed to catch in the stand of the black-board, and it fell suddenly forward upon him, as though pushed over from behind, and both together they fell to the floor. And in the crash and general darkness, he could have sworn he heard two naked feet drop gently from the black-board to the floor.

Mr. Bunce was unutterably frightened. He scrambled to his feet and groped his way towards the fire to light a taper that he knew to be lying on his mantel-piece. But as he stooped to thrust it into the flames, he glanced uneasily over his shoulder at the window by which the black-board had been standing. Before it hung two thin muslin curtains, through which the moon-light poured into a ghostly patch on the floor, and behind them in the embrasure, between him and the world outside, Mr. Bunce thought he saw a vague shadowy form, the form of a tall naked man with some strange covering to his head, leaning forward into the room with his hands at his sides, as though awaiting orders. This vision somehow angered and exasperated Mr. Bunce. He strode towards the window and pulled the curtains apart impatiently, and lo! he was staring, as of old, down at the solitary tree in the court below. Again the old feeling of nightmare flooded through his being; again he was seized with the unconquerable longing to wake himself with shouting. In another moment he had pushed open the window and was leaning on the sill, shouting his own name to the moon. And as the last reverberation of his cries rolled away from him he heard a thin, sneering voice reply from over the battlements on the opposite side of the court: "*Veni, domine, veni!*"

After this came the period of "bad dreams" to which Bunce refers, now and again in detail, but most times shortly, in his diary. His sleep was tortured at first with visions of Dr. Gerschovius and the pale nun, of Dr. Gerschovius and the black poodle, of Dr. Gerschovius prowling round the cloisters below his rooms and striking at the echoing flag-stones with his stick. But gradually the phantom changed; it was no longer the stolid German doctor that he beheld; it was the vague dark figure of an Egyptian, that lurked unseen in the far corners of his bedroom, and, so soon as he closed his eyes, tip-toed on its naked feet across the room, and stood beside his bed, staring malignantly down at him. And as it stood there, it stretched out one hand and touched his forehead, and with the touch of its cold fore-finger, all strength and will faded out of him. He awoke, struggling wildly, to find his room silent and empty, with a frantic, unreasonable desire goading him on to leave his bed and do something that the spectre of his dreams had put into his brain. For several nights he felt he must go down into the cloister and stamp upon the echoing flag-stone. He struggled and fought against this longing, cramming the bed-clothes into his mouth to stifle his screams, for if once he yielded he vaguely knew that he was a lost soul. And then, at the close of a week, he felt that he had triumphed over fate.

The Egyptian still came to his bed-side in the night but the old insidious suggestion had altered. He awoke each night possessed with the desire to do some trivial action, and with each night the action became more and more trivial. One night he rose, and felt himself compelled to wander down to the Porter's Lodge and touch a long blue mantle that he had seen hanging there a day or two before. Yet when he arrived there, the mantle was gone, and he crawled back to bed with a sense of shame and exasperation at his folly. Another night, we have seen, he rose to put out a candle in his living-room, a candle which was not alight. A third night he found himself compelled to stumble round his room in search of a scrap of scribbled paper, which, he finally remembered, he had thrown in the fire before going to bed.

And then for three nights he had a blessed respite from all dreams and all temptations. His study of astronomy showed him that they were the three nights of the new moon, and he vaguely ascribed his relief to that event. For a brief while he thought he had conquered; his dreams had been growing quieter and fainter every night, the phantom at his bed-side more and more dim and shadowy, the temptations more trivial and less compelling. But this hope faded almost at its birth: on the fourth night the shadowy Egyptian was back at his bed-side, forcing him to rise and turn the key in his bed-room door, only to find the key was not there. And he noted with a despairing terror that as the moon drew nearer to its zenith, his dreams grew sharper and more definite, and his tormentor stood out with a greater, colder intensity from the surrounding gloom. Gradually the temptations grew less and less trivial and he felt his will to resist them had grown weaker with his long obedience to them. At last one only suggestion filtered through his brain, no longer to strike the flag-stone in the cloister, but to lower himself from the window into the court below and climb the solitary tree and touch its topmost branch with his hand. Twice he awoke to find himself crawling through his window, and gripping at the stubborn ivy to lower himself down into the court.

With the approach of the three days' zenith of the moon, he grew desperate, and for several nights he scarcely slept. On the night before the moon would stand at its fullest, he knew that the crisis of his torment was drawing near, and that once more the horrid shouting-sickness would overtake him. He must escape from the college, far from the shadow of the ill-omened tree, and somewhere, in the open country, hide from his fellow-men the ignoble lunacy that had come upon him. At sun-down he hurried out through the college gate-way and struck out with rapid strides into the country. He scarcely noticed whither he went, but only wandered on and on through the long dreary hours like a man in a trance, with only one thought in his mind—to be far away from the tree and the echoing cloister.

From this unhappy state he slowly came to his senses, to find that he was leaning on a gate and gazing across a moonlit field in which a flock of sheep was peacefully sleeping. Behind him was a small wood, and far away he heard the chimes of Great St. Mary's booming out an hour that told the day was near. The tranquil scene before him, the distant chimes with their news of day-break behind him, filled him with a sense of hope and comfort. The night was far-spent, and nothing had happened; the shameful sickness had not come upon him. And even as these thoughts flashed across his mind, he lifted his eyes and stared abstractedly at the sinking moon.

At the first sound of his wild, inhuman barking, there was a noise like thunder behind him, the thunder of thousands on thousands of starlings' wings beating amid the trees as they soared out of the wood and flew screaming over his head with terrified cries, far away across the sleeping fields. With a ghast-ly sob, Bunce ceased his outcry and watched the birds flying swiftly and noisily east-wards. As he watched, he heard them break out into a wild confused babel once more, and suddenly the flock split, like magic, into two companies, which each scattered to opposite poles of the sky and faded out of sight with a faint, discordant clamour. And then, in the field before him he heard the sheep wake from their slumber with a long-drawn bleat of terror, and they, too, broke up into two separate flocks which scampered each to a different end of the meadow, as though some terrible and menacing presence were passing through their midst. Very faintly, there came a cry, as of a shepherd saluting the dawn, "*Venio, domine, venio,*" and far off, along the eastern horizon, poor Mr. Bunce saw the first silent workings of the day, and knew that, for this once, he was saved.

But drearily and despairingly, he understood that it was only a respite. The fatal night of the moon's zenith still lay ahead of him, and now he felt himself so weakened in mind and in will by shame and horror of his sickness, by the toils and terrors of that night, that he gave up hope and lost all desire to struggle against his tormentor any further. All that last day he cowered gloomily over his fire, brooding bitterly over the fate that lay in ambush for him in the coming night. A modern physician would have diagnosed his case as one of neurosis, following upon overwork; a physician with some knowledge of Hesselius and the obscure maladies that afflict the inhabitants of the Carpathian Mountains, would have seen that his neurosis had taken the unfortunate form of lykanthropy. But Mr. Bunce lived in times in which neurosis, as a disease, was not recognised, at any rate, by name. And as for lykanthropy, the stolid Cambridge of his day would have laughed it out of court as an exploded medieval superstition; in its kinder moments it might have ascribed poor Bunce's moon-struck ululations to youth or high spirits, or, perhaps, to a scholar's eccentricity, but, for the most part, it would have wagged a sorrowful head over one more lapse from learning and propriety through an all too common weakness. And he, poor man, hugging his secret to his heart and vainly pondering over it, could trace it to one source, and one source only, to the malign fate that had put the volume of Dr. Gerschovius in his hands. Somehow, with the help of that accursed book, he had given himself over to the power of some evil spirit, whom he, carelessly, unconsciously, inadvertently, had conjured up from the deep and dead past, a spirit that, in all ages and all worlds, never had been living and never would be dead, a spirit, whose sole aim in persecuting poor human nature was a grim and purposeless malevolence, older than earth itself. And why, O why, he asked, had this hateful punishment been visited upon him—for what crime of his? Dully his eyes fell upon the papers on his table, with their wasted astronomical speculations, and he thought of Dr. Gerschovius sitting in the thin shaft of moonlight, of Narcissus howling at the moon, of the moon itself, riding calmly through the sky outside, cold and serene, yet always vigilant. Was this hidden phantom that had pounced upon him the echo of his own voice, was it some revengeful "minion of the moon," sent to chastise him for his denial of her influence, his blasphemous attempt to wrest her, with his puny calculations, from her time honoured orbit? His tired brain could neither answer nor gainsay the suggestion, and so, in utter despair, he opened his journal and made that last short entry which I have already quoted. The struggle was over; his fate lay in other and stronger hands than his own, and who knows? perhaps by bowing his head and yielding to the sleepless promptings of his persecutor, he might, like Jacob of old, look on him face to face, and wrestle with him, and so either mend or end his troubles.

No man can say what passed on that last night. An undergraduate, sleeping in rooms on the further side of the New Court, was woken somewhere towards daybreak by the sound of a dog baying pitifully at the moon. Dreamily, he remembered that more than once he had seen a black poodle prowling round the tree below in the evenings, and, without further thought, he turned over on his side and fell asleep again.

The next morning, Mr. Bunce was found lying at the foot of the tree, dead, with his neck broken.

THE UNFINISHED PRAYER-MAT
(A PHANTASY)

by Ethel Archer

"I am born of all Beauty and the Music of all Sound.

"Thou hast uttered a jarring note, and now I must vanish utterly, even into the Orange Green Land of the Twilight.

"Beyond the Sunset no mortal may travel—and yet, if haply thou mayest forget, I may be reborn again of memory and thy Silence."

*

The Slave bent low above his Task. In his turban the Single Great Jewel alternately flashed and grew dim. In his ears was the sound of running water: a sense of Things that Receded mingled with a sense of Mighty Things to Come.

Blueness, and wondrous depths, beyond which frail infinite memories stirred as the rustling of birds at dawn.

"If haply thou mayest forget." Could it be, then, that he had ever known? And again the Jewel flashed and grew dim, as he drew the Thread and the Pattern grew beneath his hand.

Silence was Purple, and the Soul of all Music was Golden. But how could he combine the two? And was not one a synonym for the other? And Remembrance—must not Remembrance be Green?

And now the Pattern was a living palpitating thing. From a background of Golden Moss grew the Strange Flowers—Flowers whose shapes ever changed; as Demons intertwisted and Strange Gods turned them again, and turning were lost in the fire.

And again, as the Jewel flashed, they changed yet again, and the Golden Moss flamed into the Flower, and the Flower flamed back again into the Golden Moss, and in the heat of the blazing noon-day sun, he slept.

He dreamed of a Persian rose-garden, and over all was the Soul of Night. The great blue vault of the sky was studded with golden stars, that hung like jewelled lamps in the perfumed darkness, burning for ever in a golden mist the incense of Love.

> And the pulse of the great purple Silence
> Throbbed as tense as small harp strings at eve
> Strung by gnomes in some forest enchanted,
> Where frail infinite memories weave
> Sad mystical songs spirit-haunted,
> And spells of strange witchery cleave.
> Where ineffably, utterly tender,
> Dwelleth Tragedy darkly serene,
> Dimly veiled in her timeless seclusion,
> Born of that which Shall Be and Has Been,
> Ever Watchful, Elusive, Eternal.

Tragedy born of the Silence;—which is the Memory of the Music of all Sound.

From beyond the Sunset she had come to summon him, and gladly he yielded himself to her embrace.

❋

Had it been a day or a thousand years? He returned with a rush to Earth. The air was charged with a warm magnetic fluid; there was a ringing of tiny bells in his ears, and he was looking into a pair of mocking green-blue eyes, eyes that held a latent caress, though the mouth still smiled.

❋

"Ah!" said my friend prosaically, as he jealously drew the Prayer-Mat from beneath my feet. "I thought you'd like it. It's a beautiful thing. It grows on you."

"It does, indeed," was my answer, "but you never let me finish!"

❋

To the maker of Beautiful Things had come Beauty herself, She, the Bride of the Amir. Her cheeks flushed with joy as a warm apricot, her hair beauteous as the sun-kissed wheat. Behind her a trusty slave girl carried a mighty fan of peacocks' feathers.

Loth to disturb him, she had bent above him as he slept, lending herself to his dream. And he, waking, deemed that he dreamed still. In an immortal moment each read the secret of the other's Soul, and was silent.

How long they remained so, spellbound, who can say? Time was not. But the Shadow from the mighty fan blotted out another Shadow. And, ere they could either perceive it, a dagger flashed in the sunlight.

He fell, the weaver of Beauty, and falling, his dark blood stained the roses at his feet.

So . . . an alien hand has completed this pattern. What became of the lady? I cannot say, but she was the last thing that his eyes rested upon this side of the Sunset.

"Humph!" said my friend critically. "Not a bad little story! I am lucky indeed to be in these days the possessor of a magic carpet."

MR. OLIVER CARMICHAEL

by Amyas Northcote

MR. OLIVER CARMICHAEL was one of the fortunate ones of the world. Of good family, he was the late born and only child of wealthy, cultivated and affectionate parents, under whose auspices he received the orthodox and pleasant education of an English gentleman. After happy, though not especially distinguished careers at Eton and Oxford, he had obtained an excellent berth in one of our minor government offices and had there settled down to the life of a worthy, if not hard worked Civil Servant. In addition to this occupation he had taken up as a hobby the collection of old silver, and in the pursuit of this found all the mental stimulus that he required.

Mr. Carmichael was not a society man, in fact, he rather avoided the companionship of women, preferring the seclusion of one of our best and most exclusive Clubs, where he spent much of his leisure time and where he possessed a number of acquaintances of his own sex. Amongst these he was popular enough, for, although perhaps slightly effeminate and by no means fond of masculine sports, Mr. Carmichael was a really good fellow, ready at all times to aid with advice or purse others less fortunate than himself.

In person he was of middle size and distinctly good looking, though of rather slight frame and with a faint touch of
the feminine in him. He was, when his peculiar experiences
began, about thirty-seven years of age.

In due course of time his parents died, sincerely mourned
by Oliver, who presently parted with their old London house
and moved into smaller quarters, where he settled himself
down to lead an easy bachelor life, waited on by a staff of old
family servants, some of whom he had known all his life.

This is but a brief and imperfect sketch of Oliver
Carmichael, but it is intended to portray him as he was: an
easy-going, high-minded, good fellow, who had never been
confronted with any serious problem in life, and whose aim
was to lead a quiet and honourable existence in charity with
all men.

An event was now, however, about to occur, which brought
about a fundamental change in his nature and in his outlook
on the world about him.

One night Mr. Carmichael had a succession of unpleasant
dreams. On waking in the morning, he could not recall their
details, but he felt depressed and disturbed, and this depression and disturbance may have caused him to be a little less
careful than usual over his toilet. For, whilst walking to his
office—a custom which he kept up with meticulous care as
being beneficial to his health—he suddenly became aware
that he had left his pocket-handkerchief behind him. Though
annoying, this was a matter easy to remedy, and Oliver sought
out the nearest hosier's shop and entered it to purchase the
needed article.

The day was yet young and the shop was nearly empty
of customers. Mr. Carmichael made his way to the counter indicated and a young woman stepped forward to serve
him. Instantly he experienced a most curious and unpleasant
sensation for which there was apparently no reason. He felt

an instinctive and violent repulsion to the girl; he glanced at her more closely, but there was little externally to account for his feeling. The young woman appeared to be of the usual shop-girl class, modest and demure in manner and neatly and quietly dressed. She was a tall and strongly built person, apparently about twenty-five years of age and—was actually ugly. Not only were her features unprepossessing, but there was an indefinable look about them of something evil, not in any positive sense, but rather negatively; it was the look of one whose thoughts and aspirations were set on a low and maleficent plane.

Mr. Carmichael purchased his handkerchief and paid for it by handing the girl a sovereign. Up to the present she had paid him no more attention than was demanded by her duties, but as she gave him his change she looked him straight in the face, and he saw, for an instant, a look of exulting triumph flash into her eyes. She instantly averted them. Oliver turned to leave the shop, feeling a faint sensation of fear, an indefinite fear of something that he could not understand. As he reached the door he turned and looked back; the girl was watching him steadily.

He proceeded on his way to the office revolving the little adventure in his mind. At first he treated it but lightly and endeavoured to analyse the cause of his sudden aversion to a perfectly respectable and civil shop-girl. But gradually he found the affair taking on a more serious aspect: the personality of the girl began to oppress him, her image kept rising before him, and it was an image presaging ill and wretchedness to himself. All day the affair haunted him and, even in the evening at his Club and during his usual quiet game of bridge after dinner, that baleful look of evil triumphant in the girl's eyes continued to obtrude itself. When at last he went to bed and finally fell asleep he dreamed again, and this time the recollection of his vision remained with him the next day. He dreamed that he was alone on an apparently desert plain, enveloped in a luminous grey mist, which whirled round him in sweeping masses ever driven by the wind. Across this plain he was journeying, exactly whither he knew not, but filled with a set purpose to reach his unknown destination. Suddenly out of the mist a figure loomed up, which he instantly recognized as that of the shop-girl. She came towards him, her eyes gleaming with an evil joy. In wild panic he turned and fled, forgetting his destination, careless of his fate, seeking only to escape from the swift moving figure which pursued him. The grey luminosity around him grew darker, his confusion increased, the threatening pursuer gained upon him. He woke with a cry; daylight was stealing into the room.

He rose that morning from his bed unrefreshed and still agitated over his dream. He endeavoured in the light of a new day to look at the whole episode more calmly, and gradually forced himself to believe that he had succeeded in stilling the nervous agitation that had possessed him the day before. He found himself presently walking to his office, but it was by a new, a pleasanter route as he fondly imagined; he laughed bitterly to himself as he gradually realized that he had selected this new route to avoid passing the hosier's shop. All that day the thought of the girl haunted him and at last after much reflection he decided on a new means of obliterating her memory. His annual leave was soon due, affairs at the office were quiet, he would ask his chief to permit him to forestall his holiday, and would go away at once. No sooner decided upon than done. His chief readily gave the required permission, and Mr. Carmichael astonished his household by announcing on his return that evening that he was going to Brighton the following day, to remain there for a week before he proceeded on the round of quiet country-house visits which he had arranged for his regular holiday.

To Brighton Oliver Carmichael went accordingly, but change of scene did not serve to distract him from his prevailing obsession. He thought very often of the girl, of whom he now had an unutterable loathing, and he also found himself pursued by other thoughts. Hitherto his life's habits had induced in him a train of pleasant and amiable ideas, not perhaps marked by any special eminence in the way of ability, but the thoughts of a clean-minded, honourable man. Now he found himself imperceptibly drifting into other trains of thought: evil notions passed through his mind, views of humanity taken from a hostile and a wicked standpoint, impressions of the worst side of human nature obtruded themselves. He fought desperately against these new ideas, but he felt it was a losing fight; he began to lose all confidence in himself, his integrity, his honour; he began to despair.

He no longer dreamed of nights, but lay buried in profound slumber, slumber in which it may well be that the thing we call the soul may leave its earthly shell and wander to realms and seek affinities utterly unknown to our waking personalities.

Mr. Carmichael, deep though his sleep might he, was now in the habit of waking unrefreshed and troubled, and though he exerted himself, both inwardly for the sake of his own peace of mind and outwardly for the sake of the conventions of life, to preserve his usual demeanour it was noticed later on by his friends that he seemed distraught and to have lost his former happy and placid content and generous instincts.

His holiday over, Mr. Carmichael returned to town filled with a new resolve. He would go again and see this ill-omened girl; he persuaded himself that her haunting personality would be dissipated by another sight of her in the flesh. He had made, he said to himself, a mountain out of a molehill; because he had taken a dislike to a girl's face there was no reason that she should drive him into madness from thinking of her. A second inspection would, no doubt, show her to be just an ordinary plain-faced girl, full of her own affairs, who had never given another thought to the casual buyer of a handkerchief some weeks before. He resolved, therefore, once more to visit the shop on the pretext of making a small purchase, and, this decision being taken, he felt easier in his mind. The next morning he made the trial, and it was, it must be confessed, with a nervous although more hopeful heart that Mr. Carmichael pushed open the shop doors and entered.

His first glance around did not disclose the girl, but when he had approached the well remembered counter she stepped forward quietly to meet him. As before she moved modestly and demurely; she glanced casually at him, her manner was that of an absolute and totally indifferent stranger. Carmichael felt reassured, he was right: he had made a fool of himself, the girl had never thought of him and did not now even remember him.

She asked him his needs. Mr. Carmichael hesitated and then blundered out the first thing he could think of. Gloves. She produced them and asked him his size; Mr. Carmichael had forgotten, his valet usually bought such articles for him. Then she must measure his hand.

He held it out and she stooped to her slight task. As she stretched the glove across his hand she touched it with her own, momentarily, perhaps accidentally. The touch sent a shock as of electricity through him, all his self-possession vanished, all his belief in the unreality of the past few weeks. For one blinding instant he saw into deeps hitherto unsuspected and sensed a horror hitherto undreamt of. Scarcely knowing what he did he took the gloves, paid for them and stood for a moment looking at the girl.

So far her manner had been that of the shop assistant, doing her work carefully and politely but somewhat mechanically; she had shown no trace of recognition or of any sense of understanding. Suddenly she raised her eyes and looked straight into his own and once more he saw a blaze of exultation, a look of power light them up. She knew herself mistress of the situation; she knew and understood the secret links that bound him to her, links that he felt dimly controlled him, but the nature of which he could not comprehend.

All this passed in a moment, the girl averted her eyes and turned carelessly from him; Mr. Carmichael left the shop almost unmanned. He reached his office, but was utterly incapable of concentrating his mind upon his work, and presently his chief, seeing him to be unwell, advised him to go home. Mr. Carmichael leapt at the idea, he would go back to the shop, he felt he must go back to the shop, he would see her again, he felt he must see her again; perhaps she would explain things, perhaps he would see his way clearer. He put on his hat and left the office.

But on arrival at the shop he was doomed to disappointment; it was early closing day and all the assistants had gone home. He walked on towards his own house, in a state of mingled disappointment and relief. He felt he must see her, and yet he dreaded the interview; he knew it would be a decisive one, but how he would emerge from it he felt to be uncertain.

He found himself drawing near home and passing through one of our quiet London squares. As he turned a corner of it, he met his enemy, for so he felt the girl to be, face to face.

She was walking quietly towards him, neatly and modestly dressed, demure as ever in her expression, but with perhaps a shade of anxiety in it also. As they approached each other, she raised her eyes. There was no blaze of triumph in them now, they were deep and watchful as they rested on his face. Almost unconsciously he raised his hat; she acknowledged the salute and the next moment found him walking on beside her.

For a few minutes silence reigned, then Mr. Carmichael, collecting himself, began:

"I am glad to have met you, I was anxious to see you, I went by Messrs. —— and found the shop shut." He paused.

"Yes?" said the other interrogatively.

"I do not understand things," went on Oliver. "Ever since that day nearly five weeks ago when I came into the shop to buy a handkerchief, I have been haunted by you. I have thought of you waking, I have, I know it now, been possessed by you in sleep." Again he paused.

"Are you trying to make love to me?" said the girl with a short laugh. This notion so astounded Mr. Carmichael that for an instant he was struck dumb. Then he ejaculated:

"Love! Make love to you! Oh, Heaven forbid!"

"You are not very polite," said his companion. "Well, if you are not moved by love, perhaps you are moved by its opposite, and you hate me."

She looked keenly at him, and Mr. Carmichael hesitated for a reply. She went on:

"You need not trouble to mince matters. I know your feelings, know them far better than you do yourself."

By this time their wanderings had led them into the Park and the girl, motioning towards two vacant chairs, said:

"Let us sit down, there may be much to speak of."

He complied without answering her and looked long and fixedly at her. As always, she looked calm, demure and mistress of herself; only in her eyes there burned a sombre light, powerful, mysterious, menacing. She turned away.

"What has happened to me?" he said. "Who are you, what do you want of me? I am at sea." She answered slowly:

"You have asked several questions, the full answers to which you are not yet fit to understand, but I will tell you something. Who am I? Well, you will find out some day who and what I really am, but you may now call me by the name my parents gave me, Phyllis Rourke; I was not always, even here, what I now am, a shop-girl. My father was a man of wisdom, a gentleman who taught me how to learn"—she hesitated—"many things, truths, facts, which are obscure to you and all your like. What do I want of you? Well, much, and much that you will dread to part with, but I hold you"—she detached a blossom from her dress and held it in her hand—"like I hold this flower, and I can crush you as I do it."

She suited her actions to her words and sat silently gazing at the ruined flower. Mr. Carmichael struggled between fear and anger. Who was this boastful girl, he thought; was he not a gentleman, a man of position, what had he really to fear from the threats of an unknown girl from a second-class shop? Summoning up his courage he answered:

"These are fine words, Miss Rourke, but you do not consider what I may do in the meantime. You indulge in threats to persecute me? Have you considered our relative social positions? Do you know I am Mr. Carmichael and a man of influence and reputation? In the last place have you considered—the police? Persons who annoy others are apt to find themselves in trouble."

He spoke more bravely than he felt. As the words passed his lips he felt his courage evaporating. She listened unmoved, smiling, with something of the air of a cat watching a mouse. When he had finished, she waited a few moments and then in a low, intensely concentrated voice answered:

"Oh, you poor fool! How little you understand. Since that night five weeks ago when first I found you, before you saw my living face, have you learned nothing? You talk of your position, of your social influence; you prate of the police." Her eyes, dark and gloomy, seemed to devour him as she went on: "What can you do? I hold you and shall always hold you. I may never see you again in this body, I want nothing of your material life, I want something more, I want you yourself, I want your soul."

He shrank back in horror. "Are you the Devil?" he said.

She burst into a fit of terrible, silent laughter.

"The Devil," she said, "we are becoming quite mediæval. Do you expect to see this foot," and she pushed forward her own, "turned into a hoof? Are you waiting for me to take out a parchment to be signed in your blood?"

She laughed again.

"No, Mr. Carmichael," she went on, "I am not the Devil. Perhaps you would be better off if I were."

There was a silence. Mr. Carmichael felt like a bird in the presence of a snake. He was fascinated, he was filled with ab-horrence: he wished to fly, he could not; he wished to fortify his spirit to resist, he felt it yielding and becoming more and more plastic under the influence of her personality.

Presently she spoke again. "There is no more to be said now," she began, "we have talked long enough. You understand as much as you are yet fitted to understand: you know now what you but feared before, that I control you, control you for a purpose clear to myself, if not to you. We need not meet again, I shall summon you when I choose and you will come to me when I call you in the places of sleep."

Another shock passed through Oliver Carmichael. Like a lightning flash there passed across him the knowledge that in those deep sleeps he had had recently his soul, detached from his body, communed with that of Phyllis Rourke amidst strange and terrible surroundings. He resolved he must try not to sleep again; she answered his thought with a laugh.

"Oh yes," she said, "you will sleep as well as ever. And now," she added, "it is time to part. I live with my aunt in Fulham and the old soul will wonder where I am."

She rose from her chair. "Good-bye, Mr. Carmichael," she said. "Au revoir, my dear affinity, till tonight."

She left him and Oliver remained sitting dazed, helpless and despairing, till a park keeper warned him of the closing gates.

Mr. Carmichael returned home in a state verging on stupefaction; the amazing conversation which had taken place, the force and malevolent disposition of Phyllis Rourke appalled him. He felt, as before said, like a bird fascinated by a snake, he desired to struggle, to escape from the coils which were closing round him, but no avenue presented itself. Vainly he racked his brains and vainly he tried to summon up will power sufficient to effect—he scarcely knew what. He was threatened from a quarter totally unguarded and by dangers the very existence of which he had never hitherto suspected. And he was threatened by what? That again he did not know. Tangible evils affecting his life or his possessions he would have known how to face or to endeavour to face, but this was an evil affecting his soul. Like many other people who have always led smooth and peaceful lives, the problems of the soul had never disturbed him. He was vaguely conscious of its existence, he had in his youth been an orthodox member of the English Church, but of late years he had slipped imperceptibly into a mild form of agnosticism and, while always ready to offer a helping hand to those needing his assistance, he had never really given any consideration to the problems of suffering or wrong. He had sought to avoid them; he knew of their existence, but only after an ill-defined fashion, and he had endeavoured to retain his own happy calm by minimizing them and hiding them from his consciousness as far as possible.

Now all was changed in an instant. He found himself in the grip of what seemed to him Evil incarnate. He knew the mind of the girl to be as fertile a field for evil as he had hitherto imagined his own to be for good. And he was powerless to resist her. What would become of him? Was she destined to drag him down to her own low plane and destroy that entity, his soul, which he now for the first time began clearly to realize existed?

He thought and thought, but little help came to him. Only one way finally illumined his darkness and this he well realized might prove a will-o'-the-wisp. The girl had threatened to seek him out in sleep. Well, he would turn night into day, he would watch at night and rest in the daylight hours, when he fondly imagined that she would be attending to her waking duties. Somewhat encouraged at having at least found a chance of salvation, he passed through the rest of the evening endeavouring to collect and control himself and at the usual hour for going to rest he made up his fire and selecting a book settled down to his nocturnal vigil.

But he found it impossible to concentrate on the printed page. His thoughts wandered to Phyllis Rourke. What was she doing, was she triumphing over him, was she even now striving to approach him? He tried to dismiss these thoughts; he resumed his book.

He woke with a start. The fire was out, the lamp had died down, daylight streamed into the room and he fancied as he regained his consciousness he heard Phyllis Rourke's low, mocking laugh.

This night was the beginning of despair for Oliver Carmichael. His hope for protection against his unseen assailant had failed him and he knew of no other help.

To detail the events of the next few months would be as difficult as useless; to the end of his life Oliver Carmichael looked back upon them as a descent into hell itself. It will suffice to summarize his experiences briefly. After his one effort at an all-night vigil he decided it was useless to attempt to vary his ordinary form of life and he returned to it and lived it as heretofore. Dealing first with this external existence, it may be said, that his acquaintances found him gradually changing; the differences were not very marked, but it was noticed that he did not take quite his old placid, kindly view of human nature. His judgment grew more bitter, he became prone to attribute bad motives rather than good to the actions of others; his good temper became less marked, his desire to help others faded, he became selfish, cold, unmerciful. Socially, he became more ambitious; he frequented parties, he entertained at home, but although he thus joined more in the life of the body politic, yet he was less popular than of old. His more intimate friends grieved over the change in him, endeavoured to reason with him and, failing to convince, drew gradually away from him. In his work he did well and earned the approbation, without increasing the affection, of his colleagues. So much for the outer Mr. Carmichael. It will be harder to paint the inner man.

At first he fought desperately against the hated invasion of his personality, but from the first he felt it to be a losing fight. He was unarmed and blinded against the attack of a skilled and watchful foe. In his waking hours he was never conscious of any hostile presence. Night and she were his enemies. He rested soundly, never dreaming, or rather never being able to recall his dreams. And yet he was well aware that it was during sleep that his soul, torn from his body by the powerful spirit of Phyllis Rourke, was dragged, resisting hopelessly, through the mire of spiritual degradation. He knew this, and nightly he summoned up his forces to this losing battle and daily realized he had taken another step on the downward path.

It is, perhaps, not accurate to say that his struggles were renewed every night; it is impossible to say, but it is certain that on some nights the battle was fiercer than on others, since he would wake on certain mornings, trembling, weary and bathed in perspiration, as if indeed he had but just emerged from a frightful ordeal. And he noticed that after each one of these dreadful nights he made a very distinct step forward in his knowledge and love of evil. His love of evil! It was with a frightful pang that once, when meditating on his fate and bemoaning his lost innocence, a still, small voice spoke within him, "With lost innocence you have gained knowledge." The thought had dwelt with him and slowly he had begun to realize that, deep within himself, he had begun to prefer vice to virtue, evil to good.

Ever since the hated invasion of his sleeping personality had begun, Oliver Carmichael had striven his hardest to repel the invader. He was, as we know, a man of high principles, if not of strong will, and his waking consciousness, aware of the hostile influences acting on his soul, had set itself to resist these influences as resolutely as possible, and at first during his daylight hours with no little success. Even up to that moment he had believed that these horrible thoughts were forced upon him and were external to his real self; he now perceived that on the contrary they formed part of himself and were knit into him inextricably. Phyllis Rourke had done her work well; she had not only captured his pure soul with her evil one, but she had even intermingled her wicked personality with his so that her thoughts and his own had become one, and it was impossible for him to decide whether the impulses and reasons which guided him were his own or hers. He had lost his identity together with his principles.

This last blow seemed likely to crush him. Hitherto he had vaguely hoped that death at any rate would put a period to his sufferings, and he had from time to time even dwelt on thoughts of suicide to escape from them. He had been restrained from this last step by a vague recollection of earlier religious training and by a fear that by violating a moral law he might end by making his condition worse. All hope of final relief, however, was now cut off, he had lost himself, he was one for ever with his evil genius.

Six months of mental and spiritual anguish elapsed and during this time Oliver Carmichael never felt the faintest desire again to see his tormentor, nor did her presence force itself upon him during his waking hours. It was only subconsciously that he was aware of her approach to him during sleep, though he never doubted that she was the cause and formed the larger part of his misery. But he would pass the shop of Messrs. ——, where he presumed her still to be employed, without concern and without ever desiring to ascertain whether Phyllis Rourke was still to be found there. Nor had he made any inquiries about her, her relation to him had no connection with the things of this world, but lay, as he well knew now, entirely on another plane.

This was the position when, about six months after the first meeting between Mr. Carmichael and Miss Rourke, the former awoke one morning with the well-known signs of his nocturnal battle upon him. He was tired, trembling, bathed in perspiration, but somewhere deep within him he felt a new sensation, a sense of exhilaration; in that awful battle of the souls he had for once proved victorious. He knew it, though he knew nothing else, for throughout his long period of suffering, it must be carefully remembered, he never knew the details of those nightly happenings: he knew the results, not the causes.

Strangely gladdened he rose from his bed and dressed himself, meditating as he did so on what had happened, and even now vaguely beginning to hope that his trials might yet come to an end, and that he would, through the aid of some unknown power, be able to tear Phyllis Rourke from his personality. The day passed more happily than any had done since his first visit to the shop and on his homeward way he felt an impulse towards entering it and seeking out his enemy. He did not do so, however.

That night he dreamed, and on this occasion the dream remained with him at waking. He dreamed that he was himself again and walking in a fair country. Overhead the sun shone brightly, its rays tempered by a gentle breeze. Birds sang in the trees and hedgerows, rabbits played on the short turf and myriads of wild flowers blossomed and scented the air. In front of him a pair of lovers were strolling, arms interlocked, evidently out for a happy day. All was peaceful and serene and he walked onwards, cheery, good tempered and feeling in charity with all men. Suddenly he heard a cry, the singing of the birds was hushed, a hawk had swooped and borne off a hapless little creature in its clutches. The sight was unpleasant and marred the peaceful scene; he turned away his eyes, *he* was not to blame, it was Nature. At that moment there was a shrill scream, a stoat had sprung upon one of the rabbits, it clung to its neck viciously biting under the ear of the little beast, which struggled vainly to shake off its deadly rider. Mr. Carmichael shuddered; scenes of blood and violence were repulsive to him; he hurried on. But the wind had dropped, the heat had become oppressive, the wild flowers, withering under the glare of the sun, drooped their heads. The beauty of the landscape faded, its outlines were still there, but they were obscured and blurred by a mist, like those which, rising from the sea, instantaneously blot out the distant, sunlit shipping. He turned a corner of the road; again he saw the lovers, but they had quarrelled, high words were passing between them; on seeing Mr. Carmichael's approach they hurried on, but their angry voices came back to his ears. Now the clouds had gathered, the sun was obscured, the heat was stifling; suddenly the storm burst, the thunder rolled, the lightning flashed and rain fell in torrents. Mr. Carmichael sheltered himself and, the fury of the storm quickly passing over, he resumed his way. Refreshed by the rain the wild flowers again raised their heads and perfumed the air, the birds sang, and before him the lovers, reconciled, pursued their happy way. Trouble had come and had passed. He woke.

That morning among his letters he found one in a handwriting strange to him, but of whose authorship he had no doubts. It was from Phyllis Rourke. He hesitated for a few moments then, opening it, he read as follows:

Dear Mr. Carmichael,

I greatly wish to see you again, if it be possible. Tomorrow I leave Messrs. —— early and shall walk in the Park near where I met you before. I shall be there by 4 p.m. and will wait.

Yours sincerely,
PHYLLIS ROURKE.

P.S. Do come.

Mr. Carmichael felt no surprise at this letter. He knew now that he had expected it to come, but he was doubtful as to what course to follow. Miss Rourke evidently wanted to see him. Why should he do anything to oblige Miss Rourke? His anger against her rose, she was his worst enemy. He looked at the matter from another aspect. He glanced at himself in the glass, and saw himself a handsome, well groomed gentleman; it might be well to go and show Miss Phyllis, that, at any rate, her evil deeds had not harmed his body. Undecided, he went to his office, and he was still undecided when he set out on his walk home after lunch. Almost unconsciously he found himself in the Park and near the well-remembered spot where he had talked with Miss Rourke six months before. He found two chairs, sat down and waited, and presently saw her coming towards him.

His heart throbbed with mingled excitement, fear and hatred. As she drew near he looked at her attentively and saw that she was somehow changed: her features were less harsh than formerly, her eyes looked softer; in her dress she was as always neat and modest. She approached him quickly and quietly, there was pleasure in her face at seeing him. He rose from his seat and waited for her.

"I am glad you have come," she said, omitting any more formal greeting, "very glad. There are things I have to say to you, knowledge I must impart."

He looked coldly at her.

"What can you have to say to me?" he began. "Do you realize what you have done to me: to me who never injured you, to me a stranger to you, a harmless stranger, who sought but to live his life in peace?"

"I know what has happened," she answered "and my knowledge goes further than your own. I know what you have suffered and the change that has come about in you." She stopped.

There was a short silence, then she resumed: "But if I know what has happened to you, you are ignorant as to what has taken place in myself."

"I am indifferent as to that," said Mr. Carmichael. "What have you to do with me?" She laughed a little, but not the mocking laugh he knew so well, and said:

"When you know all, you will not say that; but now look at me, can you see any change in me?"

Carmichael looked at her.

"Yes," he said slowly, "you are changed." He hesitated. "You are changed—for the better," he went on.

She smiled again.

"I am changed," she said, "and for the better, and this I owe to you. In the struggle that has taken place between us, I have gained much and perhaps you have lost—nothing."

"I do not understand you," said he.

She turned again and looked steadily at him. As he gazed at her a new man woke within him. He saw as in a glass darkly the blurred outlines of a mighty truth; he essayed to focus it, to make clear to his mind that which his subconscious self already perceived.

But he failed, the vision faded, he sighed and said, varying his previous words: "I cannot understand you."

"Not yet," she answered, "not yet. Your inner, your true vision is still clouded by the workings of your earthly mind. You cannot yet see clearly those wonderful affinities that exist between the souls of those we wrongly call individuals. Just as darkness and light combined make the perfect day, so do the intermingled spirits of man and woman form one perfect whole. Separated in past ages, as darkness and light were separated, for some mysterious purpose, the divided souls now seek each other throughout the ages, striving once more to unite. Some happy ones have achieved their purpose, although, clouded by earthly and external thoughts, they are as yet but dimly conscious of their triumph, but most are still seekers wandering in the night."

"I begin to understand you," he said.

"Of those seekers," she went on, "I was one, and one of not the least wretched. In times far beyond our ken, Fate, Chance, what you will, severed our knit souls, and set yours on the paths of peace and joy, whilst, I, ill-fated, was turned towards the lower depths. I do not know how long I sought you, but I know that through the ages I sought in vain, and slowly there grew up in my inmost deeps a hatred of you, my joint spirit, a hatred bred of envy and despair. At last I found you, before ever you saw me in the flesh I found you in the spirit—and when you came that first day to the shop, my soul rejoiced, for I knew that I had succeeded and that you were mine. Then I began my work, to drag you down and plunge you into the abyss of those lost souls, wherein I felt myself to be. I sought to blacken you." She paused, and after a few moments, went on in a lower voice: "But I forgot that black mingled with white forms grey, and that grey may at last bleach in the sunlight to purest white."

There was a long silence, slowly the truth possessed him, the knowledge already buried in him arose and, passing through his consciousness, filled him with content.

"I think I understand you," he said.

Phyllis went on:

"And now the fight was joined and triumphantly I watched your struggles, your slow fall. Joy possessed me, the joy of evil victorious, but gradually with that joy ill ease mingled. Gradually, imperceptibly to myself even, my onslaughts slackened, and your resistance increased. Of those dreadful, silent battles of the night your earthly sense knows nothing, but even before that recent morning when you awoke victorious I knew that I had failed and, failing, I rejoiced. As you sank, I rose and, rising, helped you to rise again."

Again she stopped and again went on:

"Now you know all, and now you know that separated once we are once more knit together for ever. In this existence we shall meet no more, it will be better so, but do you go back and take up your daily life, your work, resume your friends, rejoin your family, if you have one. As for me, a small legacy has come to me, and I have persuaded my aunt to leave London and live with me in the country, where I can pass this life in quiet and thought. We have both a battle still before us, you to regain, I to attain, merit, but let us both strive after that knowledge which brings Peace, which is God."

Again there was silence, then she rose and held out her hand. "Good-bye, Mr. Carmichael," she said, "Good-bye."

He rose also and held her hand an instant. "Au revoir," he said, "till we meet again in sleep." They parted and went upon their separate ways.

BLOOD LUST

by Dion Fortune

I

I have never been able to make up my mind whether Dr. Taverner should be the hero or the villain of these histories. That he was a man of the most selfless ideals could not be questioned, but in his methods of putting these ideals into practice he was absolutely unscrupulous. He did not evade the law, he merely ignored it, and though the exquisite tenderness with which he handled his cases was an education in itself, yet he would use that wonderful psychological method of his to break a soul to pieces, going to work as quietly and methodically and benevolently as if bent upon the cure of his patient.

The manner of my meeting with this strange man was quite simple. After being gazetted out of the Royal Army Medical Corps. I went to a medical agency and inquired what posts were available.

I said: "I have come out of the Army with my nerves shattered. I want some quiet place till I can pull myself together."

"So does everybody else," said the clerk.

He looked at me thoughtfully. "I wonder whether you would care to try a place we have had on our books for some time. We have sent several men down to it but none of them would stop."

He sent me round to one of the tributaries of Harley Street, and there I made the acquaintance of the man who, whether he was good or bad, I have always regarded as the greatest mind I ever met.

Tall and thin, with a parchment-like countenance, he might have been any age from 35 to 65. I have seen him look both ages within the hour. He lost no time in coming to the point.

"I want a medical superintendent for my nursing home," he told me. "I understand that you have specialized, as far as the Army permitted you to, in mental cases. I am afraid you will find my methods very different from the orthodox ones. However, as I sometimes succeed where others fail, I consider I am justified in continuing to experiment, which I think, Dr. Rhodes, is all any of my colleagues can claim to do."

The man's cynical manner annoyed me, though I could not deny that mental treatment is not an exact science at the present moment. As if in answer to my thought he continued:

"My chief interest lies in those regions of psychology which orthodox science has not as yet ventured to explore. If you will work with me you will see some queer things, but all I ask of you is, that you should keep an open mind and a shut mouth."

This I undertook to do, for, although I shrank instinctively from the man, yet there was about him such a curious attraction, such a sense of power and adventurous research, that I determined at least to give him the benefit of the doubt and see what it might lead to. His extraordinarily stimulating personality, which seemed to key my brain to concert pitch, made me feel that he might be a good tonic for a man who had lost his grip on life for the time being.

"Unless you have elaborate packing to do," he said, "I can motor you down to my place. If you will walk over with me to the garage I will drive you round to your lodgings, pick up your things, and we shall get in before dark."

We drove at a pretty high speed down the Portsmouth road till we came to Thursley, and, then, to my surprise, my companion turned off to the right and took the big car by a cart track over the heather.

"This is Thor's Ley or field," he said, as the blighted country unrolled before us. "The old worship is still kept up about here."

"The Catholic faith?" I inquired.

"The Catholic faith, my dear sir, is an innovation. I was referring to the pagan worship. The peasants about here still retain bits of the old ritual; they think that it brings them luck, or some such superstition. They have no knowledge of its inner meaning." He paused a moment, and then turned to me and said with extraordinary emphasis: "Have you ever thought what it would mean if a man who had the Knowledge could piece that ritual together?"

I admitted I had not. I was frankly out of my depth, but he had certainly brought me to the most unchristian spot I had ever been in my life.

His nursing home, however, was in delightful contrast to the wild and barren country that surrounded it. The garden was a mass of colour, and the house, old and rambling and covered with creepers, as charming within as without; it reminded me of the East, it reminded me of the Renaissance, and yet it had no style save that of warm rich colouring and comfort.

I soon settled down to my job, which I found exceedingly interesting. As I have already said, Taverner's work began where ordinary medicine ended, and I have under my care cases such as the ordinary doctor would have referred to the safe keeping of an asylum, as being nothing else but mad. Yet Taverner, by his peculiar methods of work, laid bare causes operating both within the soul and in the shadowy realm where the soul has its dwelling, that threw an entirely new light upon the problem, and often enabled him to rescue a man from the dark influences that were closing in upon him. The affair of the sheep-killing was an interesting example of his methods.

II

One showery afternoon at the nursing home we had a call from a neighbour—not a very common occurrence, for Taverner and his ways were regarded somewhat askance. Our visitor shed her dripping mackintosh, but declined to loosen the scarf which, warm as the day was, she had twisted tightly round her neck.

"I believe you specialize in mental cases," she said to my colleague. "I should very much like to talk over with you a matter that is troubling me."

Taverner nodded, his keen eyes watching her for symptoms. "It concerns a friend of mine—in fact, I think I may call him my *fiancé*, for, although he has asked me to release him from his engagement, I have refused to do so; not because I should wish to hold a man who no longer loved me, but because I am convinced that he still cares for me, and there is something which has come between us that he will not tell me of.

"I have begged him to be frank with me and let us share the trouble together, for the thing that seems an insuperable obstacle to him may not appear in that light to me; but you know what men are when they consider their honour is in question." She looked from one to the other of us smiling. No

236

woman ever believes that her men folk are grown up; perhaps she is right. Then she leant forward and clasped her hands eagerly. "I believe I have found the key to the mystery. I want you to tell me whether it is possible or not."

"Will you give me particulars?" said Taverner.

Clearly and concisely she gave us what was required.

"We got engaged while Donald was stationed here for his training (that would be nearly five years ago now), and there was always the most perfect harmony between us until he came out of the Army, when we all began to notice a change in him. He came to the house as often as ever, but he always seemed to want to avoid being alone with me. We used to take long walks over the moors together, but he has absolutely refused to do this recently. Then, without any warning, he wrote and told me he could not marry me and did not wish to see me again, and he put a curious thing in his letter. He said: 'Even if I should come to you and ask you to see me, I beg you not to do it.'

"My people thought he had got entangled with some other girl, and were furious with him for jilting me, but I believe there is something more in it than that. I wrote to him, but could get no answer, and I had come to the conclusion that I must try and put the whole thing out of my life, when he suddenly turned up again. Now, this is where the queer part comes in.

"We heard the fowls shrieking one night, and thought a fox was after them. My brothers turned out armed with golf clubs, and I went too. When we got to the hen-house we found several fowl with their throats torn as if a rat had been at them; but the boys discovered that the hen-house door had been forced open, a thing no rat could do. They said a gipsy must have been trying to steal the birds, and told me to go back to the house. I was returning by way of the shrubberies when someone suddenly stepped out in front of me. It was quite light, for the moon was nearly full, and I recognized Donald. He held out his arms and I went to him, but, instead of kissing me, he suddenly bent his head and—look!"

She drew her scarf from her neck and showed us a semi-circle of little blue marks on the skin just under the ear, the unmistakable print of human teeth.

"He was after the jugular," said Taverner, "lucky for you he did not break the skin."

"I said to him: 'Donald, what are you doing?' My voice seemed to bring him to himself, and he let me go and tore off through the bushes. The boys chased him but did not catch him, and we have never seen him since."

"You have informed the police, I suppose?" said Taverner.

"Father told them someone had tried to rob the hen-roost, but they do not know who it was. You see, I did not tell them I had seen Donald."

"And you walk about the moors by yourself, knowing that he may be lurking in the neighbourhood?"

She nodded.

"I should advise you not to, Miss Wynter; the man is probably exceedingly dangerous, especially to you. We will send you back in the car."

"You think he has gone mad? That is exactly what I think. I believe he knew he was going mad, and that was why he broke off our engagement. Dr. Taverner, is there nothing that can be done for him? It seems to me that Donald is not mad in the ordinary way. We had a housemaid once who went off her head, and the whole of her seemed to be insane, if you can understand; but with Donald it seems as if only a little bit of him were crazy, as if his insanity were outside himself. Can you grasp what I mean?"

"It seems to me you have given a very clear description of a case of psychic interference—what was known in scriptural days as "being possessed by a devil," said Taverner.

"Can you do anything for him?" the girl inquired eagerly.

"I may be able to do a good deal if you can get him to come to me."

On our next day at the Harley Street consulting-room we found that the butler had booked an appointment for a Captain Donald Craigie. We discovered him to be a personality of singular charm—one of those highly-strung, imaginative men who have the makings of an artist in them. In his normal state he must have been a delightful companion, but as he faced us across the consulting-room desk he was a man under a cloud.

"I may as well make a clean breast of this matter," he said. "I suppose Beryl told you about their chickens?"

"She told us that you tried to bite her."

"Did she tell you I bit the chickens?"

"No."

"Well, I did."

Silence fell for a moment. Then Taverner broke it.

"When did this trouble first start?"

"After I got shell shock. I was blown right out of a trench, and it shook me up pretty badly. I thought I had got off lightly, for I was only in hospital about 10 days, but I suppose this is the aftermath."

"Are you one of those people who have a horror of blood?"

"Not especially so. I didn't like it, but I could put up with it. We had to get used to it in the trenches; someone was always getting wounded, even in the quietest times."

"And killed," put in Taverner.

"Yes, and killed," said our patient.

"So you developed a blood hunger?"

"That's about it."

"Underdone meat and all the rest of it, I suppose?"

"No, that is no use to me. It seems a horrible thing to say, but it is fresh blood that attracts me, blood as it comes from the veins of my victim."

"Ah!" said Taverner. "That puts a different complexion on the case."

"I shouldn't have thought it could have been much blacker."

"On the contrary, what you have just told me renders the outlook much more hopeful. You have not so much a blood lust, which might well be an effect of the subconscious mind, as a vitality hunger which is quite a different matter."

Craigie looked up quickly. "That's exactly it. I have never been able to put it into words before, but you have hit the nail on the head."

I saw that my colleague's perspicacity had given him great confidence.

"I should like you to come down to my nursing home for a time and be under my personal observation," said Taverner.

"I should like to very much, but I think there is something further you ought to know before I do so. This thing has begun to affect my character. At first it seemed something outside myself, but now I am responding to it, almost helping, and trying to find out ways of gratifying it without getting myself into trouble. That is why I went for the hens when I came down to the Wynters' house. I was afraid I should lose my self-control and go for Beryl. I did in the end, as it happened, so it was not much use. In fact I think it did more harm than good, for I seemed to get into much closer touch with 'It' after I had yielded to the impulse. I know that the best thing I could do would be to do away with myself, but I daren't. I feel that after I am dead I should have to meet—whatever it is—face to face."

"You need not be afraid to come down to the nursing home," said Taverner. "We will look after you."

After he had gone Taverner said to me: "Have you ever heard of vampires, Rhodes?"

"Yes, rather," I said. "I used to read myself to sleep with *Dracula* once when I had a spell of insomnia."

"That," nodding his head in the direction of the departing man, "is a singularly good specimen."

"Do you mean to say you are going to take a revolting case like that down to Hindhead?"

"Not revolting, Rhodes, a soul in a dungeon. The soul may not be very savoury, but it is a fellow creature. Let it out and it will soon clean itself."

I often used to marvel at the wonderful tolerance and compassion Taverner had for erring humanity.

"The more you see of human nature," he said to me once, "the less you feel inclined to condemn it, for you realize how hard it has struggled. No one does wrong because he likes it, but because it is the lesser of the two evils."

III

A couple of days later I was called out of the nursing home office to receive a new patient. It was Craigie. He had got as far as the doormat, and there he had stuck. He seemed so thoroughly ashamed of himself that I had not the heart to administer the judicious bullying which is usual under such circumstances.

"I feel as if I were driving a baulking horse," he said. "I want to come in, but I can't."

I called Taverner and the sight of him seemed to relieve our patient.

"Ah," he said, "you give me confidence. I feel that I can defy it," and he squared his shoulders and crossed the threshold. Once inside, a weight seemed lifted from his mind, and he settled down quite happily to the routine of the place. Beryl Wynter used to walk over almost every afternoon, unknown to her family, and cheer him up; in fact he seemed on the high road to recovery.

One morning I was strolling round the grounds with the head gardener, planning certain small improvements, when he made a remark to me which I had reason to remember later.

"You would think all the German prisoners should have been returned by now, wouldn't you, sir? But they haven't. I passed one the other night in the lane outside the back door. I never thought that I should see their filthy field-grey again."

I sympathized with his antipathy; he had been a prisoner in their hands, and the memory was not one to fade.

I thought no more of his remarks, but a few days later I was reminded of it when one of our patients came to me and said:

"Dr. Rhodes, I think you are exceedingly unpatriotic to employ German prisoners in the garden when so many dis-charged soldiers cannot get work."

I assured her that we did not do so, no German being likely to survive a day's work under the superintendence of our ex-prisoner head gardener.

"But I distinctly saw the man going round the greenhouses at shutting-up time last night," she declared. "I recognized him by his flat cap and grey uniform."

I mentioned this to Taverner.

"Tell Craigie he is on no account to go out after sundown," he said, "and tell Miss Wynter she had better keep away for the present."

A night or two later, as I was strolling round the grounds smoking an after-dinner cigarette, I met Craigie hurrying through the shrubbery.

"You will have Dr. Taverner on your trail," I called after him.

"I missed the post-bag," he replied, "and I am going down to the pillar-box."

Next evening I again found Craigie in the grounds after dark. I bore down on him.

"Look here, Craigie," I said, "if you come to this place you must keep the rules, and Dr. Taverner wants you to stay indoors after sundown."

Craigie bared his teeth and snarled at me like a dog. I took him by the arm and marched him into the house and reported the incident to Taverner.

"The creature has re-established its influence over him," he said. "We cannot evidently starve it out of existence by keeping it away from him; we shall have to use other methods. Where is Craigie at the present moment?"

"Playing the piano in the drawing-room," I replied.

"Then we will go up to his room and unseal it."

As I followed Taverner upstairs he said to me: "Did it ever occur to you to wonder why Craigie jibbed on the doorstep?"

"I paid no attention," I said. "Such a thing is common enough with mental cases."

"There is a sphere of influence, a kind of psychic bell jar, over this house to keep out evil entities, what might in popular language be called a 'spell.' Craigie's familiar could not come inside, and did not like being left behind. I thought we might be able to tire it out by keeping Craigie away from its influences, but it has got too strong a hold over him, and he deliberately co-operates with it. Evil communications corrupt good manners, and you can't keep company with a thing like that and not be tainted, especially if you are a sensitive Celt like Craigie."

When we reached the room Taverner went over to the window and passed his hand across the sill, as if sweeping something aside.

"There," he said. "It can come in now and fetch him out, and we will see what it does."

At the doorway he paused again and made a sign on the lintel.

"I don't think it will pass that," he said.

When I returned to the office I found the village policeman waiting to see me.

"I should be glad if you would keep an eye on your dog,
sir," he said. "We have been having complaints of sheep-killing
lately, and whatever animal is doing it is working in a three
mile radius with this as the centre."

"Our dog is an Airedale," I said. "I should not think he is
likely to be guilty. It is usually collies that take to sheep-killing."

At 11 o'clock we turned out the lights and herded our
patients off to bed. At Taverner's request I changed into an
old suit and rubbersoled tennis shoes and joined him in the
smoking-room, which was under Craigie's bedroom. We sat
in the darkness awaiting events.

"I don't want you to do anything," said Taverner, "but just
to follow and see what happens."

We had not long to wait. In about a quarter-of-an-hour we
heard a rustling in the creepers, and down came Craigie hand
over fist, swinging himself along by the great ropes of wisteria
that clothed the wall. As he disappeared into the shrubbery I
slipped after him, keeping in the shadow of the house.

He moved at a stealthy dog-trot over the heather paths
towards Frensham.

At first I ran and ducked, taking advantage of every patch
of shadow, but presently I saw that this caution was unnecessary. Craigie was absorbed in his own affairs, and thereupon I
drew closer to him, following at a distance of some 60 yards.

He moved at a swinging pace, a kind of loping trot that
put me in mind of a blood-hound. The wide, empty levels of
that forsaken country stretched out on either side of us, belts
of mist filled the hollows, and the heights of Hindhead stood
out against the stars. I felt no nervousness; man for man, I
reckoned I was a match for Craigie, and, in addition, I was
armed with what is technically known as a "soother"—two
feet of lead gas-piping inserted in a length of rubber hose-

244

pipe. It is not included in the official equipment of the best asylums, but can frequently be found in a keeper's trouser-leg.

If I had known what I had to deal with I should not have put so much reliance on my "soother." Ignorance is sometimes an excellent substitute for courage.

Suddenly out of the heather ahead of us a sheep got up, and then the chase began. Away went Craigie in pursuit, and away went the terrified wether. A sheep can move remarkably fast for a short distance, but the poor wool-encumbered beast could not keep pace, and Craigie ran it down, working in gradually lessening circles. It stumbled, went to its knees, and he was on it. He pulled its head back, and whether he used a knife or not I could not see, for a cloud passed over the moon, but dimly luminous in the shadow, I saw something that was semitransparent pass between me and the dark, struggling mass among the heather. As the moon cleared the clouds I made out the flat-topped cap and field-grey uniform of the German Army.

I cannot possibly convey the sickening horror of that sight—the creature that was not a man assisting the man who, for the moment, was not human.

Gradually the sheep's struggles weakened and ceased. Craigie straightened his back and stood up; then he set off at his steady lope towards the east, his grey familiar at his heels.

How I made the homeward journey I do not know. I dared not look behind lest I should find a Presence at my elbow; every breath of wind that blew across the heather seemed to be cold fingers on my throat; fir trees reached out long arms to clutch me as I passed under them, and heather bushes rose up and assumed human shapes. I moved like a runner in a nightmare, making prodigious efforts after a receding goal.

At last I tore across the moonlit lawns of the house, regardless who might be looking from the windows, burst into the smoking-room and flung myself face downwards on the sofa.

IV

"Tut, tut!" said Taverner. "Has it been as bad as all that?"

I could not tell him what I had seen, but he seemed to know.

"Which way did Craigie go after he left you?" he asked.

"Towards the moonrise," I told him.

"And you were on the way to Frensham? He is heading for the Wynters' house. This is very serious, Rhodes. We must go after him; it may be too late as it is. Do you feel equal to coming with me?"

He gave me a stiff glass of brandy, and we went to get the car out of the garage. In Taverner's company I felt secure. I could understand the confidence he inspired in his patients. Whatever that grey shadow might be, I felt he could deal with it and that I would be safe in his hands.

We were not long in approaching our destination.

"I think we will leave the car here," said Taverner, turning into a grass-grown lane. "We do not want to rouse them if we can help it."

We moved cautiously over the dew-soaked grass into the paddock that bounded one side of the Wynters' garden. It was separated from the lawn by a sunk fence, and we could command the whole front of the house and easily gain the terrace if we so desired. In the shadow of a rose pergola we paused. The great trusses of bloom, colourless in the moonlight, seemed a ghastly mockery of our business.

For some time we waited, and then a movement caught my eye.

Out in the meadow behind us something was moving at a slow lope; it followed a wide arc, of which the house formed the focus, and disappeared into a little coppice on the left. It might have been imagination, but I thought I saw a wisp of mist at its heels.

We remained where we were, and presently he came round once more, this time moving in a smaller circle—evidently closing in upon the house. The third time he reappeared more quickly, and this time he was between us and the terrace.

"Quick! Head him off," whispered Taverner. "He will be up the creepers next round."

We scrambled up the sunk fence and dashed across the lawn. As we did so a girl's figure appeared at one of the windows; it was Beryl Wynter. Taverner, plainly visible in the moonlight, laid his finger on his lips and beckoned her to come down.

"I am going to do a very risky thing," he whispered, "but she is a girl of courage, and if her nerve does not fail we shall be able to pull it off."

In a few seconds she slipped out of a side door and joined us, a cloak over her night-dress.

"Are you prepared to undertake an exceedingly unpleasant task?" Taverner asked her. "I can guarantee you will be perfectly safe so long as you keep your head, but if you lose your nerve you will be in grave danger."

"Is it to do with Donald?" she inquired.

"It is," said Taverner. "I hope to be able to rid him of the thing that is overshadowing him and trying to obsess him."

"I have seen it," she said; "it is like a wisp of grey vapour that floats just behind him. It has the most awful face you ever saw. It came up to the window last night, just the face only, while Donald was going round and round the house."

"What did you do?" asked Taverner.

"I didn't do anything. I was afraid that if someone found him he might be put in an asylum, and then we should have no chance of getting him well."

Taverner nodded.

"'Perfect love casteth out fear,'" he said. "You can do the thing that is required of you."

He placed Miss Wynter on the terrace in full moonlight.

"As soon as Craigie sees you," he said, "retreat round the corner of the house into the yard. Rhodes and I will wait for you there."

A narrow doorway led from the terrace to the back premises, and just inside its arch Taverner bade me take my stand.

"Pinion him as he comes past you and hang on for your life," he said. "Only mind he doesn't get his teeth into you; these things are infectious."

We had hardly taken up our positions when we heard the loping trot come round once more, this time on the terrace itself. Evidently he caught sight of Miss Wynter, for the stealthy padding changed to a wild scurry over the gravel, and the girl slipped quickly through the archway and sought refuge behind Taverner. Right on her heels came Craigie. Another yard and he would have had her, but I caught him by the elbows and pinioned him securely. For a moment we swayed and struggled across the dew-drenched flagstones, but I locked him in an old wrestling grip and held him.

"Now," said Taverner, "if you will keep hold of Craigie I will deal with the other. But first of all we must get it away from him, otherwise it will retreat on to him, and he may die of shock. Now, Miss Wynter, are you prepared to play your part?"

"I am prepared to do whatever is necessary," she replied.

Taverner took a scalpel out of a pocket case and made a small incision in the skin of her neck, just under the ear. A drop of blood slowly gathered, showing black in the moonlight.

"That is the bait," he said. "Now go close up to Craigie and entice the creature away; get it to follow you and draw it out into the open."

As she approached us Craigie plunged and struggled in my arms like a wild beast, and then something grey and shadowy drew out of the gloom of the wall and hovered for a moment at my elbow. Miss Wynter came nearer, walking almost into it.

"Don't go too close," cried Taverner, and she paused.

Then the grey shape seemed to make up its mind; it drew clear of Craigie and advanced towards her. She retreated towards Taverner, and the Thing came out into the moonlight. We could see it quite clearly from its flat-topped cap to its kneeboots; its high cheek-bones and slit eyes pointed its origin to the south-eastern corner of Europe where strange tribes still defy civilization and keep up their still stranger beliefs.

The shadowy form drifted onwards, following the girl across the yard, and when it was some 20 feet from Craigie, Taverner stepped out quickly behind it, cutting off its retreat. Round it came in a moment, instantly conscious of his presence, and then began a game of "puss-in-the-corner." Taverner was trying to drive it into a kind of psychic killing-pen he had made for its reception. Invisible to me, the lines of psychic force which bounded it were evidently plainly perceptible to the creature we were hunting. This way and that way it slid in its efforts to escape, but Taverner all the time herded it towards the apex of the invisible triangle, where he could give it its *coup de grâce*.

Then the end came. Taverner leapt forward. There was a Sign then a Sound. The grey form commenced to spin like a top. Faster and faster it went, its outlines merging into a whirling spiral of mist; then it broke. Out into space went the particles that had composed its form, and with the almost soundless shriek of supreme speed the soul went to its appointed place.

Then something seemed to lift. From a cold hell of limitless horror the flagged space became a normal backyard, the trees ceased to be tentacled menaces, the gloom of the wall was no longer an ambuscade, and I knew that never again would a grey shadow drift out of the darkness upon its horrible hunting.

I released Craigie, who collapsed in a heap at my feet: Miss Wynter went to rouse her father, while Taverner and I got the insensible man into the house.

✳

What masterly lies Taverner told to the family I have never known, but a couple of months later we received instead of the conventional fragment of wedding cake, a really substantial chunk, with a note from the bride to say it was to go in the office cupboard, where she knew we kept provisions for those nocturnal meals that Taverner's peculiar habits imposed upon us.

It was during one of these midnight repasts that I questioned Taverner about the strange matter of Craigie and his familiar. For a long time I had not been able to refer to it; the memory of that horrible sheep-killing was a thing that would not bear recalling.

"You have heard of vampires," said Taverner. "That was a typical case. For close on 100 years they have been practically unknown in Europe—Western Europe that is—but the War has caused a renewed outbreak, and quite a number of cases have been reported.

"When they were first observed—that is to say, when some wretched lad was caught attacking the wounded, they took him behind the lines and shot him, which is not a satisfactory way of dealing with a vampire, unless you also go to the trouble of burning his body, according to the good old-fashioned way of dealing with practitioners of black magic. Then our enlightened generation came to the conclusion that they were not dealing with a crime, but with a disease, and put the unfortunate individual afflicted with this horrible obsession into an asylum, where he did not usually live very long, the supply of his peculiar nourishment being cut off. But it never struck anybody that they might be dealing with more than one factor—that what they were really contending with was a gruesome partnership between the dead and the living."

"What in the world do you mean?" I asked.

"We have two physical bodies, you know," said Taverner, "the dense material one, with which we are all familiar, and the subtle etheric one, which inhabits it, and acts as the medium of the life-forces, whose functioning would explain a very great deal if science would only condescend to investigate it. When a man dies, the etheric body, with his soul in it, draws out of the physical form and drifts about in its neighbourhood for about three days, or until decomposition sets in, and then the soul draws out of the etheric body also, which in turn dies, and the man enters upon the first phase of his post mortem existence, the purgatorial one.

"Now, it is possible to keep the etheric body together almost indefinitely if a supply of vitality is available, but, having no stomach which can digest food and turn it into energy, the thing has to batten on someone who has, and develops into a spirit parasite which we call a vampire.

"There is a pretty good working knowledge of black magic in Eastern Europe. Now, supposing some man who has this knowledge gets shot, he knows that in three days time, at the death of the etheric body, he will have to face his reckoning, and with his record he naturally does not want to do it, so he establishes a connection with the subconscious mind of some other soul that still has a body, provided he can find one suitable for his purposes. A very positive type of character is useless; he has to find one of a negative type, such as the lower class of medium affords. Hence one of the many dangers of mediumship to the untrained. Such a negative condition may be temporarily induced by, say, shell-shock, and it is possible then for such a soul as we are considering to obtain an influence over a being of much higher type—Craigie, for instance—and use him as a means of obtaining its gratification."

"But why did not the creature confine its attentions to Craigie, instead of causing him to attack others?"

"Because Craigie would have been dead in a week if it had done so, and then it would have found itself minus its human feeding bottle. Instead of that it worked *through* Craigie, getting him to draw extra vitality from others and pass it on to itself; hence it was that Craigie had a vitality hunger rather than a blood hunger, though the fresh blood of a victim was the means of absorbing the vitality."

"Then that German we all saw—?"

"Was merely a corpse who was insufficiently dead."

THE TOKEN

by May Sinclair

I

I have only known one absolutely adorable woman, and that was my brother's wife, Cicely Dunbar.

Sisters-in-law do not, I think, invariably adore each other, and I am aware that my chief merit in Cicely's eyes was that I am Donald's sister; but for me there was no question of extraneous quality—it was all pure Cicely.

And how Donald—— But then, like all the Dunbars, Donald suffers from being Scottish, so that, if he has a feeling, he makes it a point of honour to pretend he hasn't it. I daresay he let himself go a bit during his courtship, when he was not, strictly speaking, himself; but after he had once married her I think he would have died rather than have told Cicely in so many words that he loved her. And Cicely wanted to be told. You say she ought to have known without telling? You don't know Donald. You can't conceive the perverse ingenuity he could put into hiding his affection. He has that peculiar temper—I think it's Scottish—that delights in snubbing and faultfinding and defeating expectation. If he knows you want him to do a thing, that alone is reason enough with Donald for not doing it. And my sister, who was as transparent as white crystal, was never able to conceal a want. So that Donald could, as we said, "have" her at every turn.

And, then, I don't think my brother really knew how ill she was. He didn't want to know. Besides, he was so wrapt up in trying to finish his "Development of Social Economics" (which, by the way, he hasn't finished yet) that he had no eyes to see what we all saw: that, the way her poor little heart was going, Cicely couldn't have very long to live.

Of course he understood that this was why, in those last months, they had to have separate rooms. And this in the first year of their marriage when he was still violently in love with her.

I keep those two facts firmly in my mind when I try to excuse Donald; for it was the main cause of that unkindness and perversity which I find it so hard to forgive. Even now, when I think how he used to discharge it on the poor little thing, as if it had been her fault, I have to remind myself that the lamb's innocence made her a little trying.

She couldn't understand why Donald didn't want to have her with him in his library any more while he read or wrote. It seemed to her sheer cruelty to shut her out now when she was ill, seeing that, before she was ill, she had always had her chair by the fireplace, where she would sit over her book or her embroidery for hours without speaking, hardly daring to breathe lest she should interrupt him. Now was the time, she thought, when she might expect a little indulgence.

Do you suppose that Donald would give his feelings as an explanation? Not he. They were *his feelings*, and he wouldn't talk about them; and he never explained anything you didn't understand.

That—her wanting to sit with him in the library—was what they had the awful quarrel about, the day before she died: that and the paper-weight, the precious paper-weight that he wouldn't let anybody touch because George Meredith had given it him. It was a brass block, surmounted by a white alabaster Buddha painted and gilt. And it had an inscription: *To Donald Dunbar, from George Meredith. In Affectionate Regard.*

My brother was extremely attached to this paper-weight, partly, I'm afraid, because it proclaimed his intimacy with the great man. For this reason it was known in the family ironically as the Token.

It stood on Donald's writing-table at his elbow, so near the ink-pot that the white Buddha had received a splash or two. And this evening Cicely had come in to us in the library, and had annoyed Donald by staying in it when he wanted her to go. She had taken up the Token, and was cleaning it to give herself a pretext.

She died after the quarrel they had then.

It began by Donald shouting at her.

"What are you doing with that paper-weight?"

"Only getting the ink off."

I can see her now, the darling. She had wetted the corner of her handkerchief with her little pink tongue and was rubbing the Buddha. Her hands had begun to tremble when he shouted.

"Put it down, can't you? I've told you not to touch my things."

"*You* inked him," she said. She was giving one last rub as he rose, threatening.

"Put—it—down."

And, poor child, she did put it down. Indeed, she dropped it at his feet.

"Oh!" she cried out, and stooped quickly and picked it up. Her large tear-glassed eyes glanced at him, frightened.

"He isn't broken."

"No thanks to you," he growled.

"You beast! You know I'd die rather than break anything you care about."

"It'll be broken some day, if you *will* come meddling."

I couldn't bear it. I said, "You mustn't yell at her like that. You know she can't stand it. You'll make her ill again."

That sobered him for a moment.

"I'm sorry," he said; but he made it sound as if he wasn't.

"If you're sorry," she persisted, "you might let me stay with you. I'll be as quiet as a mouse."

"No; I don't want you—I can't work with you in the room."

"You can work with Helen."

"You're not Helen."

"He only means he's not in love with *me*, dear."

"He means I'm no use to him. I know I'm not. I can't even sit on his manuscripts and keep them down. He cares more for that damned paper-weight than he does for me."

"Well—George Meredith gave it me."

"And nobody gave you me. I gave myself."

That worked up his devil again. He *had* to torment her.

"It can't have cost you much," he said. "And I may remind you that the paper-weight has *some* intrinsic value."

With that he left her.

"What's he gone out for?" she asked me.

"Because he's ashamed of himself, I suppose," I said. "Oh, Cicely, why *will* you answer him? You know what he is."

"No!" she said passionately—"that's what I don't know. I never have known."

"At least you know he's in love with you."

"He has a queer way of showing it, then. He never does anything but stamp and shout and find fault with me—all about an old paper-weight!"

She was caressing it as she spoke, stroking the alabaster Buddha as if it had been a live thing.

"His poor Buddha. Do you think it'll break if I stroke it? Better not. . . . Honestly, Helen, I'd rather die than hurt anything he really cared for. Yet look how he hurts me."

"Some men *must* hurt the things they care for."

"I wouldn't mind his hurting, if only I knew he cared. Helen—I'd give anything to know."

"I think you might know."

"I don't! I don't!"

"Well, you'll know some day."

"Never! He won't tell me."

"He's Scotch, my dear. It would kill him to tell you."

"Then how'm I to know! If I died tomorrow I should die not knowing."

And that night, not knowing, she died.

She died because she had never really known.

II

We never talked about her. It was not my brother's way. Words hurt him, to speak or to hear them.

He had become more morose than ever, but less irritable, the source of his irritation being gone. Though he plunged into work as another man might have plunged into dissipation, to drown the thought of her, you could see that he had no longer any interest in it; he no longer loved it. He attacked it with a fury that had more hate in it than love. He would spend the greater part of the day and the long evenings shut up in his library, only going out for a short walk an hour before dinner. You could see that soon all spontaneous impulses would be checked in him and he would become the creature of habit and routine.

I tried to rouse him, to shake him up out of his deadly groove; but it was no use. The first effort—for he did make efforts—exhausted him, and he sank back into it again.

But he liked to have me with him; and all the time that I could spare from my housekeeping and gardening I spent in the library. I think he didn't like to be left alone there in the place where they had the quarrel that killed her; and I noticed that the cause of it, the Token, had disappeared from his table.

And all her things, everything that could remind him of her, had been put away. It was the dead burying its dead.

Only the chair she had loved remained in its place by the side of the hearth—*her* chair, if you could call it hers when she wasn't allowed to sit in it. It was always empty, for by tacit consent we both avoided it.

We would sit there for hours at a time without speaking, while he worked and I read or sewed. I never dared to ask him whether he sometimes had, as I had, the sense of Cicely's presence there, in that room which she had so longed to enter, from which she had been so cruelly shut out. You couldn't tell what he felt or didn't feel. My brother's face was a heavy, sombre mask; his back, bent over the writing-table, a wall behind which he hid himself.

You must know that twice in my life I have more than *felt* these presences; I have seen them. This may be because I am on both sides a Highland Celt, and my mother had the same uncanny gift. I had never spoken of these appearances to Donald because he would have put it all down to what he calls my hysterical fancy. And I am sure that if he ever felt or saw anything himself he would never own it.

I ought to explain that each time the vision was premonitory of a death (in Cicely's case I had no such warning), and each time it only lasted for a second; also that, though I am certain I was wide awake each time, it is open to anybody to say I was asleep and dreamed it. The queer thing was that I was neither frightened nor surprised.

And so I was neither surprised nor frightened now, the first evening that I saw her.

It was in the early autumn twilight, about six o'clock. I was sitting in my place in front of the fireplace; Donald was in his arm-chair on my left, smoking a pipe, as usual, before the lamplight drove him out of doors into the dark.

I had had so strong a sense of Cicely's being there in the room that I felt nothing but a sudden sacred pang that was half joy when I looked up and saw her sitting in her chair on my right.

The phantasm was perfect and vivid, as if it had been flesh and blood. I should have thought that it was Cicely herself if I hadn't known that she was dead. She wasn't looking at me; her face was turned to Donald with that longing, wondering look it used to have, searching his face for the secret that he kept from her.

. . . her face was turned to Donald . . .

I looked at Donald. His chin was sunk a little, the pipe drooping from the corner of his mouth. He was heavy, absorbed in his smoking. It was clear that he did not see what I saw.

And whereas those other phantasms that I told you about disappeared at once, *this* lasted some little time, and always with its eyes fixed on Donald. It even lasted while Donald stirred, while he stooped forward, knocking the ashes out of his pipe against the hob, while he sighed, stretched himself, turned, and left the room. Then, as the door shut behind him, the whole figure went out suddenly—not flickering, but like a light you switch off.

I saw it again the next evening and the next, at the same time and in the same place, and with the same look turned towards Donald. And again I was sure that he did not see it. But I thought, from his uneasy sighing and stretching, that he had some sense of something there.

No; I was not frightened. I was glad. You see, I loved Cicely. I remember thinking, "At last, at last, you poor darling, you've got in. And you can stay as long as you like now. He can't turn you away."

The first few times I saw her just as I have said. I would look up and find the phantasm there, sitting in her chair. And it would disappear suddenly when Donald left the room. Then I knew I was alone.

But as I grew used to its presence, or perhaps as it grew used to mine and found out that I was not afraid of it, that indeed I loved to have it there, it came, I think, to trust me, so that I was made aware of all its movements. I would see it coming across the room from the doorway, making straight for its desired place, and settling in a little curled-up posture of satisfaction, appeased, as if it had expected opposition that it no longer found. Yet that it was not happy, I could still see by its look at Donald. *That* never changed. It was as uncertain of him now as she had been in her lifetime.

Up till now, the sixth or seventh time I had seen it, I had no clue to the secret of its appearance; and its movements seemed to me mysterious and without purpose. Only two things were clear: it was Donald that it came for—the instant he went it disappeared; and I never once saw it when I was alone. And always it chose this room and this hour before the lights came, when he sat doing nothing. It was clear also that he never saw it.

But that it was there with him sometimes when I was not I knew; for, more than once, things on Donald's writing-table, books or papers, would be moved out of their places, though never beyond reach; and he would ask me whether I had touched them.

"Either you lie," he would say, "or I'm mistaken. I could have sworn I put those notes on the left-hand side; and they aren't there now."

And once—that was wonderful—I saw, yes, I *saw* her come and push the lost thing under his hand. And all he said was, "Well, I'm—I could have sworn———"

For whether it had gained a sense of security, or whether its purpose was now finally fixed, it began to move regularly about the room, and its movements had evidently a reason and an aim.

It was looking for something.

One evening we were all there in our places, Donald silent in his chair and I in mine, and it seated in its attitude of wonder and of waiting, when suddenly I saw Donald looking at me.

"Helen," he said, "what are you staring for like that?"

I started. I had forgotten that the direction of my eyes would be bound, sooner or later, to betray me.

I heard myself stammer, "W—w—was I staring?"

"Yes. I wish you wouldn't."

I knew what he meant. He didn't want me to keep on looking at that chair; he didn't want to know that I was think-ing of her. I bent my head closer over my sewing, so that I no longer had the phantasm in sight.

It was then I was aware that it had risen and was crossing the hearthrug. It stopped at Donald's knees, and stood there, gazing at him with a look so intent and fixed that I could not doubt that this had some significance. I saw it put out its hand and touch him; and, though Donald sighed and shift-ed his position, I could tell that he had neither seen nor felt anything.

It turned to me then—and this was the first time it had given any sign that it was conscious of my presence—it turned on me a look of supplication, such supplication as I had seen on my sister's face in her lifetime, when she could do nothing with him and implored me to intercede. At the same time three words formed themselves in my brain with a sudden, quick impulsion, as if I had heard them cried.

"Speak to him—speak to him!"

I knew now what it wanted. It was trying to make itself seen by him, to make itself felt, and it was in anguish at finding that it could not.

It knew then that I saw it, and the idea had come to it that it could make use of me to get through to him.

I think I must have guessed even then what it had come for.

I said, "You asked me what I was staring at, and I lied. I was looking at Cicely's chair."

I saw him wince at the name.

"Because," I went on, "I don't know how *you* feel, but *I* always feel as if she were there."

He said nothing; but he got up, as though to shake off the oppression of the memory I had evoked, and stood leaning on the chimney-piece with his back to me.

The phantasm retreated to its place, where it kept its eyes fixed on him as before.

I was determined to break down his defences, to make him say something it might hear, give some sign that it would understand.

"Donald, do you think it's a good thing, a *kind* thing, never to talk about her?"

"Kind? Kind to whom?"

"To yourself, first of all."

"You can leave me out of it."

"To me, then."

"What's it got to do with you?" His voice was as hard and cutting as he could make it.

"Everything," I said. "You forget, I loved her."

He was silent. He did at least respect my love for her.

"But that wasn't what she wanted."

That hurt him. I could feel him stiffen under it.

"You see, Donald," I persisted, "*I* like thinking about her."

It was cruel of me; but I *had* to break him.

"You can think as much as you like," he said, "provided you stop talking."

"All the same, it's as bad for you," I said, "as it is for me, not talking."

"I don't care if it is bad for me. I *can't* talk about her, Helen. I don't want to."

"How do you know," I said, "it isn't bad for *her*?"

"For *her*?"

I could see I had roused him.

"Yes. If she really is there, all the time."

"How d'you mean, *there*?"

"Here—in this room. I tell you I can't get over that feeling that she's here."

"Oh, feel, feel," he said; "but don't talk to me about it!"

And he left the room, flinging himself out in anger. And instantly her flame went out.

I thought, "How he must have hurt her!" It was the old thing over again: I trying to break him down, to make him show her; he beating us both off, punishing us both. You see, I knew now what she had come back for: she had come back to find out whether he loved her. With a longing unquenched by death, she had come back for certainty. And now, as always, my clumsy interference had only made him more hard, more obstinate. I thought, "If only he could see her! But as long as he beats her off he never will."

Still, if I could once get him to believe that she was there—

I made up my mind that the next time I saw the phantasm I would tell him.

The next evening and the next its chair was empty, and I judged that it was keeping away, hurt by what it had heard the last time.

But the third evening we were hardly seated before I saw it.

It was sitting up, alert and observant, not staring at Donald as it used, but looking round the room, as if searching for something that it missed.

"Donald," I said, "if I told you that Cicely is in the room now, I suppose you wouldn't believe me?"

"Is it likely?"

"No. All the same, I see her as plainly as I see you."

The phantasm rose and moved to his side.

"She's standing close beside you."

And now it moved and went to the writing-table. I turned and followed its movements. It slid its open hands over the table, touching everything, unmistakably feeling for something it believed to be there.

I went on. "She's at the writing-table now. She's looking for something."

It stood back, baffled and distressed. Then suddenly it began opening and shutting the drawers, without a sound, searching each one in turn.

I said, "Oh, she's trying the drawers now!"

Donald stood up. He was not looking at the place where it was. He was looking hard at me, in anxiety and a sort of fright. I supposed that was why he remained unaware of the opening and shutting of the drawers.

It continued its desperate searching.

The bottom drawer stuck fast. I saw it pull and shake it, and stand back again, baffled.

"It's locked," I said.

"What's locked?"

"That bottom drawer."

"Nonsense! It's nothing of the kind."

"It is, I tell you. Give me the key. Oh, Donald, give it me!"

He shrugged his shoulders; but all the same he felt in his pockets for the key, which he gave me with a little teasing gesture, as if he humoured a child.

I unlocked the drawer, pulled it out to its full length, and there, thrust away at the back, out of sight, I found the Token.

I had not seen it since the day of Cicely's death.

"Who put it there?" I asked.

"I did."

"Well, that's what she was looking for," I said.

I held out the Token to him on the palm of my hand, as if it were the proof that I had seen her.

"Helen," he said gravely, "I think you must be ill."

"You think so? I'm not so ill that I don't know what you put it away for," I said. "It was because she thought you cared for it more than you did for her."

"You can remind me of that? There must be something very badly wrong with you, Helen," he said.

"Perhaps. Perhaps I only want to know what *she* wanted. . . . You *did* care for her, Donald?"

I couldn't see the phantasm now, but I could feel it, close, close, vibrating, palpitating, as I drove him.

"Care?" he cried. "I was mad with caring for her! And she knew it."

"She didn't. She wouldn't be here now if she knew."

At that he turned from me to his station by the chimney-piece. I followed him there.

"What are you going to do about it?" I said.

"Do about it?"

"What are you going to do with this?"

I thrust the Token close towards him. He drew back, staring at it with a look of concentrated hate and loathing.

"Do with it?" he said. "The damned thing killed her! This is what I'm going to do with it——"

He snatched it from my hand and hurled it with all his force against the bars of the grate. The Buddha fell, broken to bits, among the ashes.

He stepped forward, opening his arms.

Then I heard him give a short, groaning cry. He stepped forward, opening his arms, and I saw the phantasm slide between them. For a second it stood there, folded to his breast; then suddenly, before our eyes, it collapsed in a shining heap, a flicker of light on the floor, at his feet.

Then that went out too.

III

I never saw it again.

Neither did my brother. But I didn't know this till some time afterwards; for, somehow, we hadn't cared to speak about it. And in the end it was he who spoke first.

We were sitting together in that room, one evening in November, when he said, suddenly and irrelevantly:

"Helen—do you never see her now?"

"No," I said—"Never!"

"Do you think, then, she doesn't come?"

"Why should she?" I said. "She found what she came for. She knows what she wanted to know."

"And that—was what?"

"Why, that you loved her."

His eyes had a queer, submissive, wistful look.

"You think that was why she came back?" he said.

BACH'S FUGUE IN D-MINOR
AN INTERPRETATION

by Kenneth Morris

THE SUN rose over a world of barren mountains that were nowhere peaked or jagged, but all round of brow, and ruddy purple now that the sunrise lit them. They were all of the same height; so that you could see hundreds of thousands of them: mountaintops stretching away to the edge of the world.

Down deep in the valleys between them was the Worm of Abomination; lying half sunk in marshlands; his immense length sprawled through valley after valley. People said, 'If the Worm should awake the world will be destroyed . . . by the fetor of his breath . . . by the principle of death inherent in his coldness. Through seven-score continents nothing was so much dreaded as that the Worm of Abomination should awake.

But the Prince of the Sun thought otherwise; and determined to awake the Worm.

So now, when his Sun-car had risen over the Mountains of the Worm midway between dawn and noon, he leaped down from it on to the rounded surface of the nearest mountaintop.

His helmet of flaming gold rises in a peak above his head; he is clad in luminous golden armor intricately worked and designed, with peaks jutting out over the shoulders and at the knees. From every inch of it a dazzle of little flames arises; so that his whole mien is scintillant and quivering. His limbs are never still; their motion is flamelike; he dances rather than leaps from the sun on to the mountaintop, with a quick tremulous rhythm not easy to make out. His girdle-ornaments, the only things not golden about him, are of glowing, flaming sapphires and topazes, rubies and emeralds and amethysts, chrysoprase and diamonds and beryls; they make myriads of broken rainbows about him as he moves.

He dances down towards the valley. The mountainside is of barren rock; but where his feet fall a little life-light quivers. Here and there he drops a jewel; where they touch the rock, clearest waters bubble up from it in little pools and basins, round which, all in an instant, flowers spring up and bloom. Blue hyacinths glow where the sapphires fell; purple irises where the amethysts; the rubies have become crimson peonies, the emeralds, floors of moss.

The Prince of the Sun goes dancing down . . . and discovers at last, in the cold darkness of the valley-bottom, the head of the Worm. This is the venomous region of peril; as he enters it, his golden armor fades out; he is now shadowy in dark olive-green, trembling up from the ground.

He drops an amethyst on the Worm's head, and a diamond. . . . The head begins to glow and become luminous. Waves of light travel down from it along the spine. Through valley after valley, in which its enormous length lies sprawled, the light-waves travel.

It lifts its head out of the filth—its head that has now grown luminous and beautiful altogether. It lifts its long length, along which the waves of ever-increasing light go speeding.

It throws out beautiful and bediamonded pinions, and rises in the air singing and glorifying the Gods. Light from its scintillant gem-lit scales falls on the barren mountainsides, and flowers spring up and into bloom everywhere. The flowers are singing the praises of heaven, and glorifying the Beauty at the Heart of Things. The Worm, coiling and wreathing its lovely length in the firmament, sheds light on the worlds and on the worlds of worlds; is glorious after the fashion of a galaxy of stars; gives birth to music upon music. The world has become luminous and beautiful altogether, and there is no fear of any peril in it anywhere. But in the swamp at the bottom of the valley, where the head of the Worm once rested—there lie the bones of the Prince of the Sun.

HELL

by L. Adams Beck

THE story I am about to tell is so strange that if it were not a part of my own experience I would not vouch for it, knowing as I do through what misty zones of self-expression revelation often reaches one through others. Setting aside the charlatan, the fraud, and the self-deceiver, the most truthful people often struggle vainly and most misleadingly to relate experience, for the simple reason that we really have no language as yet to express anything but the forms of consciousness presented to us by our senses. St. Paul states the difficulty in his well-known phrase "and there saw things not possible to be uttered." They are not possible, but yet to certain persons the attempt conveys notes like the harmonic which echoes a struck string, and this impinges on their own consciousness, reviving old forms of consciousness or presenting new. St. Paul and other mystics knew that this attempt must be made if there is any hope of seeing the bud of dawning knowledge flower into the thousand-petaled lotus of day.

Therefore I say what I know, though it must be understood it was much more real than I can say.

It begins with a dream to be very briefly told. Some dreams are an open gateway to truth and this was one of them.

My body was in Canada. My consciousness was walking

in Kensington Gardens. For those who do not know the place I will say it is exceedingly beautiful, with ancient trees overshadowing great stretches of grass and wide and narrow paths where one may love to linger in the shade. There are quiet little ways where one may be alone with birds and squirrels even in the busy time of the day, and at evening time it is lovely with long shadows, a glimmer of water from the Serpentine, and the peace of the old red brick palace dreaming among its stiff Dutch gardens and stately lawns.

In my own dream I was walking slowly down a little green byway to the long stretch of water, meditating on things very foreign to the old English setting, when I saw a woman coming quickly up from the water to meet me, silently as people come in that mysterious land of sleep. Her feet made no sound. She was like a picture suddenly thrown on clear air. She was middle-aged, fretful-looking, with anxious eyes and a hurried apologetic way with her hands, which were clothed in shabby gloves. Her dress was shabby too. I believe she had once been pretty in a limp, ineffectual way. I had an impression that her voice would be shrill and a little peevish. I thought she was going to ask me the way.

No. She stood in front of me in an attitude which suggested nervous trouble in every line of face and body and said the oddest thing I have ever heard in such an encounter.

"I do wish you'd speak to me. You're the fourth silent person I've spoken to today. We live near here, but although we go out nobody ever comes in. *Nobody.* You can't think how it gets on one's nerves—always being together and nobody saying a word. Will you come?"

One does odd things in dreams. I said with some astonishment; "Yes, if I can be of any use. But when?"

She said vaguely: "Oh—well—soon. I must be going now. We have to be in before dark. Good night. It's the most hideous existence."

I said, "Good night." Trees, woman, gardens drifted away on a dream-breeze. But the impression was left for a moment clear-cut. Helpless pain and distress. A promise. But how? Where?

Not long afterwards in circumstances I had not foreseen I was in Kensington, staying within easy reach of the gardens and beautiful old palace. I often walked there, but I did not remember the dream. The impression was dormant. She had got into my world for a moment from some strange world of her own and had walked out again. Besides, my mind was fully occupied at the moment with a book I was writing and arrangements for returning to Asia.

One evening I had dined alone and early and the evening beauty of the gardens drew me. The broader walks were full of people. A few lovers sauntered along the narrow ones, so lost in their own dream that as far as the outer world was concerned they were phantasmal. They neither knew nor cared who passed. I turned down a little path I knew which leads to the upper reach of the Serpentine, quiet, lonely. As I caught the first glimpse of tranquil water I saw a woman coming towards me.

It seemed as ordinary a happening as the coming of any of the other people who had passed me on my way. I scarcely looked at her as she came slowly on. Then I saw she meant to speak to me and I half stopped. She was shabbily dressed in faded-looking black. Her clasped hands were clothed in shabby gloves. She had an anxious, slightly bewildered expression, and my first idea was that she was a stranger who had lost her way and was going to ask for directions. She walked straight up to me, nervously as if half expecting a rebuff, and said the oddest thing.

"I do wish you'd speak to me. You're the fourth person I've tried today. We live quite near here but though we go out nobody ever comes in. *Nobody.* You can't think how it gets on one's nerves—always being together and nobody ever saying anything. A dreadful life. Will you let me talk to you?"

Honestly, I thought her a little insane, or at least mentally deficient. In either case pitiable. Nothing worse. I could not have been afraid of her if I had tried. I said soothingly:

"If you wish. If I can be of any use."

She said vaguely: "Certainly it would be of use. May I walk with you a little? It's really horribly lonely."

She spoke in as many italics as Queen Victoria in her letters; every second word was underlined. It would be wearisome to give it and it was wearisome to hear. And still I did not in the least remember my dream. It all seemed one of the odd things which may happen at any moment in London. One accommodates oneself to them if they are possible. If not, one invokes a policeman. I said at once:

"Certainly. Shall we go towards the palace?"

She answered: "Oh—well—yes. But you see I want to tell you all about it. I'm *sure* I've seen you somewhere before. Shall you mind listening?"

I said, "Not in the least," convinced she must be a little daft, to put it mildly, but taking it as a gentle and milky daftness unlikely to attract attention. I tried to think how one should talk to people like that and said something about the gardens. Did she often come there?

"Fairly often! When I'm not in Kensington High Street looking at the shops. I think Barker's windows are lovely, don't you? I spend hours there watching! those adorable manikins—and now and then they have a dress parade! Have you heard? The loveliest girls—as slim! I can't think how they do it!"

I asked cautiously (with a nurse-attendant in my mind); "Do you go alone?"

"Oh, always! I can't get anyone to go with me. In the old days in my flat two or three people used to come in and have tea. Now they never come near me. I *can't* understand why."

She looked at me as if asking me to explain the situation. It might have been comic to find oneself discussing dress parades with a perfect stranger if it had not been—what? Tragic. That was the word. There was a sense of awe like thunder clouds banking up in the air. And then—

Suddenly as a lightning flash I remembered my dream. This was the woman, and instantly I saw there was something in this strange business—something to be faced and understood. The commonplace dropped. We shed it like a garment and were face to face with truth of which I could understand nothing. There was certainly nothing in the woman herself to arrest one. Her helpless fretfulness suggested feeble personality at best. But she meant something, for all that. Wary and wakeful, I asked:

"But have you no friends? Is there no one where you live? Are you alone?"

"Certainly not," she answered with a little backboneless pride. "I live at a boarding house near Holland Park. You know, you go up Church Street and turn to the left before the top. It's before you come to the rich part. A horrid little garden with Michaelmas daisies and Virginia creeper over the house."

"And several people live there?" I asked, humouring her but feeling the enigmatic something which filled the air more strongly every minute.

"Oh, yes. There's Mr. Colfax. He lost his money speculating on the stock exchange. He quite hoped to be a millionaire. Now he does nothing but advise some nephew who's trying to get on in the druggist business. And Mrs. Simmons; she was a dressmaker, quite fashionable, but now she's a little—well—mental, you know—and makes things for bazars. And Mr. Methven—he drinks, but not violently. We shouldn't tolerate it if he did. I believe he does something for a destitute aunt. And Miss Ellcot goes out once a week to look after somebody's children that can't afford a nurse. That's all."

"But," I said, pitying the dreadful stereotyped life, "you are quite a little society among yourselves."

She answered hurriedly:

"Oh no, no! We never speak to each other. And Mrs. Spinks our landlady, though perfectly respectable and the food quite good, never speaks a word to any of us even when she carves at dinner. I'm—I'm—a little afraid of her. Then we sit all the evening and stare at each other or at the wall. Very bad manners I call it. My great-grandfather was a bishop and I ought to know. . . . Would you mind coming down this way? We're so very public here."

She led the way to a quiet nook behind the trees.

Here I pause to say that one does not follow strangers in London—least of all in the parks and in twilight. But those who know the plane on which we were at the moment may on that plane go safely in perilous places. Fear is a denizen of the world's atmosphere. It dies in clear air, and where there is no fear is no danger.

We found a great elm sweeping its branches about it like the robe of a goddess. The dusk hung in it like veils of softness. In its twilights she waited for me to speak.

"Do you never try to start a little talk?" I asked.

She shook her head vaguely.

"Well—no. There's a something—let's call it constraint. They're what I call secretive—so ill-mannered. I get a little frightened sometimes. And every day I come to the gardens and speak to all sorts of nice-looking people and ask them if they won't look in on us once in a way and give us a start. Just the way I've spoken to you, you know. Perfectly friendly. And a very odd thing—" She hesitated and looked at me cunningly from sideways eyes as if to see how I would take what was coming.

"What is the odd thing?" I prompted.

"Well, you'll hardly believe it. No one ever takes the slightest notice of me. I might not exist. It's as if they neither saw nor heard me. Shocking bad manners. And I the great-granddaughter of a bishop! You can imagine how I feel it. You're the first person who ever took the trouble to answer me, I expect you're well-connected too. I feel as if I'd seen you somewhere. Perhaps you've been presented at court and I've seen your picture in the Daily Mirror."

"I feel too as if we had met before," I said. "But how very strange that no one answers you!"

"Amazing if it weren't for present-day manners. Only yesterday such a nice old lady was sitting just over there." She pointed to a seat under a tree. "Some children were flying kites and I sat down by her and made some perfectly well-bred remark about them. She never even looked at me. Can you imagine? She took out a letter and began to read."

Now as she spoke, a feeling of strangeness crept over me which I cannot describe. This is where the inadequacy of language comes in. It was utterly disconcerting. Not fear—not in the least—but the knowledge of a something deeply secret— the nearing of the supernormal. You stagger for a moment before your footing is secure. I have known it before and since, and it never deceives. And yet—a middle-aged woman, shabbily dressed, with a strong sense of gentility: Surely nothing more commonplace in the world? But yet *again* I knew the normal was rending apart and giving way to the impossible—the true.

I am going to use an extraordinary simile. I was in the state of mind drummers produce when they beat a swift tattoo like the mutter of distant thunder and it rises louder—*louder*— LOUDER—until the tension is all but unbearable and the nerves strain at the leash. Nothing was insignificant from that moment. I began to assemble my mind and subconscious and to examine her in every flicker.

Outside the trees it was still light—underneath twilight. She stood looking anxiously at me from dusk which spiritualized her until her face was like white foam flowing away on black water. I hung on her words as profoundly as if they were a thing to be earnestly considered. I said with the eagerness I felt:

"Do tell me how you came to live at the boarding house. Did you hear of it by chance?"

Her look clouded; she picked aimlessly at the beads on her sleeve.

"Odd you should ask that, for it's just what I can't answer. I often worry myself about it. It's really a horrid place. Cheap lace curtains and an aspidistra in a red pot in the window—you know the sort. And what do you think I have to do? Why, to look after the little servant-girl next door—a vulgar little slattern! She has a lover and she's going to have a baby. Revolting, I call it. What *would* my great-grandfather have said!"

I was stalking her now with such care that I almost trembled lest a wrong word should startle the whole thing into empty air.

"But why have you to do it. Who told you to?"

"No one. I just have to. I don't know why. She's wild with fear and she comes to the partition between the gardens and I go out and listen. She likes it."

"That's kind of you!" I said. "You have the gift of sympathy."

She shook her head helplessly.

"I haven't a notion why I do it. However, you asked how I got there and I can't explain. Do you think it could be loss of memory?"

"If you would tell me the story as closely as you can we might piece it together."

"Yes—I will. You can't imagine the comfort of having someone to talk to. We sit round the whole evening and never say a word. Mr. Methven drinks. Mr. Colfax smokes.

Mrs. Simmons stares at the window, and Miss Ellcot at the fireplace. I've never heard their voices. Awful, isn't it? Then they go to bed."

"And you?"

"Oh, I read novels—I like the passionate ones with beautiful rich women and sensual strong men—I always did. Then after nine I go out to the partition between the two gardens and Julia comes and cries for half an hour. I've planned for her to come as my maid if I can find a flat. I *can't* go on as I am. They're all so frightfully secretive. You never know what they're thinking. Sometimes I wonder—suppose if it were something dreadful? I could scream out loud when that comes into my head."

She whispered that and her eyes were roaming swiftly like a hunted hare's. There was unworded terror hiding in them.

"They never come out here. That's why I like it," she added with an assumption of courage.

"Then you don't know how any of them got there?"

"Not a bit. The landlady is very respectable. The eggs and butter are quite decent, and the tea is made at the table, which I always think so nice. I have a little gas stove and kettle in my bedroom and make a cup for myself when I want it."

"Do you mind telling me your story?" I ventured. "It really is like something in a book."

"Ah, you don't know yet how romantic!" she said slyly—with a kind of furtive pleasure. "If you talk of romance!—And to think of the awful place where I have to live! . . ."

An interruption here.

A young man came down the path above us, going quickly as if to an appointment. He half halted and spoke to me, slightly raising his hat.

"In case you're a stranger, madam, the gates close in an hour, and it isn't wise for a lady to be here alone so late. Pardon me!"

He went swinging on. "Alone?" she looked at me and I at her and knowledge crept through me like cold water in my veins. Now I knew why I had felt the supernormal looming up like the roll of distant thunder-drums, now I knew why no one had answered her but me, why her eyes were full of secrecy and fear. Did it frighten me? Not in the least. I have had my training in a school which understands these things and their kinship with us. But I was tense as a bow-string now with expectation. I drew as near as I dared, knowing I must not touch her.

She said fretfully: "*Now*, you see! It was you he noticed, not me. I ask you—isn't it the worst possible manners? One feels so ignored—so bewildered. It's like the awful house where I live. They never speak to me. Never. Do you know I sometimes have a feeling they don't know I'm there."

She looked at me in bewilderment. Dully. I said:

"You must allow for their ignorance. Do tell me about yourself."

That collected her as far as she could be collected. She was eager to talk about herself, as if the act of realizing and being realized would give her the kind of life she believed she still possessed. She was only holding on to shape with my realization of her, and the appearance fed on that vitality. Were we sitting between the roots of the great tree or standing looking fixedly at each other? I cannot tell.

"I had a little flat behind High Street—more down the Earl's Court way, quite superior, the bedroom opening into the sitting-room, and the use of the bathroom. My own furniture. The cabinet had belonged to my great-grandfather the bishop. People used to say, 'Ah, that speaks for itself!' My means were very small, you understand, but that doesn't touch the question of gentility, does it?"

"Not in the least. What did you do all day?"

"Oh—well—I read novels. I'm a great reader. Don't you like those passionate sex novels? And then—I had to trim my hats and mend my stockings and so on. But what I really liked best was to go up to High Street and look in at the windows and price things. They change them so often. Delightful!"

"The theater? Concerts?"

"Well—no. Seats are so frightfully expensive now. But I never found the day long. I lived in a kind of thought-world of my own. Lovely dreams of the sort of things I'd do if I could afford it. I don't know anything pleasanter than to sit by the fire with the tea-table beside you and just dream like that idly. The things you want to happen."

"No friends?"

She drew herself up with primmed mouth.

"You see, if one is well-connected it spoils one for second-rate society. No. Except Miss Maynard and the rector's wife and Mrs. Godsal— But I was perfectly happy. And now those awful people! Sitting round me like tombstones. If only I knew how I got there. Then I could get away!"

I made a mistake, I said: "May I know your name?"

She shuddered back as if a rough hand had touched her.

"No—no. It wouldn't be suitable. I'm surprised you asked!"

I should have remembered. These manifestations do not willingly tell their names. It hurts them in some way we cannot understand. I apologized hurriedly, terrified lest I should lose her and added: "Then your life was quite self-centred. No outside interest?"

"Oh yes—the shops, you know, and I had my Daily Mirror every day and the Evening News, and Mrs. Godsal who owns the flat and lives in the ground floor came in sometimes. I was as comfortable as a cat by the fire."

"Had you a cat?"

"No, I dislike animals. I could have gone on forever in perfect content and then a horrid thing happened."

She hesitated and I knew exactly why. This kind of manifestation can never bear to allude to its last earthly moments and yet cannot keep off the subject. It is like having a hidden hurt or disgrace which must be always skirted—never directly approached. I question if most of them understand at all what has happened, though the vibration hurts them.

We were interrupted again. One of the park caretakers went by and called out:

"Gates closing in half an hour, lady. Take the first turning down to Kensington Gore."

She saw him—heard him.

"Very impertinent to interrupt! Well—one snowy day just before Christmas, High Street was simply lovely. They had the manikins in ball-dresses—exquisite! I couldn't keep away, so I just went up and took it all in and then I allowed myself tea and fruit salad in the tea-room. I never enjoyed anything more. All the people coming and going—delicious! I bought some cakes and a pair of gloves—these gloves, and came home. And that very night—oh, just a trifle, but I had a sore chest and I couldn't breathe very well. People are so silly. I should have been all right if they had let me alone. And then the expense! They would have a doctor and nurse. I won't dwell on it—I hate sick-room stuff. However, they kept me on milk, and I simply got starved out, and one fine day—I fainted. Nothing more. Just fainted."

She stopped a second, her eyes glinting strangely at me in the twilight. I took it composedly as one should. They often do not know they are dead. I think she doubted and needed reassurance.

"A very common thing to happen. And then?"

She was immensely relieved and resumed her confidential tone: "You know one has the oddest dreams while one is coming to. Do you care to hear?"

"Immensely!" I said.

She simpered and went on: "I was in a meadow covered with blue flowers as thick as daffodils in spring. Millions—and the sky and sea met in the most extraordinary blue sparkling light you ever saw—like when you look out into the horizon. Blue—blue, everywhere—bathing in it. Exactly like the sea. I do so admire it off Brighton Pier. You know?"

I did know with a vengeance. This is the Clear Light after death described in a great system of thought never known in life to the little flitting fatuous being before me. I listened in awe indescribable.

"Blue—blue, piercing, flooding everything like all the arc-lights that ever were. It made my eyes dazzle. All the flowers gave out light. It flamed—flamed blue. Sparkling, rising, tremendous! I tried to hide. It was enough to blind one if one hadn't shaded glasses. All the scent of the flowers went by me like wind."

I listened breathlessly, for reasons to be told later. I knew, I knew! Again I heard the approaching roll of thunder-drums which precedes revelation. She must have been vaguely conscious of it too, but she went on peevishly:

"There was the most awful roaring noise like thunder. I had never heard the trains so loud before. I was simply blinded with light and deafened with noise, and there were the doctor and nurse chattering in the window and taking no notice of me. Me, the patient, if you please! I screamed out: 'Do put the blind down, and for goodness' sake shut the window. The arc-light at the station is shining bang into my eyes and the trains are roaring like thunder.' But it went on—perfectly awful! Someone, I think it must have been the doctor, said loudly, exactly like the booming of a great gong—so inconsiderate in a sick-room: 'When Reality is on you, cling to the Light. It is yours. It is you. Know that whatever visions you see are only your own imaginings. They are hell. Cling to the Light, the Light! It will save you.' Do you think it could have been the doctor? Or the Salvation Army in the street? They are frightfully noisy!"

"But you could not do it!" I said pityingly. "It was too bright. You could not understand!"

"Understand! It was perfectly ridiculous. I got up and pulled down the blind myself with the queerest feeling that I was lying on my bed all the time. That shows how weak I was—but I wouldn't give way to it, and presently I felt stronger. Then I said out loud so that they could hear. 'I shall report you, nurse, for neglect of duty. As to the doctor, he must be mad!' And I walked into my dear little sitting-room and sat down. Oh, the comfort of it—after that awful Light! You seem to be an understanding kind of person so you'll realize it. It was simply new life to me!"

Oh, terrible fetters and cages our own thoughts make for us! She had seen the Symbol of Divinity, and she shut herself into the base little prison from which Death had tried to free her! I looked at her with pity inexpressible. She could not read a ray of it.

"I just sat down. Heavenly! The noise had stopped and the fire was burning brightly. You know—the nice lights and shadows all flickering about. My tea-table was pulled up to it—tea and hot buttered toast, and a letter on the table. I don't often get letters. Never now! I tore it open. My uncle had died and left me Five Hundred Pounds a year." She said it in capitals. "Now I could go to Brighton and have a good room in the best boarding house on the Steyne. I could buy the five-pound dresses at Barker's. I had often and often dreamed of all that, for the poor man had an aneurism. So horrid to die so suddenly! I used always to be thinking what I would do if I had money. Wasn't it perfectly heavenly! Money! I loved it and never had it. And another letter—"

Here she minced a little. Her manner grew coy and her eyes narrowed.

"I wonder why I tell you everything. Well—long ago—he fell in love with me. You can see I was pretty. He had a wife—a perfectly horrid woman. No sympathy between them. And—well—I had a baby. Naturally I couldn't keep it. I got it adopted. He left me because of that, afraid his wife would get to know. But I was always wishing he would come back. Well, this letter was to say he couldn't do without me, and would I meet him at Tencott—our old meeting place by the Thames—on Saturday."

She paused a moment and looked at me bewildered:

"To tell you the truth I'm not perfectly certain how much I dreamed all that about him and how much was true! I used to think of nothing else—picturing things, dreaming awake and asleep, lying in my bed, crying and longing and pressing my hands on my eyes till I used to see him come into the room. My whole body wanted him. And then I used to think—Oh, but how awful if I had a baby. I got that on the brain. But we had such heavenly times. No one ever knew. Such a gentleman! He was manager of the bank where I had to go once a quarter to sign my annuity paper. It must have been there he noticed me. Don't you think so? Wasn't it a romance? Oh—his kisses, his kisses!"

Now I listened with perfect understanding. This had been her dominating complex, as modern science chooses to call it, though I know a much wiser and more ancient wisdom which not only classifies but explains causes. The complex of her miserable life was manifesting before me now in the only form in which the so-called dead can manifest in the world of appearances. The spirit—never. That is beyond all reach of human invocation. The thought-complex which sums up the experience of a lifetime, bad or good, futile or noble—that is what people pick up at the séances—the only thing which is responsive to the thoughts and prejudices in themselves. The Spirit! They might as well summon the Almighty to manifest in response to table rappings or the little out-reach of thoughts bounded by the brain. But the finite thought-complex can after death be brought in touch with other thought-complexes above or below it in the scale of evolution, as it can by telepathy or such familiar manifestations in life. Is the process desirable? This is not the place in which to discuss that point. Proof of immortality it gives none, for the atoms whirled together in a human complex take time to disintegrate and re-form. Proof of immortality there is—infinite as immortality itself, but it is not to be found along that finite road of changing moods and consciousness.

She babbled on until I caught her up again.

"And the Light was gone?" I asked, pitying this poor consciousness, shaped of illusions, manifesting in the fear and bewilderment of her abortive life. Such pity one accords to the blind beseeching faces seen behind the guarded doors of an asylum. "And you dreamed of him again?"

"Dreamed? Why, there was his letter on the tray! Don't I tell you? I was as happy as a queen. The only thing that fretted me was that the cabinet belonging to my great-grandfather the bishop was gone and they had arranged the furniture differently. So inconsiderate when I was ill! I rang to ask for Mrs. Godsal who owns the flats, but I suppose the bell was broken, and she always gave herself airs. Nobody came anyway. But I *did* enjoy my tea and I wrote to him and said I would come and went out and posted it. Do you think it was wrong? His wife simply meant nothing to him and he adored me. I love those passionate men who just take possession, don't you?"

I said: "Did the Light mean *nothing* to you? Nothing at all?"

She answered: "Oh, the light on the Thames that day! It was sunset and all the river glowed like fire. We were in the copse where we always met. We sat in the ferns—exquisite! I can smell their crushed smell now. He was beautifully dressed in flannels and a blue tie. Such a gentleman always! People used to look at him when we walked together. I had a dark blue foulard—beautifully made with the new dipping sides to the skirt. And *passionate*—oh, such a man! Love simply burning me. His wife nothing—I everything! I was even glad he was married—the secret between us was so delicious. How we cheated the dull people who couldn't guess our happiness! I thought how I'd go to the bank next week, and he would just look sidelong at me and we would know. Once he touched my foot under the table when the clerk was there. Ours was a true marriage. What's a mere ceremony compared with things like that?"

"Did you ever think of your dream-child?" I asked.

She looked puzzled. Not sorrowful. Puzzled.

"I don't think so. That was one of the things that would frighten me. But that wretched Julia talks of her baby. Of course that's quite in a low class of society. I believe the young man is a grocer's assistant. Sometimes it reminds me. But of course, if such an awful thing happened, a lady could never acknowledge it. Julia's what I call shameless. She means to pay someone to look after it until they can marry—and then she'll take it. Don't you call that very animal? But for my darling lover's sake I shall help her a little with the payments, now I have five hundred pounds a year. I had a kind of notion I might let her have the child in the flat if she turns out useful to me. She wouldn't be so likely to leave me then."

If I could only tell the thoughts that poured through me! Was she any madder than the millionaire prisoned by his counting-house, chained to his gold, the king dreaming of dominion, the shifty politician with his greased palm itching for more, the enchanting beauty whose body will be slime in a few years, the famous actress, the man or woman who pushes to any goal of success anyhow, everywhere? I declare that to me she stood an epitome of the world bartering its birthright of bliss, beauty, power, and the whole universe for a mess of pottage. I looked at her with mingled horror and sympathy. Dreams—the dreams of the lunatic asylum, the lies of the senses tossing us hither and thither, and behind them the divine spirit eternally one with the Divine. She did not even know that she could no longer react upon the world she loved. Or that she was a mere thought-form weakly manifested, soon to be disintegrated and re-formed. Until then ineffectual as a dead frost-bitten leaf. Could anyone believe her to be a spirit returning to give news of things unseen? Had she been a little more highly evolved she would have chattered of a Christian, Indian, Buddhist, or Mohammedan heaven—whatever had been the husk of symbol moulding her thought-forms in life. A more modern education would have permitted her to babble of whiskys and sodas and cigarettes.

One does not marvel at these manifestations but at the ignorance which accords them any dignity or authority. With the highest thought-forms few indeed of us can hope to come in touch for very obvious reasons. With the evil or ignorant thought-forms it can never be difficult.

When I caught up with her again she was saying fretfully:

"And then I think I must have lost my memory just a tiny wee bit! Only the effect of the illness, you know. The effect of that horrid Light and the noise in the street when they ought to have kept me quiet. Because a most extraordinary thing happened. I was just as happy as could be in my dear little flat, if they hadn't moved the furniture—and I can't *think* what's become of the bishop's lovely cabinet—but I sat there all day and nobody came, and I began to think the housemaid must be on holiday. And then it occurred to me that it would be pleasant just to run up and have a look at the fashions in Barker's windows. I do love that. Well, I went up—the street crowded, all the women simply *glued* to the windows and the things perfectly lovely. There was a dress of peach georgette with silver—five pounds. I thought, 'Well, that's the very thing if we go to the theater together. I must go back for my chequebook,' and suddenly I knew I had forgotten where I lived! Did you ever forget anything like that?"

Her weak little eyes were urgent upon me, frightened—exactly like a rabbit's if you take it in your hand without the love and understanding that all animals respond to. I said:

"I forget little things sometimes, but they come back."

She answered, shuddering: "But this didn't come back. I couldn't remember the street, the number. I couldn't even be sure whether it was Bloomsbury or Notting Hill Gate and I had got mixed up with something in Brighton. Horrible! It was simply awful. I stood as if I were looking in at the windows and women chattering all round me about hats and stockings to match the dresses. Then they mostly went home to dinner, and I couldn't stand there all night and I hadn't so much as a roof to shelter me. I couldn't think. I was half mad with fear. I felt in my pocket and even my purse was gone. Only a few loose pence."

I understood what had happened. The first thought-form after death had broken. Unconscious self-judgment (the relentless, the unbribable) was appointing her a new hell—or rather let us call it a new school for the moulding of possible thought-forms a shade higher in the scale of evolution. Then she would be turned out upon the world again in rebirth, to do the best she would for herself. I listened enthralled. Heavens, what a task before this puny creature—to hew out the divinely lovely Galatea sleeping hidden in the marble rock of her selfish futility. What ages would it take?

"So I went up to the policeman who stands at the bottom of Church Street and said"—I could see her saying it with her little mincing ineffectuality—"'I'm so worried. I've lost the address of my lodgings and I don't know the way back. Can you help me?' You can think how unpleasant it was! He looked me up and down and said, 'Haven't you any card, mum? Have you tried your pockets? Try again.' So I just felt in my pocket—very old-fashioned, but I always have one in my slip—and there I found an address. He read it and said, 'The green motor-bus takes you up within five minutes of it,' and I got in, thinking how lucky I was, and asked my way when I got out."

Her eyes filled with tears. She dried them with a raggy little handkerchief.

"I walked along, planning to have a muffin for tea and to speak very seriously to Mrs. Godsal about the cabinet when I got in; and lo and behold! there was no flat. There was a shabby garden with bushes of Michaelmas daisies—just that pale insipid colour I hate—and I went up to the house and the door was open and—oh, the very queerest thing!—I knew it was where I had to go and I just walked upstairs into my bedroom. The landlady looked out of her den and said, 'Oh, that's you,' and there I've been ever since. Now could *you* help me to remember where my dear little flat was? I would give anything to be there again."

I shook my head. "How can I? But there are other things I might help you to remember if you would let me. As a matter of fact I think Julia—who seems to be a sensible girl—will be your best help at the moment."

I had of course seen that this unwilling help to Julia was the best she was capable of as yet. It was a hopeful symptom that her mind had invented Julia and was playing with the thought of doing something for her—the only hopeful thing—a narrow chink of light in the darkness of her prison. I noticed too that everyone in the miserable household apparently had their feeble filament of care reaching out to others—all except the landlady. I felt something sinister there that I could not decipher, though no doubt she was in the scheme of the eternally right and necessary.

"Julia indeed!" she said scornfully. "A little slattern! She knows it's very kind of me to notice her at all, especially as she's lost her character."

"Do you still go for your annuity to the bank?"

Again that bewildered look.

"Not now. Some arrangement seems to have been made with the landlady and I don't have to pay her. Could it be by the municipal authorities, do you think? But I have really lovely clothes when he wants me again—a violet and grey georgette and beautiful furs and so on. My wardrobe is crammed. Five hundred a year goes a long way with a single woman's wants. Still, the place is simply awful. I wouldn't tell you at first, but I get *deadly* frightened. They never speak to me or to each other. We just sit round in the evening and stare and no one notices what I have on or thinks what an interesting life mine is. They are *extremely* second-rate."

I asked: "Do you ever think of their lives?"

"Theirs? Why, there's nothing to think of. You never saw such grim old fogies. They might all be mummies. But—I don't know who you are, but I *have* seen you before, and I see I've interested you—Couldn't you come in tomorrow evening and just talk to them a bit? The fourth house to the left after you get into Roslyn-Ware Street. You'll know the shabby lace curtains and those horrid Michaelmas daisies. Come about eight o'clock. We're always in then."

"Where do they go in the day?" I asked. Again the bewildered look.

"I don't know. You see, we don't talk to each other. I can't remember now how I heard what they do. The landlady said what I've told you when first I came. Since then she never speaks. Will you come?"

For reasons of my own I said, "Yes"—and as the words left my lips there came the usual shouting of the caretakers to clear the gardens.

"All out! All out!" It had grown suddenly dark under the trees, and they were menacing like mysterious shapes in ambush down the long paths with neither moon nor stars hanging upon the boughs. A chill breeze stirred the leaves. Before my eyes I saw her figure melting, receding, disintegrating. Her foolish shrill voice said faintly:

"Dear me, how very inconvenient! The *idea* of hustling us out like this! I was just going to say—"

All was gone but darkness. I ran as quickly as I could to the gate leading into Kensington Gore and scraped through as it clanged. I stood outside panting, but not with fear. The pitiable helpless creature! To what rebirth is she destined? Will the little lusts for little pleasures be on a plane a trifle higher? I think so. Hell is a process of education slow but sure. She will have outgrown the illicit loves of the dream bank manager and have developed into (say) platonic adoration of some gentleman who leads an influential thought-circle with Asiatic affinities. She may write soulful unrhymed verse, a meager allowance of six lines to the poem. Something after this fashion:

> A wave thundering in
>   Breaking in aimless foam,
> The ocean passions of my soul
>   Break on the rocks of fate
> And withdraw shuddering
>   Into the profundities of the abyss.

Her dress will be expressive of the depths in sexual passion and psychic implication. She will choose a modern poet for her confidences in Kensington Gardens and will show him the first chapters of an autobiography of infantile, adolescent, and adult complexes chiefly centreing on the indecent. I cannot fit the hell to this particular exposition of individuality, but since she manufactures it herself with unsparing diligence it will be ready in due course.

Meanwhile I wended my way to Roslyn-Ware Street next day guided by the omniscient policeman. A narrow street, sordid and mean, vocal with the crying of babies and scolding of overtaxed women, from open windows closely draped with cheap lace curtains the worse for soot. I found the house, the fourth on the left. Pale Michaelmas daisies bordered an untidy path with an ill-cut weed-grown flower bed on either side. A shabby Virginia creeper nourished in sooty air hung wearily about the house. The windows cried aloud for cleaning and in the centre of one, exactly between the loop of the curtains, stood an aspidistra in a red pot.

I turned the tap on the door which represented an electric bell, and after a scurry inside, a faded woman in a black apron appeared and opened it grudgingly. I said I had heard rooms were let there and she drew herself up instantly.

"Oh, dear, no! No such thing, Mr. Horner (I am Mrs. Horner) lives here and we occupy the whole house. Good afternoon."

I got a word in edgeways as she shut the door.

"Do you happen to know if there is a young woman named Julia in service in either of these houses?" pointing to the right and left.

"Certainly not. No servants are kept."

She banged the door.

I walked down the narrow path wondering many things. Did the Horners guess what terrible company they kept— what things sat in their rooms and were about them night and day? Was it a miasma of misery and shame condemning themselves to the dulness of listless despair? If I had gone into that terrible parlor, would my clearer eyes have seen Mr. Colfax, Mrs. Simmons, Mr. Methven, and Miss Ellcot sitting there in deadly silence staring at each other? Was the sinister landlady ever on the watch over her inmates, hidden in some den they could not guess? Unknown, untellable—a mystery brushing me with silent wings as it fled.

I regretted Julia. The invention of Julia with her tears and hopes and weeping courage was the only promise for the future.

To sum up. A woman to whom I told this story asked: "Why should the wretched woman have come to you?" I answered that I believed my knowledge of the subject and reaction to her wants might have helped her. But how can I tell?

Years ago, Sir William Barrett, whose work in the study of psychic events cannot be forgotten, gave me his little book on thought as a creative force and with it a powerful impetus along the line of that study. If he had known what we know now of the same study in Asia, with what tripled emphasis he would have asserted the power his own insight presaged. Remembering that book, on returning from Roslyn-Ware Street I took down another one on the art of dying (old when Tibet was young, for from that strange country it comes), that art in which so few are versed though one and all must meet the Inexorable face to face. Surely it would be well to give a little thought to a matter so inevitable and upon which personal experience enlightens only a very few. I took the book into the sunny gardens and sitting under a great elm in dappled shadow read as follows:

> At the moment of death the consciousness of objects is lost. There is what is called 'a swoon' in which is beheld the Clear Light of the Void, in other words the high consciousness which sleeps in us all under the every-day consciousness which our senses present to us. This Clear Light is seen as the glory of spring—but that is only a symbol representing an infinitely indescribable joyful

experience. If the dead man has the power to recognize that Light as his own higher consciousness he is freed from all earth bonds and passes on to perfect union with bliss. If he cannot, if the Great Light dazzles him and he shrinks from it, then his consciousness passes into lower and lower thought-forms, appearances as fashioned by his thoughts on earth. Thus entrapped by his earthly consciousness he still inhabits and exists in them. *In these his consciousness can touch other earth-consciousnesses.* By those he is gradually drawn downwards from the Light into the earthly atmosphere where he is eventually reborn to tread the sad round of earthly experience. It is said that those who have rightly practiced yoga, or the great science of concentration, recognize the Clear Light and rejoice in their union with it. For them births and deaths are ended.

Sitting under the tree with the little happy squirrels flitting beside me, I recalled how closely her earthly experiences had imprisoned the consciousness which represented my sad visitor, and how, if untrained, I, too, might have received her as a spirit and visible proof of immortality. I repeated to myself the great verse which sums up that true knowledge.

"Never the Spirit was born, the Spirit shall
    cease to be never.
Never was time it was not. End and
    beginning are dreams.
Deathless and birthless and changeless,
    abideth the Spirit for ever.
Death cannot touch it at all, dead though
    the house of it seems."

Yes, and the feeble fluttering pulse of life in her will strengthen steadily until it beats in time with the mighty heart-beat of the universe, and then—gradually, marvelously, her growth will shatter her bound crippled consciousness as an acorn shatters the vase in which it was planted and spreads into a mighty oak rooted in earth but soaring to the heavens.

> "Though I was born on earth, the child of earth,
> Yet was I fathered by the starry sky."

I shall meet her again elsewhere when the chrysalis wings tremble in their folding.

I close with the strange and beautiful prayer of these Tibetan people who have studied death as eagerly as life. The prayer of those who just are born, being dead:

> Alas, when the uncertain experience of Reality is dawning upon me, setting aside every thought of fear or terror, may I recognize whatever visions appear as the reflections only of my own consciousness! May I know them to be only apparitions. May I rejoice in the Clear Light of my own highest consciousness!

And the answer:

> When the Clear Light is seen, sparkling, bright, dazzling, glorious, be not daunted. That is the radiance of your own true nature. Recognize it.
>
> From the midst of that radiance the sound of Reality reverberating like a thousand thunders will come. That is the sound of your own true self. Be undaunted, fearless, unawed.

If you cannot recognize your own thought-
forms for nothingness, the Light will daunt
you, the sounds awe you, the rays will terrify you.
And ignorant, helpless, you will be imprisoned
in your own thought-forms and must wander
the earth again as its prisoner.

A strange thing to read in Kensington Gardens under the
ancient trees. For all such prisoners of the self-consciousness
let us pray the prayer of Enlightenment.

CAT SOULS
A RECOGNITION

by Tom Leon

FATE led me to visit a large cat show not long ago. Over six hundred exhibits embracing almost every variety of domestic or sacred cats had been brought together to compete for championships and prizes, and had attracted a miscellaneous crowd of human beings to admire their beauty or rarity.

As I wandered down the aisles of the great building in which the scene was staged my attention was attracted by a dark and slender lady, who bent tenderly over one of the pens endeavouring to reconcile its occupant to the confining wires. Her straight black hair was trimmed squarely across her brow, and her deeply-sunk eyes shone brilliantly from a bronzed and oval face, reminding me curiously of some priestess of ancient Egypt, and those far off, yet deathless days, when the cat had been held in reverent awe as symbol of all that was most sacred.

Presently she looked up and our eyes met, and with that freemasonry which a strong interest held in common bestows, we quickly introduced ourselves, and soon I was listening to a strange narrative.

"It has been asserted," said my new-made friend, "that we may sometimes obtain the answer to problems which perplex us by holding them in thought when we are about to fall asleep, and earnestly desiring their solution. With this in mind I determined one night to seek the explanation of a minor question that often occurred to me. Why is it that the many cats of which I have been the owner, have, even as tiny kittens, displayed the most extraordinary affection for me, which neither time or painful trial of their trust has ever been able to efface? Nothing in the life I consciously lead accounts for the intensity of their devotion, nor is it explainable by magnetic attraction, since not all cats, but only certain ones are thus drawn to me. There must be some occult cause. What can the reason be? I asked the question as I fell asleep, and, as if in reply, I dreamed a vivid dream.

"I thought I wandered through an ancient necropolis, and, without seeking, discovered a hidden entrance to a stonebuilt vault I vaguely remembered having seen before. In its walls small niches had been cut, and, as I looked more closely, I saw that each recess was occupied by the form of a mummied cat, which an inner vision enabled me to realise was not truly dead, but might be better described as in a state of suspended animation.

"Something within me awoke, as I gazed in wonder, and opened for me a doorway into the Past. 'Why!' I exclaimed, 'I now recollect that in the long ago I myself placed these little forms in this gloomy tomb. thinking them dead, yet with a loving hope that some day the Spirit of Life might reanimate them. There lie the dishes of food I put for their *ka*'s sustenance, and yonder burns the lamp I lighted that they might not fear the gloom. The magical ceremonies with which I laid their bodies to rest have preserved all as I left it.' Thus I mused, when suddenly a Voice from an unseen source broke into my meditation.

"'And now,' it said, 'your mission is to reconduct your former charges to the material world wherein your present lot is cast. You are to provide for them a loving home, and tenderly to guard them through another mortal life. They are not dead, but await the call to return to the sunshine, and beauty, and interest of the world that lies above this tomb. They will recognise in you the guardian of their earlier life, and feel for you a strong and grateful love of an intensity that you cannot account for, since you have drunk of the water of Lethe, and forgotten the Past. Do not be tempted to belittle your Mission, for great Trees spring from tiny seeds, and all life is of Divine Origin.' The Voice ceased, and I awoke, its accents still ringing in my ears.

"Thus was my question answered, and now I see the Hand of a Guiding Power in all things, even in our seemingly chance meeting of today."

The lady paused, her story ended, and on my listening ears there fell the sonorous note of the great hall clock, reminding me I must hasten on elsewhere. I glanced once more into the deep dark eyes from which her soul looked forth to mine, and suddenly Life seemed fraught with meaning and worthy of the suffering and effort it entailed. She had brought me a message, for I now perceived that nothing was trivial, and no creature lived in vain. Our hands met in a farewell clasp, and we murmured in unison "au revoir". To both of us a strange knowledge had come: we had met before, and our reunion, brief though it was, argued that some day we should come into contact again.

ET IN SEMPITERNUM PEREANT

by Charles Williams

LORD ARGLAY came easily down the road. About him the spring was as gaudy as the restraint imposed by English geography ever lets it be. The last village lay a couple of miles behind him; as far in front, he had been told, was a main road on which he could meet a motor bus to carry him near his destination. A casual conversation in a club had revealed to him, some months before, that in a country house of England there were supposed to lie a few yet unpublished legal opinions of the Lord Chancellor Bacon. Lord Arglay, being no longer Chief Justice, and having finished and published his *History of Organic Law*, had conceived that the editing of these papers might provide a pleasant variation upon his present business of studying the more complex parts of the Christian Schoolmen. He had taken advantage of a week-end spent in the neighbourhood to arrange, by the good will of the owner, a visit of inspection; since, as the owner had remarked, with a bitterness due to his financial problems, "everything that is smoked isn't Bacon." Lord Arglay had smiled—it hurt him a little to think that he had smiled—and said, which was true enough, that Bacon himself would not have made a better joke.

It was a very deserted part of the country through which he was walking. He had been careful to follow the directions given him, and in fact there were only two places where he could possibly have gone wrong, and at both of them Lord Arglay was certain he had not gone wrong. But he seemed to be taking a long time—a longer time than he had expected. He looked at his watch again, and noted with sharp disapproval of his own judgment that it was only six minutes since he had looked at it last. It had seemed more like sixteen. Lord Arglay frowned. He was usually a good walker, and on that morning he was not conscious of any unusual weariness. His host had offered to send him in a car, but he had declined. For a moment, as he put his watch back, he was almost sorry he had declined. A car would have made short time of this road, and at present his legs seemed to be making rather long time of it. "Or," Lord Arglay said aloud, "making time rather long." He played a little, as he went on, with the fancy that every road in space had a corresponding measure in time; that it tended, merely of itself, to hasten or delay all those that drove or walked upon it. The nature of some roads, quite apart from their material effectiveness, might urge men to speed, and of others to delay. So that the intentions of all travellers were counterpointed continually by the media they used. The courts, he thought, might reasonably take that into consideration in case of offences against right speed, and a man who accelerated upon one road would be held to have acted under the improper influence of the way, whereas one who did the same on another would be known to have defied and conquered the way.

Lord Arglay just stopped himself looking at his watch again. It was impossible that it should be more than five minutes since he had last done so. He looked back to observe, if possible, how far he had since come. It was not possible; the road narrowed and curved too much. There was a cloud of trees high up behind him; it must have been half an hour ago that he passed through it, yet it was not merely still in sight, but the trees themselves were in sight. He could re-mark them as trees; he could almost, if he were a little careful, count them. He thought, with some irritation, that he must be getting old more quickly, and more unnoticeably, than he had supposed. He did not much mind about the quickness, but he did mind about the unnoticeableness. It had given him pleasure to watch the various changes which age tended to bring; to be as stealthy and as quick to observe those changes as they were to come upon him—the slower pace, the more meditative voice, the greater reluctance to decide, the inclina-tion to fall back on habit, the desire for the familiar which is the first skirmishing approach of unfamiliar death. He neither welcomed nor grudged such changes; he only observed them with a perpetual interest in the curious nature of the creation. The fantasy of growing old, like the fantasy of growing up, was part of the ineffable sweetness, touched with horror, of existence, itself the lordliest fantasy of all. But now, as he stood looking back over and across the hidden curves of the road, he felt suddenly that time had outmarched and out-twisted him, that it was spreading along the countryside and doubling back on him, so that it troubled and deceived his judgment. In an unexpected and unusual spasm of irritation he put his hand to his watch again. He felt as if it were a quarter of an hour since he had looked at it; very well, making just allowance for his state of impatience, he would expect the actual time to be five minutes. He looked; it was only two.

Lord Arglay made a small mental effort, and almost im-mediately recognized the effort. He said to himself: "This is another mark of age. I am losing my sense of duration." He said also: "It is becoming an effort to recognize these changes." Age was certainly quickening its work in him. It approached him now doubly; not only his method of experience, but his awareness of experience was attacked. His knowledge of it comforted him—perhaps, he thought, for the last time. The knowledge would go. He would savour it then while he could. Still looking back at the trees, "It seems I'm decaying," Lord Arglay said aloud. "And that anyhow is one up against decay. Am I procrastinating? I am, and in the circumstances procrastination is a proper and pretty game. It is the thief of time, and quite right too! Why should time have it all its own way?" He turned to the road again, and went on. It passed now between open fields; in all those fields he could see no one. It was pasture, but there were no beasts. There was about him a kind of void, in which he moved, hampered by this growing oppression of duration. Things lasted. He had exclaimed, in his time, against the too swift passage of the world. This was a new experience; it was lastingness—almost, he could have believed, everlastingness. The measure of it was but his breathing, and his breathing, as it grew slower and heavier, would become the measure of everlasting labour—the labour of Sisyphus, who pushed his own slow heart through each infinite moment, and relaxed but to let it beat back and so again begin. It was the first touch of something Arglay had never yet known, of simple and perfect despair.

At that moment he saw the house. The road before him curved sharply, and as he looked he wondered at the sweep of the curve; it seemed to make a full half-circle and so turn back in the direction that he had come. At the farthest point there lay before him, tangentially, another path. The sparse hedge was broken by an opening which was more than footpath and less than road. It was narrow, even when compared with the narrowing way by which he had come, yet hard and beaten as if by the passage of many feet. There had been innumerable travellers, and all solitary, all on foot. No cars or carts could have taken that path; if there had been burdens, they had been carried on the shoulders of their owners. It ran for no long distance, no more than in happier surroundings might have been a garden path from gate to door. There, at the end, was the door.

Arglay, at the time, took all this in but half-consciously. His attention was not on the door but on the chimney. The chimney, in the ordinary phrase, was smoking. It was smoking effectively and continuously. A narrow and dense pillar of dusk poured up from it, through which there glowed every now and then, a deeper undershade of crimson, as if some trapped genius almost thrust itself out of the moving prison that held it. The house itself was not much more than a cottage. There was a door, shut; on the left of it a window, also shut; above, two little attic windows, shut, and covered within by some sort of dark hanging, or perhaps made opaque by smoke that filled the room. There was no sign of life anywhere, and the smoke continued to mount to the lifeless sky. It seemed to Arglay curious that he had not noticed this grey pillar in his approach, that only now when he stood almost in the straight and narrow path leading to the house did it become visible, an exposition of tall darkness reserved to the solitary walkers upon that wearying road.

Lord Arglay was the last person in the world to look for responsibilities. He shunned them by a courteous habit; a responsibility had to present itself with a delicate emphasis before he acceded to it. But when any so impressed itself he was courteous in accepting as in declining; he sought friendship with necessity, and as young lovers call their love fatal, so he turned fatality of life into his love. It seemed to him, as he stood and gazed at the path, the shut door, the smoking chimney, that here perhaps was a responsibility being delicately emphatic. If everyone was out—if the cottage had been left for an hour—ought he to do something? Of course, they might be busy about it within; in which case a thrusting stranger would be inopportune. Another glow of crimson in the pillar of cloud decided him. He went up the path.

As he went he glanced at the little window, but it was bluffed by dirt; he could not very well see whether the panes did or did not hide smoke within. When he was so near the threshold that the window had almost passed out of his vision, he thought he saw a face looking out of it—at the extreme edge, nearest the door—and he checked himself, and went back a step to look again. It had been only along the side of his glance that the face, if face it were, had appeared, a kind of sudden white scrawl against the blur, as if it were a mask hung by the window rather than any living person, or as if the glass of the window itself had looked sideways at him, and he had caught the look without understanding its cause. When he stepped back, he could see no face. Had there been a sun in the sky he would have attributed the apparition to a trick of the light, but in the sky over this smoking house there was no sun. It had shone brightly that morning when he started; it had paled and faded and finally been lost to him as he had passed along his road. There was neither sun nor peering face. He stepped back to the threshold, and knocked with his knuckles on the door.

There was no answer. He knocked again and again waited, and as he stood there he began to feel annoyed. The balance of Lord Arglay's mind had not been achieved without the creation of a considerable counter-energy to the violence of Lord Arglay's natural temper. There had been people whom he had once come very near hating, hating with a fury of selfish rage and detestation; for instance, his brother-in-law. His brother-in-law had not been a nice man; Lord Arglay, as he stood by the door and, for no earthly reason, remembered him, admitted it. He admitted, at the same moment, that no lack of niceness on that other's part could excuse any indulgence of vindictive hate on his own, nor could he think why, then and there, he wanted him, wanted to have him merely to hate. His brother-in-law was dead. Lord Arglay almost regretted it.

Almost he desired to follow, to be with him, to provoke and torment him, to . . .

Lord Arglay struck the door again. "There is," he said to himself, "entire clarity in the Omnipotence." It was his habit of devotion, his means of recalling himself into peace out of the angers, greeds, sloths and perversities that still too often possessed him. It operated; the temptation passed into the benediction of the Omnipotence and disappeared. But there was still no answer from within. Lord Arglay laid his hand on the latch. He swung the door, and, lifting his hat with his other hand, looked into the room—a room empty of smoke as of fire, and of all as of both.

Its size and appearance were those of a rather poor cottage, rather indeed a large brick hut than a cottage. It seemed much smaller within than without. There was a fireplace—at least, there was a place for a fire—on his left. Opposite the door, against the right-hand wall, there was a ramshackle flight of wooden steps, going up to the attics, and at its foot, swinging on a broken hinge, a door which gave a way presumably to a cellar. Vaguely, Arglay found himself surprised; he had not supposed that a dwelling of this sort would have a cellar. Indeed, from where he stood, he could not be certain. It might only be a cupboard. But, unwarrantably, it seemed more, a hinted unseen depth, as if the slow slight movement of the broken wooden door measured that labour of Sisyphus, as if the road ran past him and went coiling spirally into the darkness of the cellar. In the room there was no furniture, neither fragment of paper nor broken bit of wood; there was no sign of life, no flame in the grate nor drift of smoke in the air. It was completely and utterly void.

Lord Arglay looked at it. He went back a few steps and looked up again at the chimney. Undoubtedly the chimney was smoking. It was received into a pillar of smoke; there was no clear point where the dark chimney ended and the dark smoke began. House leaned to roof, roof to chimney, chimney to smoke, and smoke went up for ever and ever over those roads where men crawled infinitely through the smallest measurements of time. Arglay returned to the door, crossed the threshold, and stood in the room. Empty of flame, empty of flame's material, holding within its dank air the very opposite of flame, the chill of ancient years, the room lay round him. Lord Arglay contemplated it. "There's no smoke without fire," he said aloud. "Only apparently there is. Thus one lives and learns. Unless indeed this is the place where one lives without learning."

The phrase, leaving his lips, sounded oddly about the walls and in the corners of the room. He was suddenly revolted by his own chance words—"a place where one lives without learning," where no courtesy or integrity could any more be fined or clarified. The echo daunted him; he made a sharp movement, he took a step aside towards the stairs, and before the movement was complete, was aware of a change. The dank chill became a concentration of dank and deadly heat, pricking at him, entering his nostrils and his mouth. The fantasy of life without knowledge materialized, inimical, in the air, life without knowledge, corrupting life without knowledge, jungle and less than jungle, and though still the walls of the bleak chamber met his eyes, a shell of existence, it seemed that life, withdrawn from all those normal habits of which the useless memory was still drearily sustained by the thin phenomenal fabric, was collecting and corrupting in the atmosphere behind the door he had so rashly passed—outside the other door which swung crookedly at the head of the darker hole within.

He had recoiled from the heat, but not so as to escape it. He had even taken a step or two up the stairs, when he heard from without a soft approach. Light feet were coming up the beaten path to the house. Some other Good Samaritan,

Arglay thought, who would be able to keep his twopence in his pocket. For certainly, whatever was the explanation of all this and wherever it lay, in the attics above or in the pit of the cellar below, responsibility was gone. Lord Arglay did not conceive that either he or anyone else need rush about the country in an anxious effort to preserve a house which no one wanted and no one used. Prematurely enjoying the discussion, he waited. Through the doorway someone came in.

It was, or seemed to be, a man, of ordinary height, wearing some kind of loose dark overcoat that flapped about him. His head was bare; so, astonishingly, were his legs and feet. At first, as he stood just inside the door, leaning greedily forward, his face was invisible, and for a moment Arglay hesitated to speak. Then the stranger lifted his face and Arglay uttered a sound. It was emaciated beyond imagination; it was astonishing, at the appalling degree of hunger revealed, that the man could walk or move at all, or even stand as he was now doing, and turn that dreadful skull from side to side. Arglay came down the steps of the stair in one jump; he cried out again, he ran forward, and as he did so the deep burning eyes in the turning face of bone met his full and halted him. They did not see him, or if they saw did not notice; they gazed at him and moved on. Once only in his life had Arglay seen eyes remotely like those; once, when he had pronounced the death-sentence upon a wretched man who had broken under the long strain of his trial and filled the court with shrieks. Madness had glared at Lord Arglay from that dock, but at least it had looked at him and seen him; these eyes did not. They sought something—food, life, or perhaps only a form and something to hate, and in that energy the stranger moved. He began to run round the room. The bones that were his legs and feet jerked up and down. The head turned from side to side. He ran circularly, round and again round, crossing and recrossing, looking up, down, around, and at last, right in the centre of the room, coming to a halt, where, as if some terrible pain of starvation gripped him, he bent and twisted downward until he squatted grotesquely on the floor. There, squatting and bending, he lowered his head and raised his arm, and as the fantastic black coat slipped back, Arglay saw a wrist, saw it marked with scars. He did not at first think what they were; only when the face and wrist of the figure swaying in its pain came together did he suddenly know. They were teeth-marks; they were bites; the mouth closed on the wrist and gnawed. Arglay cried out and sprang forward, catching the arm, trying to press it down, catching the other shoulder, trying to press it back. He achieved nothing. He held, he felt, he grasped; he could not control. The long limb remained raised, the fierce teeth gnawed. But as Arglay bent, he was aware once more of that effluvia of heat risen round him, and breaking out with the more violence when suddenly the man, if it were man, cast his arm away, and with a jerk of movement rose once more to his feet. His eyes, as the head went back, burned close into Arglay's, who, what with the heat, the eyes, and his sickness at the horror, shut his own against them, and was at the same moment thrown from his balance by the rising form, and sent staggering a step or two away, with upon his face the sensation of a light hot breath, so light that only in the utter stillness of time could it be felt, so hot that it might have been the inner fire from which the pillar of smoke poured outward to the world.

He recovered his balance; he opened his eyes; both motions brought him into a new corner of that world. The odd black coat the thing had worn had disappeared, as if it had been a covering imagined by a habit of mind. The thing itself, a wasted flicker of pallid movement, danced and gyrated in white flame before him. Arglay saw it still, but only now as a dreamer may hear, half-asleep and half-awake, the sound of dogs barking or the crackling of fire in his very room. For he opened his eyes not to such things, but to the thing that on the threshold of this place, some seconds earlier or some years, he had felt and been pleased to feel, to the reality of his hate. It came in a rush within him, a fountain of fire, and without and about him images of the man he hated swept in a thick cloud of burning smoke. The smoke burned his eyes and choked his mouth; he clutched it, at images within it—at his greedy loves and greedy hates—at the cloud of the sin of his life, yearning to catch but one image and renew again the concentration for which he yearned. He could not. The smoke blinded and stifled him, yet more than stifling or blinding was the hunger for one true thing to lust or hate. He was starving in the smoke, and all the hut was full of smoke, for the hut and the world were smoke, pouring up round him, from him and all like him—a thing once wholly, and still a little, made visible to his corporeal eyes in forms which they recognized, but in itself of another nature. He swung and twisted and crouched. His limbs ached from long wrestling with the smoke, for as the journey to this place had prolonged itself infinitely, so now, though he had no thought of measurement, the clutch of his hands and the growing sickness that invaded him struck through him the sensation of the passage of years and the knowledge of the passage of moments. The fire sank within him, and the sickness grew, but the change could not bring him nearer to any end. The end here was not at the end, but in the beginning. There was no end to this smoke, to this fever and this chill, to crouching and rising and searching, unless the end was now. Now—now was the only possible other fact, chance, act. He cried out, defying infinity, "Now!"

Before his voice the smoke of his prison yielded, and yielded two ways at once. From where he stood he could see in one place an alteration in that perpetual grey, an alternate darkening and lightening as if two ways, of descent and ascent, met. There was, he remembered, a way in, therefore a path out; he had only to walk along it. But also there was a way still farther in, and he could walk along that. Two doors had swung, to his outer senses, in that small room. From every gate of hell there was a way to heaven, yes, and in every way to heaven there was a gate to deeper hell.

Yet for a moment he hesitated. There was no sign of the phenomenon by which he had discerned the passage of that other spirit. He desired—very strongly he desired—to be of use to it. He desired to offer himself to it, to make a ladder of himself, if that should be desired, by which it might perhaps mount from the nature of the lost, from the dereliction of all minds that refuse living and learning, postponement and irony, whose dwelling is necessarily in their undying and perishing selves. Slowly, unconsciously, he moved his head as if to seek his neighbour.

He saw, at first he felt, nothing. His eyes returned to that vibrating oblong of an imagined door, the heart of the smoke beating in the smoke. He looked at it; he remembered the way; he was on the point of movement, when the stinging heat struck him again, but this time from behind. It leapt through him; he was seized in it and loosed from it; its rush abandoned him. The torrent of its fiery passage struck the darkening hollow in the walls. At the instant that it struck, there came a small sound; there floated up a thin shrill pipe, too short to hear, too certain to miss, faint and quick as from some single insect in the hedge-row or the field, and yet more than single—a weak wail of multitudes of the lost. The shrill lament struck his ears, and he ran. He cried as he sprang: "Now is God: now is glory in God," and as the dark door swung before him it was the threshold of the house that received his flying feet. As he passed, another form slipped by him, slinking hastily into the house, another of the hordes going so swiftly up that straight way, hard with everlasting time; each driven by his own hunger, and each alone. The vision, a face looking in as a face had looked out, was gone. Running still, but more lightly now, and with some communion of peace at heart, Arglay came into the curving road. The trees were all about him; the house was at their heart. He ran on through them; beyond, he saw, he reached, the spring day and the sun. At a little distance a motor bus, gaudy within and without, was coming down the road. The driver saw him. Lord Arglay instinctively made a sign, ran, mounted. As he sat down, breathless and shaken, "*E quindi uscimmo,*" his mind said, "*a riveder le stelle.*"[1]

---

1 "And thence we came forth to gaze upon the stars again . . ." Last line of Dante's *Inferno.*

THE GRIMOIRE

by Montague Summers

The snare is laid for him in the ground,
and a trap for him in the way.
Terrors shall make him afraid on every side.

"ANYTHING in my line today, Merritt?"

The bookseller, a spare, spectacled old man, looked up quickly from "The Clique" which he was studying, blue pencil in hand, at his desk, and shot forward his scraggy neck not unlike the protruding head of some ancient tortoise, to peer hesitatingly through the half-gloom of his little shop. Even on this sunny afternoon it was not an over-light place, but shadowy and full of those dark nooks and mysterious corners stacked with bundles of dusty tomes such as the adventurer in old bookshops loves, where one hopes to find at last that uncut quarto play by D'Urfey, that elusive eighteenth-century pamphlet, or that novel of Eliza Haywood's for which one has been searching so patiently and so long.

"Good afternoon, sir. Why, yes, I have got something put aside for you. Only came in yesterday. I was posting you a card this evening about it."

"Lucky I looked in, for I shouldn't have had time to call tomorrow as I'm off to Silchester for ten days or a fortnight. Let's see it."

Mr. Merritt gingerly lowering himself from the high office-stool upon which he was perched, shambled towards a small glass-fronted Chippendale bookcase at the back of the shop. Taking a ring of labelled keys from his pocket he unlocked the door, and selected from among the array of morocco and calf-gilt bindings a podgy octavo vellum volume.

"There you are, sir."

"Not another Bodin, I hope, or one of the later editions of the *Malleus* . . . ah, I see," and the speaker did indeed see that he was handling something altogether uncommon and rare, since in spite of the fact that he had been a collector of books on alchemy, witchcraft and the occult sciences generally for a good many years he could not recollect ever before having come across the treatise whose title-page he was now scanning with such eager attention. Nor was it a work he would have been likely to forget. *Mysterium Arcanum, seu de daemonibus rite evocandis cum quibusdam aliis secretis abditissimis*, Romae, sine permissu superiorum. '*The Secret Mystery, or the Art of Evoking Evil Spirits with certain other Most Curious and Close Matters*, printed at Rome—that's fudge—no date, without the permission of the authorities. Well, whoever the writer was and I can't place him for the moment, he had a sense of humour at any rate. Early seventeenth-century printing I should guess. And the contents—they sound appetizing enough, but it may only be a hash-up of the Petit Albert and that wretched Pope Honorius."

"As you say, sir. You know more about that sort of thing than I do. Anyhow, I think it's a scarce item, and I've had a good many of these books through my hands in the past five-and-twenty years. Yet it's the first time I've seen that one."

"What date do you give it, Merritt?"

The bookseller took up the *Mysterium*, and moving to the door for a better light, held it within a few inches of his nose, blinking uncertainly. "To tell the truth, sir, I haven't examined it closely. As soon as I saw it, I said to myself, 'Now that's a bit for Dr. Hodsoll. Dr. Hodsoll will take that book.' And so I snapped it up sharp."

"And how much do you propose to stick Dr. Hodsoll for it, eh?"

Mr. Merritt, his head slightly inclined to one side, regarded the book for a minute in silence. "Ah, if you're asking me for a figure, Doctor, I am telling you that I should catalogue this item at six guineas, not a penny less. But I am going to let you have it for five."

Dr. Hodsoll and Mr. Merritt were old friends, but a histrionic palaver seemed called for by the occasion.

"Come," said Hodsoll, turning over the leaves carelessly, 'here we have a book with no date and a sham imprint, which is very probably as I've just said not much more than an adaptation of Solomon's Clavicule"—and as he spoke he lied and he knew that he lied, but such are the ways of collectors—"and you are going to ask me five pounds for it. Pooh!"

"Five guineas, sir, guineas."

"That's worse. Hang it all, Merritt, it's buying a pig in a poke."

"Well, sir, if you don't think it's worth that to you . . . but I made sure you'd like it for your collection, that is supposing you already haven't a copy. I shan't keep it long, anyhow. I expect Mr. Spicer will be interested," and the wily old man made as if to return the little volume to its shelf.

At the mention of his rival's name, Dr. Hodsoll bristled like a porcupine, and quickly put out a restraining hand. "Here, not so quick, Merritt," he cried, "let's have another peep at it first."

A very cursory glance sufficed. Five notes and two half-crowns exchanged hands, and whilst a neat parcel was being made, Dr. Hodsoll queried: "Look here, Merritt, you said it only came in yesterday, didn't you? Have you any objection to my asking where it came from?"

"Not the slightest, sir, only I'm afraid I can't tell you much. A young fellow, quite a stranger to me, brought it in, just before closing time, and asked me what I'd give for it there and then. So I bought it over the counter, as you may say."

"Ah! Well, I only wondered. No question it's an out-of-the-way book."

"Shall we send it round, sir? You shall have it within the next half-hour."

"No, I can carry it. I'm going straight home. I'll take it with me."

As a matter of fact, Dr. Hodsoll did not go straight home, for less than a couple of hundred yards from the book-shop he was buttonholed by a bore of the first water, from whom he could not escape without a promise of lunch at an early date. The delay caused him to fall straight into the arms of Miss Matty Davies, whom he must needs squire to her garden gate—it was not so very far out of his way, as she remarked, and she was sure he would be interested to know about the doings and mis-doings of her new maid. "Ah, once servants were servants," she said, with a shake of her crisp, grey curls, "and now——!"

The result was that by the time he put his latch-key in his own front door the clock of St. Matthew's at the corner of the road had struck half-past six some minutes before, and simultaneously with his entrance there appeared in the hall the excellent Burkitt, who ministered so admirably to his creature comforts and who was (be it whispered) a little bit of a tyrant in his way, to remind his master that he was dining at a house three miles distant and it behoved him not to loiter in the study over his letters and paper if he intended to be anything like punctual. In consequence the new purchase had to be put on the table, and Dr. Hodsoll dared not trust himself to open it before he went up to dress. He left it, however, with a promise to do something more than dip into it on his return before he went to sleep, a promise that was never fulfilled since the dinner was longer and more formal, the company larger, and he got back considerably later than he had expected, feeling not a little tired and very ready for bed.

The next morning Dr. Hodsoll proved quite unable to do such ample justice as his wont, in fact to do justice at all, to the tempting breakfast Mrs. Burkitt sent up from her well-ordered kitchen. He turned aside from kidneys and bacon, York ham and new-laid eggs alike, only able to manage a little dry toast with his tea. He had passed a restless and disturbed night, which left him curiously inert and depressed. He was a sound sleeper—he used to boast that he fell asleep as soon as his head touched the pillow and that he never knew anything more until eight o'clock next morning—yet not only had he tossed and turned and counted numberless sheep quite unavailingly, but when he did doze off he dreamed, and his dreams were of a singularly unpleasant nature. True they partook of that seemingly incoherent nature which appears a general characteristic of dreams, and he had, as is not infrequent, a very vague and confused memory of them upon waking, but in each there was the recurrent figure of a man, the same man, who in some way persisted and returned quite clearly every time he had closed his eyes. The man was an ordinary figure enough—he had never been able to catch sight of his face—but in some way he realized that this visitant was evil and wished him ill. The curious part was that the man seemed to be loitering up and down the corridor outside his bedroom and on the landing beyond. He had even stood outside the door with his ear bent to the keyhole listening to what was going on within. In fact, once this seemed so vivid that waking with a start Dr. Hodsoll had switched on the light, and jumping out of bed unbolted the door and flung it wide open. Of course there was nobody there, and he got back again conscious that he was more than a trifle ashamed of himself.

As he drank his last cup of tea—he was feeling particularly thirsty—and gazed out on to his gay flower-beds and smooth green lawn he passed in review his dietary of the day and particularly of the evening before, but he was unable to accuse himself of any especial indiscretion. A plain and careful liver, last night he had pointedly eschewed that rich-looking trifle with the avalanche of cream spangled with hundreds and thousands and chosen the more wholesome apples and rice. He had taken sole rather than the lobster cutlets, and avoided the mushroom savoury. No, he had nothing then with which to reproach himself. Perhaps he was ailing for something. If so Canon Spenlow wouldn't want an invalid in his house. Dr. Hodsoll crossed to a mirror and gravely examined his tongue. That looked all right at all events. Should he ring up little Dillon, and be overhauled before he went? (I should explain that Julian Hodsoll was a Doctor of Literature and not a physician). Just because he had happened to have had a bad night! It would never do to get so old-womanish. What could it be but indigestion? He had no headache, and no temperature. It was only this stupid laziness. Perhaps he had been overdoing it a bit lately. Well, at Silchester he would take a regular holiday, and slack. It was a soothing, restful place. The Canon was a model host, too, he let one do just as one liked so long as one attended a couple of services on Sunday. Of course that always became rather a bore, but then the music at the Cathedral was invariably first-rate. Why, to please the old fellow he wouldn't mind turning up two or three times on week-days during his visit. Ten o'clock or ten-thirty, he forgot which. It was worth it. Undoubtedly Silchester would do him all the good in the world.

Canon Spenlow, the only son of a wealthy Birmingham manufacturer (long since deceased), although a bachelor, kept up a large and rather old-fashioned household. Of extremely conservative views, he belonged to what was once known as the "high and dry school" of thought, and was altogether an entirely correct and proper old gentleman, who profoundly distrusted both innovations or enthusiasms of any kind. The narrowness of his intellectual outlook was to a large extent modified, it is true, by his love of books and a keen interest in ecclesiastical archaeology, and it was at a meeting of a learned Society some years before that he had first met Dr. Hodsoll, to find that although he strongly disapproved of the laxity, not to say the scepticism, of his new friend's opinions, they had many tastes and pursuits in common. An invitation to Silchester resulted, since when several visits had been exchanged. The acquaintanceship was in one sense per-force rather one-sided, for Dr. Hodsoll could not very well enter into and indeed had small sympathy with the Canon's most intimate convictions, but he was both tactful and shrewd, and with the interests they had in common their talk of books, their cult of antiquity, they did very well.

It was rather late on an afternoon towards the end of April that Dr. Hodsoll's taxi turned into Silchester Close, and as he looked out of his window he saw with great satisfaction and content the large, square, red-brick house, built by some old churchman in the reign of the second James, and mellowed to an august beauty during the passage of years. The westering sun was brightly reflected in the many tall and narrow windows, whose little panes twinkled like very diamonds. The calm nobility and stateliness of the frontage pleased and soothed him, as did the gates of elaborate iron scroll work, the broad smooth path of yellow gravel beyond, sweeping round the velvety grass with its close and sombre shrubberies until it ended in a wide oval at the foot of the imposing flight of steps that led up to the great double door.

His friend welcomed him with evident pleasure, and after an elaborately planned and served dinner—for Canon Spenlow would bate no jot of his punctiliousness because they were only two at table, and both butler and footman were required to be in attendance—they settled down to a long and chatty evening in the library, a room of magnificent proportions lined from floor to ceiling with books. Here the latest treasures had to be exhibited and commented upon and admired. The bright fire blazing merrily away was grateful on the spring night; the arm-chairs were comfortable, neither too luxurious, nor too small; the port was of the finest vintage; the Canon had acquired some genuine rarities, including several incunabula; the topics of conversation were many and varied. Midnight struck as the host was taking down yet another recent treasure trove from his shelves. "Oh! Dear me!" he exclaimed, "twelve o'clock already. Who would have thought it? But I mustn't be inconsiderate, my dear Hodsoll, and keep you from your bed. Because I'm a late sitter it doesn't follow that you are. One last glass of port? No? A brandy and soda, then? Nothing more? Ah, well, perhaps you are wise. And I think we'll be turning in. If I may say so, you are not look-ing quite so robust as I've seen you, and perhaps I've been to blame in detaining you so late as it is."

"Not at all, Canon, not at all. Truth to tell I had rather a restless night last night, and I shouldn't be speaking honestly if I were to say that I didn't feel a trifle tired after my journey."

"Travel by train is always fatiguing, I think. And personally I've never found myself able to prefer a car. But if you are not thoroughly rested tomorrow morning, take your breakfast in bed, I beg. You only have to ring or tell the servant who calls you. Perhaps you would rather not be called until a somewhat later hour?"

"No, no. I couldn't think of disturbing your arrangements. Breakfast in bed I particularly dislike. If I'm not well enough to get up, I'm not well enough to eat any breakfast. It is like your kindness to suggest it, but believe me there's not the slightest occasion for anything of the sort."

"You'll join me at breakfast at nine-thirty then? Good. You shall be called at eight-thirty. Myself, I am celebrating the Eucharist at eight o'clock, and I hardly suppose I shall have returned from the Cathedral much before nine. Good-night, and good sound sleep."

"Good-night, Canon."

When Canon Spenlow came back from the Cathedral after his celebration in the Lady Chapel he found Dr. Hodsoll walking in the garden "to clear his pipes" as Sir Roger has it, breathing the air in great lung-fulls, and watching the rooks circling about the old grey towers that pierced the somewhat watery blue, across which raced a cavalcade of fleecy white clouds. After the usual matutinal greetings and inquiries the cleric congratulated his guest with "I declare the change has done you good already.'

"I'm inclined to think it has," was the sanguine reply, "certainly your cloister air is an admirable sedative. I never felt better in my life."

The morning post brought the Canon a budget of correspondence and several book-catalogues, and as Dr. Hodsoll was indulging his bad habit of dipping into *The Times* at table, the two men exchanged only a few remarks during breakfast until towards the end of the meal when the Canon, who had been glancing through a letter with an Italian stamp and postmark, looked up and said, "I hope you don't mind, Hodsoll, beyond a dinner with the Dean, who wouldn't take a refusal, I've not made any social engagements during your visit."

"Nothing could suit me better, Canon. I am looking forward for one thing to going through some of those books again which you showed me last night. I should like to make a note or two, for example, on that early edition of Condrochius, and I'm not so well acquainted with Pordage and Jane Lead as I hope to be after a day or two in your library, for I see you have the *Mystic Divinite* and *A Fountain of Gardens* on your shelves."

"Quaint old mystics both," the Canon smiled. "But it all fits in very well, because most mornings when I get back from Mattins, I am generally busy in the library until lunch, and I know that's the time you prefer for your stroll round Silchester. I take my constitutional in the afternoon, and you can have the library entirely to yourself and browse among your visionaries as long as you please. However, I was going to say that one reason why I have declined invitations during the next few days is owing to another guest of mine who will join us on Monday. I have just had a letter," holding up the thin foreign envelope, "from him to that effect."

"Indeed? Is it anyone whom I know?"

"Not as yet. But it is someone whom, if I mistake not, you will be very interested to meet. A Dominican friar. You are surprised," for Dr. Hodsoll had indeed looked up wonderingly, "but when I was in Rome last year Father Raphael Grant showed me several kindnesses, and opened doors for me which would otherwise most certainly have remained shut. He is a very able historian, and naturally he is keenly interested in the annals of his own particular order. When I told him of the cartularies and the manuscript missal which at the Dissolution passed from the Blackfriars here to the Cathedral Library—you will remember, no doubt, that they were only discovered, or to speak more precisely, recognized a few years ago, I had an article upon them, which you may have read, in the *Ecclesiastical Review*—he expressed himself as extremely desirous of examining them in detail, and then of course there are the other codices and registers. I can be of some assistance to him there, I am glad to say, and although he is only able to spare a very few days it will be far more convenient for him to be staying here than it would be if he had to go among strangers."

"I am sure I shall very much look forward to meeting him," rejoined Hodsoll. "When do you expect your guest?"

"On Monday, so his letter says," answered the Canon. "You will find him a very intellectual, and I think I may quite safely add a very charming companion."

The morning passed pleasantly enough, but without incident. Dr. Hodsoll strolled rather aimlessly through the narrow streets and cobbled winds (as they are locally called) of the city; he renewed his acquaintance with the old Buttermarket and Sorrowing Cross; drew blank at a couple of book-shops; peeped into St. Bennet, Eastgate and St. Mildred's, shuddering at the garish magenta and gamboge window with which some pious mayor of the late Victorian seventies had outraged the latter; exchanged a word or two with the curator of the Museum; and made his way through the shadowy aisles of the Cathedral back to lunch.

Then followed two hours of unalloyed bliss in the library, where about four o'clock the Canon joined him for a cup of tea. The conversation, as we may suppose, was of books, and books, and books again.

"Yes, I acknowledge I have had one or two quite lucky finds lately," said Canon Spenlow, "but on the other, hand I had to give its full price for that Tacitus, and a good deal more than its full price for the *Don Quixote*. But what of yourself, Hodsoll, haven't you come across anything special recently? I always say I never knew a man who had the knack of picking up what he wanted in the same way as you manage to hunt your quarry down. And while the rest of us are giving preposterous figures and rummaging and ferreting you just go round the corner, and hey presto! There it is."

Dr. Hodsoll laughed as he knocked out his pipe, and replied: "I'm afraid you exaggerate, Canon. Whatever may have been the case years ago, it's all different today. Not a bargain to be had! Even Merritt's prices are soaring. Only a couple of days ago he asked me five guineas for a book—and got it. By the way, I should like to show it to you, and perhaps you could help me to trace it. It's something of an oddity. I've brought it with me, and it won't take a minute to fetch it."

No sooner said than done, and Hodsoll handed the Canon the little parcel intact just as he had received it over Merritt's counter. "There you are," he said, "I haven't even had time to look through it carefully. Open it, and see if you can tell me anything about the book."

The Canon unknotted the string with some precision and tidily folded the paper before he turned to the title-page of the podgy vellum octavo. He stared, took off his glasses and carefully wiped them before proceeding to a second inspection. "Extraordinary!" he exclaimed. "That's highly interesting. Can it be some sort of a joke? A polemic? A burlesque?"

"Oh, no. I hardly think so. At any rate, it doesn't extend farther than the imprint. The writer was in deadly earnest, I feel sure."

"Ah! so it seems." As Canon Spenlow turned the pages, scanning a paragraph here and there a heavy frown gathered upon his brow. "God bless my soul! Why, wherever did you get this thing?"

"From Merritt, as I told you. He bought it from a casual seller, and I bought it from him the very next day. Have you ever seen a copy before?"

"No, and God forbid I should ever see a copy again." The old man shut the book sharply, and slapped it down on a table with the utmost distaste. "Have you examined it, have you read it, Hodsoll?"

"No, not yet. I am looking forward——"

"Then take my advice and forgive me for speaking frankly. Put it behind the fire. Nay, I am certain you will do so when you read it."

Dr. Hodsoll stood petrified. "Put it behind the fire! Why, it may be unique. At any rate, I'm sure it's of the last rarity."

"Thank God for that. I am quite serious. Never have I seen in print such filth, such appalling blasphemy."

"Oh, I know some of these demonologists are a trifle strong, but——"

"It's not a question of being a trifle strong. Read, man, read for yourself." The Canon was deeply moved.

In some surprise Hodsoll took up the offending volume to discover the cause of so unexpected an outburst. Nor had he long to search. The very page to which he turned seemed to be some kind of liturgical ceremony, there were prayers addressed to the powers of darkness in terms of hideous profanity and rubrics of the most crapulous obscenity. What a blunder to have shown that to Canon Spenlow! He must be diplomatic and smooth the old fellow down.

"Whew!" he ejaculated, "that's pretty bad. I assure you, Canon, I had no idea there was anything like this. I'm sorry. Yet as a matter of curiosity, or rather from a bibliographical point of view, I think one ought to set on record a full description of this fellow, lewd and degraded as he is."

"Personally I should burn it here and now," retorted the Canon. "But, of course, it's not my property. It's an evil book."

"I shall certainly follow your advice. Yet I think it would be a mistake not to have a memorandum of it, and perhaps a photograph of the title-page which, you must admit, is singular."

Canon Spenlow made an impatient noise, and, pointing a long lean finger, quoted vigorously: "Many of them also which used curious arts brought their books together, and burned them before all men: and they counted the price of them, and found it fifty thousand pieces of silver."

These were regions into which Dr. Hodsoll was quite unable to follow his friend, and he therefore contented himself with a murmured "Quite," which he felt none the less to be inappropriate and inconclusive.

At that moment there came a not unwelcome interruption in the shape of the butler with a note for his master, a missive

which required an immediate answer, and Hodsoll, hastily
gathering up his book lest it should be seized for a holocaust,
was glad to escape to the fastness of his bedroom where, bolt-
ing the door behind him, he sank into an arm-chair, feeling
breathless and flurried.

"Phew!" he exclaimed, mopping his brow with his handkerchief, "whoever could have supposed that the old chap
would flare up like that! It's just it, you never know with these
religious folk where you are going to have 'em. And now let's
see what all the bother's about."

He was soon obliged to confess that the contents of the
Mysterium Arcanum were sufficiently startling. There were a
number of charms, a few to constrain love, others to compel
hate, and some with a yet more definitely atrocious aim, "*ca-
pitis damnatio*", the "death warrants", they were termed. There
were receipts for poison, and philters of the foulest ingredients. Next followed evocations of demons, cantrips and spells,
and three sections entitled respectively "the way of Cain", "the
error of Balaam", and "the gainsaying of Core". There were
litanies addressed to the fallen archangel as the patron of every
licence and abomination. There were prayers to the powers
of the pit *ante et post missam*, and a rubric which set Hodsoll
wondering, *missam autem quaere apud Missale Nigrum* (the
Mass itself will be found in the Black Missal).

Could it be that the mysterious book of the witches had
fallen into his hands, that volume which was mentioned in
more than one trial of the seventeenth century, but which
apparently had never been seen by any who was not a member of that horrid society? The *Mysterium Arcanum* showed at
any rate the signs of constant use. In the margins, here and
there, an old hand had jotted various notes and drawn strange
cabalistic signs. And to his delight he saw that a blank page at
the end was covered with fine close writing headed *Evocatio
efficacissima*, a most Powerful and Efficacious Evocation.

"Crabbed, contracted Latin! Well, I suppose I shall have to transcribe this at length, and the sooner I do it the better." Uncapping his fountain pen, and taking a quire of quarto paper from his case, Dr. Hodsoll set to work, and before long had written out in full the impious and unhallowed charm. In order to check it carefully and make sure he had omitted no word nor syllable, he then read it through sentence by sentence softly to himself.

There came a light tap at the door, and he actually started. "The servant with hot water. How time flies! I must change at once." Hastily shuffling the book and his manuscript under a sheet of blotting-paper, he called over his shoulder, "Come in."

"You wanted me, sir," said a low voice.

Dr. Hodsoll turned and saw that there had entered the room and was standing waiting his orders a tall young man with the impassive features and formal bearing of the well-trained servant. He was dressed, not in livery, but in a smartly-cut black suit, and seemed the very pattern of a gentleman's valet. At the same time there was something foreign in his appearance, which was perhaps due to his large dark eyes, full of infinite sadness and a yearning regret, and the extreme pallor of his countenance.

"Another valet of the Canon's," thought Hodsoll. "Really he has more servants just to look after himself than would be needed to wait on a family. But I suppose he entertains a good deal in this large house." Then aloud, "No, thanks, I didn't ring. I need nothing until my hot water comes."

"I beg your pardon, sir, I thought you wanted me," and the servant withdrew.

Dr. Hodsoll, reflecting that the Canon would not care for the *Mysterium* to be left about, although certainly none of the household could read Latin, and the book was quite safe unless indeed from a conscientious scruple his host purloined and destroyed it, locked it away in a suit-case. He was glad he had done so, for as he went downstairs he noticed the valet loitering in the passage not far from his door, and in these days of universal education who knows, he asked himself, whether this chap hasn't taken a course in classics and reads Horace or Livy in the servants' hall.

The Canon, he was relieved to find, made no allusion either covert or direct to the *Mysterium*, and the evening passed tranquilly, closing however at a rather earlier hour in view of the morrow being a Sunday. Upon entering his bedroom and switching on the light Hodsoll was surprised and a little annoyed to find the valet awaiting him.

"What do you want?" he asked rather abruptly.

"I was waiting for you, sir," was the reply in perfectly courteous and even deferential tones. "What can I do for you?"

"Nothing at all," answered Hodsoll. "I will ring if I require anything more." The man bowed, and left the room quietly, yet Hodsoll had the curious impression that he caught an extremely ugly look just as he was going out. "What on earth's the matter with the fellow?" he asked himself. "Is he afraid he won't get a tip when I leave. And he certainly won't if he bothers me like this. Ugh! I'm beginning to hate the sight of him," and he unbuttoned his waistcoat impatiently. "Why, he must have been up here in the dark, because the light certainly wasn't burning until I turned it on. Well, that's odd."

The next morning Canon Spenlow noticed that his guest was looking far from well, but an inquiry only elicited the information that he had passed a restless night, and as he saw that further questioning began to irritate he refrained from pressing the matter. He was somewhat agreeably surprised, however, to find that Dr. Hodsoll would not listen to his suggestion of staying away from the Morning Service at the Cathedral. In fact, he showed himself eager to attend, and at the luncheon table he spoke with a show of sympathy and understanding which he had never expressed before of the comfort and consolation those who hold the Christian faith derive from common worship and the beauty of an ordered liturgy.

That afternoon, the Canon being otherwise engaged, Dr. Hodsoll, when Evensong was over, decided to take a stroll through the meadows which lined the river's bank. Although unenclosed, these had for the extent of nearly half a mile been turned into a public garden from which one passed almost insensibly into the open country and lanes which lay beyond. There were seats, and thick hedges which formed a kind of natural wall, and although just about tea-time on a Sunday afternoon the meadows were almost empty, later in the evening when dusk began to fall and the stars crept out they would be dotted with trysting couples, since the Meads had for generations been the recognized rendezvous of every Silchester lass who was "walking out" with her young man.

Feeling tired, after a few turns Dr. Hodsoll sat down upon a bench which had been placed in a natural arbour, facing the view which for all its familiarity never lost its charm—the old huddled roofs of the city, the Cathedral towers, the sedgy banks with the stream gently flowing between. He had not been seated many minutes when he felt a sense of extreme uneasiness and disquiet; he shuddered violently as though some horrible thing was near and, as he afterwards declared, he was filled with the apprehension that a wild beast lurked in ambush ready to leap out and tear him piecemeal. In vain he tried to concentrate his thoughts on other things, books, a monograph he was contemplating, a forthcoming visit to Buxton, to call common sense to his aid. At last unable to endure the tension longer he jumped to his feet almost to ward off a blow, and as he half-turned he saw staring at him through the bushes with an expression so evil and malevolent that even now the very memory has cost him more than one sleepless night, a dead-white face in which the great dark eyes blazed like hot coals of fire. The face was instantly withdrawn. In fact, it vanished so swiftly that if he had not recognized it he might have believed it was mere imagination, a trick and play of light and shadow among the leaves. He returned to the house considerably shaken, and then, I think, that he must first have suspected who the servant was.

The next incident which seems worthy of record took place about ten o'clock that same evening when without so much as a preliminary knock or a word of warning the door of the housekeeper's room burst open, and Lucy Parkins, the Canon's upper housemaid, rushed in and almost collapsed at Mrs. Bailey's feet. That extremely correct and punctilious lady, who was reading her Chapter before the fire and sipping a glass of mulled claret preparatory to retiring to bed, arose stately from her chair, every fold of her black satin dress rustling in stern displeasure. "What can be the meaning of this, Parkins?" she began in freezing tones. "Have you taken leave of your senses?" and then, for she saw that the girl was white with terror and sobbing hysterically, she added more quickly, "What is it, you stupid girl, what has happened?"

"Oh, Mrs. Bailey, ma'am," exclaimed Parkins, "I am so frightened. I don't know what to do. Indeed I don't."

"Frightened? Shut that door at once, and tell me all about it." Then seeing the girl was shaking and shivering, Mrs. Bailey closed the door, and pushed her into a chair. From her own private cupboard she administered a small glass of brandy, and when she saw the colour coming back into her cheeks, she sharply commanded: "Stop that yammering now and tell me what's frightened you."

The upshot of Parkins' story was that she had come in at ten o'clock as usual after her Sunday evening out, and in the passage leading to the kitchen a strange man had brushed by her and looked at her horribly, he was just horrible, as she expressed it, and she had felt so terrified that she made for the shelter of Mrs. Bailey's room as a haven of safety. No amount of questioning and cross-examination on the housekeeper's part could shake her story.

"It's all those silly films. Wicked, I call it, allowing those places to be open on a Sunday night and filling the girls' and the young men's heads with trash, as though there wasn't enough badness in the world already," indignantly declared the ruffled matron, somewhat more perturbed and puzzled than she cared to admit, for Lucy Parkins had always been a most staid and sensible worker. It transpired too that so far from having spent the evening at the cinema, she had been to supper at the house of her uncle, a small shopkeeper of eminent respectability. Eventually Mr. Watson, the butler, was summoned from his pantry to hear the tale, and although evidently not believing in Parkins' strange man, he undertook to go round the lower regions of the house to make sure all windows were closed and that no burglar was lurking in a cupboard or behind a door to issue forth in the night and cut all their throats. A clean bill of safety being returned, Parkins was dismissed to her bedroom, which was fortunately shared by the second maid, "for sleep in the room alone tonight, I would not, no, not if anyone was to pay me thousands," she pathetically declared.

"Now, stop that nonsense, and get to bed, you want a good night's rest, Lucy," was Mr. Watson's unsympathetic reply.

"All the same it's funny, I must say, Mr. Watson," remarked Mrs. Bailey, gazing after the departing Parkins, "I've never known her took like this before, and she's a good worker too."

"Bilious, Mrs. Bailey, bilious. That's what it is, depend upon it."

"Well, I hope to goodness we're not going to have her in bed tomorrow, with this new gentleman coming, and all. I half wish I'd made her take a dose of salts or a pill."

Had Dr. Hodsoll confided his suspicions to Canon Spenlow I am of opinion that his story would have been received with a far greater understanding and sympathy than he imagined, but the fact remains that fearing to look a fool, he chose rather to suffer, and there can be no doubt that he suffered very acutely on that Sunday night. Although actually the servant did not re-appear—he believed he caught a glimpse of him once, a shadowy figure, at the end of a corridor—he felt that he was being closely watched and that if he was off his guard for a moment, there would come a pounce. That the Canon guessed something was amiss is evident from the reluctance with which Hodsoll said good-night, and the earnestness with which he asked for his friend's prayers.

The next morning in the course of his walk round Silchester, Dr. Hodsoll turned into the Adam and Eve, the oldest hostelry in the city and one much frequented and admired by tourists. He drank no less than four glasses of their famous brown sherry, but the waiter remarked that although at first he seemed inclined to loiter he left very abruptly upon the entrance of another customer, and what was more curious the newcomer seemed to have followed him out immediately. Perhaps he had come there to seek him, at any rate he did not wait to be served.

The rest of the morning Dr. Hodsoll spent in the Cathedral. Father Raphael Grant to whom he was introduced at the luncheon-table did not at all fulfil his idea of a Dominican. True he was dressed in a white habit with leathern girdle and black scapular, and a rosary hung at his side. But he had neither the commanding stature nor proud port of an Inquisitor. His face was not emaciated and thin, burning with the fanatic fires of a Savonarola. It was in fact rather round and fresh-coloured, whilst his eyes twinkled humourously behind his gold-rimmed glasses. He was merely a courtly, extremely well-informed English gentleman who for some reason of his own chose to wear a picturesque and mediaeval attire.

The talk which at first naturally turned upon the treasures of Silchester Cathedral and the manuscripts Father Raphael particularly wished to collate, soon began to range over the whole field of literature and it was evident that the friar had worked in most of the big European libraries.

"By the way, Hodsoll," remarked Canon Spenlow, towards the end of the meal, "I took the liberty of mentioning to Father Raphael that very extraordinary little book you picked up recently and which you showed me the other day. He is very anxious to see it, and I'm sure you will have no objection to letting us examine it."

"Oh, no, naturally, not at all," Hodsoll was conscious that he had blushed guiltily and was almost betrayed into a stammer, "I shall be most pleased to show it to you. Certainly, yes. Only . . . or . . . I ought perhaps to warn Father Raphael . . . to say . . . that is, I . . ."

"You are afraid, Dr. Hodsoll, that it will be something of a shock?" asked Father Raphael. "Please make yourself perfectly easy on that account. After all," with a smile, "you didn't write it, and you can't be held responsible for the contents, however unpleasant they may be."

"Father Raphael may be able to tell you something of its origin," interpolated the Canon, "he has a knowledge of these things, and I think you would be very well advised to let him see it. Nay, I make the request as a personal favour to myself."

"Oh, of course, Canon, of course. If you put it that way. And I am sure that Father Raphael quite understands . . ."

The Dominican bowed courteously without speaking.

"Then, if you will excuse me, I'll fetch it for you now."

"Bring it into the library, Hodsoll, where we are going to have coffee," said the Canon.

Dr. Hodsoll was coming downstairs, a little quickly perhaps, the *Mysterium Arcanum* in one hand, when from an angle of a landing, a rather dark spot even on the sunniest day, there seemed to leap out at him a black shapeless shadow, and it was only by fast clutching the balusters that he avoided an abrupt and dangerous fall. When he had steadied himself, and turned to look, he saw nothing.

The Dominican attentively scanned the pages of the vellum octavo Hodsoll had handed him. His expression did not alter in any degree of astonishment or distaste. It was merely the calm, careful scrutiny of a scholar examining a rare and curious work. Once he nodded to himself as he came across some phrase or passage which seemed not unfamiliar.

"Yes, Dr. Hodsoll," he said at length, as he closed the *Mysterium*, and placed it on the table, "you certainly have there a most scarce and uncommon book. It will perhaps seem to you an impertinence on my part if I proffer any comment on the nature and purpose of this treatise, and yet I must risk your displeasure. I cannot see anyone standing in such deadly peril without a word of warning on my part, a word I trust you will not take amiss. Believe me when I say in all seriousness that I had rather put a lighted match to a train of gunpowder than pronounce certain of these incantations. The very possession of the book is apt to bring you into most undesirable company."

My impression is that Dr. Hodsoll was a good deal upset as well as not a little perplexed by the friar's words. On the one hand he shuddered to think that already he might, however unwittingly, have attracted attentions on the part of those whom he would certainly be most desirous to avoid, yet of whose existence philosophically he was far from resting assured. The incidents he had observed were (he argued) in themselves quite capable of a natural explanation and possibly merely subjective. A man who had always prided himself upon his mental poise and balance, who boasted in religious matters a "healthy agnosticism", to use his own pet phrase, he was loath to confess his fears to another. Ridicule or polite incredulity he would beyond anything have resented. There was also the powerful motive of the book, which, as a bibliophile, he could hardly bring himself to destroy. It might be cased in morocco, yes; and kept in a locked bookcase, certainly; but to burn these pages which were not impossibly unique, was unthinkable.

Begging to be excused on account of certain duties, Father Raphael Grant retired early to his room that evening, fortunately not to sleep.

Dr. Hodsoll and the Canon parted company somewhere past eleven o'clock, and it was with a sensation of relief that the former as he switched on his electric light saw there was no intruder in his bedchamber. A small but cheerful fire was burning in his grate, and after undressing somewhat slowly he slipped a dressing-gown over his sleeping-suit, and sat down to review the situation. It was only natural that two clerics such as Canon Spenlow and the friar, each in his own line of extremely orthodox views, should regard such a book as the *Mysterium* with abhorrence, and speak out pretty freely concerning it. No doubt he himself had been a little off-colour lately and fanciful, and he had allowed himself first to be vexed by and then to weave a regular romance around the officiousness of a new and over-zealous valet, who doubtless had been specially ordered to look after guests in the house. Add to that the mere accident of an ugly tramp having peered round a bush at him when he was tired and half-asleep, and— why he was yawning already. It was striking twelve.

As he turned towards the bed he saw standing but a few paces behind him the servant, and at that moment his heart chilled with deadly paralyzing terror, for in a flash he knew who he was and whence he came. Only a few seconds can have passed before the stranger spoke in low tones of horrid menace, but those seconds seemed to Hodsoll a fearful eternity, and it is fairly clear that he came as near to madness as a man may and not wholly lose his reason.

"You wanted me, sir."

"No . . . no . . . no . . . go away!"

"You called me, fool. And do you think I am to be dismissed so lightly?"

His eyes blazing furiously with exulting hate, and crooking his lithe white hands which to his horror Hodsoll saw were armed with great sharp horny nails that curved like the cruel talons of a vulture or some foul beast of prey, the demon suddenly and silently leaped upon the unfortunate wretch, who, frantic with physical fear and an even intenser mental loathing, reeled backwards uttering a hoarse stifled cry.

In that moment the door was flung wide open and the Dominican friar advanced stern and unflinching into the room. Around his neck hung a purple stole, as with upraised hand he marked swift sacred signs in the air and spoke certain Latin words of might in a tone of imperious command. Hodsoll, who extremely dislikes being questioned about the incident, on one occasion acknowledged that he really remembers nothing of what transpired. He can only recall that he heard the Most Holy Name, and that with a moan of brute agony his assailant seemed to slip away—as he expressed it—into nothingness.

As may be supposed the struggle aroused the house, and the Canon followed by Watson and a footman in a state of *déshabillé* very shortly appeared on the scene. Father Raphael, however, was able completely to re-assure them by briefly stating that Dr. Hodsoll had been taken ill, but that he was better, and since he himself intended to pass the night in his room no further assistance would be necessary or required.

If I am not much mistaken, on the following day the Canon was privately enlightened as to the correct state of affairs by the Dominican, to whom Hodsoll confided the whole story. At any rate, the *Mysterium Arcanum* was burnt to ashes that morning, a cremation at which the Canon expressed highest satisfaction.

It does not require a very active imagination to appreciate why Julian Hodsoll, the cultured and intellectual agnostic, fasts much and prays, and a Tertiary of the Order wears around his neck against his skin the brown scapulary of Carmel.

MAPPA MUNDI

by Mary Butts

PARIS is not a safe city. It is never supposed to be, but so often for the wrong reasons. Perhaps the only place in the world that is really and truly both a sink of iniquity and a fountain of life at one and the same time; in the same quarter, in the same place, at the same hour, with the same properties—to even the same person.

It is no use, or not much use, to know it only as a spree, or as an aesthetic jolt, returning very sophisticated about it. Like all the great feminine places, behind its first dazzling free display, you come quickly upon profound reserves. After the spree a veil is drawn, a sober, *noli me tangere* veil. Isis, whose face on a first swift initiation you think you have seen, even to the colour of her eyes, Isis you believe you have kissed, withdraws, well wrapped-up, grown instantly to her own height—as is the property of a Goddess. Colossal, as Apuleius saw Hecate, and made of stone which is goddess's material; and for lover and mistress you are left with an image, remote as St. Geneviève where she stands looking upstream, an inviolable city behind her.

Properly snubbed, or enchanted, if you remain, above all if you live there, you learn that the delights of that first spree are repeated and confirmed as pleasure does not often repeat itself. Not only these, you find that there are others, possibilities of thrilling ways of life that do not depend on wealth or sex or the excitements between midnight and dawn; vistas of wellbeing that touch the commonest acts with the service of the goddess and her law, the quality of sheer living, sufficient in itself, as Tamar Karsavina tells in her book.

That is as far as most people get. Wise men stay there; more than the ghosts of good Americans settle down to the bliss of it. Only remember we are dealing with the goddess Isis. Her forbidding veil is off and not for a long time replaced. She moves now in transparencies. Only do not pretend to yourself that you have seen her eyes. Still less her smile. Least of all perhaps, do not ask what she is smiling about.

If you do you must be prepared for other things to happen.

There are people who do. That is how I account for what became of Currer Mileson, the american boy I met outside the Café des Deux Magots. Who was seen, who was seen less, who was not seen. Until he was never seen again. It was a business people explained in various ways—so far as it was explained at all. Until they gave it up. For he had come to Europe, so I gathered, all by himself out of the Middle West; and there one supposes were a few people who said: "that wicked Paris got him." Which about sums up, perhaps omitting the adjective, all that was ever said.

Yet american boys usually take some killing—if Currer Mileson is dead. As nuts they are tough, and as eggs hardboiled. Their imaginations having less historic exercise than ones over here, they are inclined to be superficial—that is, romantic. Or, their national culture not yet achieved, when they do not despise they gobble. Or, anxious to assert their capacity, become culture-fans.

Enough about american boys. As rare and no rarer than rarity the world over, there are some of them who do not fit into any convention of their land.

I knew he was a rare one when I saw him, sitting alone on the round-the-corner part of the *terrasse*. The beautiful lean body, immense strength the generations had fined, even to over-fineness. All length that old age would make gaunt, and wild bright hunter's eyes. Eyes that were looking east, towards the shabby end of the Boulevard St. Germain where behind the Boul' Miche rises the Sorbonne, and behind the Sorbonne, the Rue du Cardinal Lemoine, where Strindberg ran away from two crossed sticks when he was finding the philosopher's stone.

We had met before. I sat down beside him and we each looked. The spring sun made one's senses ache as they ache nowhere but in Paris.

"Have you ever thought?" we both began at once. Both meaning the same question, but it was he who explained.

"Have you ever thought what lies behind this city—above all behind the ancient part we're sitting looking at? What, if you go at it long enough, comes through, comes out, what you walk into when you're awake and when you're asleep?" I stared at him. He went on:

"It's easiest on the Quai Notre-Dame, by the little old shop where they sell books on how to raise the devil. There it's pretty well done for you."

"What about when you're asleep?" said I.

He turned half round to have a good look at me, as though to be sure of my face for the first time:

"So you go there too?" he said. I nodded.

"Here? In Paris? But I might have seen you."

"Here and other places—places I have really known, got inside of, worked into myself."

Like him I sat, my face lifted towards the quarter which is the womb of Paris, where her young still go and her secret poor. Down the street where the broken bits of Julian's baths lie about, which he built when the legions occupied the little city of the Parisii called Lutetia. Stones cluttering the grass railed off from the pavement, round the house full of symbols of the real story, the Cluny Museum. All the Parises were about us, behind us, on our right and our left. Only before me, invisible behind the high roofs, stood the matrix of Isis' temple, the darkened shrine. He went on suddenly:—

"What do you think is the meaning of it? What do you see there when you go? What is it, that kind of sleep?"

"Well," I said, "I think, I'm nearly sure, that then, in *that* way, we are seeing, or even being shown, as much as we can see of what is really there."

"Why do you say 'sometimes'?" I hesitated.

"You know what dreams are—even these sometimes begin and sometimes fade away into quite ordinary dreamstuff."

"Mine don't. They're as sharp and separate as two kinds of being alive. But this other thing that happens when we're awake, that we're watching here right now, sitting on the edge of the Boulevard St. Germain—that's different, that's another thing, isn't it?"

"Yes," I answered slowly, "I'm pretty well sure by now that it's not the same thing at all; that these two experiences are different. If your sleep and mine are a pair, then we are moving about in places we know, and we can recognise this place or that. Only more real. Only in splendour. Great houses and courts and terraces climbing the sky from squares and steps and streets. A perfectness.

"When we're awake, as we are now, sitting together, it is much more like ordinary living, extended in time." He interrupted: "That's it. Trailers for half the films that have made Paris, or a hundred and one ways of Queer Street."

I agreed. I have a weakness for Queer Street, and people who have that are soon past being astonished at anything. So I did not ask him the questions I might have asked, but took it as I found it that a boy from the other side of the world should have walked straight up one of my own particular streets. A long way further up than I had ever gone.

I followed his eyes again, pitched high on the roofs on the other side of the street beyond the trams.

"It's there it all begins," he said. "Every corner you turn will be the next and the last. How'd you describe that?"

I tried again: "An extraordinary, a unique sense of all sorts of mixed pasts, a sense of the ancient city and all the fury of life that went to make it. Especially for me, in Villon's time and in the seventeenth century. That and"—he gave me a quick look—"that and something else. Like something out of which they *all* came. A matrix, which is Paris and the secret of Paris."

"The pot-boiling," he said, "and the bubbles coming off the stew."

"You can go home," I said, "when you've prowled enough, and pick it over and make plans and patterns. Even maps. But I think we're right to be careful, to keep this wholly separate from what we see in sleep. For there is nothing glorified about it." The look in his eyes troubled me, the look of a hunter of his race at a terrible quarry approaching from a long way off, a quarry that made him the hunted as much as the hunter.

"'Glorified' is the word," he said. "Alone there in a light of a finer quality than day. Funny I didn't meet you. D'you know the white cliffs with the poplars and the fountains, east of the city near the old fortifications?" (I did, it was one of my "places," and I knew the Orphic tablet too.)

"No one to speak to—just a few lovely quiet people about on their own blessed business. All Edens man's been working on. But what are the great birds?"

"Of course you're right. It is two different things. But what luck on my first trip to have walked back straight into the lot. History by day and Plato's patterns by night—Garçon!" He ordered two long, golden, starry drinks.

Like two travellers we compared notes. Yes, any time of day did, but a misty dusk was propitious in the broken hill-country at the back of the Sorbonne. Yes, and we both knew the ancient church at the foot of the wicked slum, called after Port Royal; and I had broken new country in the three great parallels along the river, of which the lowest was the Rue de l'Université and the highest the Rue de Grenelle. To us both had come the moment when walls slid in and out, to reveal others; both understood *crains dans le mur aveugle un regard qui t'épie.* Pure past or pasts, with their mystery and their passion; and as it were *through* them, the over-powering sense of one energy roaring through each, the crucible, the power-house in which each was formed.

After such wandering you could go home, turn over in your mind what you had walked through. That was why I had spoken of maps. For by now I had in my mind a chart of the place, of a Paris upon which the city of our time was no more than superimposed. One aspect of a central fire, or the womb of Isis, eternally fertile, eternally bringing forth. An activity of which we were the latest *eidola.* Admitted perhaps to this knowledge because we had not been content with her carnal gifts, had never boasted that we had seen her face.

Not even in our dreams, though there was no intellectual work, remembering or researching. There we strayed. Into the courts of her perfected work, the threshold of the completion of her labours; within and beyond the *simulacra* which were all we, in our bodies, could share.

It is one of the curious things about such experiences, whatever their reality, their ultimate significance or insignif-icance, that no one can discuss them for long. (It has been years before I could bring myself to write this.) After that morning we saw a good deal of one another, Currer and I; and though we knew perfectly what each was doing, what each was thinking about, we never spoke of it again.

Yet I thought of him as well, this young man, strayed round the side of a planet, carried across an ocean to stray again, awake or asleep, in two wholly new forms of experience.

The dreams, so I concluded after some meditation, were safe. So long as you woke up in time. Nor could you prevent them, nor had I ever come to harm in that country. Rather I loved them, as a promise and an exquisite reassurance; knowing too that like the "sensible fervours" of prayer, they were not to be sought or asked for or even longed after, but, like the grace of God, only to be enjoyed.

So much for the Goddess's more legitimate work. No, it was the other business, this waking awareness of what one could only describe as the "goings-on," the furies of dark energy, for which our Paris, with its brilliance, its exquisite sobrieties, was the mere shell—it was there that I felt less happy about him.

He did not know (for one instance) that along the line of my three glorious streets was once the waste place where the witches met—*quartier des Sorciers*; that when it was known what had happened in the little church by the river, the judge ordered a cloth to be hung over the crucifix, in sign that man if he could would spare God the knowledge of what had been done there.

He did not know, and I shied at my own guess, why the Tour St. Jacques stands alone as it does, or who the Child is who visited there.

He did not know the things Strindberg did not tell—even less than the things Joris Karl Huysmans told—in part.

He did not know that it is a curious fact that Madame de Montespan could not even get buried properly.

He did not know that the work of Isis implies the opposite of its own activity, that the Courts of the Morning stand on ground won from the Waste Land. He did not know that there was a were-wolf in Paris as late as the Franco-Prussian War.

He did not know what Hugo meant when he wrote about the Wicked Poor.

Any more than he knew what the Surréalistes were up to.

He did not even know the Song of Paris, how every century she had taken civilisation and made it dance to her tune. Built it and sung it and dressed it, prepared it for the table, for the assembly, for the bed. For prayer, for wit, for treachery, for rhetoric, for devotion; for its life and for its death.

Nor understand what goes with this and what must go; until the ἀνακατάστασις, the renewal of all things, which Paris will be the last place to notice.

Puis ça, puis là, comme le vent varie—that most dreadful line of a terrible poet, the most dreadful line in French literature of the dead men rotting on Montfaucon, might have been written about a girl's scarf, fluttering in the Tuileries in a spring gale. Might be said of the Goddess, flirting with her admirers.

I went across the river, to the Paris of the Empire and the Third Republic, but only depressed myself by the sight of women buying lovely things I should never be able to afford.

Across the Seine, still high, still racing last winter's rains, ancient Paris sat watching the light splendours that had risen across her stream. So that it seemed that a giant, straddling the river, would have one foot in time and one foot out of it; and little doubt, for all the contrast and the easy splendours, on which side the Bird-Priestess who under Isis is the city's daimon has her nest and lays her eggs.

Anyhow all mine were in that basket, and I walked home across one of the bridges that have a spring to them like a bent bow.

II

The next time we met was in the Rue de l'Happe— this was in the days before the playground of the Wicked Poor had become one of those spots for vice without tears in which Isis specialises the first time you meet.

I had not thought to find him there, "on the zinc," and the centime-in-the-slot jazz, among the youth in their coloured linen and skimpy suits.

It appeared that he was expecting someone. A friend just over and calling loudly for adventure? He did not want to tell me about it and he did. It was an exquisite night. I suggested a cooling walk along the quays, away from, not towards, the Tour St. Jacques.

We strolled west under the moon. The Paris moon, of all moons the most nostalgic. For what? For everything. Love-in-a-mist at eighteen; for a night spent with a vampire in a vault; for a court ball; for an adventure at sea. For staying in Paris forever; for running away from it at once. For delicate vice, for sanctity, for a great laugh—the moon who creates out of all these longings the final mood of divine high spirits, for which again only Paris has the receipt. The laughter no other city can evoke—except Vienna before we murdered her—the joy and daring she distils out of one like a dance, a running up and down between the alcove and the stars.

Shadows on the moon-candied stones, cat-black and sharp. It was late. Spring night or no spring night, the city was indoors at its play. My companion in his tuxedo was black and white too, the stones not paler than his young cheeks nor the night brighter than his eyes. Nor any hunter moved on a lighter step—I thought of great woods, and of his forbears' watching in the woods for the feathered, silent warriors of the Five Nations, stepping, score by score, on the war-trail in the night. Then noticed him (we were silent) glancing right and left, checking his step as if to listen. For this friend?

With my mind on secular things, "Who are you looking for?" I said.

As though already I was not there, and his question to the wide world (as our questions often are), to anyone who would answer:

"Have they never spoken to you in sleep?"

As I have said, you cannot dwell for long on these things. My active mind was on the Boeuf sur le Toit and the friends I had left. "No," I said, was suddenly glad, now I came to think of it, that they had not. Even if they were the souls of just men made perfect (as one hoped).

"No, they never speak—Why?"

"Well," he said, with again that flash across his shoulder—"believe it or not, when it happens in the other way, there are some about who do."

"They're *not* the same thing—" I began, pedantically. Then suddenly felt as if I were pulled up short. By an intense cold. As though the little perfumed breeze that rose across the river were iced. Blown off some glacier—a breath, but a more than polar chill. And if you are to believe Dante, there is ice in hell. Then from behind a shadow I could not account for all but caught me up. Came up and dropped back into an angle in the walls. A little dark that had been following us, catching up and falling back, all the way, a thing that I had noticed and I had not noticed. A shadow thrown from one tree to another, traveling with them as they bent in the night airs on the embankment over our heads? I did not think so. Somehow I was wanted away. Instantly I wanted myself away also.

An interesting adventure, a perception to play with from time to time, wet one's toes in that sea. This man by my side had plunged straight in, with more intuition and even less knowledge, was already past hailing distance from the shore.

Argument and near-panic raced up on me together.

"Don't," I managed to cry, "come away. It's not safe. Come tomorrow, and I will tell you everything I know about it"—I caught his arm and it felt as if it was something a long way—an infinite distance—off, and cold, and made of something else; and between us something that was not space, and cold from where cold comes from, was separating us. I heard myself saying:

"Ariadne it's like. You can't go without your thread."

Hearing his answer:

"He's got it. He's past the Minotaur he said. Round the next corner he'll wait."

We had been standing facing one another. Now we began to walk again, and into my mind flashed images of men who had been too far. The young publisher who vanished on Olympus; the man in Buchan's story who discovered the corridors and that space, like murder, is "full of holes." We hurried as though driven. Already our feet were on the incline that leads up to street level again; as with the tail of my eye I saw the shadow dart out of its hiding-place.

Just at that moment a taxi drew up to the curb at the top.

He did not follow even so far as to put me in; nor the taxi wait so long as for me to see what happened to the American left alone on the white moon road below the street, beside the stream.

It was an hour later, at the Boeuf, that I remembered to wonder who had paid that taxi, and how he had known that he was to bring me there.

I was with friends. But not to one of them could I say: "I've been out with a man who was followed by a ghost, and I left them making friends; and because I was upsetting its vibrations, it drove me away."

Next day this dumbness Montagu James describes as "common form" still held me; and it was three days before a mixture of conscience, curiosity and Paris high spirits sent me out to try if I could find him again.

I learned nothing at all; or rather that he had been seen, and that he had not been seen; alone and not alone (or possibly with a friend beside him, or with a bad character at his heels) by the concierge of his hotel, the *dame du bureau*, a waiter at the Deux Magots and one or two of his acquaintances.

Pensive, I left them, and walked east towards Notre-Dame along the Quai Voltaire.

Oh but the place was sweet! On the Quai des Fleurs I bought some. Country flowers, larkspurs and *giroflées*, and the orange marigolds the French call *soucis*. Looking up at the towers of Our Lady of Paris, thinking of Our Lady at Chartres, who could believe—in the demon who from her roofs looks down upon the city of Paris? That ubiquitous demon they can make into a door-knocker and the simple tourist's souvenir; who may even be a fake, a restorer's idea for a devil. Who, set in the crown of Our Lady in Paris, is yet the best known portrait of the Evil One that exists.

On my way back I passed again by the very dirty deserted house, beside which an alley runs back into the web of old streets at the wrong end of the Boulevard St. Germain. A house that saw the Musketeers in and the Revolution out, high-pitched, crazy, the kind of house etchers love, rat-worn, with something abominable about it. On my secret map a black spot and a question-mark—*crains dans le mur aveugle*— and the alley beside it is filthy. If you could not see the far end nothing would make you walk up it. You never meet anyone in it, and from the river end I was half-way up when I saw him cross the mouth of it; and I could not be sure if the figure at his heels was accompanying him or not.

I hurried up, to find myself in a street market, in a crowd walking round in circles, and on the Boulevard a knot of trams, all starting at once.

It was clearly, perfectly clearly Currer Mileson, seen with something of the small perfection of a figure seen down the wrong end of a glass.

Reassured, I walked back to the Café des Deux Magots.

It began to get about that he was gone, to get about and be contradicted. I said nothing, and as I have told, he was new to Paris and he had no close friends. No one to start the inquiries which set the machinery of society in action. It was some time after that a man from the *Sûreté* came to see me; and I suggested, which did not please him, that Paris was a city in which one might easily be lost.

"Have a look round here," I said at last, "and see if I'm hiding him." It was the quietest of still days. The turquoise and gold dust of early summer—*maquillage d'Isis*—lay upon the city. Yet a picture, a map of old Paris, suddenly clattered on the wall, the *agent* turned his head, and a curious silence fell between us, like a shutter between his incredulity and my reserve.

You can only really give to people the kind of truth that is serviceable to them. I dined early, and when dusk came shut myself in to consider very carefully what I knew that I could be sure I knew, in the policeman's sense, in any sense, and possibly in another.

I ought to be able to believe that Currer Mileson was doing no more than wander about, neglectful of his meals or the people he knew or his bed. That overwhelmed by his discoveries, by the release of certain imaginative and intuitive faculties, he was working off a crisis in himself. That in time he would either snap out of it or be picked up by the police. "Partial loss of memory" was the phrase that rose—until I considered the sense of it and began to laugh rather shakily.

Yet it was the obvious way to approach it. It was what I should ordinarily have believed, even in the face of far stranger-seeming evidence. Only this time I did not believe it, I could not believe it, a single image recurring to my mind continually—of a young man to whom an order had been given: "step out of your body." An order he would obey (the means given, the means would certainly be given) as lightly as he would change his shoes.

Swept up, hurried off into an extension of that knowledge we both shared. Only an extension I had the sense to keep out of or the inability to pursue. "*Something far more deeply interfused.*" That was it. So far that he would never return.

It was after this that people came to see me. Americans mostly. People I had met and people I had not met. Few, or very few, with the idea that I had harmed him or even had some private knowledge, but (as I did not at first understand) as if some of them, at least, had a question to ask me they could not ask themselves. They came for help, and I had no help to give that would have helped them. Yet they seemed to feel that I felt something, and would one day produce it on a plate. One of them got so far as to hint about "vibrations"— but they none of them knew Paris.

Now and then I would try them out. "In the Rue Férou— did they remember who had lodged there?" Or did they know Jean Goujon's fountain, in a panel of which the inner genius of water is shown in stone? Or who had died on the Pont Henri-Quatre, calling upon a Pope and a King to meet him within a year before the Court of God? (A point which taken only provoked a reaction about the Templars and homosexuality.)

Or at Versailles even—had they noticed the silver birch that stands alone in the rough field beside the choked tank between Petit Trianon and Hameau?

Or that in the Bibliothèque de l'Arsenal there is the manuscript with the squares, and the receipts for letting out what, as Montagu James says, most certainly ought to be kept in? Or the emptiness of Boulevard Arago where, for all its broad leafiness the horses shy because of the work that the guillotine does there? Or? Or?

It was during this time, too, more than once, as I had seen it that night on the quays, a shadow would follow me home. A slip of dark I could not account for; and like Punch hiding behind the curtains, so it used my windows. Hanging half in, half out when my back was turned, as though keeping an eye on me to see if I knew enough either to be drawn in or to interfere. One evening it leaned out, shamelessly stretched up over my shoulder, as though to follow the page on which I had been writing down my helplessness. An eye it had on me, but I did not know and I could do nothing; and that was what it wanted, what it had come to find out. And all the time I was aware of this also; that there was a step I could take, simple and obvious, that I was a person with a key in one hand, a box in the other, without the wits to make them fit. Like Punch it sniggered at me, like Punch it was somehow annoyed.

Until one night it gave it up; and this time I was so certain of it that I hurried to the window, to see what appeared like a thin blackness swarming down the face of the house, dart across the moon bar in the narrow street, to be swallowed up in the dark of the opposite wall.

"Goddess," said I, "keep an eye on your servants."

But it seemed, too, that she was laughing at my ignorance; and as the summer drew to its height began to be bored with me, having given me, and in more ways than this, of her best and of her worst.

✳

The agent came once more. This time he was more amiable. It seemed that Authority was still asking questions. Strange as it seemed, even the most insignificant of Americans were not allowed to vanish utterly. As one European to another, he implied that I would see the point. As if one of them, supposing they came from the place they said, supposing there was such a place for them to come from, mattered more or less.

Especially, as I pointed out, the object of his inquiries did not seem to have made a good job of it. There always seemed—just to be a little ghost of evidence that he was still occasionally seen. Then, for the sake of trying to say something, I added:

"Last time, Monsieur, you would not admit that your city was a bad place to be lost in. Yet would you admit that it is a place where you might make a bad friend?"

His answer surprised me:

"I entreat you, Madame, to tell me what you mean."

"I have told you all I can tell you, and you know that." Again there was silence, again our eyes met, and this time it was his eyes led mine to the map on the wall.

Then he surprised me even more. He crossed himself:

"I am not of Paris—I am from Corsica, I; and I do not mean its brothels or its criminals, but I say there are parts of this city that were better burned to the ground."

I nodded: "That is why I do not think you will ever see him again. Can you not get a corpse, any corpse, and satisfy them as to its identity?"

"That," he said simply, "will no doubt be done." Then surprisingly: "It is not you, Madame, who could bring him back?"

"No," said I, "then there would only be two of us. Besides, I assure you that if I could I would have done so long ago."

He stood there, no longer the Paris policeman but a tall man from the pure mountains in the South. And he believed me.

"He met then?"

"A shadow. Who has drawn him into the shadows. But remember, he was good. He may come to no harm there."

"How is that possible?"

"I mean that on the other side of the shadows there is another country, the Courts of the Morning that lie only just outside the gates of Paradise. When you are off duty, pray for him."

The map on the wall was still.

ABOUT THE AUTHORS

ETHEL ARCHER (1885-1962), the daughter of a clergy-man, was born in Sussex, and expelled from school at the age of fourteen for asking questions in Scripture class. In 1908 she married the aspiring artist Eugene Wieland, and lived with him in West London. The couple made the acquaintance of Aleister Crowley, joined his A∴A∴ magical organization, and set up a publishing company called Wieland and Co., to publish Crowley's periodical *The Equinox*, as well as other texts, including Archer's first poetry collection *The Whirlpool* (1911). She published two other books, *Phantasy and Other Poems* (1930) and the occult novel *The Hieroglyph* (1932). For a number of years she contributed book reviews and other prose pieces to *The Occult Review*, the September 1921 issue of that magazine being where "The Unfinished Prayer-Mat" first appeared.

L. ADAMS BECK (1862–1931), who also wrote under the names E. Barrington and Louis Moresby, was born Elizabeth Louisa "Lily" Moresby, in Queenstown, Cork, Ireland, the daughter of Rear Admiral John Moresby, who she accompanied on his many expeditions, travelling and living in places such as India, Tibet, Egypt and Japan. She married Edward Western Hodgkinson, a Royal Navy commander, and after he passed away married, in 1912, the solicitor Ralph Coker

Adams Beck. She began her writing career publishing short stories in *The Atlantic Monthly* and elsewhere. Her work was heavily influenced by the beliefs of the East, theosophy, and the occult. Her numerous books include *The Way of the Stars: A Romance of Reincarnation* (1925), *The Way of Power: Studies in the Occult* (1928), and *The Openers of the Gate and Other Stories of the Occult* (1930), the latter volume being that from which "Hell" is taken.

E. F. BENSON (1867-1940) was an English novelist and short story writer of considerable fame, mostly remembered today for his Mapp and Lucia series of novels. His interest in the occult is evident in a great many of his works, including several of the pieces in *The Room in the Tower and Other Stories* (1912), from which "The Confession of Charles Linkworth" is taken.

ALGERNON BLACKWOOD (1869-1951) was one of the foremost writers of supernatural fiction, some of which he also presented on radio and television. A member of the Hermetic Order of the Golden Dawn, many of his novels and short stories are heavily informed by the occult, including "The Wings of Horus" which first appeared in the November 1914 issue of *The Century Magazine*.

MARY BUTTS (1890-1937) was an English modernist writer. In 1921, in Cefalù, Sicily, at the Abbey of Thelema, she received magical training from Aleister Crowley, an account of which she told of the following year in *The Sunday Express*. Among her writings are the novels *Ashe of Rings* (1925) and *Armed with Madness* (1928). "Mappa Mundi" was most likely written in 1937, or shortly before that, and was first published in *Last Stories* (1938).

"D.N.J." was the pseudonym employed by the author of two stories which first appeared in *The Cambridge Review*, the second of which, "The Moon-Gazer," was published in the June 9, 1920 issue of that periodical.

JACK EDWARDS was the name, or pseudonym, under which, from 1910-1921 a large number of stories, many with occult and supernatural themes, appeared in various English periodicals, primarily *Yes or No* and *The Weekly Tale-Teller*. "The Ghost Friend" is taken from the December 12, 1912 issue of the latter magazine.

"DION FORTUNE" was the pseudonym of Violet Mary Firth (1890-1946), a medium and author and one of the foremost British occultists. She was a member of the Alpha et Omega order, before being expelled and joining the Christian Mystic Lodge of the Theosophical Society, of which she became president. Being dissatisfied with some of the views of the latter lodge, however, she left and formed the Community of the Inner Light. She wrote prolifically, both fiction and non-fiction, her works including *Psychic Self-Defense* (1930) and *The Mystical Qabalah* (1935), and the novels *The Demon Lover* (1927) and *The Winged Bull* (1935). "Blood Lust" originally appeared in May 1922, in *The Royal Magazine* and was subsequently reprinted in *The Secrets of Dr. Taverner* (1926).

WILLIAM T. HORTON (18641919) was a mystic, illustrator and author. With the aid of W. B. Yeats, he gained initiation into the Hermetic Order of the Golden Dawn. His illustrations, which appeared in numerous places, including the Symbolist-Decadent leaning periodicals *The Savoy*, *The Dome*, and *The Green Sheaf*, are replete with occult themes, as is his book *The Way of the Soul: A Legend in Line and Verse* (1910). "A Legend of Life" is taken from the December 1912 issue of *The Occult Review*.

PRINCE IMMANUEL OF JERUSALEM (1874-1949), was the pseudonym of E. I. Goldreich, an eccentric Welsh-born Jew who, after leaving his native land, appeared in Jerusalem, and then Egypt, where he published *The African University College Journal*, and then the United States, where he joined the "faculty" of the spiritualist Helmuth Peter Holler's Oriental University. He believed himself to be a direct descendent of Jesus and was the founder of the Most Supreme Inviolate and Universal Grand Lodge of King Solomon's Temple and the creator of a language which he called "Universl." Among his other literary endeavours was the book *Criminals of Chicago* (1921), and *Prince Immanuel's Journal*, which promoted the work of the G.R.O. (the Golden Rule Order), the mission of which was, at least in part, to "find you a friend somewhere on this great earth." The story "When I was Dead" was released as a mail order pamphlet, most likely in 1918.

JESSIE DOUGLAS KERRUISH (1884-1949) was born at Seaton Carew in Durham and, according to one biographical note, was raised on the "legends of witches, warlocks, ghosts, submerged forests and sea-swallowed lands that colour the mental atmosphere of the wild North Coast." Though mostly remembered today for her classic werewolf novel *The Undying Monster* (1922), she was also a productive short story writer, many of her pieces appearing in *The Weekly Tale-Teller*, the January 16, 1915 issue of which contained "The Swaying Vision."

C. W. LEADBEATER (1854-1934), though originally an Anglican priest, became a student of H. P. Blavatsky and, in 1884, travelled to India where he was, according to himself, trained by the "Masters". The next year he travelled with Henry Steel Olcott to Ceylon where they founded the Buddhist Society. He was the author of numerous books, including *Clairvoyance* (1899) and *The Perfume of Egypt and Other Weird Stories* (1911), from which the tale in the present anthology was taken.

TOM LEON, which might or might not be a pseudonym, is an author about which nothing is known, outside of whatever information might be gleaned from his few writings, one of which appeared in *The Occult Review*, and a second, "Cat Souls," which first appeared in the May 1931 issue of *The Seer*.

NEVILLE MEAKIN (c. 1876-1912) was, aside from being an Adeptus Minor of the Stella Matutina, also Grand Master of the Order of the Table Round, an order which he likely invented himself, but which he claimed had been founded in the time of King Arthur. He wrote a novel titled *The Assassins: A Romance of the Crusades* (1902), and collaborated on two books with H.T. Sheringham. "The Paper Man" was first published in the September 1915 issue of *The Occult Review*.

KENNETH MORRIS (1879-1937) was a Welsh author and theosophist. When he was a child, his family moved to London, and then to Dublin, where he became friends with George William Russell, the author who wrote under the pseudonym "A.E." From 1908 to 1930 Morris lived in California and worked at the Theosophical Society headquarters at Point Loma. The last seven years of his life were spent in Wales, where he founded seven Welsh theosophical lodges. During his lifetime he published three novels and numerous short stories and items of non-fiction, often employing pseudonyms, such as Walshingham Arthur, Aubrey Tyndall Bloggsleigh, Hankin Maggs, Ambrosius Kesteven, Maurice Langran, Fortescue Lanyard, Venon Lloyd-Griffiths, Ephraim Soulsby Paton, Bingham T. Molyneux, Sergius Mompesson, and Quintus Reynolds. "Bach's Fugue in D-Minor" originally appeared in the February 1929 issue of *The Theosophical Path*.

AMYAS NORTHCOTE (1864-1923) was the seventh son of Sir Stafford Northcote, 1st Earl of Iddesleigh, and Cecilia Frances Farrer, sister of Thomas Farrer, 1st Baron Farrer. He was the author of a single book, *In Ghostly Company* (1922), from which "Mr. Oliver Carmichael" is taken.

RALPH SHIRLEY (1865-1946), a direct descendant of Robert Devereux, Earl of Essex, was born and educated in Oxford. Aside from being the author of several books, including *Occultists & Mystics of All Ages* (1920), he was, from 1892 until 1925, director of William Rider & Son, the most important British publishers of occult literature. He founded and edited *The Occult Review* and was also vice president of the International Institute for Psychic Investigation. "The Man Who Killed God" was first published, under the by-line "R.S.", in the February 1920 issue of *The Occult Review*.

"MAY SINCLAIR" was the pseudonym of Mary Amelia St. Clair (1863-1946), a British writer of some fame. She was a member of the Society for Psychical Research and a close friend of Evelyn Underhill, to whom she dedicated her book *A Defence of Idealism* (1917), the publication of which gained her election into the Aristotelian Society. She wrote numerous novels, as well as two volumes of supernatural tales, *The Intercessor and Other Stories* (1931), and *Uncanny Stories* (1923), the latter volume being that from which "The Token" is taken.

MONTAGUE SUMMERS (1880-1948) was an English clergyman, occultist, poet and man of letters. His most famous products were a series of colourful studies of vampirism, lycanthropy and witchcraft, such as *The History of Witchcraft and Demonology* (1926) and *The Vampire: His Kith and Kin* (1928). Among his other literary endeavours was an English translation of the *Malleus Maleficarum* and his works on English Gothic fiction, *The Gothic Quest: a History of the Gothic Novel* (1938) and *A Gothic Bibliography* (1941). "The Grimoire" first appeared in an anthology which Summers edited, titled *The Grimoire and Other Supernatural Stories* (1936).

CHARLES WILLIAMS (1886-1945) was a British poet, novelist, playwright, theologian and literary critic, who with C. S. Lewis and J. R. R. Tolkein formed the group The Inklings. He was, for ten years, a member of the Fellowship of the Rosy Cross, a group which descended from the Hermetic Order of the Golden Dawn, where he led initiates in practising various occult arts, such as alchemy, Cabalism, and divination with tarot cards. He wrote seven novels, all of which have mystical and occult themes. "Et in Sempiternum Pereant" originally appeared in the December 1935 issue of *The London Mercury*.

W. B. Yeats (1865-1939) was an Irish poet and writer and a significant part of the Irish Literary Revival. In 1890 he joined the Hermetic Order of the Golden Dawn and later, in 1911, became a member of The Ghost Club, a paranormal investigation society. "Rosa Alchemica" originally appeared in *The Savoy* in 1896 and subsequently in the book *The Secret Rose* in 1897. Yeats, however, was dissatisfied with that early version, which he said was "written in that artificial, elaborate English so many of us played with in the nineties" and he later revised it with the help of Lady Gregory. The present version of the story is taken from *The Collected Works in Verse and Prose* (1908).

OTHER BOOKS IN THE SERIES

The Zinzolin Book of Occult fiction (edited by Brendan Connell)
The Vermilion Book of Occult fiction (edited by Brian Stableford)
The Alabaster Book of Occult fiction (edited by Brian Stableford)

A PARTIAL LIST OF SNUGGLY BOOKS

G. ALBERT AURIER *Elsewhere and Other Stories*
CHARLES BARBARA *My Lunatic Asylum*
S. HEZOLNRY BERTHOUD *Misanthropic Tales*
LÉON BLOY *The Tarantulas' Parlor and Other Unkind Tales*
ÉLÉMIR BOURGES *The Twilight of the Gods*
CYRIEL BUYSSE *The Aunts*
JAMES CHAMPAGNE *Harlem Smoke*
FÉLICIEN CHAMPSAUR *The Latin Orgy*
BRENDAN CONNELL *Metrophilias*
BRENDAN CONNELL *Unofficial History of Pi Wei*
BRENDAN CONNELL (editor)
   The World in Violet: An Anthology of EnglishDecadent Poetry
RAFAELA CONTRERAS *The Turquoise Ring and Other Stories*
DANIEL CORRICK (editor)
   Ghosts and Robbers: An Anthology of German Gothic Fiction
ADOLFO COUVE *When I Think of My Missing Head*
QUENTIN S. CRISP *Aiaigasa*
LUCIE DELARUE-MARDRUS *The Last Siren and Other Stories*
LADY DILKE *The Outcast Spirit and Other Stories*
CATHERINE DOUSTEYSSIER-KHOZE *The Beauty of the Death Cap*
ÉDOUARD DUJARDIN *Hauntings*
BERIT ELLINGSEN *Now We Can See the Moon*
ERCKMANN-CHATRIAN *A Malediction*
ALPHONSE ESQUIROS *The Enchanted Castle*
ENRIQUE GÓMEZ CARRILLO *Sentimental Stories*
DELPHI FABRICE *Flowers of Ether*
DELPHI FABRICE *The Red Sorcerer*
DELPHI FABRICE *The Red Spider*
BENJAMIN GASTINEAU *The Reign of Satan*
EDMOND AND JULES DE GONCOURT *Manette Salomon*
REMY DE GOURMONT *From a Faraway Land*
REMY DE GOURMONT *Morose Vignettes*
GUIDO GOZZANO *Alcina and Other Stories*
GUSTAVE GUICHES *The Modesty of Sodom*
EDWARD HERON-ALLEN *The Complete Shorter Fiction*
EDWARD HERON-ALLEN *Three Ghost-Written Novels*